The intimacy of the moment
wound around them,
filling her head.

She set down the pliers and began to move back. A broad hand wrapping around her hip stopped her.

She stilled, energy rushing down her torso.

They were alone and in real time. No dreams, no fantasies, just reality.

Zane stood, brushing warmth against her front. So much taller and bigger than she. He slid his free hand along her jaw to the nape of her neck, tilting her head up. Keeping her in place.

She wanted to say something, but words fled. Instead, she lost herself in his green gaze, finally dropping her concentration to his full lips. Intrigue, curiosity, and need kept her still.

Just one. Just one kiss.

Right now, in person, just to feel if any of her dreams could become real.

He lowered his head slowly, adding anticipation to the moment. As if waiting two decades wasn't long enough. "Belle?" he asked, his breath brushing her lips.

"Yes."

Marked

REBECCA ZANETTI

LYRICAL PRESS
Kensington Publishing Corp.
www.kensingtonbooks.com

LYRICAL PRESS BOOKS are published by

Kensington Publishing Corp.
119 West 40th Street
New York, NY 10018

First electronic edition: December 2014

ISBN-13: 978-1-60183-154-5
ISBN-10: 1-60183-154-4

First print edition: December 2014

ISBN-13: 978-1-60183-231-3
ISBN-10: 1-60183-231-1

*When I created Janie Belle Kayrs,
she didn't have a dad until Talen took her in.
At that moment, her world became much better,
because a good dad makes the world a safer place.
This book is dedicated to my dad, James Michael English,
because he has always made the world as safe as possible
for his girls. He's the person we all go to when we need help,
and he's always been there for us. From the excellent softball
coaching to the disastrous downhill skiing lessons,
he's been our umbrella in a big universe.
Now, he's Bampa to my kids, and he can do no wrong.
Thank you, Dad. I love you.*

ACKNOWLEDGMENTS

I'd like to thank the many loyal readers who started with *Fated* and have read the entire Dark Protectors series while leaving reviews on sites as well as e-mailing me. I can't tell you how much your support means every day! I hope you've enjoyed Janie's story, and I hope you'll also enjoy our spinoff series with the very tough, very sexy witch enforcers, beginning with Kellach Dunne.

Thank you to Tony, Gabe, and Karlina Zanetti, my very patient family, who remind me that there's a fun life outside of my make-believe worlds. I love you all so much.

Thank you to my talented agent, Caitlin Blasdell, who is incredibly dedicated, insightful, and wise. I am so grateful to be working with you. Thanks also to Liza Dawson and Havis Dawson for your hard work and support. We started together with this series, and it has been an incredible journey so far.

Thank you to my amazing editor, Alicia Condon, who is so sharp, kind, hardworking . . . and also wears incredible shoes when the occasion calls for it.

Thank you to all the folks at Kensington Publishing, especially Alexandra Nicolajsen, Vida Engstrand, and Justine Willis, because they're such a joy to work with. Thanks also to Arthur Maisel for the excellent copyedits, and to Steven Zacharius and Adam Zacharius for taking a chance on a new author. Thanks also to Megan Records, who picked up this series and gave me my first "call." The only difficult thing in working with Kensington is remembering how to spell some of the last names. ☺

Thank you to my critique partner, Jennifer Dorough—who one day said . . . "I think you should submit this book to Kensington. I heard Megan Records is looking for paranormal novels." Thank you as well to the myriad of terrific review sites and bloggers who have gotten behind this series.

And thanks also to my constant support system: Gail and Jim English, Debbie and Travis Smith, Stephanie and Don West, Brandie and Mike Chapman, Jessica and Jonah Namson, and Kathy and Herb Zanetti.

Prologue

Twenty-one years ago

Janie snuggled down in her bed, her four-year-old arms wrapped around her favorite stuffed bear. Mr. Mullet snuggled right back, although he didn't move much. Probably so she could get some sleep and see what was coming. Her recent dreams promised their lives were about to change.

Janie's dreams always came true.

In the next room, her mama slept quietly. Maybe Janie should warn her. But maybe not.

Bad people were coming, but so were good people. The ones with fangs. Especially the really big man with the golden eyes who she'd one day call daddy. She'd always wanted a daddy, and one with fangs would be nice.

But first, she had to dream again.

So she tightened her hold on Mr. Mullet and sank into a dream world. This one she'd created at the side of a sparkling lake way high up in the mountains. She left the water blue but made the surrounding trees purple.

She loved purple.

Glancing down, she straightened her favorite shirt. White with bright pink flowers in the front, it made her feel pretty. Maybe her new friend would like it, too.

He peered out from behind a tree.

She waved.

Even from across the small distance, she recognized his green eyes. Very deep green eyes. She'd been dreaming about him forever. Maybe even before she got borned.

He slowly stepped out of the trees and walked toward her, glancing all around. This close, he was a lot bigger than she'd thought, and had to be at least five years older than she was. Probably.

"This is a safe place. We're both asleep," she said.

He scratched his head, rumpling long black hair. "Who are you?"

"Janet," she said. "You're Zane."

He stopped moving. "How do you know my name?"

She shrugged. "I dreamed about you. About us being friends and ending the war."

"What war?" he asked, frowning and looking around again.

"It hasn't started yet." But boy, things were about to get bad. "We can meet here in dream worlds where nobody can hurt us." Janie smiled.

"You're human?" Zane asked, focusing on her.

"Yep." She peered closer. "You gots fangs?"

"Maybe." Zane glanced toward a ripple in the dream, where the trees kind of jiggled funny. He somehow stood taller. "Who's there?"

Janie swallowed. "Um, it's another boy, but we won't let him in yet. He's bad."

"How bad?"

"Dunno." But she knew not to let him in yet. She'd dreamed about Kalin for a while now, too. "But we'll save everybody we love. I promise."

Zane focused down on her, his shoulders relaxing. "Janie?"

"Yep. Janet Isabella Paulsen." If things worked out right, she'd have a new last name soon.

Zane grinned. "You're too small for that name."

"It's still my name."

He shook his head. "How about I call you Janie Belle?"

Janie grinned and fought to keep from clapping her hands. They were gonna be friends. "Okay."

Chapter 1

The present day

Sometimes destiny arrived with the crash of a bomb detonating in the trees.

Janet Isabella Kayrs perched on a rock wall facing the tarmac as men in full combat gear loaded helicopters. A young vampire had accidentally launched a rocket into the Oregon forest, but the blaze had already been contained. Unlike the smell.

Dawn began to peek over the horizon, bringing a flash of sunlight lacking in warmth. A breeze slithered through her black silk shirt, but she'd chosen carefully, and she didn't want a jacket. Just in case she needed to fight.

Tension battled with oxygen, mingling with power. The vampires, each and every one, had a power more daunting than oxygen molecules. With destiny all but riding her, Janie fought to control her emotions. Indulging in fear would get her killed.

With a screeching protest, a heavily secured door opened to her right. She turned and forced a smile. "There's my favorite firefighter."

Garrett Kayrs, her younger brother, wiped soot off his forehead. "I helped put out the fire, but it wasn't me." He leaned back against the wall, long legs extended, worry cutting grooves next to his generous mouth. "I haven't accidentally set off an explosive since the fifth grade."

"I remember." This time her smile arrived easily. "You were playing in the armory and blew up several trucks."

"Dad was mad."

The understatement widened Janie's smile. "Yeah, but he was amused, too."

Garrett's odd gaze sharpened as he watched a missile being loaded. "I don't think you should go."

"I know." She took a deep breath and studied him. At twenty years old, the young vampire stood well over six feet tall. He'd inherited their father's broad shoulders and rugged features, but the unique metallic gray eyes were all Garrett's. She slipped her arm through his, impressed by the solid muscle. "I have to go."

He shut his eyes, the cords in his arm vibrating with a dangerous tension. "Then I should be there."

Janie leaned against him. With almost five years between them, she'd vowed to protect him at his birth. Even after he'd outgrown her when she'd turned twelve, she'd known how to make him laugh, how to ease the pressure he must surely feel as the sole Kayrs born in the new generation.

Vampires produced only male babies, and not very often. So far Garrett was the single progeny of the Kayrs ruling family.

"You're needed here to protect headquarters," she said. "And Mom."

His massive body shuddered. "I'm torn." Garrett lifted his chin. "I need to be here for Mom but want to be at the peace talks with you."

In profile, he looked just as dangerous as their father.

"I'm trained, Garrett."

"You're human, Janie." Garrett hunched his shoulders forward. "No matter how well trained you are, you're still human."

Janie nodded. The breeze whipped around them, and she pushed hair out of her eyes. When her mother had mated Talen Kayrs, he'd adopted Janie. He was the only father she'd ever known. While she loved her family, she'd never lived a normal life. "Sometimes I forget I'm human."

"I don't," Garrett said softly.

When had his voice deepened so much? She hoped to whatever God watched over them that she'd see him again. See him grow fully and become who he wanted to be in this life. For today, she couldn't leave him in such a worried state. "For as long as I remember, I've had visions of the peace talks to end the war. I'm present to play a part, and I know I have to be there."

His head slowly turned to face her. "But no visions about the outcome."

"No." She swallowed. Visions had filled her dreams her entire life, and sometimes she even saw different outcomes to different events, depending on the actions of the people involved. Free will always trumped destiny. But the last vision she'd had of her life included the peace talks about to commence so deep underground. "I've never seen past the peace talks."

Garrett exhaled. "I don't like this."

She nodded. A chill skittered down her back, and her stomach churned. For the rest of the Realm, she needed to appear calm and determined. But with Garrett, she could be herself. "I'm frightened." God, she was scared—on so many levels. What if she failed?

"Then don't go."

Why did men try to fix everything with an absolute? While she wanted to tell him everything, she just couldn't admit the horrible sense of foreboding hanging over her head and tightening her neck muscles into a headache. "We have the chance to end a terrible war that has cost us so many lives. Good lives. How can I not go?"

"Is peace worth your life?" Garrett's jaw hardened.

"Yes." She drew out the response, while truth filled her with regret and fortitude. Surely her fear of failure was coloring her entire outlook right now, although maybe not. Sacrifices were made in war, and more important, to gain peace. "I don't want to die, but if that's what it takes to find peace for our people, I'm okay with it."

"I'm not."

She shook her head, drawing on a courage she'd stored up for a decade. "Don't get me wrong. I want to live, and I've given this a lot of thought. This isn't ego or a quest to be a hero or to fulfill any destiny."

"Then what the hell is it?"

"A chance for less bloodshed." There had been so much for nearly two decades. Vampires, witches, shifters—even Kurjans and demons, who were the enemy. Too many people had died.

Enough death, and she didn't want to be included in the toll at the age of twenty-five. "Besides, we've taken every precaution possible. Just because I don't see visions of myself after the peace talks doesn't mean I don't have a future."

"That doesn't make sense." Garrett's nostrils flared in warning of his rare temper.

"Sure it does." Unfortunately, fate never played fair. "Maybe the peace talks will change the future for all of us, and thus I can't see any outcome until after they occur." Oddly enough, the idea made sense to her.

The sun grew in brightness, and Garrett glanced down at her neck. "You think that'll bring you luck?"

Janie lifted a shoulder and fingered the silver horseshoe necklace her best childhood friend, Zane, had given her on her fifth birthday. How the shiny gift had made it from the dream world where he'd presented it to reality remained a mystery. "Luck can't hurt."

"You sure about that?" Garrett scuffed his size fourteen boot in the dirt.

"He saved your life." Janie elbowed her brother, who recently had been kidnapped by Kurjans, their monstrously creepy, white-faced enemies who couldn't go into the sun, unlike the vampires, who enjoyed the sun. Zane had rescued Garrett as a favor to Janie.

Garrett shook his head. "Yes, but we don't know why he helped me. Zane is only half-vampire, and I'm pretty sure his other half is more dominant—whatever that may be."

Janie rubbed her chin, nearly burning with curiosity. She and Zane had met in dream worlds her entire life, and she'd seen him change from a good-natured vampire into something else when he'd moved to live with his mother's people after his vampire father's death. "Maybe he's a mystical dragon who will save the world."

Garrett snorted. "There's no such thing as mystical dragons."

"Most people don't believe in vampires." Janie had no clue what genes thrived in Zane, but they had to have some good in them.

"No. My guess is that he's a shifter—a member of an outlying clan that does not align with us. That makes us his enemy, and if he wants to attack, doing so while we're preoccupied with the peace talks is great timing." Garrett softened the harsh words by sliding an arm around her shoulders.

"Zane helped you, Garrett."

"Just because he saved my life doesn't mean I won't take his. If he's a threat to you." Garrett tugged her closer.

Janie shook her head. Her younger brother should be joking about going off on adventures and meeting girls—maybe hitting the beach somewhere tropical. Definitely not talking about killing another soldier. The mantle of responsibility had landed as formidably on Garrett's head as on her own.

A shadow fell across them as their father approached. "Janie?" Talen asked.

"I'm ready, Dad." She smoothed her calm smile into place and released Garrett.

Talen looked down at them, his golden eyes softening. "I don't like this."

"Me either," Garrett muttered, standing to his full height.

"Then it's a good thing we all believe in fate." Janie hugged her brother and fought as tears pricked the back of her eyes. Clearing her throat, she pushed away. "I've already said good-bye to Mom and that I'll see her later tonight."

Talen nodded, looking beyond vampire dangerous in tactical gear and wearing his heading-to-battle expression. "We've been training for weeks. Do you understand the plan and all escape routes from the meeting cavern?"

"Yes." Janie eyed the helicopters, trying to remain calm. "We also ran simulations yesterday."

"This is a bad idea," Garrett said, facing their father over her head.

Talen nodded and clapped his son on the arm. Emotion glowed dark in his eyes, but his expression remained stoic and hard. "You have your orders. Protect headquarters in case the peace talks are just a diversion for an attack. We'll be back tonight." Taking Janie's arm with a gentle touch, he escorted her to the nearest helicopter, where he jumped in beside her.

Dage Kayrs, the king of the Realm, turned from the pilot's seat. He'd tied his dark hair back, probably in case of a fight, and his silver eyes were somber. "You ready?"

"Yes." Janie folded her hands in her lap, meeting her uncle's gaze as the sense of destiny clicked into place. "I'm ready."

* * *

Two hours later, deep underground in an impossibly dangerous cavern, Janie settled onto a stone bench, her hands clasped on the stone table. The ride down into the earth had taken forever, yet she'd arrived much too quickly at one of the four entrances, each controlled by one of the species attending the talks.

A mutation in the laws of physics made survival in the room possible, allowing them to breathe so close to the earth's core. The possibility existed that the safeguards put in place might fail, and she swallowed to keep from panicking.

The king sat to her right, looking nearly bored. He eyed the fire burning in the center. "Ever feel like we've challenged quantum physics one time too many?" he muttered.

Yes. God, yes. "I shouldn't have, but I Googled fault lines on the Internet. The one beneath this cavern connects with the Andreas Fault," she whispered.

He nodded. "If our safeguards fail, we'll trigger the largest earthquake in history. Millions will die."

Anxiety flattened her chest and compressed her lungs. She swallowed. "Great."

Behind them stood her father, at guard. He was the only person who'd be allowed to stand in the room. Everyone else had agreed to sit behind solid rock.

It was more difficult to attack from a seated position.

But Talen could stand as a concession because Janie was attending the talks. Every species on earth had prophesied her birth, and her attendance was mandatory. But fate had failed to whisper why Janie was prophesied. She had no clue what to do to fulfill destiny, and the fear of failure squeezed like a vise.

"I'm sure our safeguards will hold. You okay?" Dage asked quietly, his gaze remaining on the roaring fire in the middle of the stone tables. The fire was necessary both for light, and because somehow the element assisted the quantum physics protecting the occupants.

"Yes," she lied. "Just ready to get started." Another lie. Why did the Kurjans and the demons have to arrive last? It was as if they wanted to make a big entrance. Enough with the waiting. She glanced around the tavern.

To her left sat the three prophets of the Realm. While they advised the Realm, they stood as the true spiritual leaders of the immortal world, and all species respected them. Prophet Lily sat regal in a flowing gown, her blue eyes sparkling like a lake in the peace of summer. The ancient Prophet Guiles wore a brown overcoat and had dark bags under his eyes. As a traitor to the Realm who'd tried to aid the Kurjans, he was fortunate to be breathing.

And finally, Prophet Caleb, Lily's mate, looked pissed off and ready to hit anybody at any time. It was his normal expression, so Janie wasn't alarmed.

Lily looked toward Janie and winked.

Misplaced humor bubbled up from Janie's stomach. "Lily's trying to calm me."

Dage nodded. "I hope she can keep us all calm."

Calm would be good.

Dage cleared his throat. "If something goes wrong, you run for the lift behind your father. Don't hesitate."

"I understand." They'd been over the plan many times.

Frustration twisted Dage's lip. "I can't teleport from here. You know that. We're too deep in the earth."

"Yes." Janie patted his arm. Vampires had extra abilities, but Dage was the only vampire she'd ever heard about who could teleport from one place to another. Probably because he was the king and from the ruling family.

Janie glanced past the prophets to the two men representing the shifter nations in the talks; they'd shared the vampires' entrance to the cavern. Jordan Pride, head of the lions, and Terrent Vilks, head of the wolf nation, both sat without moving, attention on the openings in the rock where the Kurjans and demons would enter.

When shifters remained motionless, things were about to blow up.

Janie exhaled and counted to ten, trying to slow her heart rate. Immortals could sense fear, and she had to be a beacon right now. To keep her mind occupied, she glanced past Dage to the witches sitting regally at their table.

Vivienne Northcutt, the leader of the witches, sat at proper attention, waiting with no expression on her intelligent face. Next to her sat Moira Kayrs, Janie's aunt, and a witch enforcer. Moira's curly red hair had been pulled back, and her green eyes flashed five shades of plasma electricity. Deadly and ready.

They were to continually monitor the quantum physics keeping the group safe, so the meeting didn't set off the worst earthquake in human history.

To their right, on a sharply cut stone edge, lay the Prophecies of Arias. A book bound in worn green leather, an ancient text sought by all species. The witches had possessed the volume for at least two centuries after having stolen it from the demons. Janie had dreamed about the book for years, but she still couldn't see inside its pages. As she watched, the book began to glow.

Welcoming her?

A rustle sounded, jerking Janie's attention to one of the vacant openings. Tall and whipcord thin, a Kurjan she didn't recognize entered through the detector that would immediately vaporize him if he dared bring a physical or chemical weapon. Seven feet tall and dressed in all black, the white-faced predator had the typical Kurjan red hair with black tips . . . and purple eyes. He took his seat, obviously weaponless.

Kalin, the current leader of the Kurjans, entered next, his odd green gaze immediately seeking her out.

Her smile came naturally.

His arrived with a flash of fangs. He bowed. "Janet. It's good to see you again."

"You too," Janie said, even though Dage stiffened next to her. She'd met Kalin in dream worlds since childhood, and they'd formed an uneasy, unlikely sort of friendship. He was a butcher, and he killed easily, but he'd also saved her life once. Maybe they could find peace together in order to save their families.

He took his seat, his black hair and slightly darker skin a contrast to the Kurjan soldier sitting next to him. With a bit of makeup, Kalin might appear human.

Janie said a quick prayer that Kalin really wanted peace. The Kurjans had created a deadly virus, Virus-27, which attacked the chromosomal pairs of vampire mates as well as witches, and Janie's mother had the illness. Hopefully Kalin had a cure to share.

"Now we just need the demons," Moira muttered. "Are they still dressing, or what?"

Dage growled low.

Janie swallowed. Suri, the demon leader, had captured and tortured Dage's youngest brother for nearly five years. Janie wanted Suri dead as badly as Dage did, because it had taken Uncle Jase years to recover.

How were they ever going to find peace?

Power permeated the air when Suri stepped into the cavern. Broad and tall, the demon had presence. White hair and black eyes showed his purebred lineage. He glanced around the cavern, and his chest puffed out.

Dage shifted his weight next to Janie.

She kept her gaze on the enemy. Whatever demon soldier he'd brought with him didn't matter. Only this man did. If he would agree to peace, no more blood would be shed.

He took his seat, his dark gaze landing squarely on her.

Dage eyed his enemy. "You come alone, Suri?"

"No. I brought my nephew." Suri didn't break eye contact.

A large body suddenly overwhelmed the doorway behind him.

Heat rushed down Janie's throat to burn her lungs. A roaring filled her ears. Her hand involuntarily sought the necklace at her throat. The soldier standing behind Suri, so tall, broad, and deadly, was the one person she thought she'd be able to trust forever.

"Hi, Janie Belle," Zane said.

Chapter 2

Zane's a demon. A demon. A demon. A demon. The mantra ripped through Janie's head in an endless loop of pain. *A fucking demon.*

He sat directly across from her, the firelight flicking shadows across his familiar face. Somewhat familiar, anyway. In reality, in person, a hardness angled his features in a way the dream world had masked. A scar ran along the right side of his face, proclaiming battle and near death. He'd once told her a pissed-off demon had scarred him.

Had he lied?

The boy she'd known, the teenager she'd loved, had grown into a predator studying her with eyes a deeper green than she'd realized.

Strength, power, and determination all cascaded around him, enhancing a wildness at his core he didn't bother to conceal.

Half-vampire and half-demon? What kind of power would mixing two such predatory races create? Even surrounded by deadly creatures, he stood out as something unique. Deadly. The mere uncertainty of his birth made him an excellent ally or a deadly enemy. As he sat next to Suri, the one being Janie hated more than any other, his allegiance became all too clear.

Enemy.

"Well, that explains why we couldn't find Zane's mother's people when his father died," Dage muttered quietly just for her.

Janie lifted her chin. Even if she'd wanted to speak, her vocal cords had frozen.

A demon.

Shock and hurt chilled her, until slowly, with a sure burn, the fire of fury banished the cold.

Pure, raw, *female* fury.

She didn't know him. Maybe she never had. Even so, the sense of betrayal failed to mask the feelings she'd harbored for him. Deep and real. Her focus narrowed, and Zane's chin slowly lowered, his nostrils flaring like a wolf's accepting a challenge.

As their gazes clashed, a silent war cry resonated through the unnatural physics in the chamber so deep in the earth. The protective walls morphed, and the immortals all around tensed.

"Take it easy, Jane," Dage whispered.

She nodded and exhaled slowly, allowing anger to replace the pain. Her human emotions didn't have the strength to affect the mutated quantum physics keeping them safe.

Zane's emotions did.

At the realization, triumph lifted her lips in almost a smile. Yeah. She'd gotten to him.

His eyes blazed ten shades of fire, but that hard face remained expressionless.

Dage leaned in. "So Zane's the *Ghost*. He must be."

Oh. The demon assassin whispered about at campfires and in strategic meetings. The deadly demon close to Suri who had nearly supernatural powers and a fatal ability to kill. Janic swayed and quickly tightened her thighs to keep from falling. How could the sweet kid she'd known so long ago be the feared *Ghost*?

Prophet Lily cleared her throat. "Well, then. Ah, shall we get started?"

Whispers of movement sounded as attention turned toward Lily. Yet Zane kept his focus on Janie, and she couldn't look away. He gave her no expression, no inkling of what he was thinking or even feeling. Nothing. How could he be a demon?

She wanted to run across the chamber and touch him. Feel the real man and get him to say this was all a mistake. That he still cared for her, and they'd work together. That what she remembered wasn't some silly girlhood dream. That she mattered.

But he sat across the room next to her biggest enemy. It was time for Janie to grow up and let go of childhood dreams. Her chest actually hurt as if somebody had kicked through her breastbone to her heart. Direct hit.

Lily cleared her throat. "Since nobody put demands in writing, we'll go around the room and state our initial demands. I'd appreciate it if everyone waited to respond until all demands have been made."

Janie blinked and tried to concentrate, but so many questions swirled through her head, she couldn't focus. How could Zane keep this from her? Had any of their friendship been real? It had to have been. She'd known him as a scared kid, way back when, and he'd cared for her.

Did he still?

Dage leaned forward. "The Realm demands all warring stop, the demons return any prisoners of war immediately, the Kurjans turn over all research and data concerning Virus-27, and any contracts out on any Realm citizens or members of the Kayrs family be immediately rescinded. In addition, we demand a treaty prohibiting biochemical warfare." His deep voice held power and echoed around the cavern. "And we want possession of the Prophesies of Arias, as it must be our turn."

Janie broke eye contact with Zane to glance around the group for reactions. Damn immortals. Nobody even twitched.

Vivienne Northcutt clasped her long fingers together on the stone. "The Coven Nine demands all information regarding Virus-27 be turned over immediately, and any contracts on witches be rescinded." She glanced at Dage. "The Prophecies of Arias remains in our possession. In addition"—she turned to face Suri and Zane—"we want Eastern Europe. The former Soviet Union and all the Baltic States. The lands were settled by witches, so get out."

Janie wanted to nod but instead kept still. The witches needed the land because of a dangerous mineral inherent in the rocks there that harmed witches, and they wanted Virus-27 information because the damn illness affected witches as well as vampire and probably demon mates who had once been human. Apparently witches had fewer chromosomal pairs than other immortal species and thus lacked the protection vampires, demons, and Kurjans had with their additional pairs. The witches' demands seemed fair.

Jordan Pride's eyes flickered just like a cougar's as he straightened.

"The shifter nation wants all prisoners of war returned immediately, and considering Virus-27 turned shifters into werewolves until we found a cure for shifters, we want all research associated with the virus."

It was too bad they hadn't found a cure for witches or mates yet. Janie took a deep breath.

"In addition"—Terrent Vilks eyed the fire crackling in the center of the room—"we want information regarding any werewolves still alive, and we demand autonomy in dealing with werewolves. Nobody hunts or kills our own but us."

Wow. Janie hadn't been expecting that one from their allies, and by the stiffening of Dage next to her, neither had he.

Kalin tapped bony fingers on the stone table. "The Kurjans demand all research regarding our biology and aversion to sunlight from every species in here, because we know you've been studying us. We also demand the return of any imprisoned Kurjans, as well as our turn taking possession of the Arias book." He turned his odd green/purple gaze on Janie. "Finally, we demand access to the chosen one."

Janie blinked. What did *access* mean? Her father moved closer to her, bringing the reassuring scent of pine.

Kalin didn't move. "We want a dialogue and the right to conduct some noninvasive tests to see why Janet Kayrs has been prophesied by our oracles."

Was *access* a euphemism for *mating*? It wasn't a secret Kalin wanted to mate with Janie to gain access to her psychic abilities, but she had to appreciate his mild approach.

Janie blew out air. It had to be killing some of the immortals in the room to refrain from responding to the demands. Round two of the talks would certainly be more explosive. "The Prophesied One has her own demands," she said.

Dage's head jerked toward her, and her father growled low. She kept her face calm, not having realized until right that second she'd need to make her own statement. "The war ends, and all prisoners will be returned to their homes. No more bloodshed, no more biological weapons, and no more secret agendas—and the Prophecies of Arias comes home with me."

The book flew up into the air, hovered, and zip-lined for her head.

She put up both hands, and leather slapped into her palms. Her eyes widened, and her stomach clenched. How could a book fly? With great care, she set the book on the table.

A hush fell on the room, and even the fire's crackle lulled.

The book pulled at Janie. Holding her breath, she flipped open the cover.

Dage sucked in breath. "Nobody has ever been able to touch the book with bare skin. Ever. Even the witches had to transport the book with heat-resistant gloves."

Janie smiled, entranced. Pages rustled, opening to nearly the middle.

Blank pages.

"What do you see?" Dage asked.

Janie blinked. Slowly, symbols took shape and then words. She smiled. "Strengths. Weaknesses." Of different species. The weakness of witches was listed as phenakite, also known as planekite and phanakite, depending on region. Maybe the information there could help her find a way to end the war. Reaching out, she began to turn the page.

"Enough!" Suri bellowed through the room. "Nobody reads the book until we reach an agreement."

"Apparently nobody but Janie can read the book," Dage said dryly. Even so, he nodded. "For now, close the prophecies."

Janie faltered, fighting the drive to read more. To understand more. Maybe the weathered pages revealed her destiny. But as Suri began to rise from his desk, she closed the book.

The demon sat back down.

Janie swallowed and kept one palm on the rough leather. Somehow the object heated her hand.

"I believe it's our turn for demands," Suri said.

Janie turned her focus to the demons, her heart thumping upon meeting Zane's gaze again.

He apparently hadn't looked away.

Tingles spread through Janie's abdomen, and heat rose from her chest. Even across the room, the man held a magnetic pull.

She met his determined gaze without flinching. Irritation filled his eyes. An odd tension had permeated the room from the moment the Kurjans had demanded access to her. Probably because to end the war, she'd grant it.

Yeah, she had known the moment would come when she must choose between her own happiness and the future of her people, but even so, unease skittered down her spine as Zane's gaze sharpened and his jaw set. She stared at him across the fire; he was no longer the kind older protector or even the mischievous boy playing in her dreams.

He was all man.

And he wanted her to know it.

His full lips formed the word, "no," his eyes hot and daring on hers. She gave a quick jerk of her head, and her own focus narrowed in anger. This was her choice to make.

Next to Zane, Suri puffed out his silver medals. "The demons demand the release of any demon in custody, all contracts on demon heads, especially mine, be rescinded, and sole possession of the eastern side of the current United States be granted to us. We also demand the return of the ancient Arias text, considering it was stolen from us in the first place." He sat back, white hair gleaming in the firelight.

The book jumped beneath Janie's hand, but even then, she couldn't look away from the determination and intent on Zane's face. What was he going to do? Her breath caught, and anticipation lit her from within.

"One more demand." Zane kept her gaze hostage. He leaned forward, his jaw hard. "There will be no Kurjan *access* to Janet Isabella Kayrs, and she will make a choice as to her destiny."

He kicked back from the table and broke all the rules by standing. A massive man, a true predator, a dangerous warrior. His deep voice easily reached around the cavern. "At the end of these talks, regardless of books, science, and geographic boundaries, Janie becomes mine."

Chapter 3

An abandoned gold mine and adjacent ghost town comprised the demon temporary headquarters in a lost section of Idaho. Near enough to the peace talk site to make travel convenient, but far enough away to allow for a decent getaway if necessary, the lonely ghost town hinted of lives lost and fortunes wasted.

In the madam's office of a refurbished whorehouse, Zane accepted the full punch to the jaw from his uncle, allowing his head to jerk back before slowly turning to face Suri. The hit pissed him off less than the futile eight hours underground at the so-called peace talks. Thank God the first day was over. "Was that supposed to hurt?" he asked. They stood eye-to-eye, and there was no doubt Zane cut a harder warrior now. The last few years warring in hellish conditions had guaranteed his fighting condition.

Being an assassin tended to rip the soul from a man.

Suri hissed out. "How dare you?"

"What?" Zane lifted a shoulder and sauntered across the room to drop onto a bright pink settee. The furniture groaned under his bulk. Odd that Suri had kept the feminine piece. "I improvised."

"Improvised?" Moonlight glinted through the window to illuminate Suri's eyes a pissed black. "*Janie Kayrs is mine?*"

"Janet Isabella Kayrs is mine." Zane stretched and ignored the pounding pain in his jaw from the punch. "Using her full name had more impact, I think." Plus, the words rang true. He knew her; she had decided she'd sacrifice herself to the Kurjans years ago. Even so, he was surprised she thought he'd allow it. She had set her destiny the first time she had invaded his dreams; she should've stayed out if she'd wanted to choose her own path.

While his own future remained uncertain, he couldn't go out knowing Janie had sacrificed herself. He owed her more than that— just for being his friend.

Suri growled and swept an antique desk clean of a myriad of maps and papers. Three Degoller Stars fell to the floor, their deadly sharp points glinting. "Putting aside the fact that you acted independently and without orders, what in the hell was your purpose in making that claim?"

Zane kept his expression calm. "I meant what I said. Janie is mine." Even if he never truly claimed her, she wouldn't belong to the Kurjans. No doubt he'd die soon, but he'd ensure her safety first.

Suri's upper lip curled. "I thought I'd beaten the vampire out of you."

"You certainly gave it a try." Every hit Zane had taken had protected his two younger brothers, and it had been fucking worth the bloodshed. "Each prophet, oracle, and seer in the world has decreed that Janie's twenty-fifth year is crucial, and her powers will be known. She's twenty-five. If we give access to her to the Kurjans, Kalin will force her to mate with him. The Kurjans can't have her, and the vampires have no clue what to do with her. I do."

"Oh, you do?" Suri snarled, his broad face contorting. "She needs to die."

The simple words punched Zane in the gut. "No. We need her powers, her gifts, whatever they turn out to be. If I mate her, I'll get those gifts." He had no intention of binding Janie to him for a lonely eternity, but he needed to keep Suri off balance. Zane eyed his watch as he bluffed. His brother should be checking in any minute, and he needed to get away from Suri.

Suri picked up the Degoller Stars and leaned back against the desk. "My prophets have declared in no uncertain terms that the Kayrs woman will destroy the demon nation if she lives. She will die, and you will obey orders. Don't ever forget I own you. One phone call, and your brothers die in battle, or your mother disappears."

Anger slowly burned down Zane's spine. "My mother? You mean *your sister.* You'd end her so easily?"

"Yes." Suri lowered his chin, the medals on his chest proving his prowess in battle. The guy was a master in hand-to-hand and had never lost a fight. Most brutal bastards who enjoyed inflicting pain won every damn time. "She betrayed me when she mated a vampire and is lucky I didn't kill her when she came crawling back."

Zane slowly stood. "I've done everything you've asked to ensure her safety." God. The things he'd done in battle, in the name of war, just to keep his family safe would plague him for eternity.

"Yes." Satisfaction coated Suri's deep tone. "Keep that in mind."

Zane bit back a growl and gestured toward the devastating De-goller Stars. If thrown correctly, the weapon neatly sliced off an immortal's head, leaving no chance of survival. All immortal races on earth had reached a rare agreement to refrain from using them. "Those are banned by treaty, and you know it."

Suri glanced down. "We're at war . . . and treaties be damned." He shook his head. "After the talks tomorrow, we need to take the Arias book. Make it happen."

Zane lifted an eyebrow. "Everyone agreed to keep the book on that rock ledge for the duration of the talks." Though he could see how badly Janie had wanted to take the bound volume home. Her hands had actually shaken when she'd returned it to the ledge.

Suri shook his head. "I don't care. Get the book."

"Why?" What the hell was it about the ancient text?

"The book has prophesies beyond our oracles, and it has details about our enemies we need, and information about us we must hide." A knock sounded on the hand-carved oak door. "Enter."

Nikolaj Veis, Suri's head strategist, walked in. His gray eyes sizzled, and his white-blond hair had been ruffled. Harsh lines cut grooves into the sides of his generous mouth, proof of the difficult exile he'd endured the last decade when Suri had sent him to the Arctic to fight after he'd plotted strategy regarding land holdings with a beautiful witch. Suri had required Nick's help with the peace talks and had finally ordered him home. He'd only been back in civilization for a week. "We need to talk."

Suri nodded. "Zane and I are finished."

The hair on the back of Zane's neck rose from the tension now vibrating through the room. What were the two demons planning?

Nick eyed him. "How did the talks go?"

Zane strode toward the door. "Just peachy," he muttered. Then he paused. An odd vibration shivered through him. He pivoted just in time to catch a view of a red laser beam sliding toward Suri's neck. "Duck," he bellowed, leaping across the room and pummeling Suri to the floor. The entire wall exploded over their heads.

Without missing a beat, Zane turned and jumped through the window, falling two stories to the muddy street. He landed on his feet, crouched, and let the demon in him free.

The night narrowed in scope to heartbeats and unfamiliar scents. He ran through the town, quicker than any vampire, faster than most shifters. A heartbeat echoed in the distance, and the smell of an unfamiliar oil coating a weapon flared his nostrils. His *prey.*

His boots made no sound as he scaled rocks, bending against the wind, single-minded in his focus. Sights and sounds exploded in a myriad of colors, in a million individual scents. As he reached the top of the nearest hill, he paused to listen. The guy was good. Only the tiniest sound wisped through the night as the other soldier jogged down the mountain, probably heading for transport.

Zane sniffed the air. Shifter. Wolf shifter. Interesting.

He ducked his head and forged on, dodging tree limbs and branches with an instinct he'd learned to accept. Sliding around a tree, he lunged for the would-be assassin and took him down. They skidded across mud, and Zane flipped him over, straddling the wolf. "Who are you?" Zane asked, sliding his knife from his boot.

The man's eyes widened. "The Ghost," he whispered.

"You've heard of me." Zane pressed the razor-sharp blade against the wolf's carotid artery, shoving any humanity he might have once had to hell. "Answer my question."

The shifter blinked. "You're, ah, *real.*" The stench of fear clogged the oxygen molecules around them.

"Yes." He'd earned the nickname fighting across the globe because of his uncanny ability to reach an enemy, to kill, without warning. "Who are you working for?" Slowly, Zane sliced into rough skin. "I won't ask again."

The guy's eyes widened. "The Baltic Consortium. It's just a mission."

Zane nodded. He'd figured the loosely organized shifter organization in the Baltics would make a move at some point. Suri had been laying siege to the Baltic States for the last century. The mines there were rich in minerals, and war took money. "You failed," Zane said, shoving the knife in just as the wolf tried to shift.

A cacophony of boot steps pounded behind them.

Then Zane twisted the knife, slicing through cartilage, bone, and thick muscle. The wolf's head rolled a foot away.

Zane wiped his blade off on the guy's shirt and stood, turning to find Nick and two soldiers standing near.

The first soldier coughed. "Jesus. You cut off that guy's head like it was made of butter."

The other soldier nodded, his gaze wide on Zane. He appeared as if he'd like to cross himself but didn't dare.

Nick raised an eyebrow, his gaze inscrutable. "Wolf shifter?"

"Yes. Baltic Consortium." Zane slipped his knife back home, his gut rebelling at saving Suri's life. But Suri most certainly had orders in place to have Zane's mother killed if Suri died, so Suri couldn't die. Yet.

Zane pushed past the men, ignoring it when the two demon soldiers stepped hastily out of his path. "Have them dispose of the body," he told Nick. Without waiting for a response, he jogged down the hillside.

Even so, he didn't miss the second soldier's rough question, "What the hell is he?"

Zane exhaled. He was a demon, vampire, shifter mix . . . but that wasn't all. Even he didn't truly understand the beast deep inside him resulting from those dangerous unions. What was he?

A purebred killer. Plain and simple.

Zane shrugged off his reaction to the killing, to who he really was, and plastered on his soldier persona. Things were going south and fast. He reached the whorehouse and hurried up two flights of just repaired stairs to a room on the top floor with a spectacular view of the mountains. Dragging his cell phone from his pocket, he dialed his brother.

Sam came into view on the screen. "How did the peace talks go?"

Zane paused. A gash marred his younger brother's forehead, and mottled bruises covered his face. Dirt and grime were embedded in the wound. "Holy hell. What happened to you?"

"Big fight in Iceland where a bunch of werewolves jumped in. Fucking hate werewolves," Sam muttered. "Did you get anywhere in the negotiations?"

"No. We go back tomorrow." Zane paused and glanced around. His uncle would be watching him, and ears were everywhere. "Are you prepared?"

Sam sat up, green eyes sparking. "Yes."

"Good." Enough said.

"How did it go? Did the king react to your being half-demon?" Sam asked.

"No." In fact, the king had appeared bored the entire day. Impressive effort to remain unaffected, actually. Zane's gut rolled. "Don't worry about me—you need to find Logan before all hell breaks loose."

"I know." Sam wiped a grimy hand over his brow. "I have feelers out everywhere, but I don't have a location yet. There's no way to get word to him."

Zane swallowed. Their youngest brother Logan was only in his early twenties and shouldn't be fighting alone. "My guess is Suri sent Logan to deal with the African shifter uprising." A group of African shifters was trying to force all demons, vampires, and witches out of southern Africa, and the fighting had reached a brutal level. By keeping Logan so far away, Suri held a deadly trump card over Zane. "Suri won't tell me where he is, but I'll see what I can find out."

Sam frowned. "Be careful. Suri's twitchy with peace near, and he's gonna want to get rid of you at some point. You're too much of a threat to his rule."

Zane had already figured that one out, although nothing in him wanted to rule the demon nation. Ever. Once he took care of Suri, he'd be a dead man, anyway. "For now, I'm useful because of my ties to the Kayrs family. Janie and I have spoken for years, and I saved Garrett Kayrs from the Kurjans a while back."

"The Kayrs family probably wants your head on a mantel about now," Sam drawled, the concern in his eyes contrasting with his low tone.

Zane nodded, keeping his face stoic. Sometimes in life there wasn't any choice. "Not sure I blame them."

"They're all about family and should understand that we are, too. Even when it fucks up our lives royally." Sam scratched his chin. "For now, keep on your toes. The second you're no longer useful, Suri is going to have you killed."

Zane was more worried about his brothers. "I'll have a contingency plan in place for Mom, just in case." At the very least, he'd be able to get their mother to safety.

Sam shook his head, his eyes blazing. "I need to get home to back you up. Now."

Zane hardened his face into an expression he'd learned from his sadistic uncle. "No, you need to find Logan and get to safety. Period."

"Zane—"

"Enough. You have your orders." They couldn't go into details on the phone. "Wait for my signal." He clicked off.

Lead weights seemed to hold down his shoulders. A clock ticked over his head, and he truly had no clue how to protect the people he loved. *All of them.* But as the moon glared over the snowcapped mountains, he continued to plan.

He'd have just one shot, and if he failed, all was lost.

Chapter 4

Janie Kayrs eyed the three full shot glasses lined up at the bar. A tumultuous Oregon storm raged outside, throwing up whitecaps from the turbulent ocean, but the entertainment room behind her remained quiet and empty. She lifted a glass and tossed down two fingers of tequila.

The liquid burned her throat, and she sputtered, taking a deep breath.

"I've found tequila doesn't fix much." Cara Paulsen sauntered into the room, her voice clear and concerned.

Janie turned to see her mother skirt the pool table to sit on the adjoining bar stool. Cara's blue eyes were clouded, her face pale. Smudges of dirt marred her sweater and jeans. "You've been in the lab?" Janie asked.

Her mom nodded. "Yes. I was working on genetic mutations of some African plants that might have healing properties for Virus-27."

Janie took a deep breath, her face heating. Feeling sorry for herself was stupid, especially since her mother was fighting a deadly virus and apparently losing, if her pale skin provided any indication. "Any luck?"

"No." Cara eyed the alcohol and grabbed a glass. "What the hell." She tipped back her head and swallowed, coughing immediately.

Janie smiled and patted Cara on the back. How odd that they now appeared to be about the same age. "You just said alcohol doesn't help."

Cara set down the empty glass. "True, although it does numb

things a little." She pushed Janie's hair out of her eyes. "I'm sorry about Zane. A demon? I truly would've never guessed it, although it does make an odd sort of sense, considering we've never been able to find him."

Janie nodded, the lead ball in her stomach heavy. "I just can't figure out why I've never had an inkling about Zane. So many psychic visions have flashed through my head for years, and not once did I see the truth." Maybe she hadn't wanted to see the truth? Hurt cut through her chest. "How could he not tell me?"

"I don't know." Cara slid one arm around Janie's shoulders for a hug. "But I can't imagine it was easy for him to leave the vampire encampment as a child and go live with Suri. Suri is such an ass."

Janie leaned into her mother's strength and shut her eyes. "I know, but I can't afford to see Zane's side in this. Not right now with everything so up in the air."

Cara kissed her forehead. "Maybe you'll have to see Zane's side."

"I just, I don't know. Feel like I've lost something." The reality failed to make sense, and she struggled to relax as she straightened on the stool.

"You have." Cara tapped on the remaining tequila shot. "Zane has always been your soft place to land in this crazy world we forced you into. Turns out he's not so soft."

Janie blinked. "I love this world."

"I know." Cara's voice softened. "Do you ever think about what you gave up? A normal childhood, schooling, vacationing with friends?"

Yes, but then she felt guilty. "No. I need this family we've built." Hell. She *owed* the family. Everything.

Cara chuckled. "It's all right to regret what you missed and even be angry at this pressure cooker of a destiny you've been slammed over the head with. You didn't get a normal childhood, and it looks like your adulthood isn't going to be much different. That's what you feel you lost."

Janie bit her lip. True. She'd spun dreams about her and Zane ending the war and having a happily-ever-after that included kids, trips to Disneyworld, and even the PTA. "God. I've been so stupid."

"No." Cara patted her hand. "Not stupid. Your path isn't an easy one, sweetheart. But it might just end up being spectacular." She turned brilliant blue eyes on her daughter. "You have to fight for what you want, and I know you'll win. Every damn time."

Warmth flushed through Janie. Now she just had to figure out what she wanted and how to fight for it. Did she even know Zane enough to factor him into the equation? "I love you, Mom."

"Love you more."

Heavy boot steps echoed down the hallway, and they both turned as Talen stalked into the room.

He lifted one dark eyebrow over a golden eye. "You two drinking?"

"Yes." Cara tilted her head toward the remaining glass. "Want one?"

"No." He frowned and strode closer, his gaze on his wife's face. The massive vampire loomed over them, in an awesome shelter of protectiveness. One Janie had always counted on. "Headache?" he asked.

Janie blinked and turned toward her mother. No wonder Cara was so pale. "I'm not sure alcohol is a good numbing agent for headaches," she said slowly.

"No, but this is." Talen wiped two knuckles across Cara's forehead, smiling when she leaned into his touch.

Cara moved back, her eyes clearing. "Now you have the headache."

Talen shrugged. "It'll go away within seconds. Besides, you know I can't stand to see you hurting."

Janie's heart warmed. Her dad could be half-dead, and he'd still try to take their pains away. She'd always thought it very cool that vampires could take most illnesses or aches from their mates. Unfortunately, Virus-27 seemed impervious to the vampires' talents and refused to be unwound from mates. Her dad would definitely get rid of the virus if he could. She shook herself into the present. "Any news on the peace talks?"

Talen sighed and shoved a large hand through his dark hair. "Just the same. We go back tomorrow to fight some more."

"Fighting for peace?" Cara shook her head. "Was anything accomplished today?"

Talen lifted a muscled shoulder. "We all gave our demands after the demons dropped the bomb about Zane."

Janie rubbed her eyes as the alcohol started to slow the blood pumping in her veins. "Why wouldn't he have told me?" She lifted her head.

Talen grimaced. "It's irrelevant at this point. I'm sorry, but there can be no more contact with Zane, and you know it. Whatever they're planning is now in motion."

Cara slipped off the stool. "Do you think the demons are against peace?"

"Yes." Talen tangled his fingers with hers. "Let's grab something to eat. You hungry, Jane?"

"No." She'd probably never be hungry again with this stone in her stomach. "You two go ahead. I need to think."

Talen leaned in and brushed a kiss across her forehead. "Make sure you eat something today."

Janie nodded, wanting nothing more than to dive into his arms and have him fix the world for her like he'd done when she was young. Even now, as an adult, she knew Talen Kayrs to be invincible. But it was time to grow up and fix her own problems. "I just need a little time to think and will see you both later."

Cara paused, her blue gaze taking in her daughter. Understanding lifted her top lip. "Don't think too hard, and be careful." She stressed the last with a knowing tilt of her chin and then allowed her husband to lead her from the room.

Janie watched them go, her head reeling. She'd never sleep if she didn't at least talk to Zane and find out what was going on. Yeah, she was thinking with her heart and not her head. Silly woman. More than anything, she wanted him to tell her that she was right about him and that he cared for her. That they'd work together to save their peoples.

Realistically, she needed to find out his agenda. Friend or foe?

So, with a resigned sigh, she crossed the room and headed through the main lodge and outside into a drizzly day. Ducking her head against the rain, she hurried down the sidewalk to her home with its spectacular view of the ocean.

Once inside, she flipped on the fire and settled down at a pillow.

Warmth surrounded her, and the fire's crackle helped soothe raw nerves. She took in several deep breaths, exhaling slowly. The alcohol helped her to drop into a meditative state almost immediately.

The dream world environment matched her mood. Gray, wet, and stormy. She stood beneath a sheltering pine, her gaze on the ocean. Rain splattered against rocks, competing with the spraying waves. She shivered, even in the dream world.

He didn't keep her waiting.

Zane walked across the sand, combat boots leaving large indents. Rain beat against his dark T-shirt, outlining ripped muscles in an impressive chest. Cargo pants covered his powerful legs as they ate up the distance between them. Even through the rain, his green eyes sizzled in a masculine face. Soon, he reached her, his expression guarded.

So many questions whirled through her that her mind blanked. "Why?" she whispered.

Something flashed in his eyes, and those generous lips smirked. "Why what?"

That easily, that quickly, she roared from sad to furious. In one smooth, well-trained motion, she slid back a foot, pivoted, and nailed him in the cheek with a right cross. The hit shocked her probably more than him.

Zane's head jerked back.

Pain ripped from her wrist to her shoulder. His jaw was made of granite.

Thunder split the imaginary sky in waves of blue and red.

He pivoted back toward her, danger cascading off him.

Her wrist aching, she punched again.

This time he blocked her, easily capturing her fist in one broad palm. "No fighting in dream worlds, remember?" he rumbled, closing his hand over hers in warning. The thunder clapped again as if in agreement, a deadly reminder of when Zane and Kalin had come to blows in a dream world that had nearly exploded.

Violence wouldn't be tolerated in the dream worlds, and Janie tried to pull herself back to reality. To start thinking and stop feeling.

Too late. Regret, pain, sorrow—every emotion slamming through her ripped to the surface, and all she could do was fight. She slammed a fist into his gut and then pivoted to nail him in the thigh.

With a low growl, he took her down.

Hard.

Her butt hit the sand first, followed by her head. Zane sprawled over her, one hand manacling her wrists above her head, his jeans soaking hers.

Fire lanced through her so quickly her breath heated. Well over two hundred pounds of hard-muscled warrior pressed her into the soft sand, making it nearly impossible to gain purchase and fight. Air panted out of her lungs, rubbing her breasts against him.

Desire flared her nerves awake, multiplied to the nth power by the fury consuming her. She struggled futilely against him, her hips bucking. This was her dream world, and she'd change it.

Sucking in air, she tried to concentrate.

"Stop." Zane gripped her hip, yanking her closer.

The world stilled as his groin met hers. An erection harder than steel pressed against her. Heat pooled at the apex of her legs, stunning her with need, and lava unleashed through her body with an intensity unmatched by any other feeling. Ever.

He groaned. "Don't try to leave the world. We're not done yet." His hold tightened.

She bit back a whimper at the unreal thirst, fighting the very real urge to pin him with her thighs and rub against him to find relief. Any relief from the fierce demand gripping her body.

His hardness shut down her brain, and she needed to think. To focus and plan. "Let go of me," she breathed out.

"No." He lifted his head to pin her with a hungry gaze. "I hadn't wanted to talk this way, but here we are."

Oh yeah? She blinked and tried to wake up in Oregon. Frustration welled through her when she remained in place. Worse yet, a horrible relief loosened her muscles as her body remained enveloped by his.

"I have as much power as you here since I took your blood." Pure fact and no triumph colored his words. "And you're going to goddamn stay here and talk this out whether you like it or not."

Okay. A bit of a vampiric ego there.

Janie glared up at him. So much for two decades of training.

Against a vampire/demon, her human strength didn't amount to much. But she had more tricks up her sleeve. Flashing him a smile, she slightly spread her legs, wiggling her butt in the sand.

His erection jumped against her, while his eyes darkened and his chest hitched.

"Problem, Zane?" she whispered, throwing challenge into every syllable. The sensations coursing through her threatened to reduce her to a begging mass of nerves, and she had to fight herself as much as him. Yeah, fury filled her, but even so, he felt so damn good. She'd always wondered, and now she wanted more. So much more.

His gaze dropped to her mouth. "You've pushed enough, Belle." His voice lowered to a guttural tone that licked right across her skin. Demon low and far too sexy.

If he didn't get his hard body off her, she just might explode. She slowly licked her bottom lip in one last desperate attempt to force his retreat. "I'm just getting started."

He sucked in air. "You want to play, baby? Fine." His hard shaft slid against her, and even through their clothing, she could feel him pulse. His chest flattened hers with restrained strength.

She swallowed, bombarded with instant hunger. "This isn't real."

His heated breath brushed her face. "Feels real though, doesn't it?"

Yes. God yes, and she was seconds away from offering him everything. "No. Although you weigh a ton. Get off."

His upper lip quirked. "I'd love to."

She rolled her eyes and tried to struggle, but he'd effectively pinned her in place. The wet sand cooled her backside, while the heated male warmed her front. Too much. "Say your piece and get the hell off me."

He settled into place, his jaw hardening. "I appreciate your need for the smart-ass attitude, and usually I rather enjoy it, but I suggest you refrain for the moment."

"Or what?" she asked, meeting his gaze evenly.

"Don't push."

She tried to focus on anything but the desire uncoiling too fast inside her. He covered her head-to-toe, and each nerve begged for movement. For release. "I don't need to be a smart-ass."

"Sure you do." His gaze finally gentled. "You're a small human

surrounded by vampires who think you're going to save them all. The smart-ass attitude reassures them and keeps you from spiraling into fear."

She blinked. Twice. How was it possible he could see her so clearly when they'd only met in person once across a deep cavern? Nobody knew her that well. "You don't know what you're talking about." The rain continued to batter the sand around them, while the tree boughs protected them for now. "You lied to me." As hard as she tried, she failed to keep a tendril of hurt from her words.

He sighed, his gaze softening. "I didn't lie. I just didn't tell you I'm a demon."

"Half-demon," she muttered.

His smile broke out, a flash of white against his bronze skin. "Half-demon." The hold on her hands relaxed. "My uncle ordered me not to tell you, but I wouldn't have anyway."

She frowned. He didn't trust her? Hurt competed with desire inside her. "Why not?" she whispered.

He lifted an eyebrow. "Because you would've told the king, and he would've figured out a way to use it to his advantage. Like I would in his place."

True. Janie flexed her hands. Nope. Still couldn't move. "Did you know about my uncle Jase?" she asked.

"No." Sympathy twisted Zane's lip. "I was fighting in Iceland for years and had no clue Suri had taken your uncle or was torturing him. Once I did find out, I tried to discover where, but Suri kept the truth from me. I am sorry."

So perhaps Zane and Suri weren't on the same page. Relief helped Janie to focus. She hoped he was telling her the truth. Her body relaxed, and his pressed her harder into the sand, flushing desire through her again. Could she trust him? "How did you get the scar on your face?"

He blinked. "Suri. Training with him, was . . . difficult."

Sympathy softened her. "I'm sorry." She didn't want to let emotion rule her, but she felt so much for him it was difficult to maintain logic. "What's your plan, Zane?" she asked.

He glanced toward the tree line and frowned. "My plan is in place and includes you staying out of the way for now."

"Out of the way?" she spit. "I'd love to stay out of the way, but that's impossible. Either let me in on your plan, or get the hell out of my way." If he wasn't going to help her, then he was part of the problem. "Make a choice."

His focus returned to her. "Just because our people are enemies, doesn't mean we have to fight each other."

She shook her head, sand spraying. "You don't really believe that, do you?"

He exhaled, his shoulders dropping. "No. Anything I tell you, you'll tell your uncle."

Of course. Her family came first, and they wanted to end the war. "Ditto."

"I know," he said softly, his gaze going to her mouth.

Her lips tingled. Just from one little glance. "Zane?"

He shook his head, a low growl rumbling from his chest. "This is madness."

Her breath caught. "What is?"

He blinked and slowly, so damn slowly, lowered his mouth to hers. "This," he whispered against her.

Yeah. True, crazy, and untamed. Without thinking, she allowed her tongue to dart out and lick his lips. Yum.

His chest hitched, and a new tension spiraled around them. "Belle." A question—a warning.

She did it again.

He growled again, and his mouth enclosed hers. Warmth, fire, and male surrounded her, plunged, and went deep.

She opened her mouth, taking all of him, feeling every inch of his body covering hers. His mouth consumed her with a primal force that both ignited and startled her. Hard and pulsing, his arousal pressed against the apex of her legs in an overwhelming demand.

Her entire body burned for him, and she kissed him back with everything she had.

His shoulders stiffened, and he broke away.

No!

He lifted his head toward the tree line, his focus cutting hard. "I have to go." Desire, lust, and something all male darkened his tone. Rising to his knees, he slowly stood and tugged her to her feet. "Stay out of trouble until I figure things out." He released her and stepped back.

She glanced toward the quiet tree line, her body on fire, her mind fuzzing. "What's going on?"

"I don't know." He leaned down to brush sand off her legs.

Warmth vibrated to her core, and she forced down a moan. Then she glanced around and shook her head to regain reality. "I'm surprised Kalin didn't jump in here." Ever since Kalin had bitten her in a dream world, he'd been able to come and go at will.

Zane frowned. "Me too. Since he's not here, he must be busy, which is a bad sign."

Yeah, it was. She tilted her head and cleared her throat. "You're not forgiven for lying to me."

His instant grin reminded her of better times, of when he had been young and rather carefree. "Of that, I have no doubt."

"Are we going to find peace together?" she asked, hope weakening her knees as she tried one last time while trying to calm her rioting body.

Regret filled his eyes. "I'd like to find peace." Turning on his heel, he strode toward the tree line, stopping to glance over his shoulder. "Be safe, Belle." With that, he disappeared behind two pine trees.

That wasn't exactly a yes.

Chapter 5

Zane stood on the balcony, his body rioting with a hard-on strong enough to punch through concrete. If they hadn't been in the dream world, he might not have been able to hold back.

Janie wanted him as badly as he craved her, but now was a bad time.

A seriously bad time.

Plus, the first time he took her, he wanted it to be real. She needed to make the decision facing the real him and not a dream-world mellowed-out version of the killer he'd become. Even so, one more minute, and he might have taken what she'd offered on that sandy beach.

But something had alerted him to head home, and he lifted his head to the moon-filled night.

Power. A different sort of power hinted on the breeze, bringing a tension that tightened his gut. No fucking way.

Turning on his heel, he jogged into his quarters and through the old whorehouse, reaching Suri's door within seconds. A wave of power slammed into him, and he gasped.

Schooling his face into calm lines, he nudged open the door. Suri faced a Kurjan across a battered desk. A Kurjan with long black hair tipped with red.

Kalin stood and turned to face him. "We finally meet in person and not in a dream world or an underground cavern surrounded by vampires."

It took every ounce of Zane's control to keep his composure. Just the tension in the room from the Kurjan made his fingers itch to hold a blade. He looked beyond Kalin to his uncle. "What in the hell are you doing?" Stepping inside, he closed the door.

Kalin laughed, flashing incredibly sharp canines. "Peace makes for strange bedfellows, demon."

Zane glanced up about four inches to Kalin's face. At six-foot-six, Zane didn't look up to many people, but Kurjans were a tall race. "We going to bed, Kurjan?"

Kalin's eyes morphed from odd green to a flashy purple. "You'd be ruined for all other beings." His blood-red lips twisted. "Even Janet."

Explosions detonated inside Zane at the mention of her name. Going on instinct, he yanked free his knife and lunged toward his enemy. They impacted with a boom louder than the thunder in Janie's dream world.

Papers flew and a stapler ricocheted into the window as they collided against the desk. The antique oak smashed to the ground, splintering into pieces.

Kalin punched the knife out of Zane's grip, following up with a shot to the jaw.

Zane's vision fuzzed, and he struck out, nailing Kalin in the nose. A desperate fury raced through Zane, and the need to kill ignited the beast within him. Blood arced and burned Zane's neck as he continued throwing punches.

"Stop it!" Suri yelled, kicking shards of wood out of his way.

Rough hands, tons of them, yanked Zane off Kalin, who continued to punch.

Zane struggled furiously, swearing in multiple languages at once. The Kurjan had to die. A treaty between demons and Kurjans would mean a disaster for Janie, without question.

His uncle cocked a gun. "You want to get shot?"

Zane stopped fighting and shrugged off the three demon soldiers who'd stopped him. "Who the fuck are you, Suri?" he asked. Demons held Kurjans lower than beetle shit, and his uncle went and aligned himself with them?

Kalin shoved rubble out of his way and rose to his impressive height, taking a moment to dust off the medals at his breast. "We're not done here, demon."

Zane snarled through a busted lip. "Name the time and place, asshole."

Kalin wiped blood off his face. "Don't worry. Our time will come." He turned and bowed to Suri. "The deal stands. Good day."

As simple as that, the ruler of the Kurjan nation sauntered out of the demon's office. The three demon soldiers followed him.

Zane spit blood onto the floor. "I never thought I'd see the day a demon conspired with a lowly Kurjan." His uncle was a bastard, it was true, but even bastards had standards.

Suri eyed his destroyed desk. "I never thought my sister would whore herself out to a vampire. Life often takes unexpected turns."

Zane's hands clenched, despite his shredded knuckles. "Stop talking about my mother like that."

Suri lifted a thick eyebrow. "Or what? You finally going to try to kill me?"

Zane turned and slowly surveyed his uncle. His mind spun and then cleared. "We both know I could."

Suri scoffed. "Bullshit. I'm twice the fighter you are." He kicked kindling out of the way. "Besides, if anything happens to me, your mother and brothers will instantly pay the price. I do have my safeguards in place."

"Where is my mother?" Zane asked quietly. The day was fast approaching when he'd have to torture Suri for the information, but right now too many of Suri's followers surrounded them.

"Safe for now." Suri shrugged. "Have you made contact with Janet Kayrs?"

"No. Apparently she's pissed I'm a demon and won't enter the dream world." Zane kept his gaze level as he lied. "Not that I'm surprised."

Suri smirked. "The vampires hate you because you're part-demon, the demons despise you because you're part-vampire, and the Kurjans just want you dead. You're lucky I've provided you shelter all these years."

"Why have you?" Zane asked, not bothering to react to the truth of the rest of the statement. The reality of his birth had been dealt with long ago.

"Your gifts with the chosen one," Suri said. "You are about to become very handy."

Chills cascaded down Zane's back. "What did you promise the Kurjans?"

"None of your damn business." Suri reached down to an orphaned desk drawer to grab another laser gun. "Your only concern is keeping your mother alive, and don't you forget it."

Zane hadn't been able to forget that fact since the first day he'd arrived at demon headquarters. "I deserve to know the plan with the Kurjans. Did you promise them Janie? If so, in exchange for what?" He couldn't get his mind wrapped around that possibility.

Suri shrugged. "It matters little what I promised Kalin, although I did say we'd fetch Janet Kayrs for them. Once I get what I want, all deals are off the table."

"What do you want?" Zane whispered.

"This whole damn mess to be over, and for the vampires and Kurjans to go back to killing each other off without involving us." Suri straightened his perfectly pressed uniform. "For decades, even before Janet Kayrs was born, the doom attached to her life hung over our heads. The Seers are never wrong, and they've envisioned a destroyed world if she's allowed to fulfill her destiny."

Zane reached down to retrieve his knife to sheathe in his boot. "Changed how?"

"Nobody knows, and that's the crux of the problem. Change for immortals is never good, and there's a sense of the dystopian to the visions. Can't you sense the danger?" Suri's eyes flashed black and hard. "If you were a true demon, a real leader, you would instinctively feel the weight of disaster in the very oxygen around us."

The spit dried up in Zane's mouth. "The Seers are wrong, and I don't want to lead the fucking demons. Stop threatening me, stop threatening my family, and let us be."

Suri cracked his massive knuckles. "To think I had such high hopes for you."

Zane shook his head. "I care little for your hopes. What do you want?"

Suri chuckled, and the sound coated the roam with invisible oil. "You're a killer, plain and simple. *The Ghost.* So kill."

Zane's blood heated until the liquid burned his veins. "My destiny isn't to kill Janet Kayrs."

"No?" Suri kicked a mangled piece of desk out of his way. "The choice is, of course, yours."

"Meaning?" Zane asked softly.

Suri smiled, fangs glinting. "Your mother or your whore. One will die by the end of the week."

A blade weighed heavily against Zane's calf, almost pulsing with the need to slice into his uncle. "I've expected that ultimatum for a while now. But it does beg the question, if you want me to kill Janie, why make a deal with Kalin and the Kurjans?"

"Plan B." Suri glanced pointedly down at Zane's leg. "I'm not entirely sure you won't sacrifice your mother."

Zane's head snapped up, rage heating his breath. He rushed across the desk, grabbed Suri by the shirt, and pummeled him against the wall. Old plaster rained down, covering them both. "I will never sacrifice my mother." Zane leaned in close, surprised he had to look down a couple of inches. "Besides, as I recall, my mother has kicked your ass more than once."

Suri flushed. "Your memory is faulty."

Zane's fangs lengthened as memories rushed through him. Once, during training, Suri had beaten Zane so badly he couldn't see for several days. Felicity, although petite, had taken Suri down in a bundle of parental fury. Female demons were rare, notoriously tiny, and fucking deadly. "You're afraid of her, aren't you?" he asked.

Suri growled. "No."

"Liar." Zane leaned in even closer, pleased to see Suri's pupils dilate. "Female demons are dangerous as hell and stronger than their counterparts. Why else would you have her sequestered by soldiers away from here. Coward."

Suri slammed both hands against Zane's chest and shoved him across the room. Zane's shoulders hit the wall, knocking in old wooden beams. Pain flared along his spine. Sometimes he forgot how much power his uncle leashed daily.

"Watch yourself, boy." Suri yanked down his uniform top. "We both know I could end you in a second. In addition, the fact remains that I have your mother contained and surrounded. The moment I give the order, she dies. So, nephew, you have one week to figure out how to end Janet Kayrs in that dream world you share."

Zane loped into a run through the old mining town, jogging past a ramshackle saloon fronted by one sagging door. If he concentrated, he could still hear the clatter of horses and bustle of women's skirts. Even as he tried to calm his thoughts, fear punched him in the gut. He'd lost contact with both of his brothers as well as his mother and could only hope Suri hadn't ordered their deaths yet.

That time was coming.

Suri allowed Zane's family to live only to use them against him, and the second the mess with Janie was straightened out, Zane and his family would be of no further use to Suri. In fact, their royal blood made them a threat to the demon leader and his rule, which meant they needed to be eliminated.

So Suri could rule his fiefdom alone.

Crazy bastard.

Zane exited the town and increased his pace to wind through a barely there dirt road through the forest. How many dreams had been lost in the old town? How many loves had been sacrificed for silver and gold?

For years he'd sacrificed, doing Suri's deadly bidding. Not even his brothers knew all the terrible things he'd done. Now Suri demanded the ultimate sacrifice on Zane's part, and he couldn't do it. He kept running through the chilly night to prevent himself from jumping back into a dream world where Janie would be warm and willing. There had to be a scenario where both his mother and Janie Belle lived through the week, but as hard as he tried, he couldn't find a plan.

Footsteps echoed in his wake, and he kept pace until Nikolaj Veis reached his side.

"Running from or to something?" Nick asked evenly, falling into step.

Zane glanced at the scarred soldier dressed in sweats and a ripped T-shirt. The Veis whom Zane had known a decade ago wouldn't have been caught dead in damaged clothing. "Nice shirt."

Nick shrugged. "What else would one wear to a midnight run?"

Zane grinned. "Good point."

"We could just spar, if you wish. I've missed sparring with you."

Zane nodded. For years, they'd trained, and the older demon had often tried to find some sort of protection for Zane from Suri. But it had been ten years, and now Zane and Nick stood as equals. "Neither one of us needs more violence." Zane ducked a branch. "Was the witch worth it?" he asked.

Nick jumped over a boulder. "Absolutely. What's ten years of hard labor and exile compared to the fire of a witch?"

Zane's feet pounded rhythmically on the path. "What exactly were you doing conspiring with Simone Brightston of the Coven Nine?"

"Have you seen the woman?" Nick said dryly.

Zane stretched to hurdle a mass of huckleberry bushes. "Yes, and I agree that she's a stunning witch. But you helped her with land use matters in Russia against Suri's interests, and I've never figured out why." He'd missed his friend when he'd been sent away. Frustration clenched Zane's hands into fists.

"Simone and I have a history . . . one I don't want to discuss right now." Nick shoved a small pine tree out of his way. "As for Russia, let's just say the witches have a problem with our land holdings there."

Zane slowed to a lope and then a walk. He'd already surmised Nick and Simone had once been lovers. But the land dispute didn't make sense. "Russia? They did ask for the territory during demands yesterday."

"I'm sure," Nick said, stopping to twist his torso.

Zane leaned back against a white pine, wondering how well he really knew Nick. "What's in Russia?"

"Russians?" Nick rolled on his feet. "Witches and their issues are irrelevant to us right now. Focus."

Zane scratched his jaw. "Is there an *us*?"

Nick stilled. "What are you asking me?"

Zane eyed the dark face of someone he'd once considered a friend. But years of hard labor often destroyed a man, especially when demons designed the labor. They hadn't talked in too much time, and even now, Nick might be desperately loyal to Suri. Demons lived for subterfuge. "Are you broken?" Zane asked.

Fire flashed through Nick's gray eyes. Muscles rippled along his arms and broad chest. "No. Are you?"

"No." Zane's shoulders settled into place.

"Well then." Nick studied him. "I wonder where this leaves us."

Everything in Zane wanted to trust his old friend, but he'd learned young that trust could be bought. "Can you get into the main control room?" Zane asked.

Nick jerked his head, blinking. "Yes. Why?"

"Suri and Kalin. I need to know the plan."

"I already know the plan. Tomorrow Suri is going to double-cross Kalin and take out the Realm forces in order to kill Janet Kayrs." Nick rocked back on his heels. "The strategy is nearly perfect, actually."

So Suri had given up on Zane's killing Janie? "How do you know?" Zane settled his stance, realization dawning. He had no allies.

The smile Nick flashed could only be termed malevolent. "Because I came up with the plan."

Chapter 6

The Realm helicopters spread out in a defensive formation, all unmarked, all fully armed on the way to the underground cavern. Far below, the ocean rioted, flinging up whitecaps like a child throwing a tantrum. Rough weather issued an ominous warning against the second day of peace talks.

Janie sat back in her seat, her mind spinning. Instinct raised the hair on the back of her neck, foretelling a monumental day about to occur.

Why or how, she didn't know.

As always, the mantle of destiny weighed down her shoulders, and as always, she shrugged through the heaviness with a smile for those around her.

A smart-assed smile Zane had apparently seen right through.

She didn't feel the smart-aleck persona, and she never had. Fighting to find the lightness in their situation wore on her, and sometimes she just wanted to escape.

Her father sat next to her, his gaze out the window, tension vibrating from his tough body.

Uncles Dage and Max sat in the front of the helicopter fully armed and prepared to wage war. Well, continue waging war.

Could peace actually be accomplished? If so, how could she make it happen? There must be some truth to all the prophecies, so there had to be something she could do to end the war. To end the bloodshed.

Leaving the Arias volume in the cavern the previous day had

actually hurt deep inside. As if she'd left a part of her, one aspect she needed for survival. To breathe and live.

What in the world was she meant to do?

Could the book actually help her meet destiny? Finally?

A wisp of sound echoed, and water whooshed through the early morning. Gray and fast, a spinning missile barely missed her side of the helicopter.

Fear flushed down her body like pricking needles. Janie's scream caught in her throat.

Dage yanked the controls to the right, and the helicopter banked dangerously to the side. "Evasive maneuvers, attack from water," he growled into his earpiece.

Janie smashed her palm against the side of the craft, her heart racing, her breath rushing out. Cold metal scraped her skin. She reached out and clutched her father's thigh for support.

He turned toward the window on his side and drew a gun from his waistband. Fury vibrated along his back. "Missile from the ocean?" Leaning against the opening, he scanned the ocean below. "Three rafts—very small."

Another missile winged by, barely missing the craft. The helicopter banked sharply, and Janie cried out. Only Dage's incredible reflexes kept them from being hit.

"How do they know this is us?" Max growled, yanking open the passenger-side door for a better shooting angle. He fired rapidly down, half-leaning outside, one large hand keeping him from falling.

Dage banked hard left. "They're attacking every helicopter."

Janie swallowed and tugged a gun from her back pocket. Her terror panted out. She wouldn't have much range, but if they went down, she wanted to be prepared. Although the missiles were kill shots and not an effort to merely take them out of the air, they might get a chance to fight.

"How the hell did they get near enough to bring in rafts?" Talen yelled.

Janie peered closer, her nose pressed to the bulletproof glass. "We're far enough away from headquarters that we wouldn't have seen them." Plus, the rafts were incredibly small—it was possible the vampire's security measures wouldn't have tracked them.

The gun lay heavy in her hand, and she fought the urge to fire. Her gun was too small to reach a target this far up, and she might need the weapon upon landing.

Dage punched a yellow button in the ceiling. "Load up."

Parachutes dropped from the roof. Janie reached for one, buttoning up with trembling fingers and getting ready to fly. The blood echoed as it roared between her ears. The vampires suited up.

An explosion rocked the sky.

Panic swept Janie's mind clean. Who had been hit?

Dage jerked his head around. "Shit. Jase? Come in."

God. It had been Uncle Jase. Emotion clogged Janie's throat, and she pivoted to look out the window. Blazes of fire and smoke spiraled through the gathering rain. Jase's craft spun, descending in slow motion toward the churning ocean.

She squinted as hard as possible but failed to see through the debris and smoke. Were there bodies? Her breath held while she tried to make out yellow parachutes. Nothing but black smoke and billowing fire filled the sky.

Her gaze took in the gray day and the other helicopters, and her throat closed.

Talen ripped open his door and leaned out. A burst of cold air swirled inside. "Does anybody see Jase?" he yelled.

"No." Max kept firing down and nailed a raft. The rubber exploded, spraying salt water up. Several men fell over the side into the dangerous water, and the other two rafts maneuvered to fetch them.

Max bellowed a warrior's cry and aimed at the rescuers. Talen leaned out and added his firepower to Max's.

"Get us down to the water," Talen ordered. "We need to find Jase and his squad."

Dage nodded. "Give me a minute. We're still taking fire." He glanced over his shoulder at Janie. "Get ready to shoot."

"Not a problem." Janie took several calming breaths, but her heart still beat erratically against her breastbone.

An intense wave of shrieking pain lanced into her brain. Images of death and disease flared alive, dancing with the physical agony. She cried out and clapped a hand over her forehead. The pain intensified, and her ears grew numb.

Talen groaned. "Fucking demon mind attack."

A missile hit their chopper, sending it spinning through the smoky air. A burn lanced along her arm. They spun around and around, and a high-pitched squeal erupted from the engine. Smoke billowed past the window.

"Everyone jump. Now!" Dage bellowed.

Talen turned to grab Janie's arm just as the air snapped around them.

A heavy body landed hard in front of Janie and rocked the entire vehicle.

She gasped. "Zane?" In the helicopter out of nowhere? "How?" she breathed.

He lifted his head, a grim smile tilting his lips while he crouched in front of her. Instantly, a healing balm slid around her brain, banishing the images and agony from the demon mind attack.

Talen swiveled from the open doorway, gun out.

Zane grabbed her arms. "Hold on."

Dage turned and fired at Zane. Zane hissed in pain, his body shuddering.

Janie reached for him, panic fuzzing the day. She had a moment to feel the hard warmth of his palms around her biceps before the world spun away. No sight, no sounds . . . nothing.

Chapter 7

Liquid fire rippled through Zane's blood as he teleported through dimensions. He kept a tight hold on Janie, and within seconds, they landed on frozen ground. Ice shards slipped up the back of his shirt. He tucked himself around her fragile body as they rolled across rocks.

Sharp points ripped into his damaged shoulder, but he kept Janie off the jagged rock edges.

Finally, they slammed into a massive pine tree and sent snow spraying.

Zane lay on the ground with Janie on top of him, his wound bellowing, his heart racing. "Belle?" he asked.

She slowly lifted her head. Wide blue eyes focused on him. Shock, fear, bewilderment, all raced across her expressive face in seconds. Her pink mouth opened and closed.

"Are you all right?" he asked, sliding his hands down her arms. She smelled like fresh peaches, sweet and wild. Even through their clothing, he could feel her heat. Her toned body fit against him perfectly, her softness a comforting contrast to his hard angles. He'd wanted her for so damn long. "Belle?" he asked again.

That quickly, fury darkened those spectacular eyes. "No!" she exploded, lifting her head and dropping her forehead sharply on his nose.

Agony zipped through his face, and his eyes watered.

She scrambled off him, kicking snow and debris.

"Wait—" He reached for her, only to receive a boot planted hard in his gut. "Oof." He leaned up toward his stomach to sit, grabbing his nose. "Jesus, Belle. You broke my nose."

She slid in the snow, trying to find purchase with the large parachute still on her back. Her anger vibrated on the wind. So when she shifted her stance to kick him again, this time he was ready.

He caught her small boot in one hand right before it connected with his ear. She hopped on her other foot to keep her balance.

"No more kicking." He gently placed her foot on the ground and stood to maneuver into her space, forcing her to lift her head to keep eye contact. "Get your bearings. Teleporting takes a few minutes to get used to." Although the woman had launched into fight mode in an impressively short amount of time.

"Where the hell are we?" She shrugged out of the yellow chute and dropped it on the ground.

He cleared his throat and mentally popped his nose back into alignment. "Alaska wilderness . . . weeks away from any civilization."

Red spiraled across her classic cheekbones. "Take. Me. Back."

He lifted an eyebrow. "Into the war zone? Hell no. This rescue took me all night to arrange." The tone came out more irritated than he would've liked, but right now, his nose hurt, his gut hurt, and he was bleeding from a bullet wound inflicted by the King of the Realm. Plus, Nick had helped him plan, which would get his friend killed if Suri found out.

Janie gasped and reached into her waistband, only to frown.

"Weapons don't teleport." Thank God. Zane didn't want to deal with another wound. His nose repaired, he sent healing cells to the shoulder injury.

Janie glanced around at the forest of snow-covered trees. "So you can teleport." Anger rode every consonant. "That's a rare talent."

He shrugged. "About twenty percent of demons can teleport."

Janie stepped away from him. "My uncle Dage is the only vampire I know who can do so." Hurt slid across her face. "Why didn't you ever tell me you had the gift?"

He didn't like the sudden blue tinge to her lips. "The less you ever knew about me, the safer we both were." Sad, but true. He gestured toward a trail between two trees. "The cabin is that way. I would've landed in there, but the bullet wound threw me off."

She shuffled her feet in the snow. "Are you all right now?" Her unwilling concern warmed him. "Fine."

"Good. Then fucking take me back." She put both hands on her hips, challenge in every line of her human body even as she shivered in the cold.

He did love a good challenge. "No."

Her gaze narrowed. "Fine." She glanced up at the cloudy sky and then turned on her heel. The snow came above her knees, but she pushed doggedly down an invisible trail.

"Where are you going?" he called out. She couldn't be that stubborn, could she?

"Screw you." The words came back clearly on the breeze.

He grinned. Though he certainly didn't have time for this, he liked the real Janie showing up. All grit, all woman—no fake smiles or smart-aleck reassurances. "Get your ass back here."

Her snort reached his ears.

As did a shiver rumbling through her body.

A human wouldn't survive very long in the cold, and Janie wasn't even wearing a jacket. He sighed and reached her in several long strides through the light powder, trying mentally to close his bullet hole. "We need to get you to warmth."

She ignored him, her chin on her chest as she battled the wind.

Admiration welled through him along with aggravation. "Janie, we really don't have time for this."

She whirled around, eyes flashing. "We don't?" Her now blue lips pursed. "Do you have a plan?"

"Yes." He gently grasped her arm. "The plan is to get you to the warm cabin and then go take care of business."

She blinked. Several snowflakes landed on her pale skin. "You're leaving me here?" Her arms swept out toward the wilderness.

"Yes." Thank God. She understood. He turned to lead her to the cabin.

She jerked back. "Forget it, Fucktard." She turned and made it several steps before his brain kicked into gear.

"Fucktard?" He barked out a laugh. While that might be funny, his patience was dwindling. Time mattered. He strode through freezing snow again to clasp her arm and turn her around. "Enough of this. You're minutes from freezing to death."

Her teeth clenched in a chatter. "Either take me back to help my family, or I'll walk. Your choice."

What would it be like to have her loyalty to such a degree? Though he could certainly understand her desire to help, the woman needed to stay safe. They'd been friends their entire lives; surely he could reason with her. "Listen, Janie—"

The kick to his shin shocked the hell out of him.

He'd spent years taming his temper, yet five minutes in her company and he wanted to growl. "That's it." In one smooth motion, he ducked his head and tossed her over his shoulder to stride toward the hidden cabin. He clasped a hard arm across the back of her thighs to protect his gut from her swinging boots. "We're going to have to address your penchant for kicking," he said conversationally, his good humor restored.

Janie's furious hiss emerged as warning when she struggled on his shoulder, her fists punching his back.

The woman could seriously squirm, but her weight didn't even register. They reached the darkened cabin, and he kicked open the door. Several steps inside, he dropped her on the bed.

She shot up, and he planted her back down with a hand against her upper chest.

"Son of a bitch." She shoved his way again, and he set her back down.

"I feel like I'm playing Whac-A-Mole," he said with a grin. God, she was cute when furious, but he knew better than to say those words out loud.

He reached his limit the fifth time he sat her down. "Enough." Dropping to his haunches, he ripped off her boots and socks.

"Hey—" She stood up in bare feet. Adorable, small feet with nails painted a stunning scarlet. Delicate, feminine, and sexy. His heart thumped. Hard.

Sucking up air in an application of string theory, he concentrated and ran through space and time to end up in Seattle, where he threw the boots in a trash can. His temples pounded, and his gut churned in warning. Ignoring the risks, seconds later he returned to the cabin and landed on his feet. Each teleport weakened him, and he needed to knock off the quick jumps.

Janie stood where he'd left her. "Where are my boots?"

"Near the Space Needle." Even stubborn Janie wouldn't try to traverse the freezing ground without shoes. Zane ignored his headache and flipped on the lights to reveal the cozy one-room cabin. He had Janie right where he wanted her, and the responsibility sobered him. "The generator is full of gas, but I'll light you a quick fire."

A stone fireplace took up one entire wall, while the bed lay opposite it. A small kitchenette made up the other wall. He'd left kindling, wood, and paper in the fireplace the day before and just had to light it now. He made quick work of the materials, and soon the crackle of warmth filled the space. "There's a bath just off the kitchen." He stood and pointed.

Janie remained in place, her skin pale. "Did you arrange the attack on my family?"

"No." Zane dusted off his hands, wanting more than anything for her to believe him. He had to see that trust in her eyes again. It was shocking how much he missed it. "Suri and Kalin reached an agreement yesterday, but Suri decided to double-cross Kalin and kill you. I spent a good portion of the night coming up with a counterattack to get you to safety before a bomb took you out."

She gasped. "At least Kalin doesn't want me dead." She pushed auburn hair out of her face.

Zane sighed. Why did she have to be so damn appealing? All he wanted to do was cuddle up with her by the fire and chat. Flirt. Maybe kiss and forget who he was and what he'd done. Yet instead, he had to go wage a fucking war and probably commit more acts to damage any humanity he still had. "Suri wants you dead, and he had no problem betraying Kalin."

Janie blinked. "Please take me back. I have to know they're all okay." Vulnerability chased fear across her face.

Zane's chest hurt. "I'm sure they're okay, Jane. I'll check on them as soon as I can."

"Where are you going?" She glanced around the cabin as if looking for a way out.

"To protect *my* family." He wanted to touch her, to try to reassure her. How could he make her understand? "If Kalin gets to you, then my family is no longer necessary to Suri. I have to get them to safety." And keep Janie safe. Nobody knew where she was. "This keeps you out of danger, too." He needed her to trust him.

"I don't want to be out of danger." She shook her head. "I have a job to do, and hiding in the Alaskan wilderness won't accomplish anything."

"Just give me some time." He brushed snow off his hair.

She reached him in two strides. "I'm sorry, but I can't. We have to go back."

He slid a knuckle down the side of her face. Silk and cream . . . softer than he could've ever imagined. "I'm sorry, Belle." He closed his eyes and began to teleport, stopping short as pain ricocheted up his spine.

Maybe he should let his system recharge a little bit. If he destroyed his body, he'd be no good to anybody.

She shivered, while her lips remained a pale blue.

"Damn it." He drew her toward the two chairs fronting the fireplace and gently pushed her into one. "At least warm up while we argue." Keeping her hand, he settled into the other chair.

"Let's not argue." She flipped her hand under his and laced her fingers through his.

He bit back a smile. While she might not recognize the gesture as one of trust, he did, and it warmed him somewhere deep inside that was always cold. "I like that idea."

She smiled, looking so pretty something hurt in his chest. "Let's go back and make sure everyone is all right, and then we can go to headquarters and work on a plan with my uncle. We can save your family."

Fuck, she was naïve. He tried to gentle his voice and not sound like a demon. "I know you think involving your family will help, but doing so will negate my bargaining power with Suri. I have to do this alone."

Her fine eyebrows arched. "Isn't that how you do everything? Alone?"

The soft question held a sharp edge. "No. Soldiers follow me, and I have a mother and two brothers."

Janie began shaking her head before he'd finished speaking. "Do you work with them or around them? Protecting them without sharing what you're doing?" Her eyes darkened. "What you've done?"

Either insightful or psychic, the woman had nailed him. He removed his hand and settled back in his chair. Away from her . . . and the truth. "I do what I have to do."

She glanced down at her hand and frowned. Taking a deep breath, she pushed off from the chair and landed between his knees, her palms on his thighs. The fire lit her from behind, turning the highlights in her auburn hair into compelling flames. "Working alone gets you killed. The people in your life, the ones who love you, they need to *share* in the burden. To help and to plan."

Did she consider herself one of the people who loved him? "That's sweet, Belle."

Her fingers dug into his legs. "I'm not being sweet. This is smart, and you have to trust somebody at some time. Duty doesn't always have to be painful."

"Doesn't it?" His voice lowered as he leaned toward her, his senses on alert. "When was the last time you *shared*? Stopped being a reassuring smart-ass and told somebody, *anybody*, how scared you are? How overwhelmed by fucking fate?"

Her eyes dilated, and her mouth opened and closed before she pushed out words. "That's different."

"Is it?" Taken aback and getting pissed at her accurately profiling him, he flattened her hands under his. "Look at the position you've put yourself in, trying to share. You're on your knees, as vulnerable as a woman can be." Shit. He could break her neck without flexing a muscle. The woman needed to realize her precarious position and back the hell off.

Instead, she lifted her head and stared him right in the eye. "I do understand my position, and I do realize how dangerous you are. Yet I'm willing to take the chance, to be fragile, to show you what trust looks like. What courage can look like."

The calm statement burned his ears and sped up the blood in his veins. She was braver than any soldier he'd ever met. Lifting his hand, he allowed himself one moment to touch the smooth skin along her cheekbone, humming at the delicate structure. "You're so soft, Belle," he rumbled.

She swallowed and leaned into his touch.

Heat flowed into his torso, expanding him into somebody strong enough to protect her. Determination slid just beneath his skin.

As if reading him, sadness filled her eyes. "You're not listening."

He helped her up and stood, backing her into the wall. "I listened." One knuckle under her stubborn chin lifted her face. Her scent surrounded him, driving him to follow his plan. "I just didn't agree."

Temper brushed a muted red across her cheeks.

Ah, the pretty one usually got her way, now didn't she? He grinned, even knowing he played with fire. "Thanks for the suggestion, though. For the record, any time you want to get on your knees, I'm there."

The punch to the gut was expected and thus didn't hurt. But it did deserve a response.

His mouth connected beneath her jaw, pressing a hard kiss to her neck. The simple touch nearly knocked him back on his heels. Soft and sweet, her skin felt too smooth to be real. Her head fell back, anchored by the wall, her legs parting to grant him access.

He'd conquered before, and the urge now held a resemblance to battle. To triumph and take. So badly he wanted her under him, pinned for good. Sighing his name.

He kissed down her jugular, feeling the pulse pounding. She slid her hands up into his hair, holding him in place as she plastered her soft body against his. The soft tug awoke the beast inside him. The one who scented his mate. Those incredible curves molded to his hardness, giving way and cushioning him. The driving urge to pleasure her forced him to slow down and explore. To taste and tempt, wandering up to the soft spot behind her ear.

He wouldn't go near her mouth, because if he kissed her, he wouldn't stop. One taste of that mouth, of her, would seal his fate.

Drawing back, he took a moment to remember her. Dazed blue eyes, smooth skin, pursed lips. As if waiting for his kiss. So damn perfect he'd do anything to protect her. To defend her from what wanted to hurt her.

He stepped back, allowing his face to harden. "Stay warm until I return." His hoarse voice sounded more demon than vampire, and he fought a wince.

"Don't leave," she breathed.

"I'm sorry, Belle." Drawing on the universe and controlling her dimensions, he teleported out of Alaska.

Chapter 8

Zane landed hard outside the back entrance to the old whorehouse. Pain ratcheted up his spine. A green laser beam whizzed by his head, morphing into a bullet as it impacted the warped wooden siding. Two more bullets slammed into his upper shoulder.

Shit.

He ducked and dove through a damaged window, hitting the ground and rolling. Pain rode him hard, and he shoved all feeling down to deal with later.

Nick Veis nodded from a crouched position in the thick smoke. Blood covered his face and poured from several wounds along his neck. He grunted before straightening to shoot through the window. "Nice of you to join us." A bomb went off in the distance, and wooden beams dropped from the ceiling.

Zane ducked and crab-walked closer to the shards of glass. He smelled *Kurjan*. "Gun."

Nick spun a laser weapon through burned embers on the floor.

Zane clasped the handle, rose up, and fired a volley of shots toward the tree line. "How badly are you hurt?"

"Not bad," Nick groaned, leaning against a side wall. "Just need a minute to repair the damage."

"Humph." Metal glinted in the forest, and Zane took aim, neatly hitting his target. Kurjan blood sprayed. "Status?" Zane asked.

Nick grunted as a bullet hole closed next to his trachea. "Status? Our status is that a holy fuck of a shit-storm has descended upon the demon nation."

Zane nodded and took aim again. As hard as he tried, he couldn't shut the bullet wounds in his shoulder after having just teleported. The best he could accomplish was stemming the blood flow. "Kalin didn't like Suri's double-cross today?"

"No." Nick kept low and took position on the other side of the destroyed window. "The second we attacked the vampire helicopters and tried to kill Janet Kayrs, the Kurjans figured out our double-cross and attacked us here." He dodged as a series of green bullets ripped by his chest. "Suri promised Kalin delivery of Janet Kayrs on a platter, and the Kurjan wants to feast."

Zane grimaced. "Gross."

"There's more." Nick leaned up to take a shot.

"There's always more." Zane fired a series of shots into the forest, listening closely for any impact. His head reeled, and his knees weakened. Teleporting three times in an hour after just getting shot had taken too much of a toll. He needed protein and fast.

Nick paused as another explosion rocked the earth. "After we shot out their helicopters, the vampires immediately struck back, hitting us in Eastern Europe, Africa, Iceland, and Florida."

"Florida?" Zane wiped grime out of his eyes.

"Yeah. How they discovered our holdings there is beyond me." Nick drew a smartphone from his pocket. "No updates."

That wasn't good. "So Suri's double-cross put us in the crosshairs of the vampires *and* the Kurjans." Zane took a deep breath and then coughed out soot and powder. He had to find his mother and youngest brother. "Any chance they'll gang up on us?"

"Sure. Why the hell not?" Nick lifted the phone to his ear. "Suri? What is going on?"

Zane frowned.

Nick nodded as he listened. "Keep us apprised." He slid the phone back into a pocket.

"Well?" Zane rubbed his still damaged shoulder and tried again to close the wounds. No luck, but the blood flow trickled.

"Suri and Kalin are communicating now. The vampires are so pissed, they're attacking worldwide with shifter and witch backup. The Kurjans need us to counter, and it looks like we need them now, too—regardless of our double-cross." Nick spit out blood.

Dread dropped like a lead weight into Zane's gut. "Janie will be the bargaining chip. Kalin won't deal this time unless it's a guarantee and we hand her over."

All sounds of a fight stopped outside.

Nick's eyebrows rose. "Apparently Suri and Kalin are reaching an agreement." He wiped off his neck. "Were you successful in your mission?"

"Yes. Janie is safe." Zane studied Nick. Just how much could he trust the older demon? "How about you?"

A bullet popped out of Nick's jaw to ping across the dirty floor. "Logan is fighting in southern Africa, and I should have a location on him soon. I haven't found any trace of your mother, but I will. Sam is prepared to move on orders."

Zane dropped down to lean against the soot-covered wall. "What's the Intel on Janie and the vampire helicopters?"

Nick slid a fresh clip into his weapon. "Total damage on the helicopters and several yellow parachutes with shooting vampires as they plunged into the ocean. Their backup arrived amazingly fast, so I assume no deaths. Good injuries, though."

"And Janie?" Zane whispered.

"No news." Nick grinned. "The Kurjans and your uncle are afraid the vampires got her to safety."

Zane's shoulders relaxed. "So we're the only two who know that I have Janie safe."

"Well, and the vampires must know you captured her. But they're not talking." Nick slid down to sit.

No, the vampires would be waiting for Zane to make demands. While they attacked the hell out of every demon stronghold in the world, that is. "So much for the peace talks."

His phone buzzed, and he glanced at the face. "Sam?"

"What the hell is going on?" Sam sounded beyond pissed. "We were just besieged by both vampires and Kurjans, who then turned on each other. It's fucking chaos in Iceland."

"Hang tight and duck low." Zane stretched to his feet. "You'll be out of there shortly. As soon as I find Logan, I need you to get him." Sam could teleport, unlike either their mother or Logan. "Be ready, and if you need to flee, do it."

"I'm not fleeing."

Zane nodded. His younger brother was a warrior and a loyal one. He'd fight to the death. Pride and fear filled Zane at the thought of losing Sam. If they all made it out of the current mess, it'd be a miracle. "Stay safe—I need you." He ended the call, searching for a miracle.

The phone buzzed again, and Zane read the face. "Suri wants us."

Nick shoved to his feet. "He's holed up in the center of the building." No expression crossed Nick's face, but judgment echoed in his words.

Zane nodded in agreement. "Any chance you want to lead the demon nation?"

"Fuck no. You?"

"No." Zane shoved damaged beams out of the way to hustle to the heart of the whorehouse—the private bar area. "Neither does my mother, unfortunately." He loped inside to find Suri pacing the wall before a blank screen. "I told you not to double-cross the Kurjans."

Suri slowly turned, his eyes a burning black. "Where have you been?"

"Scouring wreckage for Janet Kayrs," Zane growled. "Then I was fighting downstairs, defending this place, as you were . . . in here."

Nick shut the door behind them.

Suri snarled. "I was negotiating with Kalin for another chance at peace and to double our efforts against the vampires. It's time to take them all out."

Zane's head jerked up. "Did you manage to kill any of them?" God, he hoped he wouldn't have to break bad news to Janie.

"No." Suri shook his head. "Our sources indicate we injured several of the vampires, but nobody died. We didn't really expect anybody to die from bombing their transport."

"No. You did expect Janet to die, however." Zane's fingers clenched with the need to slam his fists into Suri's face.

Suri nodded. "Yes, well . . . that didn't work out. So we'll have to go with Plan B for sure."

Zane's blood chilled. "What did you promise Kalin?"

"Janet Kayrs, of course." Suri clasped his hands behind his back. "If she survived the attack, then she's back at the vampire headquarters in Oregon. You can teleport, and you can find her there."

"Or what?" Zane asked softly.

Suri flashed sharp fangs. "You have twenty-four hours to bring Janet Kayrs here. One minute after that deadline, and I have your mother killed. Painfully."

Janie finished stashing knives around the tidy cabin, her mind spinning. She'd wrapped her bare feet in kitchen towels and climbed outside to the top of the cabin, but only trees and snow had met her gaze. A lone antelope had wandered by, and several birds had flown above. Weren't they supposed to fly south?

Finally, with shudders racking her body, she'd climbed down and headed inside to warm up when it had become too dark to see. When feeling had returned to her feet, she had to bite back tears, but she wouldn't allow them to fall.

She had to get home.

Was her father all right? He had to be. So did her uncles. The idea of losing one of them, so close to the end of the war, sliced a sharp pain through her heart. They'd protected her for decades, and it was her turn to protect them. Somehow. By doing whatever it was she was meant to do.

Which couldn't happen in the wilds of Alaska—if she really was in Alaska.

The silly kitchen blades she'd hidden might harm Zane, but she couldn't force him to teleport her home. Frustration filled her until she couldn't help tapping her foot. Several deep breaths calmed her until she could plan. She glanced out the double-pane window to the quiet world outside. Still and silent with only snow pummeling down. As if just waiting for her to look, the wind picked up, whistling an eerie tune through the trees as the world turned darkly white. A tantrum of freezing cold and no visibility.

She'd never make it to safety if she ventured out.

The fire crackled, warming the interior. A hand-stitched quilt covered the inviting bed, and carved cupboards made up the kitchen walls. The space would be very comfortable if she hadn't been kidnapped.

Was this Zane's getaway?

The area smelled of fresh cleansers, pine, and something indefinitely male. For years she'd wondered at his scent. In dream worlds, she hadn't been able to smell him, but now that she'd transported through dimensions, his scent all but covered her. Something out-doorsy and free, like a forest right before spring. Dark, dangerous, and ready to live.

Even as furious and determined to get home as she was, her body felt electrified. Alive as if for the first time.

The air fizzled by the door. She stood, reaching for a knife tucked in her back pocket. Her heart kicked right back into full gallop. Sparkles zipped through the oxygen.

Zane plunged to the ground and impacted the polished wood floor with a resounding boom. He groaned and rolled to his feet. Both dark eyebrows rose at her defensive stance. "You going to stab me?"

She tightened her grip on the handle, fighting relief that he'd returned. "Would it do any good?"

"No." His eyes sizzled an electric green, and harsh grooves cut into the sides of his generous mouth. Power and tension vibrated from him. All of his earlier humor had disappeared, leaving a full-grown, battle-scarred, pissed-off male. Though he remained still, his stance whispered he could pounce at any second. Fast and without warning. "Put the knife away."

An order. Definitely an order.

Janie was accustomed to dealing with angry vampires, but this one was different. This one looked at her as if he'd either like to eat her alive or toss her on the bed. She swallowed. Her abdomen flut-tered, and her breasts grew heavy. The cabin suddenly shrank in size, overwhelmed by Zane. She kept her stance steady, studying him, and then gasped. "You're injured."

"Yes." He held her gaze. "Either put the knife away or attack. Let's get this over with."

Chapter 9

Stabbing Zane wouldn't get her home. Janie slowly slid the blade into her back pocket, trying to banish concern over his bleeding chest without success. "Who shot you this time?"

"The Kurjans are irritated Suri double-crossed them." Zane snapped open his black vest, dropped it on the floor, and then yanked his shirt over his head, turning to stride into the kitchen.

Janie's mouth dried up. Smooth, hard, predatory muscles shifted in Zane's back as he moved. He'd always been big, but seeing him in person, seeing his ripped, corded body in real time, stole her breath. The sweet boy had grown into a magnificent creature. "Are you more vampire or demon?" she whispered as he retrieved a first-aid kit from beneath the wide sink.

He turned and dropped into one of two kitchen chairs, which creaked under his weight. "Hell if I know. Add in a feline shifter as a great-grandmother and a wolf shifter several generations back, and I don't belong with any race." Loneliness flashed across his face to be quickly banished as he removed a set of pliers from the box.

Wow. Such a pedigree made for an explosive combination. Although he certainly shared his genetics with his brothers, he seemed so alone. An island in the middle of nowhere and responsible for everyone. Without even taking a breath, he shoved the pliers into his flesh.

Janie rushed forward, panic heating her lungs. "What in the world are you doing?" She wrapped her hand on top of his, not coming close to covering it.

He stilled and glanced down at her hand to look back up. Curiosity filtered through his gaze. "Teleporting weakens me, and I can't shove out the bullets. So I'm removing them."

Oh. Not for one second had he even thought to ask for assistance. That idea saddened her more than the fact that he'd been shot twice in a day. She gently pushed his hand off the tool. The man needed to learn how to accept help. "Take a deep breath and hold it, remaining perfectly still."

He lifted an eyebrow. "You know how to remove a bullet?"

"Of course. My life is surrounded by war, Zane." She studied the wound. Circular and small. His vest had done the trick and protected him from a through-and-through. "Did you think I just hung out and did yoga all the time?"

He shrugged and winced as his shoulder pulled on the wound. More blood slid out. "I guess we don't know much about each other's real lives, now do we?"

"Apparently not."

"I, ah, imagined you more involved in the intellectual side of the Realm. Planning and strategizing."

Her upper lip twisted. "Didn't see me getting my hands dirty, did you?"

"Bloody." He leaned back in the chair and stiffened. "Your hands are bloody, sweetheart."

"Not for the first time." Probably not for the last, either. She took a deep breath to settle herself and slowly probed inside the wound, trying to get a good grip on the bullet.

Zane didn't twitch. Only watched her with that thoughtful gaze that flared all her girly parts to life.

As gently as possible, she drew out the first bullet. While she winced, he didn't move, although his tissue tore. So she went to work on the second bullet. "You're doing great," she murmured.

He gripped the table. "I checked on your family. No deaths after the attack this morning. Everybody is fine."

Relief caught in her solar plexus, and she stopped probing until her hands regained steadiness. "Are you sure?" Her voice thickened.

"I'm sure." He reached up with his free hand and brushed a curl off her cheek.

Thank God. She blinked back tears and kept working. Even though the scent of copper hung in the air, and the sense of danger threaded the oxygen, intimacy filtered through the small cabin and kept her voice soft. They were alone in the middle of nowhere. Although administering first aid, her body began to hum from his nearness. She struggled to find something to talk about. "The demons in rafts shot a mental attack up at us. You countered the pain and terrible images for me?" she asked.

"Yes."

She nodded and forced herself to remain calm. "Can you attack minds?"

"I can, but I choose not to rip into people's brains." His voice lowered a little on the last.

"So if you wanted, you could crush my mind." Although she trusted him, the idea of anyone holding that kind of power stole her breath and set her nerves on alert.

He cleared his throat. "Yes, but I fight with my body and don't play mind games."

She paused and glanced at his implacable face. In times of war, why would anyone ignore an advantage? "Why?"

"So I'm not like him. Ever." Vulnerability flashed for a second in Zane's emerald eyes before being veiled.

"Suri?"

"Yes." Zane's monotone said more than if he'd shouted the words.

The need to offer comfort gentled her movements. If only he'd share his pain and let her heal him. He seemed so alone that pangs attacked her heart, but she continued working, instinctively knowing he wouldn't appreciate her seeing his hurts.

A twist of her wrist captured the second projectile. Only a twitch of his jaw showed his pain. Man, he was tough.

After removing the bloody bullet, she covered the wounds with gauze, pressing lightly against his chest. His hard-as-steel chest.

"Thank you," he said softly.

The intimacy of the moment wound around them, filling her head. She set down the pliers and began to move back. A broad hand wrapping around her hip stopped her.

She stilled, energy rushing down her torso.

They were alone and in real time. No dreams, no fantasies, just reality.

Zane stood, brushing warmth against her front. So much taller and bigger than she was. He slid his free hand along her jaw to the nape of her neck, tilting her head up. Keeping her in place.

She wanted to say something, but words fled. Instead, she lost herself in his green gaze, finally dropping her concentration to his full lips. Intrigue, curiosity, and need kept her still.

Just one. Just one kiss.

Right now, in person, just to feel if any of her dreams could become real.

He lowered his head slowly, adding anticipation to the moment. As if waiting two decades wasn't long enough. "Belle?" he asked, his breath brushing her lips.

"Yes." She stepped into him, stretching up to meet his mouth, her hand flattening against his bare abs.

The second their lips met, something clicked into place deep inside her.

He made a sound low in his throat—a sound of welcome. Then he immediately took control. Firm lips curved over hers, taking and forcing her to feel. Too much. Definitely too much.

But it was too late to turn back.

As he hauled her closer, her breasts flattened against his chest. Sparks flew from her nipples to her sex. His grip tightened along with every nerve inside her body. Sensation after sensation bombarded her as his tongue tangled with hers, pushing deep, retreating, and demanding. Desperation and loneliness colored his touch, along with hunger.

The hunger penetrated her skin, clawing deep and taking hold.

He took his time, exploring her, building a firestorm inside her. A desperate craving. Finally, he slowed and sucked on her bottom lip. The pull careened right down her center to her core.

Her knees buckled.

The hand at her hip gripped harder and kept her upright. So much strength. Her mind spinning, her body aching, she reached for his belt.

He stilled and lifted his head. "You sure, Belle?"

She blinked. Shook her head to regain reality. Her knuckles brushed very ripped abs. Dangerously ripped. A small whimper rose from her chest.

His nostrils flared, and the growl that rumbled up was all vampire.

Her panties dampened even further. Was she sure? Her body bellowed a *hell yes*, while her mind slowly cleared. "You've kidnapped me." She released the leather.

"I know." No apology lived in his tone, but raw desire glittered in his eyes.

Enough to make her pause. Even if she wanted to, could she handle him? Her body wanted to be overwhelmed and overtaken, but her brain knew better. "Not like this."

His eyes darkened to storm clouds reflected in a pure-green riverbed. "Then how?"

She coughed. Leave it to Zane to cut to the heart of the matter. "As part of whatever is happening. I won't be the woman you stash in safety as you fight." Reasoning with a turned-on vampire was crazy. Add his demon lineage into the mix, and she should just stab him and be done with it. "We work together, or we work *against* each other. Friends or enemies. Your choice."

He released her and stepped back. "What if I don't want either?"

His low rumble full of desire rippled through her as if he licked her skin, and she swayed in place. When aroused, his voice lowered to a hoarseness that sounded like a full-blooded demon's. "What do you want?" God, she should not have asked that.

"Same thing you do. One night before we go back to war." He shoved a rough hand through his dark hair, leaving him tousled and dangerous. "We've been moving toward this since the first time you invaded my dreams. I want you. You want me. One or both of us aren't going to see next year." He glanced at the bed. "We have tonight."

She followed his gaze to the large bed. The flutters in her abdomen increased to full-out vibrations. She'd loved him since she was four years old, and through the years, that sense had only increased. He could've overtaken her with seduction but instead was making sure she fully acquiesced. Maybe the sweet kid she'd known hadn't changed completely. She returned her focus to him. "Tomorrow you'll take me back?"

He stilled and put up a large-boned hand. Make that a humongous hand. "Whoa. I'm taking you back whether you moan my name tonight or not. This isn't a bargaining chip."

Heat swarmed into her face. "I *know* that. God." She'd stab him in the heart before she'd bargain her body for freedom.

"Oh." He cleared his throat.

She grinned. How had they gone from panting to awkwardness? "Our history makes this kind of difficult."

He nodded. "You're worried we have too much to lose."

"Perhaps too much to live up to." Her shoulders relaxed. "It's too much of a risk."

He rubbed the dark stubble along his sharp jawline. "Risks make life worthwhile." His gaze direct, he crossed flexed arms. "Take a risk, Janie Belle."

Yeah, that low tenor shot straight to her clit. But she had a brain, and she needed to use it. "I'm not some stupid female who'll jump your bones without knowing the plan, without being part of the plan. This isn't to scratch an itch, Zane. It's you and me." If he didn't get that, then one night together wouldn't make a difference. He had to let her in for them to make a go of it. Of them.

"You're special to me." Frustration twisted his upper lip.

"Then let's come up with a plan, and hopefully we'll have more than one night." Plus, although she'd never admit it, she needed time. Time to make sure she wanted the real Zane, the deadly soldier, and not the Zane she'd invented in her fantasies. For years she'd only known glimpses of him in safe dream worlds.

This man was nowhere near safe. In fact, he'd always been her escape from the violence of her life, and here he was, a man *intimate* with violence. With death and destruction. Even she had heard of the *Ghost*, and the thought that the feared assassin was actually her childhood friend warned her to proceed with caution. To make sure reality meshed with her impressions.

Even so, giving up wasn't in her nature, and she had to hold on to some hope they'd survive the war. She frowned, trying to use her brain and not screw the consequences and jump his hot body. "Why are you agreeing to take me back tomorrow?"

His chin lowered. "I have twenty-four hours to find my mother and get her to safety, or she's dead."

Janie tilted her head. "I don't understand the correlation."

"That's the amount of time I have to take you to Suri so he can give you to Kalin." Zane shoved his hands in his pockets, his eyes glittering.

"Oh." Janie exhaled, her mind spinning. How did that make any sense? "Are you taking me to Suri?"

Zane's face hardened. "No. Which means if I don't find my mother before the clock counts down, then I need to get you to the vampires for protection."

Janie sighed, her heart warming. Nice that he didn't want to sacrifice her, but maybe there was another way. He needed to listen to her. "Why not take me home now?"

Zane leaned back against the wall. "Because that's not the plan." The unyielding tightening of his jaw guaranteed he wouldn't reconsider. Any semblance of the man she'd known disappeared, leaving only the warrior behind. The one she didn't know. "Believe it or not, we have sources in the Realm, and if Suri discovers I've taken you home, he'll kill my mother," he said.

Janie fought to control her temper. "Where does Suri think you are right now?"

"Scouting the Oregon compound to best figure out how to take you." Zane reached behind his back to gather paper blueprints. "This is the sketch of the Realm headquarters I have, but I was hoping you would fill in the details for me."

"Why?" Janie shook her head. "If you're taking me back, why do you need to know about headquarters?"

His lids lowered in a curiously dangerous way. "Because I'm going in alone first. To negotiate."

The breath caught in her throat. "For what?" she murmured, already knowing the answer.

"For your release."

Chapter 10

When the King of the Realm was pissed, the world darkened. Literally. Outside the Oregonian lodge serving as Realm headquarters, black clouds rolled above while thunder bellowed. Hail the size of golf balls assaulted the earth, pummeling buildings and vehicles.

Dage must be seriously angry.

The storm suited Talen Kayrs and his current mood. A desperation only a father could feel hollowed him out until he could barely breathe. A demon had taken his baby girl. On his watch. He sat at the round conference table, facing the most dangerous warriors in existence. Family. His brothers. "Any news?"

"No." Frustration glittered a molten silver in Dage's eyes. "No demands, and none of our sources have reported in with sightings of Janie."

Garrett Kayrs sat to Talen's left, anger vibrating off the young vampire. "You're sure Zane took my sister?"

"Yes. After Dage shot him," Talen ground out.

Dage nodded, steepling his fingers under his chin. "He'll be weakened but should've been able to transport to his destination. Wherever that may be."

Talen forced down bile. He was the strategic leader of the fucking Realm, and he needed to think. "Who the hell would've thought the bastard could teleport?"

Nobody answered him. Really, there was no answer.

He cleared his throat, falling back on training to keep from going insane. "The demons attacked the helicopters, and the second we fought back, the war escalated around the world. Even between the demons and the Kurjans."

His younger brother, Conn, leaned forward. "About three hours after a multitude of skirmishes, all fire ceased between Kurjans and demons."

Talen growled. "Which might mean Zane turned Janie over to the Kurjans in exchange for an alliance."

Jase, the youngest Kayrs brother, rubbed his chin. "Yeah, but the demons want Janie dead. They've always called for her death, so if Zane is working with Suri, he wouldn't have turned her over to Kalin. He would've, ah, killed her, which I don't think happened. It couldn't have happened."

"Right. If the demons had killed her," Kane, the brilliant brother, said quietly, "then the Kurjans wouldn't have stopped attacking the demons. They stopped fighting for some reason. She has to be alive and being held as a bargaining chip. Either between them or against us—probably both. Hopefully Zane will make contact soon."

"So where the hell is she?" Max, Janie's bodyguard and honorary uncle, hissed. He shoved away from the table—a massive vampire alight with fury. "I need something to charge."

They all needed a target.

Garrett drummed his fingers on the table. "There's always a possibility Zane took her to safety. Out of the way of whatever the demons and Kurjans were planning."

Talen concealed a wince at the hope in his son's statement. "True."

"Besides, Janie can fight. She's excellent," Garrett said.

Max turned and punched a wall. Sheetrock exploded around the room. "Zane is a demon-vampire hybrid. That kind of power is unparalleled." Max flexed his fingers, eyeing his dust-covered knuckles. "Janie is . . . human."

He might as well have said *breakable*. Talen exhaled slowly to keep from exploding. "Jane is smart, she's psychic, and she's determined. Be ready for her to get word to us."

"We're ready to move on demand," Conn said quietly. He stood. "I'll go make sure the forces are suited up." He, Kane, Jase, and Max left the room.

Dage eyed Talen. "You okay?"

"No. You?" Talen ground out.

"No." Dage flattened his palms on the onyx table, his hands vibrating. "How's your mate holding up?"

Rage poured through Talen. "Not well. Cara and your mate are meditating, trying to find Janie in a dream world." It was a long shot, considering only Janie, Zane, and Kalin had ever been able to enter the dream world. But his mate had to do something to get her daughter back.

Dage nodded and stood. Helplessness and frustration cut harsh lines in his strong face. "I'm going to reach out to any allies we have and will report back with news." He turned on his heel and strode from the room.

Talen slowly stood, feeling much older than his three and a half centuries. His son stretched to his feet, standing shoulder-to-shoulder with him. When had Garrett gotten so tall? They grew up too damn fast. Talen slammed a hand against Garrett's back to offer comfort, oddly proud when his son didn't move. "Janie will be all right."

Garrett turned, meeting his gaze directly. "I know."

The hint of fear in the air proved neither one of them believed their words. Talen cleared his throat. "Zane saved your life once, and I understand your need to think he might be a good guy." Shit. Talen needed to think so, too.

The smile Garrett flashed showed fangs. "I owe him, it's true. But he took my sister away from family and into danger." Garrett's metallic gray eyes morphed into a startling aqua. "That means he fucking dies."

Zane shoved through time and space, the molecules in his body tearing apart. Drawing deep on a rapidly waning strength, he opened the air and fell to land flat on his face back in Idaho.

Agony burst through his nose.

Again.

Jesus. How many times could a guy break his nose in one day? He rolled over onto his back to find Nick Veis staring down.

"How many times have you teleported today?" Nick nudged him with a size sixteen flack boot.

"Too many," Zane croaked, accepting a hand up. Each jump weakened him, and he hadn't had time to restore his strength. He blinked blood out of his eyes, and his large intestine cracked. The small computer room swayed around him, and he stood still until things settled. "Please tell me you've found my mother."

"No." Nick dropped into a chair facing a computer and tossed him a cheeseburger from a bag. Then, taking a good look, he threw the whole bag at him before turning back to the screen. "I have narrowed her location down to Maine, Brisbane, or Hong Kong."

Three different continents. Zane polished off a burger in two bites and reached for another one. "And Logan?"

"Nothing." Nick punched in keystrokes, and Sam took shape on the screen. "We do have an idea, however," Nick murmured.

Bruises and blood covered Sam's face, clearly visible in HD.

Anger burned through Zane's gut. "Are you all right?"

"Of course." Sam spit out red. "The fighting here is dying down, and I thought I'd head to Africa."

Zane frowned and took the seat Nick kicked toward him, eating his third burger. "Where?"

Nick tapped more keys and split the screen to show a map next to Sam's face. "We have troops here, here, and here." Nick pointed to the three places. "Since Sam can teleport, we thought he'd check them out one by one."

"What if Logan isn't in Africa?" The last thing Zane needed was Sam weakened by multiple jumps. With their demon and vampire mix, they could jump more consecutive times than any other demon, but they still had limits and needed to recharge. He eyed Nick. Too bad the older demon couldn't teleport. So far, neither could Logan, although he was still young. Sometimes the talent took a century to develop. Zane had been able to teleport since puberty, and so had Sam. Rare indeed.

Sam shoved to his feet, a pained grimace twisting his lip. "This is our best shot—and it's all we've got. As soon as you get a lock on Mom, we need to get there. If I'm already with Logan, we save a step." He leaned toward the camera in his cell phone, his eyes the same green as Zane's. "I can't just sit tight any longer. I need to go find him."

Zane cracked his nose back into place. He did like the idea of Sam being off Suri's radar and out of Iceland, and if Sam found Logan, even better. "All right. Um, Sam? Suri has given us twenty-four hours to turn over Janie, or he'll kill Mom." Zane swallowed, his gut churning. "I can't turn her over."

Sam's jaw clenched. "I don't want to be the kind of people who'd turn a little human woman over to the Kurjans, Bro. No matter who she is or what she might mean to you." He glanced over his shoulder. "Let's find Mom."

Emotions clogged Zane's throat. His brother was a damn good man. "We will. Keep in touch."

The screen went black.

The door opened, and Suri stomped inside. "Status?"

Zane finished chewing and remained sprawled in the chair. "The best time to hit Realm headquarters is tomorrow morning at ten a.m. There's a shift change, and several of the forces will be out on training drills, if they stick to their current schedule." Part of his report was true and the rest complete bullshit. "Too bad you can't teleport to help tomorrow."

Nick shot Zane a warning glance.

Zane half-shrugged. At this point, he was done. "Where's my mother?"

"Safe but well hidden." Suri's vocal chords sounded more mangled than usual. Stress must be getting to the leader. "If you attack at that time, you'll have less than an hour to get to Janet Kayrs and bring her here. To save your mother."

Zane slowly stood to look down at the dangerous leader. "Once my mother is safe, I'd like to put her in the ring with you." If provoked enough, a female demon could easily take a male. Even Suri.

Suri's head jerked up. "I never should have let you live."

Zane flashed his fangs. "Yet you did, and now you need me." Nobody else could get close to Janie, and Suri thought he had Zane where he wanted him. "For now."

Suri growled low. "For now." He glanced at Nick and then back to Zane.

Shit. He couldn't get a clue Zane and Nick were working together. Zane snarled. "When this is over, I'm done being your puppet. My family and I are out of here."

Suri snorted, disbelief twisting his lip. He'd never believe Zane didn't want to rule. "Just get the job done."

Zane nodded and headed for the door. "That's my plan."

Janie heard rather than saw Zane drop out of nowhere this time. She sat on the rug before the fire, her legs crossed, her eyes closed. "Back so soon?" she asked, keeping her face to the flames.

"Yes," he groaned.

A chair scraped across the wooden floor. "Try to be quiet," she whispered.

"What are you doing?" he asked.

"Meditating." She'd needed to clear her head and possibly reach out. Zane was ticking her off, and contacting Kalin seemed foolish. Although, she could contact him just for information and not reveal her location or current situation.

"No." Strong hands slid under her arms and jerked her up.

She gasped and spun around to shove Zane. "What are you doing?" Her eyes flipped open.

His lids half-lowered, giving him a sexy, dangerous look. "No meditating." Even with the fierce growl, he couldn't mask the paleness under his fine skin. A dark shadow covered his jaw and contrasted with his colorless face.

Janie frowned. "What is wrong with you?"

"Tired," he slurred. "Shouldn't have jumped so many times."

No way could he teleport her out of there right now. She sighed, wanting nothing more than to hold him tight and offer comfort. But she knew better. "What do you need?"

"Sleep." He grasped her upper arms. Even weakened, his hold was unbreakable. "Did you eat?"

"Yes." She shuffled her feet. A part of her wanted to thank him for the food he'd left, while the other part still wanted to kick him for kidnapping her. "Thank you." Damn it. Good manners always won.

"Welcome." He turned and led her over to the bed, his normally graceful gait lurching.

She struggled. "No."

"Yes." He shoved her down and crawled up to spoon around her. "Just sleep."

It was like being wrapped by a bear. Heat cascaded along her back until he jerked her into his hardness. God. The man was a brick freakin' wall. With a pleased murmur, he tucked his head against her neck, one arm firmly around her waist and one leg tossed over hers.

Her butt settled pressed against a defined erection. Desire blasted into her and stole her breath.

His hand flattened out, spreading across her entire midriff. Holding her close.

"Janie?" he whispered against her nape, his breath warm.

A shiver wound through her entire body. Her nipples peaked, and her abdominal muscles clenched. "What?"

"I'm sorry I'm not who you thought." His lips moved against her skin.

She forced instant need down along with a definite groan. "I like who you are."

He chuckled. "You do not."

"Yes, I do. You're strong and loyal. I just wish you'd share."

"I'll share anything with you," he mumbled.

Did he have to sound so damn sexual? She wiggled to get more comfortable and ended up rubbing his erection.

He groaned.

"Sorry." She stilled. Maybe she could get him to open up since he was almost out. "What are you so afraid of, Zane?"

He sighed, his mouth near enough to her ear to cascade a tremble down her back. "Failing. Losing family. Losing you." With his hand flattened, the tips of his fingers brushed the underside of her breast.

She bit her lip to keep from turning around and jumping him. The guy needed sleep, and she had to think. Thinking was good, right? "What do you want?" she breathed. "For everybody?"

"Peace and to be left alone."

Her eyes fluttered shut, captivated by his warmth. "You don't want to rule the demon nation?"

"God, no." His voice quieted. "Never."

"What if you're needed?" she asked. Life was all about duty, and Zane's might suck. But surely he'd step up.

"Too bad." He buried his face in her hair. "Smell so good," he whispered.

She swallowed. "Night, Zane."

"Night. And Janie?"

"Yeah?"

"Don't try to find Kalin. I'll know, and you won't like the result."

Even his threat was sexy. She opened her mouth to retort, but a soft snore stopped her. He was out cold.

She blinked and shifted her weight. He tightened his hold, continuing to snore. Protective warmth surrounded her. All muscle, all strength . . . all male. She'd never slept the whole night with a man, nor had she ever been held so tightly. As if she were the only thing anchoring him to earth.

Zane.

The raw heat cascading off him loosened her muscles, and her eyes remained closed. A few hours of sleep wouldn't hurt her any, and then she'd come up with a plan.

She awoke hours later, while darkness still ruled outside. The fire had dwindled to a crackle of embers, yet the vampire holding her close kept her warm. Or was he more demon? More important, did it really matter? He hadn't moved an inch during sleep, except the erection against her butt seemed to have grown. How the hell was that possible?

He breathed evenly against her neck, still sleeping soundly. After teleporting so many times, it was amazing he could still function. Maybe something about crossing the two deadly races had given him extra stamina, because no way could her uncle Dage teleport that many times in a day. Nobody could.

Janie breathed deep, her body softening further at the scent of Zane. He smelled even better than she'd dreamed.

But for now, she had to get home to her family. Though she wouldn't tell Kalin her location, she could seek him out for information. So she closed her eyes again and opened up a dream world, hoping Zane was too exhausted to take heed.

She slipped into the impossible realm between dreams and reality, making the sun bright in a pretty meadow lined with outcroppings of rock. Birds trilled high above, and a sweetly scented breeze lifted the rough wheat. She sat on a rock, swinging her leg and enjoying the mock sun.

Kalin stepped out from behind a row of trees, his white face already turned to the sun, which glinted off the red tips of his black hair. Long strides propelled him to sit beside her. "I appreciate your always making the sun available to me here." His low voice carried across the meadow, filling the oxygen. Even in the dream world, he wore his Kurjan black uniform with the impressive red medals above his breast.

She took in his size, barely recognizing the boy she'd once known. "I've always felt bad that you can't see the real sun." Did it make a difference? Would he be a kinder person, less of a killer, if somehow he'd known true outside warmth?

His eyes flashed open—a melding of green and purple. "I'm glad you're alive. When the demons attacked your helicopter, I was . . . worried." His frown darkened his entire face. "Damn demons."

She blinked. "I'm fine. Why didn't you ever tell me Zane was a demon?"

Kalin lifted a muscled shoulder. "If you'd known, you would've told the king, and he would've reached out to the demons. We couldn't have you ganging up on us."

"Yet you've aligned yourself with the demons now," Janie said, sitting up.

Kalin stilled. "How do you know that?"

Oh. "Our Intel is pretty damn good, and you know it." Had she just given herself away?

Kalin studied her, his face implacable. "Interesting." Reaching out, very slowly, he pushed a piece of hair behind her ear and away from her face. He frowned as if confused by his own gentle touch. "I suppose you're barricaded right now behind a hundred vampire guards?"

She met his gaze and kept her expression blank. "What's your end-game here? I mean, with the demand to study the chosen one?" As hard as she tried, she couldn't help rolling her eyes at the last.

Kalin grinned and flashed sharp canines. "Initially, I just wanted access to you and figured we'd mate."

She stilled. "What if I don't want to mate?"

Regret twisted his red upper lip. "Destiny is destiny."

She sighed. "You think we're destined to mate?"

"I think it's one of your possible destinies, and it's the one that is going to come to fruition." His gaze hardened along with his impressive jaw. "I'm meant to have your psychic powers."

A vampire or Kurjan mate, probably even a demon mate, often shared her powers, and Janie's psychic abilities were above par. "Is that all?" she asked softly.

"No." He reached out to cup her jaw, his hand cool. "I've always been drawn to you like no other. Whatever it is between us, I would never hurt you."

Sometimes life made no sense, but instinct whispered Kalin believed his words, even if they turned out to be impossible. The vampires had documented Kalin's frightening history of violence, and she'd memorized every word. Although he'd saved her life once from a crazed werewolf, he still had the need to kill. Often. "You like to hurt women," she said.

He nodded. "I truly do. You're special, though."

Her heart started to race and not in a good way. Nobody was special enough to banish that type of urge. Yet now she had a job to do. "So what's the plan now that the peace talks have blown up?"

He smiled. "Things are going according to plan. Soon you'll be where you're destined to be."

Janie opened her mouth to ask another question, and a sizzling pain cascaded along her scalp. She cried out as she was ripped from the dream world.

She flipped her eyes wide open. Flat on her back, helpless, she looked up into furious green eyes as Zane pinned her to the mattress, his hand clenched in her hair.

Chapter 11

Janie swallowed and tried to shove Zane off her. Embers from the fire lit the room, encasing them in a cocoon of intimacy.

His gaze narrowing, he grabbed her wrists and yanked them above her head, easily pinning them with one warm hand. She shifted against him, her breasts rubbing his bare chest, her hips cushioning his. The hard ridge of his shaft pressed against her cleft, and she bit back a moan.

Crimson spread across his daunting cheekbones, giving him the look of a furious jaguar. "I said no dream world."

She struggled against him, fighting the raw desire rippling along her every nerve ending. "Too bad I don't take orders from kidnappers."

The flash of white against his now healthy looking face surprised her. His smile held an amused menace. "Did you tell Kalin I have you?" Zane asked quietly.

"Of course not." She settled into the bed and tried not to move against his hard body. He was just too damn tempting. "Apparently Kalin thinks he and I are going to be together soon."

Satisfaction lightened Zane's eyes. "Good. So he thinks I'm going to infiltrate Realm headquarters, kidnap you, and deliver you to Suri, according to plan."

"Probably." Her eyes wanted to flutter shut and just enjoy the heaviness of the delectable body pinning her. Her brain tried to focus. "Speaking of your grand plan, you can't just walk into Realm headquarters and try to negotiate today. They'll shoot you in the head before you get a word out."

"Not a chance as long as I have you."

The double entendre whispered along her skin, yet she still felt the need to warn him. "They'll torture you until you give up my location . . . I promise. My family is ruthless." She shifted against him, unable to stop herself. Electrical zaps cascaded through her at the contact. "Besides. You don't *have* me."

"I'd like to." His gaze dropped to her lips, and with a small groan, he brushed his mouth against hers.

The contact was soft and sweet, the result explosive. Every nerve in her body sprang to attention, clamoring for release. Impossibly demanding. "What are you doing?" she breathed.

"This." His mouth covered hers, pressing her back, driving into her with a desperation she felt in her own bones. He stroked her cheek, his thumb pushing against her jaw, forcing her mouth to open.

The second she granted him entrance, he dove in. Deep and hard, all consuming, his mouth worked hers.

She thought she'd been kissed before. Hell no. This was carnal, animalistic . . . everything. A flush of heat sparked her nipples and cascaded down to her sex, opening her legs. For him. Only for him. He moved against her, mimicking the sex act, rubbing her nearly into a frenzy. Finally, he whipped his head up, freeing her lips.

His breath panted out, his rock-hard chest moving against hers. "I want this." His direct gaze held no subterfuge and allowed for no evasion. "I want you. Just once and before all hell breaks loose again. Our odds aren't good." He blinked and pressed a soft kiss to her nose. "Just you and me. Us. For once, in case this is all we have."

She moved restlessly against him, needing relief.

"Janie." Firm. Commanding. A tone that made her still. In the dream worlds, he'd hidden this side of himself. The side demanding control—pure Zane.

She blinked. "I know our odds of survival stink." The war had just strengthened, and Zane had now defied the demon leader. Or rather, he was about to. "I don't want to miss this night." It was the truth, and he deserved to hear it. No matter what happened. For so many years she'd hoped for a future with him, and then as she'd grown, she'd seen the destruction of hope and dreams. Those with destinies often had to sacrifice.

She had a hell of a destiny. "I want this time."

"You're sure?" He loosened his hold on her wrists. "I can't decide for you."

She met his gaze levelly, too much emotion roaring through her to find the right words. Even if they ended up on opposite sides of the world or worse, she'd take this night for herself. Something just for her. "I'm sure. You and me. Now."

His eyes flashed a sparkling black through the green. Ah. A vampire's secondary color brought out only when he was seriously pissed or dangerously aroused. She'd done that. Brought out his hidden colors. The black signified a purebred demon, and it made sense it'd be his color.

He released her to nimbly unbutton her shirt, a low growl rolling from his chest.

The sound surged through her and ignited a darker desire. "Do demons growl like vampires?" she breathed.

His fangs flashed to be quickly withdrawn. "I don't know." He flicked open the clasp on her bra. "You're beautiful, Belle." Lowering his mouth, he flicked a nipple.

"Ohh." She arched into him, digging her head into the pillow. Sensations bombarded her—electric and sparking fast. Those fangs. She'd never been bitten by a vampire. Ever.

He turned his attention to her other breast, nipping, tugging, and teasing. Janie spread her hands over his shoulders, marveling at the undulating muscles. She caressed down his back, digging into ridges, trying to memorize his body. Just in case this was their only chance, she wanted to remember everything.

Her shirt and bra flew across the room, even while he kept loving her chest. Bedclothes rustled when he sat up and unzipped her jeans.

Her breath caught. He pulled her clothing off, leaving her nude.

Vulnerability flushed through her. "I, ah—"

"Perfect." His eyes flashed full black with a rim of green around the cornea. All primal being. "You're perfect."

Heat slammed into her along with a rare feminine confidence. At her small height, she had no choice but to be curvy, no matter how many hours she logged on the training field. Those extra ten pounds she'd wanted to lose weren't going anywhere—ever. But Zane thought she was beautiful.

Half-sitting up, she reached for the buckle of his belt. Her hands trembled as she slid the tough leather free and unzipped his cargo pants. His cock sprang free. She stilled, her gaze caught. Huge. Unbearably huge. The small giggle that escaped her was full of nerves.

Zane grinned and shoved off the bed to drop his pants and kick off his shoes. "It'll be okay, Belle." He rested a knee on the bed.

Gingerly, she reached out and ran a finger along the hard ridges of his penis. His breath hitched. The skin was softer than she'd expected, but the overall shaft much harder. She hummed as she explored. "I should, ah, probably tell you something." She tore her gaze from his dick to see his face.

Desire glittered in his eyes, and a masculine tension vibrated along his arms. But his expression. Full of hunger. "What's that?" His voice lowered to demon guttural.

She swallowed. He needed to know the truth to make his decision, and she'd rather not get hurt too badly. "I haven't done this before."

The world stilled. Or maybe just Zane stilled, but everything else stopped moving, too. He kept her gaze, the black overtaking the green but leaving enough to be him. To be Zane. "Why not?" he murmured.

She coughed out air, not expecting the question. Zane always was a head-on type of guy. "Bodyguards, dangerous destiny, busy life." She wanted to look away, but he wouldn't let her.

A very dangerous masculine satisfaction curved his upper lip. "Did you wait for me, Belle?"

She sighed and picked at a string on the bedspread. Years ago, she'd figured they'd never really meet like this, but she'd hoped. "I don't know. I think I may have waited for the *possibility* of you."

His gaze warmed even further. "Your sweetness flays me every time." He leaned into her and slid a hand to tangle in her hair, his mouth against hers. "I won't hurt you."

Relief washed through her that he hadn't turned away or given her some baloney line about waiting for her soul mate. If she had a soul mate, it was Zane, even if their souls wouldn't be on earth long. "I'm not sweet."

His lips curved against hers. "When you're not reassuring everyone and acting tough, you're as sweet as they come. The real you."

He kissed her, deep, a man finished with waiting, showing her how much he wanted her. All consuming, he kissed her until she could do nothing but take what he was giving. Only after she'd softened against him, relaxing into the bed, did he release her mouth to pepper kisses along her jaw, over her breasts, and down her abdomen.

Desire wasn't sweet, nor was it soothing. The craving coursing through her actually hurt. Beyond an ache, desire was a painful need, and only Zane had the balm. She moved against him, her hands gripping his flanks.

His mouth enclosed her clit.

Surprise bent her at the waist before her entire body detonated. She flopped back down, her fingers threading through his thick hair as waves of intense pleasure sheeted the room white. Her body shook in release, forcing her to ride waves bigger than she could imagine. The orgasm overwhelmed her and stole her breath.

Finally, she looked down. Zane lifted his head and chuckled against her, sending more vibrations through her core. "That was quick," he rumbled.

She swallowed. Twice. Vulnerability made her blink. "Too quick?"

"No." He wandered back up her body. "Perfect. Although later I want to play there for a while, so try to control yourself next time." Charming humor creased his cheek.

She smacked him and settled her butt into a more comfortable position, her breath still panting out. Who knew that sex with Zane would be fun as well as overwhelming? She widened her legs to make room for his hips against hers. "I'll try not to hurt you too much," she whispered.

He chuckled again. "I appreciate your restraint." One broad palm slid down her rib cage and over her hip until he found her. His eyes closed. "You're so wet." He slipped one finger inside her. "And tight." His forehead dropped to hers. "This *is* going to hurt, Belle." Regret echoed on his low groan.

She arched into his touch with a small gasp. Nerves flared to life under his talented fingers, and she fought a whimper of desperate need. She slid both hands into his thick hair and jerked his head up to meet her gaze. "I know." The man had both her heart and her trust. "It's okay." To emphasize her point, she tilted her hips to give him better access, rubbing along his shaft and making them both groan.

He removed his finger and positioned himself at her entry. "I'm sorry, baby." Slowly, he pushed inside, pausing several times to pull out and maneuver back in. "God, you're tight."

Erotic pain filled her, and she fought the dual urges to pull away and get closer. As he reached her barrier, finally, she began to panic. Zane captured her mouth in a kiss, going deep, taking everything she had. She fell into the firestorm, kissing him back, her body rioting for relief. He shoved the last couple of inches, taking her virginity.

She cried out into his mouth as pain overtook all pleasure.

He released her mouth and lifted his head. Waiting, his odd black/green gaze seeing everything.

Finally, the pain ebbed. She moved against him, testing. Then she smiled, her breath catching. "Move."

He grinned and slowly slid out to glide back in, watching her carefully. Yeah, it hurt. But as he moved more, pleasure replaced the pain. Desire rippled through her again, stoked higher than before. She grabbed his hips, meeting each thrust. "More," she gasped. Wow. This was . . . new.

His concentration solely on her, he increased the speed and strength of his thrusts. Harder. Farther. More.

The sound of flesh slapping flesh filled the small cabin.

One thought centered her. Zane. This was Zane inside her, filling her. The reality was so much more than any dream she'd concocted. "Zane," she whispered.

A coiling in her belly grew like electrical fire. She climbed, getting so close, wanting with everything she was to fall over and into bliss. The need stole her breath, her very mind.

Fangs flashed.

In an instinctive move older than time, she turned her head, baring her neck.

He struck swift and deep. Those fangs pierced her flesh in a pain way too erotic to define. She cried out, her body flying way. The orgasm hit her deep, striking through her body and uncoiling everything she was. Everything she'd ever been, and everything she'd become. She shut her eyes, letting the explosions destroy her.

Zane growled low, pounded harder, and grabbed her hips for better leverage.

She couldn't move.

A searing pain spread along her lower back, and then Zane held her tight, her name on his breath as he disintegrated with her.

Chapter 12

Zane sprawled in the chair, his mind spinning, his body impossibly sated. The fire crackled with subdued energy, glowing through the cabin. What in the fucking hell had he just done? He kept his gaze on Janie as she slept so peacefully in the big bed. After mind-blowing sex, the woman had drifted to sleep.

He'd waited a few moments before yanking on his pants and fetching a towel to clean her up. Blood had dotted her thighs, giving proof of their union. She'd waited for him, which both humbled him and filled him with masculine pride. Already in dreamland, the woman hadn't moved as he'd administered to her.

Finally, he'd dropped into the chair.

The burning across his palms forced him to look again.

Both fucking palms.

A rare Z cut hard and deep across his hands. From the name of his demon ancestors, the Zane family. He'd been named for them.

God. *He'd mated Janie.*

She was going to kill him. Rightfully. He hadn't planned to bind them and sure as hell hadn't realized the mating would happen. But once inside her, his body and instincts had taken over. They'd agreed to one night, just to know each other. Now she was trapped.

If he died soon, and surely Suri already had a contract on Zane's head ready to go, then Janie was stuck for life. A demon/vampire hybrid mating a human was so damn rare, and there was no way out of it.

She murmured in her sleep and rolled over onto her stomach. As

if drawn, he stood and quietly leaned over her, tugging down the
bedclothes. Twin Z's, along with his large handprints, spread almost
magically across her lower back. Her entire lower back and around
her rib cage—right above two perfect globes. His woman had a
great ass.

Primitive satisfaction filled his chest and pissed him off even more.
Yet the *'mine'* that rumbled from his chest wouldn't be silenced.

The world began to lighten outside, and he pulled on his shirt.
Should he leave her a note? If so, what the hell should it say? *Sorry,
baby, I just mated you so you'll never find anybody else when I die?
XOXO, see you soon, if your family doesn't cut off my head the
second they smell you on me.*

Fuck. No way.

Maybe she'd sleep until he returned. Grumbling, he strode into
the kitchen to grab a notepad.

Janie Belle,
We need to talk.
Zane

He rubbed his chin as he left the note on the table. Then he took
one last good look.

She slept on her stomach, her head turned to the side, her expression one of peaceful abandon. Firelight kissed her delicate features
and highlighted her stubborn chin. Her skin was smooth, her muscles
toned, and a sense of innocence and sweetness all but surrounded her.

His heart thumped. Hard. "Mine."

Keeping his gaze on her until the last second, he drew power up
through his feet to his head, filling himself with the universe and
naturally bending the binding of physical laws. Visualizing the computer room in Idaho, he allowed his molecules to separate and then
regroup, finally closing his eyes.

This time he landed on his feet.

Nick looked up, his eyes bloodshot, three empty coffee cups next
to him. "'Bout time you got here. Learn to jump with a damn cell
phone, would you?"

Zane shrugged and shoved his guilty hands into his pockets.

Besides the brand, the damn things were shaking. He had to stop jumping so often. God knew what was happening with his internal organs. "Can't. A phone won't make the jump." He frowned to see Sam up on the screen, and then Logan came into view. "Thank God," Zane muttered, taking a deep breath finally.

Logan grinned, his green eyes sparkling in a bruised face. He'd cut his black hair short, and a three-day stubble covered his square jaw. "Hi, Bro."

Zane nodded, his shoulders relaxing. "You all right?"

"Fine. Just fighting vampires in Zimbabwe." Young and earnest, Logan's face nevertheless held a new hardness. Killing and surviving stamped them every time.

A twenty-year-old shouldn't be fighting, damn it. Zane clenched his hands into fists in his pockets and leaned closer to the screen. "Sam, get him out of there. Now."

Nick spoke before Sam could. "I found your mother."

Zane jerked his head. "Where?"

"Island off the Florida Keys." Nick typed and brought up a schematic on a second screen. "I decided to look where they'd be least likely to keep her and followed the money trail there."

Relief buzzed through Zane along with apprehension. "Do we have friendlies in Florida?"

"Yes." Nick handed him an address. "Teleport to this locale, suit up, and rent a raft to take the island. It's guarded, but a lot of Suri's forces have been pulled to fight around the world, so you have a chance."

A chance was all Zane had needed. Finally, he could get his mother to safety. His muscles bunched with the need to move and fast.

Sam pushed Logan off the first screen. "We'll meet you there in a minute."

"No." Zane lowered his voice into command. "Get Logan to safety, and I'll be in touch."

Logan's head popped up next to Sam's. "We're going, Zane. You need backup, and she's our mom, too." Fire and determination lit his face.

Zane paused. She was their mother, too, and he'd trained them since day one, so they'd be good backup. He couldn't exclude them. "Very well. See you in a minute; wait for me outside." He flicked off the screen and turned toward Nick. "Thanks for your help. I owe you."

Nick rubbed his whiskered chin, fatigue lining his face. "We've planned for every contingency, I hope." He held out a hand. "Godspeed, buddy."

Zane accepted the hand and shook. "You're a good friend."

Nick frowned and flipped over Zane's palm. "Oh, you fucking didn't."

Yeah. That pretty much summed up his situation. "I did." With the last remark, Zane teleported out of Idaho.

Zane held the automatic weapon low and against his bulletproof vest as he emerged from the water. He'd met his brothers and suited up, paying a fortune for the guns. They'd rafted out and then swum the rest of the way, reaching the seemingly quiet island from three different vantage points.

As always, he'd take the front entrance. Sam had the rear, and Logan a side entrance where he shouldn't see too much resistance. Hopefully.

Taking a moment, Zane tied a bandanna over his hair to keep it from getting in the way. If he survived the next week, he really needed a haircut. Clasping his gun with leather-covered hands, he leaned against a series of rocks and listened. No sounds. No vibration of power on the wind.

Either the coast was clear . . . or they knew he was coming and they'd shielded.

Only one way to find out.

He swung around the rock and edged toward the tree line. Infrared photos of the island had revealed a plantation-type home in the middle, with many heat signatures. To contain a female demon, Suri's forces had probably dug a basement and encased the walls in both concrete and steel.

The thought of Zane's mother imprisoned in such a way clogged his throat with fury. He shook his head to center himself. Anger would get him killed, and he had a job to do.

So he calmed and allowed the beast deep down to lurch forward.

The beast could hunt, track, and kill without mercy, and for now, he'd show none.

Gunfire ripped through the peaceful morning.

Shit. He ran into the forest to jog through the trees, wondering which of his brothers had taken on fire. They had orders to back each other up, and he had to trust they'd fall back on training. His job was to go in.

He reached the edge of the trees and dropped to one knee, shooting the guard at the door, hitting him in the neck. The demon had remained at his post, even with a gun battle going on behind the house, and Zane had to appreciate the fact. But he still had to go down.

Running forward, Zane leaped over the body and hit the front door with his left shoulder. Wood impacted, and he flew through, his gun ready. A bullet whipped into his thigh, and he dropped, rolling to fire toward the shooter. Pain pierced his leg, and he ignored it to dodge behind a purple settee. Powerful visions and screaming agony stabbed into his brain.

Sucking in air, he forced shields around his mind. All demons could fight with mind games, and all could shield. As part-vampire, his shields weren't as good as a full-blooded demon, thus leaving fingernails of pain still clawing through his brain.

But he could still function.

So he jutted up and shot toward the grandfather clock in the corner.

The demon guard jumped across the room and hit the small couch, shoving shards of wood into Zane's vest. Zane reached up and pulled the demon down, scissored around him, and stabbed him in the neck. Blood arced across Zane's vest, bubbling like acid.

He pushed the demon off only to be tackled to the ground again. Relying on training, he flipped around and punched his attacker in the eye. They grappled, both going for the fast kill.

Smoke filled the room while gunfire continued unabated outside.

Zane sliced his blade into the demon's neck and shoved him away. Ducking low to peer under the smoke, he dodged through the room and headed down a long hall to a doorway. Kicking it open, he grimaced at the narrow stairs leading down.

A whisper of sound alerted him, and he half-turned, only to get hit mid-center by a guard. He flailed for the railing and missed, hitting three steps and breaking his ribs. He and the demon fought each other while plummeting down the concrete stairs, finally land- ing at the bottom with Zane on top. Three hard punches to the demon's face knocked him out cold.

Zane stood and placed a hand against the wall to keep from falling again. His leg burned, and the world had gone fuzzy as his brain swelled against his skull. Swallowing bile, he turned and jogged down a concrete surrounded hallway to a door with a keypad next to it. He drew out his pistol and shot the keypad, fizzing the wires until the door lock released.

Heavy boots echoed behind him, and he turned to find his brothers. Bloody, sooty, and wounded. Sam half-carried Logan.

Logan grimaced. "A couple of wounds and no big deal. I'm healing as we speak." He eyed the closed doorway warily.

Sam shook his head. "He's been shot too many times and needs to recuperate. Somewhere safe." Sam jerked his head toward the stairway. "The outside is cleared." He pushed Logan against the wall and took a defensive position in front of his brother.

Zane turned and kicked open the door, keeping his body between his family and whatever lay on the other side. Then he stilled.

Felicity rose from a feminine settee and put down a book. As cells went, it had been decorated for royalty. Apparently Suri hadn't wanted to piss his sister off too badly.

Zane swallowed and felt like a kid again. "Mom?"

She took a deep breath and ran into his opened arms. "Are you all right?" she asked, leaning back to look at him and wiping blood from his chin.

He nodded, unable to speak. Sometimes he forgot how tiny she was, and she'd lost weight during captivity. Long blond hair flowed down her back in contrast to her midnight black eyes. Faint lines of fatigue and worry fanned out from her eyes.

Zane's heart clenched. "I'm fine. Did they hurt you?"

"No." Felicity turned with a happy cry and launched herself at first Sam and then Logan, staying clear of his injuries. Finally, she turned to smile at Zane. "I knew you'd find me."

Her trust humbled him, but she'd have to dig deep to keep it when she heard what he had in mind. He took in his family. "We have to go before Suri's reinforcements get here."

Sam nodded and reached for Logan.

Zane slid an arm around his mother's petite shoulders. "Sam, take Logan to Alaska and have Janie patch him up. She, ah, may be a little angry when you first get there."

Sam frowned. "Why?"

Zane shrugged. His brothers had been too occupied with the rescue to take notice of him, and that was fine.

Logan grimaced. "We go with you."

"No." Zane shook his head. The vampires were pissed, and the smart move would be to take out everybody with him and then torture him for information to find Janie. He didn't think they'd kill a female, but his brothers would be perfect targets. "Do as I've ordered." He dismissed his brothers and glanced down at his mother.

She studied him as if considering something she couldn't quite grasp. "I'd like to go face my brother, if you don't mind." Her rough voice sounded more like a bar singer's than a demon's, but the anger was there.

Zane tightened his hold and kept his gaze level. "I have a different plan."

Felicity lifted a pale eyebrow. "Which is?"

"How do you feel about meeting the Realm vampires, Mom?" he asked.

Chapter 13

Janie leaned back against the ice pack, her mind furiously running. Zane had *marked* her. Burned Z's into her flesh.

Permanently.

While she'd always thought the marking a bit romantic, actually carrying a brand came with a heavy sense of finality. Of ownership.

She carried *his* mark.

Not the other way around.

What the hell was he doing marking anybody, anyway? The only people who marked their mates were the Kayrs family, and that's because they ruled the vampires and had since the beginning of time. The marking was unique to them, and the burn included a K for their surname. What was Zane doing branding her with a Z?

Just one of many questions pummeling through her head.

Was it possible he'd mated her on purpose? To gain her gifts and preclude her mating anybody else? A part of her scoffed at the idea, but a kernel of insecurity still irritated her like popcorn caught between two teeth. He'd seemed as overtaken as she had been the previous night, but it had been her first time, so what did she know?

Still, a dangerous tingle of happiness threatened to destroy her anger. Zane as her mate. A dream she'd had since she was too little to understand what mating meant. He'd always had her heart, and now she had a chance at his. She'd seen love overcome fate and destiny, and in order to mate, Zane had to love her—at least a little.

She shook her head. Again, she felt the twin bite marks in her neck. A slow shiver wandered down her body. Zane.

He'd better show up and provide some answers.

Standing, she glanced again at the brief note he'd left. They needed to talk? Oh, hell yeah.

The air shimmered by the fireplace. She jumped up and fetched a worn, cast-iron skillet from the stove. If Zane didn't talk, she was going to brain him. With a lurch of sound, two bodies dropped onto the wooden floor.

She gasped and stepped back, reaching for a knife.

Slowly, the men stood. Green eyes, black hair, familiar features. One was bleeding out all over the rug.

The one with darker eyes smiled. "Hi, Janie, I'm Sam. This is Logan, and we're Zane's brothers."

Janie tightened her hold on the handle. "Where is Zane?"

Logan coughed out, "Meeting with the king of the Realm. Um, do you have a Band-Aid I could borrow?" He groaned and fell onto a chair.

Janie swallowed and studied him. His eyes were lighter and his jaw more square than Zane's, but there was no doubt they were siblings. The kid looked to be about twenty—Garrett's age. She plopped the pan onto the table and slid into big-sister mode. She couldn't allow Zane's little brother to bleed to death, nor would she let the kid sit there in such pain. At one point, Zane had saved her brother. Now it was time for her to help Logan. "Yes. Let me help."

"Thanks," Logan said.

As she reached for the first-aid kit, she stilled. "Zane went to meet my family?"

"Yep," Logan muttered, shaking his head.

Oh God. They'd be able to scent her on him and might even figure out about the mating. She bit her lip, her stomach clenching.

They'd kill him.

Zane landed right outside the main lodge of Realm headquarters. Nicely manicured lawns spread out in every direction in front of stately homes, while the cedar-walled building before him stood proudly against the rolling Pacific Ocean. A sense of foreboding rode the breeze, and he promptly set his mother behind him.

Soldiers came out of nowhere to surround them, guns pointing and ready to shoot.

He lifted his leather-gloved hands in the air.

As usual, no weapons had teleported with him, which might be a good thing.

Although he'd give his right nut to have a knife to protect his mother if necessary. The vampires surrounding them remained still, but his gut still ached with the danger of a twitchy finger. It only took one.

The king strode from the main building, followed by his brothers—all dressed for battle. Zane knew each one of them from dossiers he'd studied. When Dage had nearly reached him, he lifted a pistol to point between his eyes. "Where is Janie?"

Felicity hustled around Zane. "Really, King. Put down the weapon."

Zane grabbed her arm and tried to push her behind him again. She struggled—a determined female in harmless white pants and shirt. The idea of blood marring her silk prompted Zane to try harder.

The king watched the interplay with no expression on his face.

Finally, Zane stopped fighting. "King Kayrs, may I introduce my mother, Felicity Kyllwood of the demon ruling family." He edged her closer to him so he could jump in front of any bullet fired before it hit her. "Mother, this is Dage Kayrs, King of the Realm."

Felicity glided forward, her hand outstretched. "It's good to make your acquaintance, young man."

Zane fought a wince. While his mom was probably a century or two older than the king, the woman looked thirty. Tops.

Dage blinked and took her hand, his grip appearing gentle. "Ma'am."

That mother tone got them every time. Zane's shoulders slowly relaxed. "I'd like to request asylum for my mother. She was mated to a vampire."

Dage lifted a dark eyebrow. "I'd grant asylum regardless of mating. Where the hell is my niece?"

Felicity slowly turned. "Why is the king asking you that question?"

"Because he kidnapped her," Garrett growled from next to his father, a furious vampire with golden eyes.

Zane nodded at Garrett. "Hi, kid. Good to see you survived your ordeal." Reminding the kid that Zane had saved his life couldn't hurt.

"You won't," Garrett ground out.

A woman ran out of the building, dressed in a worn sweatshirt and faded jeans. She headed straight for Zane, and only the strong arm of Janie's father stopped her. "Where the hell is my daughter?" she asked, looking downright miniature next to her massive mate.

Felicity frowned. "Why is everybody asking you that question?"

Zane cleared his throat. "I took Janie out of a helicopter before the Kurjans could kill her." True. But he'd also mated her, and the second Talen found out, Zane was a dead man. He needed to secure his mother's safety along with his brothers' security before that happened.

"Oh." Felicity eyed the king. "Well, that was nice of you."

"So. Where. Is. She?" the king asked again.

Felicity turned. "You saved her, but you didn't bring her home. Why?"

Zane fought to keep from shuffling his feet. "I wanted to secure your safety first."

Felicity rolled her eyes. "Oh. A simple misunderstanding then. Zane, go get the girl."

Guns cocked.

Felicity stiffened. "Apparently not." She sighed. "King, I do hope you know we don't support my psychotic brother, Suri, and we are sincerely sorry for what happened to your brother. If we'd been in a position to find him and help him, he wouldn't have endured such pain."

The king slowly lowered his weapon. "If I'd known you were a prisoner, I would've laid siege to gain your freedom."

Felicity smiled sadly. "As you know, my mate didn't align with the Realm, so we weren't on your radar, but thank you for the kind words."

"Enough kind words." Cara Kayrs pushed forward again.

Zane pivoted to face her, to reassure her that Janie was fine, but Garrett planted himself firmly in front of his mother. Zane gave him a *Dude, do you really think I'd hurt your mom* look of irritation.

Garrett returned a very simple *fuck you* expression.

God, Zane liked the kid. He focused back on Dage. "I'd like to request asylum for my brothers as well."

"Granted." Dage tucked his pistol in his back pocket.

The forces around them drew nearer. Apparently the soldiers didn't like the king being unarmed.

"What about you?" Dage asked dryly.

Zane shrugged. "I have a job to do after I bring Janie home."

"Which is?" his mother asked.

He paused. "You know."

She shook her head, and for the first time that day, real fear filled her eyes. "You can't take on Suri by yourself."

"I'm the only one who can," Zane said gently.

Dage gestured to a soldier. "Please escort Felicity to a room." He turned to Felicity. "I hope you'll join my mate and me for dinner tonight, once Janie is home. Perhaps we can come up with a plan together to deal with your brother."

Felicity stilled, her worried glance turning to Zane.

He nodded. "Go with the soldier, Mom. Sam and Logan will be here soon."

She turned with obvious reluctance to follow the armed man.

Zane relaxed his stance and finally lowered his hands, waiting until his mother was out of earshot. "You don't need to say it. I understand." The last thing he wanted to hear was how Dage would skin Felicity alive if Janie wasn't returned home.

Dage slowly nodded. "Good enough. I like your mother." *Although I will kill her.* The last part of the sentence remained unsaid but fully expressed.

Zane didn't know whether or not the king was bluffing and had no intention of finding out. He glanced at the brewing storm clouds. "I'll be back shortly."

"I'm going with you," Dage said.

"No." Zane kept his gaze level and his stance nonthreatening. "Janie and I need to have a quick, private conversation before I bring her back. Shouldn't take more than fifteen minutes."

"About what?" Garrett asked, crossing his arms.

"The word *private* should've clued you in that it's none of your business," Zane said levelly. Whether the Realm vampires liked it or not, Janie was now his mate and his responsibility. *His.*

Talen stepped forward, his face hard, his muscles tense. "One of us is going with you. So choose."

Zane faced Janie's father, awareness dawning as to how frightened the man must've been. Janie was a human, and a fragile one at that. The idea of somebody taking her from Zane sliced deep into his soul, and he couldn't imagine the hell Talen had been feeling. "I'm sorry," Zane said. "I'd never hurt Janie, but you didn't know that."

"Decide," Talen said through gritted teeth.

Zane swallowed. He could take somebody with him just to provide some reassurance to the Kayrs family. But they all weighed a fucking ton, and his strength wasn't at full power, considering he'd already jumped twice. "Fine. The kid weighs the least. I'll take him."

Garrett stepped forward.

Talen stopped him with a hand on his arm, keeping his gaze on Zane.

Zane waited for Talen to refuse to allow his son to leave with Zane as well. The vampire couldn't want two of his children in Zane's hands.

Talen flashed dangerous fangs. "Don't kill him until Janie is safe."

Garrett nodded and stepped forward to grasp Zane's arm. "No problem."

Zane grinned. Janie came from an amazing family, to be sure. "You ever transport, kid?"

"No." Determination filled Garrett's odd gray eyes.

"Hold on to your lunch." With a shifting of time and space, Zane jerked them out of the pan and into the fire.

Chapter 14

They landed near the fireplace, and Zane had to stagger back to lean against the worn rocks. "Do you have boulders in your pockets?" he growled at the young vampire, releasing his arm.

Garrett slowly looked around, his gaze finding his sister as she stood near the kitchen. "Janie. Are you all right?" Both menace and relief echoed in the vampire's low tone.

Janie nodded and jumped into her brother's arms with a sigh of relief.

Jealousy, odd and unnecessary, whipped through Zane. What would it be like to have her leap at him without a care in the world, sure she could trust him and that he'd catch her? Whether the woman knew it or not, he'd never let her fall. Although his relationship with her family was surely suspect.

Man, he hoped he didn't have to kill any of them.

He glanced at his two brothers sitting quietly at the table. The cabin wasn't large enough for four men and one tiny human. The climate grew heavy with the sense of power and testosterone. "Everyone patched up?" Zane asked.

Logan nodded and then eyed him head to toe. "You seem . . . different."

Sam's head jerked up as if to scent the air. He looked from Zane to Janie and then back, his eyes lightening. "You didn't."

"Didn't what?" Logan drawled, a dimple winking in his left cheek.

Zane cut them both a look to shut up.

Garrett Kayrs lifted his head and took a deep breath. Slowly and way too deliberately, he set Janie away from him. "Janie?" he asked.

Her hands fluttered together, her eyes wide. "It just happened."

Garrett growled, his eyes flashing a bright aqua, and then rushed Zane.

Zane dropped into a fighting stance just before the vampire slammed him into the rock chimney. Shards ripped into his back and pinged off the floor. "Knock it off." He cuffed Garrett on the side of the head the same way he would Logan before punching Garrett's thigh and knocking him to one knee. "I have ten years of combat experience on you, kid. Wait for the right time to battle."

Garrett shot a punch up into Zane's groin.

Zane doubled over, waited, and then groaned when the agony hit. His eyes watered, while his temper flew. "Damn it." He slapped his hands above Garrett's ears, careful not to break his skull. Then he grabbed the young vampire by the nape, pivoted, and threw him across the room.

Garrett landed on the table and smashed to the floor.

Holy fuck. Zane leaned over, trying to breathe again. He'd forgotten vampires fought dirty.

"Zane!" Janie rushed forward and bent to help her brother up. A table leg rolled across the floor. "Stop hurting Garrett."

Son of a bitch. Zane was the one with swollen balls. "Everyone calm down," he groaned.

Garrett swore and leaped through the air at him.

Logan intercepted Garrett with a tackle a second before he hit Zane, the two young soldiers impacting the door and flying right through it. Snow billowed up and covered the floor.

"Garrett!" Janie jumped to her feet and rushed toward the outside.

Zane reached out with one arm and caught her at the waist, forcing her to a quick halt. She struggled against him. "No," he said. "Stay away while they're fighting." If one of the men accidentally hit her, they could take off her entire head. They were young and out of control . . . and both defending family.

"Screw you," she muttered, turning and aiming a punch at his dick.

He turned at the last second, but she still grazed his groin. Nausea skidded through his gut. Damn fucking Kayrs family—they all went for the balls.

The sound of punches and grunts echoed from outside, and Janie fought him hard, trying to get outside.

"Stop." Zane was done being gentle. He picked her up by both arms and strode across the room to drop her on the bed. She bounced, her eyes on fire, fury spinning a glorious red across her stunning face. He leaned in until his nose nearly touched hers. "Get off this bed, and I'll flip you over my knee, regardless of who's here."

She blinked, rage darkening her eyes to a midnight blue. Then the combative woman tried to kick him in the balls again.

He swiped her foot away from his junk and pivoted to glare at Sam, who sat on a chair in front of the demolished table, a bowl of carrots in his lap. Sam finished chewing one and swallowed. "What?"

"Stop them," Zane ground out.

Sam shrugged. "Why? They're evenly matched and have too much energy. Let them beat the shit out of each other."

The soft cry of distress from Janie struck right to Zane's heart. A tree crashed to the earth outside. He turned. "Stay here and I'll get them." He pinned her with the glare he gave young demons during training and waited until she nodded.

He didn't believe the nod for a damn second.

The young fighters burst through the door frame, ripping half of the wall apart. Furious hits and kicks punctuated groans and growls.

"Enough!" Zane reached down and dragged them both up by the hair.

Logan punched him in the ribs, and Zane threw him down hard. He bounced twice.

Garrett snorted and hit Zane in the knee. Zane tossed his ass down, and the vampire bounced three times.

"Let's try again." Zane hauled them both up again. Bruises and cuts marred their faces, while anger vibrated around them. He shoved Garrett. "You're scaring your sister." Then he pushed Logan the other way. "You're pissing me off, and you ruined my cabin."

Both young soldiers turned to view the missing wall. Snow drifted around, and the heat from the fire dissipated.

Garrett turned again, his gaze finding Janie. "How the hell could you?"

Zane stepped to block his view, his voice lowering to deadly. "Watch your tone with your sister."

Janie scrambled to her knees on the bed and leaned around Zane. "Are you all right, Garrett?"

Garrett snarled. "Sure. The demon here hits like a girl." At Janie's indrawn breath, he hastily added, "A girl who hasn't been trained to fight."

"A girl?" Logan lunged for Garrett, propelling them both into Sam. He crashed to the floor. Carrots flew in every direction and rolled through the snow. "God fucking damn it," Sam muttered, standing and yanking both kids up by the ears.

Logan howled in surprise, and Garrett hissed in pain.

Sam eyed Zane. "What's the plan?"

"Take them to Realm headquarters and land right outside the main lodge. Check on Mom, and tell the king I'll bring Janie within the hour." Zane ignored the fist she plowed into his kidney. "Now, Sam."

Both Garrett and Logan began to protest, and with a wink, Sam zipped them all from sight.

The wind whistling, his cabin demolished, Zane turned to view his mate.

It was time to reach an understanding.

Janie eyed Zane warily. "Is Sam strong enough to transport both Garrett and Logan?"

"Yes," Zane said. The guy had been punched in the groin too many times, and irritation glowed a bright green in those amazing eyes. She realized she didn't know him.

Not really.

The kid she'd played with was gone, and this man had fought battles she couldn't even imagine.

He'd overpowered both Garrett and Logan, two predatory vampires, with an easy grace and an effort not to injure them. With the controlled authority of a warrior. Underestimating him would be a mistake.

Even so, they needed to get a couple of things straight, and she couldn't let his earlier threat go unanswered.

"You ever try to spank me, and I promise you'll lose a hand." She kept her voice level and as pleasant as possible.

His cheek creased, while his eyes warmed in amusement. "Ah, baby. I accept that challenge."

The low tone zinged right through her body to land between her legs. She shivered.

He frowned and leaned down to gather her up, blankets and all. She squawked and grasped his shoulders as he strode toward the still crackling fire to deposit her on the large ottoman.

Then, with a sigh, he turned back, grabbed the entire mattress, and propped it over the gaping hole in the wall. "I liked this cabin," he grumbled.

Janie swallowed, watching him move. All predatory grace and economical movements—just like a big cat considering dinner. "What did you think would happen when you brought Garrett here?"

Zane grimaced and scooped her back up, dropping into the chair with her on his lap. "I thought I'd have more time to get them out before fists flew."

Right—because vampires were so quick to think before acting. She tried to sit primly on his lap and not sink into his muscled heat. This was all just beyond her. As if disagreeing, the markings across her back began to burn. She shifted against him.

He exhaled slowly. "We need to talk."

"I know."

"So stop moving."

Heat filled her face. Oh. Well then. She half-turned to see his face. "Did you mark me on purpose?"

He paused, his eyes searching. One thick hand banded around her nape, caressing. "No." He didn't expand, just waited and watched.

She nodded, while both an unexpected hurt and a welcome relief flowed through her. She'd hate him if he'd tried to manipulate her like that, but even so, he hadn't *wanted* to mate her, and that made her heart ache. "Okay."

"But I'm glad the mating happened." Nothing else on earth was the true green color of his eyes.

Her shoulders hunched. "Right. Because now you can use my powers and keep me from the Kurjans."

His hold tightened. "No. Because you've been mine your entire life, and I'm tired of waiting."

A humming erupted in her core. The guy sure liked to control everything around him, and the strong hold and possessive tone promised the real Zane was showing up. So much for the sweet kid she'd once known. That kid she could've easily swayed. This guy? Not so much. A new determination hardened his jaw and made her pause. She tried to lever herself back but didn't move.

"Let me go," she murmured.

"Not a chance." He stretched his neck. "I'm tired of fighting what I want. I want you, Belle, and now I have you. No regrets, no recriminations. *Mine.*"

That humming exploded into flapping wings, igniting an ache just for him. "I'm not into the whole vampire caveman routine, Zane."

"That's unfortunate."

Her hand folded into a fist. For years she'd wrapped the most dangerous immortals in history around her finger, even while carrying an impossible mantle of responsibility. For once, a predator looked at her, and she had no clue how to handle him. No clue if she *could* handle him. Irritation swept through her at his changing the game. "You're nicer than this," she whispered.

He slowly shook his head. "I've never been nice, Belle."

"What do you want?" she asked, digging her free hand into the quilt.

Satisfaction lifted his upper lip. "Glad you asked. Want to know what I like best about you?"

He'd thrown her off balance, and she didn't like it. Not one bit. "Sure."

"Your independence and willingness to throw yourself into danger for those you love." His free hand flattened over the blanket, capturing her thigh.

"Thank you." She eyed him, wondering at his point, even as her nipples hardened.

"That ends today."

Damn it. "You are such a vampire."

"Vampire-demon hybrid," he said without a hint of a smile. "I protect what's mine, and nobody, including you, will change that."

All right. The possessive words shouldn't thrill her in such a way, so she frowned. "Listen, you can't just start issuing orders because you chose to mark me. I choose to go my own way."

His smile seemed more of a warning. "You chose to get into bed with me, and any consequences we'll accept together."

She lifted an eyebrow. "You consider marking me and binding us together for eternity a consequence?"

"That's not what I meant."

All control had been wrestled from her, and she needed to reclaim some power. "I make my own way. Just because we mated doesn't mean you're responsible for me."

Amusement, genuine and dark, sparkled in his eyes. "That's exactly what it means." He cocked his head to the side. "You are now my number one priority, and even you aren't going to hinder my ability to ensure your safety."

She blew out air. "God, you remind me of my father."

Zane's head jerked back. "I do not."

"Do too." Although she'd always thought her father rather charming and his overbearing ways cute. It felt different coming from Zane, and she wanted to rebel instantly.

Zane licked his lips. "Maybe there's more vampire in me than I thought, because I meant exactly what I said. Get on board now, Belle."

What an arrogant ass. "Speaking of your vampire-demon heritage, how the hell did you mark me with a damn Z?"

"All demons mark their mates with the first letter of their demon family name." That amusement deepened. "Didn't you know?"

"No." Her mind spun. "I thought only the Kayrs family marked their mates because they're the ruling family. Most vampires just mate with a good bite during sex."

He chuckled. "Pride. So much pride in that Kayrs family."

"Meaning what?" Anger prickled her skin.

Zane leaned closer. "Vampires don't mark mates. Demons do. Figure it out."

She blinked. Once. Twice. A third time. "Oh."

"Yes. *Oh.* Not only that, vampires can't teleport. Well . . . except for the king. Many demons have the gift." Zane settled back. "The Kayrs family wants people to think they're purebred vampires, but there's a dirty little demon somewhere in their far past. Like it or not. *That's* why they can mark their mates."

Well. Unfortunately, that did make sense. Janie shrugged. "Doesn't matter."

"Didn't think it would." Zane caressed her nape, sending tingles through her entire scalp. "I care little about your family's heritage, so long as you understand mine."

Why did that sound like a threat? "So the vampire in you bit me, and the demon in you marked me." Talk about doubly bound.

He nodded. "I'm just as mated and marked as you are." Slowly, he opened his free palm. "See?"

She traced the lines on his hand. Zane Kyllwood was *hers*. A deep thrill coursed through her, warming her heart. "The design really is beautiful."

"You should see it on your back," he rumbled, an erotic tension cascading off him.

"I saw." She glanced up and frowned. "Why two markings? I mean, both hands?" All the Kayrs men had one marking on one palm.

Zane shrugged. "I haven't figured that out. It's unheard of as far as I know."

Well now. Sounded like destiny, fate, and a whole lot of pressure. But she'd known Zane her entire life; she could reason with him. "Even so, no marking and mating is going to keep us from doing our jobs. You understand that, right?"

"I completely agree."

Relief filled her. Good. Zane was Zane. "I'm glad."

"So long as you now understand your job."

Damn it. Time to take the bull by the horns. She flattened both hands over his chest, wanting to purr at the warm hardness. Instead, she leaned in, and he allowed her to inch toward his face. "Stop dancing around with innuendo and vampire-esque orders. What are you saying?"

His expression didn't change. All thoughtful determination. One that dampened her panties while ticking her off. "I'm saying that you stick to the plan," he said softly.

"What plan?"

"Mine. Which means you stay safely at Realm headquarters until I deal with both Suri and Kalin."

Janie shook her head. "Just those two?" she asked, trying to refrain from rolling her eyes.

"And anybody else who threatens you." He captured her lips in a hard kiss, going deep until she sagged against him. Then he leaned back, satisfaction gleaming in his eyes as he slowly stood, keeping her in his arms. "Hold on, and when we get to your home, stay out of the way when your father tries to kill me."

Chapter 15

Zane landed in a war zone: barricades, vampire special forces, so many guns pointed at him, he couldn't focus. The Realm had quickly prepared for his return. Slowly, he set Janie onto her feet and pushed her behind him.

She tapped his shoulder. "They won't shoot me."

Maybe. Maybe not.

The demons had spies in the vampire organization, and Zane had no doubt one would take the shot if possible. "Just stay back," he said, blocking her the best he could.

Barricades parted to allow for Dage and Talen Kayrs to stalk his way. Fully armed and wearing combat gear, they allowed no expression to lighten their hard faces.

Zane relaxed his stance although his mind reeled. He needed to know that Sam and Logan were all right. "Where are my brothers?"

The two vampires came to a stop.

"Janie?" Talen asked.

Janie peered around Zane. "I'm fine, Dad."

"Walk this way, please," Dage said evenly.

Janie stepped to Zane's side. "I'd really rather you didn't shoot Zane."

Zane nudged her toward safety. The hulking vampires wouldn't let anybody harm her, and it was too difficult to concentrate with so many weapons pointed her way. "Go to your family."

"If I go to my family, there's a good chance you'll get shot," she muttered under her breath. "Kidnappers don't get much leniency from the Realm."

"I understand. Now go." He had to get her out of the line of fire. There hadn't been time to fully recuperate from the previous day's jumps, and today he'd already teleported three times. His strength was subpar at the moment. He focused on the king. "Where are my brothers?"

Talen stepped up. "Release my daughter."

"I'm trying to." Zane nudged her again.

She sighed. "I don't suppose Garrett or your brothers broke the news to my family?"

Doubtful. The young soldiers were all too smart to be the messengers of bad news. "No." Zane angled to the right to prevent a clean line to Janie, hoping the vampires crossed to the left. "Please get out of the line of fire." Every instinct he owned pushed him to grab her and toss her to her family, but if he moved too quickly, somebody would shoot. He couldn't risk her safety.

Rioting red hair came into view as Moira Dunne Kayrs shoved her way past a barricade. "Where the hell is my cousin?"

Zane frowned. Dark circles marred the pale skin under the witch's furious eyes. "Which cousin?" he asked, a weight sinking into his gut.

"You know what cousin." Moira pressed her hands to her hips, electric blue energy gathering on her arms. Her mate, Conn Kayrs, jogged up behind her, fury darkening his expression.

Shit. Zane was about to take a plasma ball to the face from a pissed-off witch. "For the sake of argument, let's pretend I don't." He kept his voice calm and his stance nonthreatening. "Which cousin?"

She swallowed. "Simone Brightston."

Zane huffed out a breath, his mind reeling. The witch Nickolas Veis had gladly risked exile to help. "Did Suri take Simone?" Zane asked quietly, his gut churning.

"You know he did," Moira spat. She turned to the side and sneezed.

Did witches sneeze when angry?

Zane closed his eyes. Okay. He needed to think. "Get me a phone and I'll see what I can find out." If Simone had been taken to influence Nick, then Suri would know Zane had betrayed him. For the witch, Nick would've talked. Time was counting down too rapidly. "I didn't take your cousin."

Talen growled, the sound vibrating through the tense air. "Kidnapping's your specialty, right?"

"No." Zane eyed Janie's father. At over three centuries, the soldier was in fighting shape. Incredible fighting shape. "Get your daughter to safety, and we'll talk."

"I'm not leaving you," Janie snapped.

"Now, Janie," Talen ordered.

The hair bristled down Zane's neck. "Don't yell at her." Then he gave her a small push. "Go."

Janie dug in her heels, exasperation escaping on her sigh. "Everybody calm down and listen. Dad, let's go inside and have a discussion . . . with Zane."

Talen's eyes morphed into a glittering gold. "Not a chance. Get inside, Janet."

Janie faltered and scanned the bristling weapons surrounding them. "We really need to talk privately."

"Okay. Go inside and wait for me," Talen said, his gaze never leaving Zane.

Zane shook his head. Talk about stubborn, and he could see where Janie got it. "Would you please go inside so I can talk to your father?"

"It's a little late for that talk, isn't it?" Janie shot back.

Talen's chin lowered. Slowly. "What does that mean?"

Janie held her ground. "You can't shoot Zane if he's my mate."

"He won't be if I kill him," Talen said conversationally. "That's not a decision you're ready to make."

Zane's ears rang. "Okay. Everyone just calm down a little bit. How about I follow Janie inside, and then you can shoot me?" That way, at least he'd be able to cover her back until she reached safety.

"How about I shoot you right now?" Talen growled.

Enough of this shit. "Fine. Shoot me. But first make sure Janie is covered, damn it." Zane had about had it with vampires. With the Kayrs family, actually. There were too many of them. "Get inside, Belle."

She grabbed his arm, trying to slide in front of him.

To take a bullet meant for him? Zane saw red. "Take your daughter out of the line of fire, Kayrs." He couldn't say it any plainer than that.

Talen took a step toward them.

Janie planted her feet. "I will not let you harm my mate."

God. She had to quit saying that before somebody figured out they'd actually mated and started shooting.

Talen snarled. "He's not your mate, and he won't be if I cut off his head. Please go inside, Janie."

She sighed and her shoulders went back.

Oh shit. She wouldn't—

"We mated last night," Janie said clearly.

The damn earth ground to a stop. A weapon hit the pavement a yard away. Dage Kayrs's eyes widened, and Moira Kayrs gasped.

Zane sighed and focused just as a locomotive the size of Talen Kayrs tackled him midsection, throwing him ten yards and landing hard on his chest. Zane's head crashed onto the asphalt. Stars exploded behind his eyeballs, and unbearable pain cut into his brain. He tried to concentrate, to say something, when a fist plowed into his face.

Unconsciousness was a fucking blessing.

Janie paced in front of the long window in the gathering room of the main lodge, her hands flailing. "And then Dad *hit* him." Why did the vampires always hit first and then hit again? Forget *ever* asking questions. She turned toward the two women watching her with their mouths open. "Can you believe it?"

Her aunt Emma glanced sideways at Janie's mother as they sat side-by-side on the wide sofa. "Um, no?" Emma whispered.

Cara didn't move. "You, ah, mated."

Janie paused. "Yes." She studied her mother closer. "Are you okay?"

"Am I okay?" Cara asked, her voice rising two octaves. "Am I okay?"

Emma slid an arm around her sister's shoulders. "I think maybe your mom is a bit taken aback, Jane. You know. With the mating and all."

Frankly, Emma sounded taken aback as well.

Janie's face heated. "Right."

Emma, ever the scientist, leaned forward. "Only demons have markings, huh? Interesting, and it clears up a couple of questions I've had. Can we see it?"

Janie paused, embarrassment flooding through her. "Sure." She turned and lifted her shirt.

Her mother made a sound similar to a cat being strangled.

Janie dropped the shirt and turned around. "I know this is, er, a surprise."

"A surprise," Cara said weakly.

Emma cleared her throat. "Are you okay, Janie? I mean, he didn't force this on you, did he?"

Cara's head jerked up, her blue eyes darkening. "Janie?"

Janie shook her head. "No, he didn't force me. The marking took us both by surprise, but I, ah, fully participated." Her blush actually burned her face. "I care about Zane—I always have. Please help me keep him alive."

Emma swallowed and shoved dark hair away from her face. "Ah. Hmm."

Cara nodded. "Yes."

Janie frowned. Somebody needed to speak in a complete sentence. "Are you two all right?"

Cara stood. "I don't know." Emma tugged on her arm, and she fell back to the sofa. "Mated. To a vampire-demon." She turned her gaze on her sister. "Mated. Like *mated*."

Janie lifted her chin. "Wait a minute. You're upset because he's part-demon?"

Emma patted her sister's hand. "I think your mom is overwhelmed by the thought of you mating anybody. It's not like you've had dates, gone to prom, had your heart broken a couple of times."

Yeah. She knew she was odd, with a heavy destiny. "So?" She'd gone from indignant to ready to defend Zane to plain old confused.

"Well"—Cara played with her hair—"mating is pretty heavy duty, well, you know . . ."

"Sex?" Janie asked, her face heating again.

"Beyond sex," Emma snorted. "Waaaay beyond."

"And before, you haven't, I mean that you really haven't, um . . ." Cara lifted her chin and squinted. "Have you?"

"Ah, no." Janie coughed into her hand. "I've been a bit busy for sex. You know?" God? Could this get any more embarrassing?

Emma straightened her shoulders. "Yes. I do know. So. Well. Um."

For Pete's sake. One of the most brilliant women in the universe was spitting out nonsense words. Janie sank into an overstuffed chair. "I liked the sex." Wasn't she supposed to?

Cara coughed out a garbled expletive.

Emma sighed. "That's actually good, right?" She turned toward her sister. "If she's having sex, we want her to enjoy it. To have a good experience."

Janie buried her face in her hands. This was unbelievable.

Cara cleared her throat and waited until Janie looked back up. "Sex is good and natural."

Oh holy fuck. "I know that, Mom." Janie rubbed her temples. "I don't understand why you're both so surprised. You had to know I'd end up with a vampire or immortal someday."

Cara swallowed. "Sure, but to end up with a soldier, a warrior? It's not the easiest of roads, sweetheart. No matter how much you love the man."

"Although it is totally worth it," Emma said.

"Yes." Cara exhaled slowly.

Janie shook her head. "Who did you think I'd end up with?"

"A nerdy scientist," they answered in unison, identical blue eyes flashing.

Wow. "Why?" Janie asked.

Cara wet her lips. "You've been surrounded by soldiers and war your entire life, and I figured you'd find somebody calm and mellow to love. A brilliant man who wasn't deadly or so over-the-top dominant like, well, the Kayrs men."

Emma nodded. "Yeah. What she said."

"Huh." Janie rubbed the still healing puncture marks on her neck. "What about Zane? You didn't think fate brought us together?"

"Fate, schmate," Emma muttered. "I figured Zane was a nice, sweet boy you met in dreams who'd always be your friend. Someday, I thought you'd move on."

Cara focused on Janie. "Do you love him?"

Janie rubbed her chest. "I'm not sure 'love' explains how I feel."

Cara nodded. "I understand that. What do you feel?"

"Too much." The words popped out, and once Janie started, she couldn't stop. "I thought he was safe and sweet, too. Maybe a lone shifter trying to protect a small pack, who'd give up war and live a gentle life. One who'd give me flowers, forget our anniversary, and do the crossword puzzles with me. And I loved him like that—who I thought he was."

A dimple in Emma's cheek winked as she grinned. "Sounds like a nice human life that goes on forever."

"I know," Janie whispered.

"And the reality?" Cara asked.

Janie inhaled and then let out the air. "He's powerful and dangerous. Deadly and so damn wounded I just want to ease his pain—but he won't let me. When he kisses me, the world makes sense, and when he orders me around, I want to kick him in the balls." She plucked at a loose string on a pillow. "And more than anything, I want to be his everything."

Cara sighed and smiled. "Yeah, that sounds about right."

Janie relaxed. "I feel safe with him, and I don't want to live this life without him."

Emma grinned. "Nicely put."

For now, she had to figure out a way to broker peace between her mate and her family. "Mom? You're the only person in the universe who can deal with Dad, and I need him to accept Zane."

Cara's eyebrows arched up. "Where did they take Zane?"

"To the infirmary," Emma whispered. "Talen knocked him out."

Cara nodded. "I'm sure he did." She shook her head like a dog with a face full of water. "Janie, do you have any questions? I mean, you know—"

"God, no." Janie stood up. "We had the sex talk years ago."

Cara coughed. "No, I mean about the mating. The actual process."

Good. Science and biology. Janie stilled. She'd never really thought about it. "Well, other than being a little tired from all the teleporting, I don't feel much different. What happens now?"

Emma leaned forward. "Your human chromosomal pairs will

combine to form several more until you're immortal, and you might even gain Zane's gift to teleport." She frowned and tucked a piece of dark hair behind her ears. "Vampire mates reach twenty-seven chromosomal pairs, but we have no idea how many demon mates reach. You're unique since Zane is so different. There's a chance you'll get enough to be impervious to Virus-27, since it attacks at the twenty-seventh and winds down." She stood. "I need to take your blood."

It was just a matter of time until Emma pulled out a needle. Janie nodded. "I know. But first, I really need to see Zane." To make sure his head was still attached to his body.

The door opened and Garrett strode inside with Logan on his heels. "Are you all right?" Garrett asked, just as Logan piped up, "Where's my brother?"

Janie eyed the two young soldiers. "Are you two done hitting each other?"

"Yes," they both muttered.

"I'm fine, and I'm trying to find Zane right now." Janie frowned. "I'm surprised Dad allowed Logan out of custody."

Garrett shrugged. "No weapons, and he's supposed to stay with me. Sam is with their mom." He grinned at the demon. "Logan can't teleport."

"Yet," Logan groused. "I may be able to soon, while you'll never be able to move your weak body through dimensions."

Garrett punched him in the arm. "Shut up."

"You shut up."

Janie shook her head. After trying to kill each other earlier, they now seemed the best of friends. Males made no sense. "I need to see Zane."

Logan cleared his throat. "My mother would like to meet you as well."

The spit dried up in Janie's throat. Zane's mother would like to meet her, of course. She tried to swallow. What if Zane's mother didn't like her? She slowly nodded. "I'd love to meet her." The lie must've been unconvincing, because Emma chuckled.

Logan grinned, looking like a young and carefree Zane. "My mom will love you."

Sure, why not? It wasn't like Janie's dad had just caved in Zane's head. "Where is Dad?" she asked Cara.

Cara stood. "He's planning strategy in the war room with Uncle Conn."

Janie nodded. So far, she'd done a pretty crappy job of fulfilling her destiny and saving people. The peace talks had dwindled, and war had broken out in full force across the world. "Any hope for the peace talks?"

"No," Garrett said quietly. "The demons and Kurjans are still allies."

"That'll end once the Kurjans discover Janie mated Zane," Logan said just as quietly. A flush covered his high cheekbones, and he shuffled his feet. "Though I'm sure that's not why it happened."

Garrett cut him a hard look. "I said not to talk about it."

"We weren't. We were talking war and strategy," Logan said. He nodded toward the door. "Come on. You said you'd show me the new weapons that disintegrate flesh."

Garrett smiled. "Yeah, and we have some new ground missiles that are just as awesome. Let's head out to the northern tree line." Chattering away, the two young soldiers loped out of the lodge.

Janie's shoulders went back. A lot of people would assume her mating was a political union, and that was just fine. Only she and Zane had been in that bed, and she believed him when he'd promised he hadn't planned the marking. Although, it wasn't as if he'd declared any deep, abiding love for her. She turned toward the door. "I'm heading to the infirmary."

Emma hustled by her side. "That's perfect. Let's swing by the lab first, and I'll take some blood and do tests there so we can monitor how your chromosomal pairs react. I'm quite curious."

Janie nodded and slipped her arm through her aunt's. She turned to her mother. "Are you coming?"

"No. I'll go head off your father and see what I can do." Determination tilted Cara's petite chin.

God, Janie loved the women in her family. Living with vampires took strength, brains, and courage. More than she'd ever realized. "Thanks, Mom."

Cara patted her cheek and hustled by. "Don't worry, sweetheart. This will all work out." The words came out too brightly.

Janie nodded. "I know." For really, what else could go wrong?

Chapter 16

Zane opened his eyes, instantly alert. Talen Kayrs hit like a truck. Not a sturdy Ford or even one of those new Mack haulers he'd seen on the highway. Kayrs hit like a rusty, well-formed, farm truck made from solid steel.

A groan tried to erupt from his gut, but Zane bit all weakness down. He'd never have a daughter because vampires only had males, but he could imagine how pissed a father of a mated female would feel. Take into account the fact that Zane was half-demon, and thus an enemy? Yeah. Talen had the right to hit him.

Once.

A quick glance down at his arms confirmed the vampires had cuffed Zane to thick rings permanently set near the bed. Jesus. How often did the Realm give medical care to the enemy?

Better just to go for a quick kill.

He jerked on his restraints, testing their strength. Strong. Very strong. Well, he'd have to teleport.

"I wouldn't," came a low voice from the doorway.

Zane turned his head.

A blond vampire leaned against the wall dressed in dark jeans and a pressed T-shirt, a weapon pointed between Zane's eyes. "I'll shoot you in the head, and I doubt you'll reach your intended destination." Casual boredom hardened his hazel eyes.

Zane lifted an eyebrow. "Chalton Reese. Don't you have a computer to play with?"

The vampire didn't react in the slightest to his name. If anything, he appeared even more bored.

Zane drew on strength to teleport. His research on the Kayrs organization had included a full dossier on the vampire who was not only the Realm's prime computer expert but a deadly assassin. Something about numbers lining up evenly. Though Chalton would certainly shoot him, Zane had no choice but to jump.

He gathered his strength and paused as a commotion sounded by the door. "What the hell?"

A bloody Garrett half-carried in a groaning Logan. Cuts marred Logan's neck, and a wicked piece of re-bar stuck out from his right shoulder. "What happened?" Zane growled.

Janie hustled in from the other side of the infirmary, her eyes wide. "I heard there was a bombing."

Garrett dropped Logan onto an examination bed. "I was showing Logan the perimeter along the western forest, and all of a sudden, we detonated a bomb."

Zane glared at his brother. "You didn't scent the bomb?"

Garrett glared at Zane. "Neither one of us smelled anything."

How odd. The young vampire was defending Logan.

Logan hissed and reached for the re-bar, Garrett leaped forward to stop him, and Chalton came off the wall, his gaze hard on Zane. Zane gathered deep again to teleport, knowing he was about to be shot—

"Stop." Janie held both hands up. "Everyone freeze right there."

At her soft order, four dangerous, deadly, well-trained warriors all froze.

She moved toward Logan, her face calm, her voice soothing. "First things first, let's remove the steel from your chest, sweetheart."

Logan blinked.

Janie paused at a cabinet and drew out bandages, tape, and a syringe. "I have a painkiller here, but if your metabolism is anything like Garrett's, it won't work for long."

Logan shook his head, agony etched into his face. "Just get it out."

The scent of blood filled the room. Vibrations of terrible pain echoed through it.

Janie nodded. "Garrett, hold Logan from behind, and keep him still." She turned to glance at the bindings around Zane's wrists. "Chalton, unbind Zane."

"No," Chalton said. "I'll take out the re-bar."

"Hell, no," Logan hissed. "Only my brother."

"Please, Chalton," Janie said softly.

Zane could only gape. The woman had taken control of the entire room and somehow kept everybody from turning on each other. She truly was magnificent.

With a pissed-off growl, Chalton stalked forward and ripped off the offending cuffs. "If you bolt, I'll shoot you in the head." He backed toward his earlier vantage point.

Zane slipped to his feet, concern for this brother slowing his normally quick movements. "Give him the painkiller, Belle."

Logan opened his mouth to protest, but Janie was already sliding the needle into his shoulder. She nodded to Garrett as she removed the syringe.

Gingerly, and far more gently than Zane would've ever suspected Garrett could be, he slipped an arm beneath Logan's good arm, tugged his back to Garrett's large chest, and held tight. "I've got him," Garrett said.

Logan gasped in pain and grimaced. "We'd better not be having a gay moment here, buddy. I like women."

Garrett snorted. "Ditto, and I bet you don't even know what to do with a woman."

Zane reached for the end of the re-bar. "Neither one of you idiots knows what to do with a woman." He hated seeing his brother in pain, and he was about to cause a hell of a lot more. "On the count of three. One—" He yanked out the projectile.

Logan bellowed and then sagged against Garrett, who placed him down on the bed.

"Holy fuck, brother," Logan hissed. "You're supposed to go on *two*."

Janie quickly pressed a bandage against the wound. "Zane said *three*."

Garrett leaned over his sister to supervise the treatment. "Yeah. You're supposed to say *three* but go on *two*. Everybody knows that."

"Which is why I went on *one*." Zane eyed Janie. She'd surprised him, and he wasn't sure he liked it. While he'd always felt her nurturing qualities, the woman patching up his younger brother had brains, strength, and serious depth. Her calm in the middle of chaos humbled him. "You seem used to healing injuries."

She shrugged and finished taping down the gauze. "I've worked in infirmaries most of my life, and the doctoring part comes easily."

"She's studied for years," Garrett said, his chest puffing out.

Janie flushed. "Well, field training and Internet classes. I like helping people." She brushed dirt off Logan's cheek. "You're okay. Take some deep breaths and try to heal your wounds."

Logan's eyes warmed and his cheeks colored. "Um, thanks."

Zane bit back a grin. Which he quickly lost as Dage and Talen strode into the room.

"We had a bomb close to the perimeter?" Dage asked Garrett, his gaze silver and hard.

"Yes." Garrett wiped blood off his chin.

Talen glared at Zane. "Why the hell isn't he restrained?"

Janie smoothly inserted herself in front of Zane. "Enough."

Oh, hell no. Zane grasped both her arms and set her behind him. Then he held up a finger to Talen Kayrs. "Give me a minute." Turning his back on one of the most dangerous vampires in history, he glared down at his mate. "Never, and I mean fucking *never*, get between me and somebody who wants to hit me. Got it?"

Blue flashed hard and pissed in her gorgeous eyes. "Right now *I* want to hit you."

He barked out a laugh. The woman was asking for a good taming, and he needed to set some ground rules. Later and without witnesses. He turned back around to catch a glimmer of grudging respect in Talen Kayrs's golden eyes. "I'm happy to go a round or two with you, Kayrs, and I have time now."

Talen stepped forward, but Dage stopped him with a hand on his arm. "Don't be an asshole. Either of you," Dage rumbled. "What's your plan with Suri?"

The king did like to get to the point, now didn't he?

Zane shrugged. "I plan to kill him."

"Any time soon?" Talen drawled.

Irritation clawed up Zane's throat. "Well, the plan was to get my family to safety here and then go take care of Suri. But it seems the Realm has lost a witch, and now Suri has her, which might be a problem."

"Are you working with Nicholas Veis?" Dage asked.

Zane's shoulders went back. So it was true. Nick was still aligned with the Realm, or Dage would never ask the question. Well, there wasn't a reason to lie. "I was working with Nick, but since Suri now has Nick's lady love, I'm thinking I'm on my own."

Janie slid out from behind Zane. "So you can't go back. It's a trap."

"Yes. The trap is most likely being set right now." Zane tried to soften his voice. "But I have to go, Belle."

Dage rubbed his chin. "Nick hasn't reached out yet, but he will. My guess is tomorrow morning, since he's ignoring our calls right now. So let's head to the main conference room to come up with a strategy."

Zane eyed the king. "I'm better off alone in this."

Dage lifted one dark eyebrow. "Nick's with us, and we'll go in for him. Either get on board, or get out of the way."

Damn, Zane liked the king. "I'm the only one who can get to Suri. He'll mind-fuck you to death before you get near."

"I can shield," Dage said calmly.

"Not against Suri." Zane shook his head. The demon leader had more mind power than anybody Zane had ever met. "He's beyond gifted, and even other demons have trouble shielding against his psychic powers."

"But you can shield?" Talen asked.

Zane lifted a shoulder. "I can shield better than most, and I've spent decades working on the skill against Suri." He allowed his voice to lower into its natural state, sounding almost like a pure demon. "Suri frightened my mother and hurt my brothers." *And he tried repeatedly to break me.* "So he's mine. If we're working together, you need to agree."

Dage nodded. "And when he's dead?"

Zane caught himself. There was no way Zane would live through killing Suri. That kind of power unleashed in death would fry Zane's brain, but it was worth the sacrifice to rid the earth and his family of the monster. "Afterward? Figure it out. Maybe Nick will step up to lead until either Sam or Logan want the job."

Dage surveyed him. "You're the rightful heir."

"Hell no." Zane shook his head again. "I refuse to rule the nation—I'm a soldier, not a king."

A wide grin split Dage's hard face. "Welcome to my world."

Janie finished her last yoga move while the fire crackled peacefully behind her, and the Pacific Ocean pummeled the world in front of her. The moon peeked through the rolling clouds periodically to illuminate the slashing rain and crashing waves.

A knock on the door brought her up short. Her heart thrumming, she stood and hurried to open the door.

Zane stood on her rough stone porch, his dark hair wet, his fit body encased in combat gear. Black vest, cargo pants, loaded weapons.

She stepped back, her throat drying up. The weapons fit his personality and appeared right at home. Vulnerability swept through her as she looked so far up into his implacable face. In her yoga pants and tank top, she had few defenses. "Come in."

His boots clomped across the tiles. "You didn't have to wait up."

Of course she did. "I have leftover lasagna, if you'd like."

He shrugged out of the bulletproof vest and placed it by the door. "We ate earlier, but thank you."

The polite talk was going to make her sick. "Did you come up with a strategy for helping Nick?"

"I think so." Zane kicked off one boot and then the other. Three knives and two guns then found places by the vest.

Butterflies winged through Janie's abdomen. She couldn't gauge his mood and was reminded once again of how little they really knew each other. The man moved with contained energy, and she instinctively tensed. The markings on her back began to burn.

"I'm surprised you made it to my house without being jumped." She tried to lighten the tension filling the room.

He turned toward her, his focus suddenly and absolutely on her. "Your family and I reached an understanding, and now it's time we do the same." His tone deepened to one of determination.

Janie took a step back. "Why are you in Realm combat gear, anyway?" Changing the subject seemed wise.

He stepped toward her. "When I teleport tomorrow, there's a good chance I'll be shot immediately. The king thought maybe combat gear would give me a leg up, and we've been working on it. The gear is good."

She backed up again and kept going until her butt met the coat closet door.

He matched her steps, bringing the warmth of male with him. "Are you ready to talk?"

Talk? Oh. She swallowed. "Yes. Talking would be good." Giving up any pretense of decorum, she slid away from him and forced herself to walk calmly to the sofa. She settled into place and crossed her legs.

Zane took measured steps around the sofa and stopped to peruse the DVD and book collection on the shelves by the fireplace. "All romances and contemporary comedies," he mused.

She licked her lips. What was going on in his head? "So?"

He turned and that gaze pierced right into her. "No thrillers, paranormals, horror stories?"

"God, no." Her everyday life sometimes fit that description.

Understanding tilted his lips. He turned and shocked the hell out of her when he crouched down between her legs, his broad hands flattening on her thighs.

Heat flared along every nerve ending, driving up and into her core. "Um, why don't you sit up here?" She was so out of her element.

"I'm fine." Even crouching he had to look down a little to meet her eyes.

She tried to smile. "If you're trying to put me at ease by not looming over me, you're not succeeding."

"I'm not trying to put you at ease." The green in his eyes darkened.

Hail spattered against the windows, and she jumped. "What are you trying to do?"

He frowned as if choosing his words. "The dream worlds weren't real. You know that, right?"

She fought to concentrate while his rough hands remained on

her legs, but her body rioted against any thought. "They were real enough. We were there."

"No." His hands flexed. "It was playtime and make-believe—an escape for me." His features darkened.

Living with Suri must've been hell. She'd known Zane suffered, but he'd never shared the truth with her. "I know," she said softly.

"Good. Then you understand I'm not the guy you played with by the make-believe ocean. I wish I could be, but that's not who I am." Even his voice had deepened.

What was he getting at, and why was her body suddenly on fire? "Okay."

"Do you trust me, Belle?" he asked, his chin lowering.

"Yes." She didn't have to ponder the question, as she'd always trusted Zane. Through everything.

His shoulders relaxed, and approval lightened his eyes. "Thank you."

"You're welcome." She reached out and cupped his whiskered jaw. "Do you trust me?"

"Yes. Always have and always will." He turned into her palm and kissed her love line. "I need you to go underground while I hunt Suri."

She smiled. "No."

He blinked. "Yes. If word gets out that I've mated you, and it will, you'll be in more danger than ever. At least go into hiding until Suri is dead."

Her heart warmed. While Zane might think he wasn't the sweet kid she'd known in dream worlds, he had a kindness to him nonetheless. "If we're about to fight, and you know we are, I'm needed in the infirmary. I have to help, too."

"I can't concentrate on the job if you're in danger." He released one of her legs to run a rough hand through his hair, leaving it tousled. "So you'll go underground. The second promise I need from you is that you'll move on if I don't make it back."

Her head jerked up, and she ignored the fact that she hadn't made the first promise. "You're making it back here."

"Chances aren't good. Your scientists are getting closer to finding a cure for Virus-27, and when they do, they'll be able to manipulate the virus to end other mating aspects if needed."

Janie swallowed, and hurt bloomed in her chest. A vampire or demon mating was absolute, and any other being that tried to become intimate with somebody else's mate would become horribly ill. Until the virus was created that negated the mating bond. One day, when it was managed, mates could separate. "You want me with somebody else?" It was stunning how badly that hurt.

"Hell, no." His nostrils flared. "Not in a million years. Just the thought makes me want to wage war."

Oh. Well, all right then. Her heart warmed, filled with him. "How about you survive and we figure the future out together?" she asked.

"I'll do my best."

She removed her hand to place it on the pillow. "What if you do survive?" He had to survive.

He exhaled slowly. "We'll have to jump off that bridge if it happens."

God, she hoped they had a chance together. Her blood began to burn even hotter. For the briefest moment in time, after so darn long, this amazing warrior was *hers*. "So, then. I guess that leaves us with this one night."

Chapter 17

Everything in Zane stilled. Maybe even his blood. "This one night?"

"Yes." A very pretty pink flushed up and over Janie's high cheek-bones.

The primal being at Zane's core stretched awake, and his blood started to hum. "There's nothing in the world I want more than to spend one more night with you." She'd been his only friend during his childhood, and when she'd grown, she'd been the woman who tortured his nights and gave him a far-fetched, desperate hope for an impossible future. "Although I'm not looking forward to your family beating down the door." But for one more time with his Belle, he'd fight them all.

Sweetness lifted her lips. "Nobody will bother us tonight. My mother and aunts have promised me."

His head lifted. The slow burn inside him burst into a full-blown inferno. "The women do seem to run things around here."

"Shhh. Don't tell the vampires." Janie grinned.

He reached for her and stood, turning to drop into her seat with her straddling him. "You know that's not how I operate, right?" It seemed only fair to be honest with her.

She reached for the bottom of his T-shirt and tugged the material over his head, humming while tossing it across the room. "Like to be in charge, do you?" she murmured, her gaze on his bare chest, her hands flattening on his pecs.

"I am in charge." He'd led soldiers for too many years to know any other way. With a quick move, he captured her hands. Her thighs heated his legs, and he spread them, widening her.

She tried to move back, her body tensing as he kept her in place. Open and vulnerable. Intrigue and arousal narrowed her focus, while defiance lifted her delicate chin.

Truth be told, he liked every damn expression filtering across her face. The intrigue and arousal he'd heighten; the defiance he'd tame. The woman took too many chances and failed to understand her limitations as a human—especially since her chromosomal pairs wouldn't increase overnight. So easy to harm and too easy to end. Just using her hands, he pulled her closer. "Who's in charge, Belle?" he asked softly.

She frowned and started to spout a denial, so he captured her lips and fused their mouths together. When she didn't open soon enough for him, he nipped her bottom lip. She gasped, and he dove in. He loved that he could take her, could penetrate her, could really make her his after so much time. For eons, she'd owned his soul.

Janie was good and kind . . . and reckless. Smart as hell and ready to give the world the finger while also sacrificing her life for the greater good.

That he couldn't allow.

So he took over, showing her strength, providing her a safe place for now. He tasted red wine and woman as he inhaled her, intent on devouring her very essence. Her scent of peaches went right to his head, while her gyrating body shot straight to his cock. Hard and needy, he wanted in her. Now. Yet he kissed her, enjoying her response as she somehow maneuvered closer to him, her core against his groin, her chest plastered against his.

He released her hands and growled low as her nails bit into his bare chest. His mission tomorrow would most likely finish him off, and the ticking clock over his head pushed him to take. But this was Janie, and he needed to go slow. To make sure she remembered him, and more important, that she remembered to be cautious. The woman deserved a long life.

If he could leave her with nothing else, he'd leave her safe.

Finally, when she sagged against him, he allowed her to breathe. "Who's in charge?" he asked.

She blinked, her gaze unfocused. A spunky smile lifted her swollen lips. "I'm on top."

He matched her grin, allowing the predator to glow in his eyes. The woman's innocence was intoxicating, while her naiveté challenging. "You certainly are." Years ago he'd learned the value of patience. Keeping her gaze, he slipped her tank top off. Gorgeous breasts sprang free. Round, firm, and topped with the loveliest pink nipples he'd ever seen.

Almost reverently, he swept his knuckles across one. The small bud hardened instantly.

Janie gasped and pressed her heated sex down on his shaft.

A roaring filled his ears, and he battled back the beast. "You're so beautiful, Belle." Fighting every instinct he owned, he carefully lifted her with one arm and drew off her yoga pants and tiny blue panties, settling her back down on him.

She blushed, her arousal and embarrassment mixing on her sigh. So sweet and innocent, and he didn't want her ever to be unsure of him. Of how much he cared and how much he wanted her. Apparently he needed to get her out of her head.

He ducked his head and captured a nipple, drawing hard. She leaned into him, digging her hands into his hair, her moan slithering through him to his pounding cock.

Taking his time, truly enjoying himself, he played with her breasts. Nipping, licking, and kissing, he lost himself in the silky feel of her skin, in the throaty moans from her lips.

Finally, he leaned back. "Tell me if I'm too rough."

Her eyes had darkened to the color of deep sapphires. "I, ah, kind of like you rough." She ducked her head against his chin.

His heart thumped and seemed to swell. That sweet honesty from the incredible woman cut right into him and took hold. Even so, he tangled his hand in her hair and forced her to meet his gaze. "I appreciate the honesty, sweetheart, but there will be no hiding between us. How rough?"

She gave a small laugh, the sound happy and free. "Heck if I know. I don't have a wealth of experience here, Zane. But I like that you're so strong, and you make me feel safe. Protected. But not in the usual way."

He frowned. "Usual way?"

"Yeah." She shrugged, her hands sliding through his hair to trace his jaw. "You know. Little human among big vampires to be wrapped in bubbles and kept from all harm." She slid along his shaft, her breath quickening. "You make me feel whole and alive. Like a woman."

"I definitely see you as a woman." *His woman.* Though she was still inexperienced, and he had to be careful.

"Good." She unbuckled his belt and released his zipper.

His dick sprang free, and cool air washed across his skin, tantalizing firing nerves. Janie touched him gingerly, exploring. Being breathlessly careful.

"You can't hurt me, baby." His voice went demon low.

"Okay." She encircled part of him, playing with the tip, her soft touch gaining strength.

His balls drew up tight, and he fought a hard groan. If the woman wanted to explore, he damn well wanted to be the man who taught her. Everything. "I like that you're not shy."

"Oh, I'm shy. But I'm curious, too." She bit her lip and leaned down to cup his balls.

Holy fucking hell. Appeasing her curiosity was going to kill him—if her sweetness didn't completely undo him first. He lived with demons, with soldiers fighting to live and killing often. Now, with Janie's smooth hands on him, he wondered when he'd last touched something good. Somebody kind? "What else are you?" he asked.

"Hmm?" She tucked her fingers into his waistband. "Lift up."

He lifted, and she pulled his pants off to leave them both nude. Seeming comfortable now, she settled back down on his legs, her gaze still on his shaft.

"Are you wet, Janie?" he asked, already knowing the answer, considering she perched on his thigh.

That blush returned. "A little."

"Let's see what we can do about that." His gaze dropped to the imprint of the heels of his hands on her ribs. Going on instinct, he encircled her waist, stretching his fingers around her back . . . in perfect alignment with his markings.

Her entire body shuddered, and her mouth opened in a silent "oh."

Yeah, he felt it, too. A deep sense of belonging, and a dangerous urge to take.

She levered herself up. His leg dampened more as wetness spilled from her core. "I want you. Now," she said.

"You're not ready." God, he wanted her, too.

She smiled. "I'm ready."

Well, they did have all night to play and explore. He supported her weight as she rose to her knees and tried to take him in. "Take your time," he said.

She nodded and worked him in, slowly and barely an inch at a time. Wet warmth wrapped around him, squeezing hard.

His hold tightened while he kept himself in check. While he let her explore and play . . . learning her body. Learning his, too. Finally, a fucking century or two later, her body relaxed as her butt hit his groin. His muscles vibrated with the effort to stay still, and his heart thumped hard enough against his ribs to ache.

She glanced up, delight in her eyes. "I took all of you." Even so, her mouth remained pinched, and her body stiff.

"Yeah, but it hurts, right?" he rumbled. He'd told her she wasn't ready.

She grinned. "Yeah. You're huge."

Warmth filled him, and not just from the compliment. The woman was beginning to mean everything to him. "Maybe next time you'll listen to me?"

"Probably not." Using his chest for balance, she slowly lifted up . . . and winced.

Enough. He shoved her back down, his eyes nearly rolling back in his head at the heated contact. Hot and wet, she gripped him hard enough that the beast inside him yanked against any chain of restraint. "You need to learn to listen, Belle."

She gasped and struggled against him.

He kept her in place, waiting patiently until she stopped moving. "If you'd listened and gone slower, you wouldn't be in pain." He'd much rather be pounding into her and making them both happy than teaching a lesson, but she'd given him no choice. "Understand?"

She wiggled a little. "I'm not in a lot of pain, and if you'd start moving, I think it wouldn't be so bad."

He snorted. The minx was impossible. "I can do better than 'not so bad.'" Flexing one hand around her hip in warning, he tweaked her nipple with the other one, just hard enough to add a little bite.

She breathed out, and her sex softened around him. More wetness coated his balls.

Sliding his hand down her torso, he appreciated her toned abdomen before zeroing in on her clit. The small bundle of nerves protruded, begging for a caress. He indulged her, making circular motions.

She whimpered and tried to gyrate against him, but he wouldn't let her move. "My way, Belle."

Frustration curled her lip, while the hand in his hair tugged.

He pinched.

She gasped and stilled, her eyes widening.

"Let go of my hair." He punctuated each word with a little tug.

She released him hastily, her internal walls clenching his shaft like a vise.

"Better," he murmured, continuing to play. He played with her clit, his other hand caressing her hip and butt, continuing until she writhed against him, her breathless moans echoing right through his body.

The beast inside roared for him to take, the leash nearly broken. Zane grabbed her neck and yanked her down for a hard kiss, mastering her mouth, taking what he wanted. She kissed him back with abandon, free and giving. So damn sweet he'd do anything to keep her safe.

He released her mouth. "Who's in charge?"

She blinked, surprise mingling with the need in her eyes.

Not for one second had he forgotten. "Belle?"

"You are," she breathed. So much need crossed her face, he doubted she cared about the words. But it was a start.

He released her. She might have given the words he'd wanted, but she'd also taken everything he was. Body and soul, Janie Kayrs owned him. Always would. "Now you're ready, baby. Go for it."

She breathed out and grabbed his arms, rising and then dropping back down. Her soft cry echoed along with his low groan. Heaven. The woman was heaven.

Her smile held brilliance as she tried again, slowly finding a rhythm that tortured them both.

"Wait," Zane said, grasping her hips and tilting slightly. "Try this."

Her eyes widened and she let out a low moan.

Yeah. That was it.

Passion caught her, glazing in her eyes, as she increased her pace.

He let her lead as long as he could, finally giving in to help her, moving her faster. Harder. Every time he pulled her back down, he thrust up with his hips. The slap of flesh against flesh drowned out the ferocious storm outside. His balls pulled tight, and electricity ripped down his spine.

Reaching between them, he scraped his thumb across her clit.

She stiffened, crying out, her hands curling around his shoulders. Wave upon wave shuddered through her body, while she gripped him fiercely inside, taking him with her.

He held her tight, shoved himself home, and exploded.

Finally, she gasped against him, her body going lax. Her nose snuggled into his neck, while her hair curtained his face.

Contentment whirled through him, almost hinting at peace. The feelings boiling inside him, the dark and dangerous spurs a vampire felt for his mate, the desperate need to protect and defend, nearly suffocated him. She was everything. He ran a hand down her damp back.

She sucked in air. "I think you killed me."

He smiled and hugged her tight. "We're just getting started." They had one night together, and he wanted to savor every second. Remaining connected to her, he stood and glanced around. "Which way to the bedroom?"

Chapter 18

Janie snuggled deeper into the heat of Zane, her mind at peace for the first time in weeks. Months maybe. For so many years she'd wondered about him. The reality was better than any fantasy.

The man hogged the bed. Just knowing that intimate detail about him rushed warmth through her. He sprawled without a care in the world, a powerful animal at rest.

She turned on her side to study him in the scattered moonlight.

Hard features, straight nose, solid jaw. The scar lining the right side of his face added to the sense of danger cascading off him.

His features failed to soften even in sleep.

Possessiveness swept her as she slid a dark piece of hair off his forehead. Hers. For the moment, for the night, Zane Kyllwood was hers. A part of her had always claimed him, and she'd accepted that truth years ago, regardless of where fate pushed them.

He'd shoved the bedclothes down to his waist, and she took a moment to appreciate his muscled chest. Warm, smooth strength filled her palm as she caressed him.

Even after a wild night in which he'd showed her passion she'd never dreamed about, her body wanted him. Maybe not with the hard edge of hunger she'd felt earlier, but with enough of a yearning to give her pause.

She wanted more than the night.

There had to be a way to end the war and find peace.

Sighing, she snuggled closer and slid her thigh over his, her hand over his heart, and her nose into his neck.

He murmured and tucked an arm around her, providing warmth and protection.

She liked that.

Fate and destiny had held enough power over Janie for this life-time, and she was done waiting for the sky to fall. Taking several deep breaths, she slid into the meditative state she'd perfected so long ago.

Her body went lax as her mind created a safe haven on a long wooden dock surrounded by calm waters. Misty, beautiful, gray waters.

"Fate?" Janie called out, having met the gorgeous woman in a dreamland before. It was time the elusive creature showed up and helped out.

Not even the water lapped or made a noise.

Nothing. Janie turned toward the shore as the mist parted.

Kalin.

Janie glanced down at the yoga outfit she'd naturally donned when creating the world. Once again, she faced a predator in vul-nerable clothing. Maybe she should wear combat gear in the pretend worlds.

At the thought, her lips twitched.

Kalin strode through the fog, the medals across his breast appearing dingy in the colorless day. His boot steps thunked against the worn dock as he drew near.

She took a deep breath. "Kalin."

He half-bowed. "Janet. Ready to broker peace?"

"I'd love to broker peace," she said quietly, her mind beginning to spin. "How about you?"

He lifted his aristocratic features to the damp air and sniffed. His eyes morphed from green to purple and back again. "What did you fucking do?" he growled as sharp fangs dropped low.

She gasped. The Kurjan had never really shown emotion before, and to see him furious shot adrenaline through her veins in a warning to flee.

Yet she held her ground. There was no way he could scent her mating in the dream world. "Excuse me?"

"You mated that demon," Kalin spat.

Damn. The Kurjan had always owned his own gifts in the dream worlds. "Can you smell things here?" she asked, without thinking.

"Yes." He shoved his large-boned hands in his pockets. "I can smell the stench of vampire-demon mixed with your normally sweet peaches scent."

She swallowed, looking closely. The soldier didn't seem hurt . . . only furious. "Since this is a done deal, how about we end the war now before either one of us loses more people. You care about your people, right?"

His gaze turned cold—far harder than he'd ever looked before. "You have no idea what you've done."

Her own temper began to stir. "I know exactly what I've done. Fate didn't make my choices . . . I did."

Kalin scoffed. "Bullshit." He sighed and ran a hand through his dark hair, his gaze cutting to the foggy forest. "I suppose this part of the story was inevitable. Just remember, when you decide you need help, I'm here."

She blinked, an ominous shiver winding down her spine. "Why would I need help?"

He shook his head. "Do you really not believe I've covered every contingency? My people have had plans in motion before your birth."

She stepped back, her breath accelerating. "Tell me what is going to happen."

Sorrow twisted his blood-red lips. "I tried to protect you, but you'll have to endure so much now before you become mine. For that, I truly am sorry."

She shook her head. "I mated Zane and can't ever become yours. You know that."

"No." Kalin turned and began to stride down the dock toward the shrouded forest. At the tree line, he turned around, his gaze nearly glowing in the dim light. "Your mating only changes the timeline, not the outcome." With a slight shrug, he turned and disappeared.

Janie rubbed her nose, suddenly freezing. What had the Kurjan been talking about? A hard ball of dread slammed into her stomach.

She could handle this.

Taking several deep breaths, she pulled herself out of the dream world and into reality.

Heat. God. So much heat. She burrowed into Zane's body, her mind spinning. No psychic vision tingled in her brain—no warning of the problems to come. In fact, she hadn't had a decent vision since her birthday.

Even so . . . she knew the problems would arrive. Soon.

Zane tugged down his combat vest and ignored the itch between his shoulder blades. "I'm ready."

Dage nodded from behind the control window. "All set."

Zane slid his finger across his smartphone, and Nicholas Veis popped up. "Nick. I saw you called earlier." In truth, Zane had ignored the call so the king could control the frequency.

Nick nodded, no expression crossing his face. "Yes. Status?"

Zane forced a smile. "I'm sure you've heard my status. I have my mother and brothers locked down in a safe location. Suri can't fucking touch me."

Nick nodded. "Sounds like a dumbass move."

Dumbass. Their code word for "all hell has broken loose."

Zane rubbed his chin. "I know, but getting my family to safety has always been my priority." He kept his tone genial and serious for those listening in. But a quick nod hopefully conveyed he'd received Nick's distress call and knew all about Simone Brightston being taken.

"What's your plan now?" Nick asked.

Zane shrugged, trying to appear unconcerned. "I thought maybe I'd just sit out the rest of the war and let it end. Want to meet up in Cabo for drinks and barmaids?"

Nick's smile seemed forced. "Mexico is too warm for a full-bred demon, you know. Let's go somewhere cooler and relax."

So Simone was being kept close by. Zane chuckled. "Fair enough. When shall we meet?"

"Actually, how about you meet me at the Idaho compound and we work to end the war." Nick leaned closer to the camera on his end. "Suri wants the same thing we do—let's just get it done and then go on our way."

Zane feigned a frown. "Suri wants my head on a platter now that I have my family safe."

"No. I talked to him and can guarantee your safety. As you know, he needs your skills in battle now more than ever. Come home, and we'll plan together." Nick would've been convincing had Zane not known the truth.

"Are you sure?" Zane pretended to waffle.

"Absolutely." Nick glanced down and then back up. "Meet me in an hour. You have my word you'll be safe."

Zane nodded. "I'll be there." He clicked off. Slowly, he stood and waited for the king to enter the room. "I have to go. Suri will kill Nick and Simone if I don't."

Dage nodded. "I know, but you're not going alone."

Talen and Conn stepped into the room, both dressed for war.

Zane straightened his shoulders. "I'm not taking you." God. All he needed was Realm vampires in the way.

"Too bad." Talen shoved an arm through Zane's. "Don't fucking put me into a tree."

Conn clasped Dage's arm. "We'll meet you thirty yards to the north of Suri's Idaho headquarters. Let's do this." They disappeared.

Shit. Zane shook his head. The damn Kayrs family. How the hell had they found Suri's headquarters? Drawing deep through his feet, he made peace with the universe and began to bend her laws.

He had to get there before the king did.

Zane maneuvered through time and space, acutely aware of the massive vampire riding his wave. Talen weighed a freakin' ton, and Zane had to actually fight the laws of physics to transport him.

Finally, they landed flat on their backs on snowy, muddy pine needles.

Talen groaned and rolled over. "Nice finesse."

Zane jumped to his feet. "Not my fault you're heavier than a truck." He stretched his back and rolled his neck, feeling like he'd been through a meat grinder. His hands trembled, so he shoved them in his pockets.

Dage and Conn dropped next to them. On their feet.

Talen smirked.

Zane ignored him and eyed the cloudy sky. "I have a cache of weapons stashed a mile to the north."

Dage growled. "Then why did we land here?"

"Because you took off before I could tell you," Zane responded without heat. For some reason, he understood the Kayrs family. His father would've liked them.

Dage rubbed his chin. "You're right. Sorry."

Zane blinked. "No worries. This way." He turned and jogged through the forest while three vampires followed behind him.

War made for odd allies. Or was it the war? He and Janie were always meant to be, as far as he was concerned. Even if their mating was short-lived.

For the first time in a long, time, he wondered. Was there a way to survive his destiny?

They reached the hidden trunk and quickly suited up with knives, laser guns, and automatic rifles.

Dage glanced up. "No Degoller Stars?"

"No. Banned by treaty," Zane returned.

Dage nodded, his gaze thoughtful. "Will Suri abide by the treaty?"

"No." Zane shoved one more knife in his boot. "So watch your heads." Then he turned and led the way toward the abandoned town.

Vibrations of power filtered on the breeze.

Talen growled.

Yeah, demons and vampires didn't usually mix. Zane paused at the tree line. "Stay away from anybody with more than five medals on their chest. You can't handle the backlash for killing one of the elite."

Arrogance lifted Dage's eyebrow. "I've killed demons."

"None of these." Zane dug deep for patience. "Killing one of these will send out a mental shock wave strong enough to fry your brain."

"Bullshit," Conn muttered.

Zane shrugged. "Believe me or not. Your choice."

Dage eyed the quiet building. "I have heard stories. If this is true, can you shield against Suri if you kill him?"

"Yes," Zane lied. Something down deep told him the king would sacrifice himself for Janie's mate if necessary, and Zane couldn't let him do it. If anybody had a sliver of a chance of healing from Suri's unleashed powers, it was a demon like Zane.

No vampire would ever survive.

"I'll take the interior. Wait for my signal." Without looking back,

Zane hustled through the early morning and climbed the outside of the whorehouse. He reached the balcony and slipped inside an abandoned bedroom.

A gun cocked.

He stilled.

Nick walked out from behind an oriental dressing screen, his weapon pointed at Zane's head. "I'm sorry."

Suri shoved open the door and stomped inside, a Degoller Star in his hand. "Bind him."

Nick zip-tied Zane's wrists before frisking him head to toe and finding every damn weapon.

Zane growled. "Traitor."

Nick shrugged. "Says who?"

Suri tucked his gun at the back of his waist and stepped into Zane's space. He inhaled, his nostrils flaring. "You mated the human bitch."

Fire ripped through Zane's blood. "Watch how you talk about my mate."

Suri growled. "Considering she's dead in about an hour, you might want to lose the posturing."

Zane's head jerked up. Dread whipped down his spine. "What are you doing?"

Nick sighed. "The trap is a bit bigger than just you. We're taking your mate right about now."

God. The king and two of his brothers waited harmlessly outside for Zane's signal, leaving Realm headquarters three soldiers down.

"Why, Nick?" Zane asked, his gaze remaining on his uncle.

Suri snarled in a parody of a smile. "I have the only person Nick has ever cared about secured in a concrete cell lined with phanakite three stories down."

A muscle in Nick's jaw twitched. "And here I thought we called it planekite. Did you get that, Zane?"

It had been surprisingly easy to discover Simone's location. Suri was losing his edge. Zane nodded and threw himself into his buddy, yanking power up through his toes.

Lights flashed in wild succession as they tumbled through time and space to land in the dungeon below.

Zane landed on his back, and Nick fell into the wall.

God. Air. Zane needed air. He gasped in, his kidneys and spleen swelling with pain. At some point, he'd figured the numerous jumps would catch up to him. Apparently that time was now. Slowly, he rolled to his feet, his gut lurching. He ripped open the ties binding him.

Nick grasped metal bars to pull himself up. "Simone?" he called.

The witch paced the small cell, her features pale, her eyes a wild black. "Get me out of here." Her voice emerged weak.

Zane glanced at the walls. Yep. Pure phanakite—the mineral that negated a witch's powers. If ingested, the harmless looking sparkles could maim or kill.

Nick growled and aimed a well-placed kick against the metal lock. The door swung open.

Men shouted far above, and heavy boot steps pounded down the stairs.

Nick tugged Simone from the cell and shoved her into Zane's arms. "Take her."

"No." Simone struggled against him, but she hadn't regained her strength, and Zane easily overpowered her. She tried to reach for Nick, who shook his head.

Bodies fell down the stairs, landing hard. The King of the Realm straddled a demon and neatly sliced off his head. A smattering of power rushed out. Dage turned, blood sliding out of his left eye.

"Hi, Simone," he said.

Simone winced and nodded. "King."

An explosion rocked the building, spinning shards of wood and Sheetrock down. One cut into Zane's neck, and he grimaced. Damn good thing the dead demon hadn't had much power.

Nick punched Zane in the arm. "Get the hell out of here."

Zane tried to catch his breath and reduce his internal injuries as he focused on the king through the raining debris. "Get to headquarters. Big trap."

Dage's eyes shot silver through the blue. "I'll grab my brothers and meet you there."

Zane ducked as a beam slammed into his shoulder.

Dage paused. "You align with us."

Zane lifted his chin, fate clicking into place. "Go. Now." He'd worry about alliances later. Right now survival mattered more.

Another explosion ripped through the day, and a body fell from above, slamming Nick to the ground. His head thunked against the cement, and blood sprayed.

Simone cried out and reached for him.

With a growl, Zane tucked Simone close and manacled his buddy's arm. If he was aligning with the Realm, he was taking his one friend with him. Before Nick could fight him off, he ripped open a portal and crawled through.

Chapter 19

Janie finished patching up two young vampires who'd thought to experiment with rocket fuel and laser bullets. Burns marred their arms, but those would soon heal.

Their pride was another matter.

Garrett had put out the fire and hustled both boys into the infirmary and now leaned back against a wall of cupboards, his arms crossed, his face cold.

He didn't have to be such a tough taskmaster. Janie's heart ached for the two wounded kids.

She patted one on the back. "It's okay, Freddie. You should've seen Garrett when he first learned how to blow things up." Truth be told, it was a miracle headquarters still stood.

Garrett shot her a look.

The teenager grinned. "I've heard. But, ah, don't tell my mom, okay?"

Janie bit back a grin. "No worries. Doctor-patient privilege and all of that." The kids had learned their lesson, so she figured they'd be safe for a while.

The two patients hopped off the tables and hurried from the room, no doubt heading to find something to eat. Protein always helped immortals to heal.

Prophet Guiles sauntered inside, his wrinkled silk pants matching his hangdog expression. Two guards reached the doorway and turned to protect the exit. "I cut myself," Guiles muttered.

Janie glanced down at the deep slice across his forearm. "So heal yourself." Since the bastard had tried to turn Prophet Lily over to their enemies the previous month, Janie hadn't had much use for him.

Garrett pushed off from the wall.

The prophet perched on an examination table, his gaze raking Garrett and then finding Janie. "Fine. I thought we could talk."

Janie turned and leaned against a table, her arms crossed. "I'm not sure we have much to talk about. You kidnapped my friend after trying to manipulate her into killing me."

The prophet sighed. "Sometimes people get lost. Regardless, fate has made me a prophet, and there has to be some respect given."

Garrett stepped closer to his sister. "The fact that you're still breathing shows respect."

Janie nodded. It was a damn miracle her father or one of her uncles hadn't cut off the prophet's head for his betrayal, but even big bad vampires balked at messing with fate. And only fate could permanently tattoo the prophesy brand on one of the chosen three.

Well, probably. Prophet Caleb had other ideas, notably that the marking was transferred like a virus when its host died. But Caleb disliked being a prophet, and he hated fate.

So who the heck knew.

Prophet Guiles crossed muscled arms. "Help me and I'll help you."

"No," Garrett said.

Janie lifted an eyebrow, her instincts flaring to life. "How so?"

Prophet Guiles's brown eyes glimmered. "You're not the only physic here, Miss Kayrs."

She lifted her chin. Could she still be considered a "miss" since she'd been mated? Not married but mated? Somehow, she didn't think so. "What are you offering?"

He glanced around and then leaned toward her, his voice low. "I know why Fate wants you."

"Bullshit," Garrett muttered.

Heat rushed down Janie's torso. "Why does Fate want me?"

Triumph curled the prophet's lips. "Help me get free, and I'll tell you everything. The big reason you're prophesied, and more important, why so many species want you dead."

Well. "Don't sugarcoat it, Guiles." The man didn't deserve the title of prophet. "As far as I remember, you wanted me dead because I'm going to end up wearing your prophesy mark, which means you die."

He shook his head. "No, no, no. That was just a manipulation on Fate's part. You don't end up with my marking . . . but you do end up changing the world."

"For the better?"

He lifted a lean shoulder. "There are two paths, as usual, and it depends which one you choose. I can offer guidance as well as a road map."

She couldn't trust him, but he might be telling the truth. "What do you want from me?"

"Freedom," he said simply. "Help me get away from the king and out from under his thumb. I just want to be left alone."

Janie eyed the guards at the door. "Not sure we can take them, Guiles." She had absolutely no intention of helping the betrayer, even if he did have useful information.

"Fair enough." He coughed. "Now."

The first guard turned and shot Garrett in the chest. He fell back, blood arcing.

Janie cried out and reached for her brother. In a surprisingly smooth movement, Guiles dodged forward and slid a needle into her neck but did not depress the plunger.

Janie stilled. What the hell? She hadn't even seen him move, and she was trained. What was in the syringe? Fear buzzed through her brain, and she had to shove the sensation aside to concentrate. "This is a good way to get yourself killed."

The guards at the doorway slipped inside and shut the door.

Janie blinked. Why weren't they reaching for weapons?

The prophet chuckled against her hair. "You're not the only one with allies."

Janie gulped and glanced down as Garrett shoved himself to his feet. Blood flowed from his chest, and his eyes had turned a furious aqua.

"Shoot him again," Guiles said.

"No. Wait." Janie kept still so he wouldn't inject her. "Don't shoot him. Let's talk."

Prophet Guiles tightened his hold. "Now you want to talk?"

"Sure." She kept her gaze on Garrett so she'd be ready when he made a move.

Garrett planted a hand on his wound. "What's in the syringe?"

"Cyanide," Prophet Guiles said. "Your sister hasn't been mated long enough to become immortal. If I release the liquid, she'll die. Painfully and in front of your eyes."

Garrett eyed the two guards. "When I'm done with this Fucktard, I'm ripping your heads off." His tone remained nearly conversational.

God, he reminded Janie of their father so much lately. She cleared her throat and struggled to keep calm. The guards would shoot her brother again, and if they ganged up on him, they could probably kill him. Sure, he was trained, but so were they, and they seemed a lot more seasoned. "Let's all get out of here alive, shall we?"

Guiles breathed into her neck. "I like you being accommodating, Miss Kayrs. Too bad you mated that demon. I always thought we'd make a nice pair."

She swallowed as bile rose in her throat. Gross. The man was like centuries and centuries old. "What's your plan here?"

"My plan is for my two friends to stow us away and drive right out of here. Then we'll get to safety and my allies." He pulled her away from Garrett and toward the door.

Janie held back a wince. "Are you still working with the Kurjans?" If he traded her to Kalin, she might have a chance at surviving. She'd go along with the plan if she could keep Garrett alive.

"No." Prophet Guiles tugged her toward the doorway. "The demons have a much better offer for me. In fact, I just informed Suri that three of the Kayrs brothers are in his local. Let's hope he gets my message in time."

God. They'd walked into a trap. "If you've hurt any of them, I'll kill you myself, Prophet," Janie ground out between clenched teeth.

Garrett angled around to the right. "What's your plan with Janie?"

Prophet Guiles shrugged. "Alas, I do believe Suri wants her head cut off." Guiles wrapped an arm around her waist from behind to push her along. "Although she's quite charming. Maybe she can get

Suri to change his mind and let her live. How are you on your knees, sweetheart?" His breath smelled like old coffee and stale bread.

Garrett hissed out air and stalked closer. "One chance, Prophet. Let her go, and I won't cut off your head."

Janie blinked. She'd never heard that tone from her younger brother.

Guiles paused at the doorway, his gaze on his guards. "Kill him."

"No." Janie struggled and grimaced as the needle dug into her neck.

"Hold still," Garrett ordered. Then he smiled at the two guards. "Let's go, assholes." He dropped into a fighting stance, anticipation lighting his lips. Blood matted the front of his shirt, but the wound appeared to have closed.

The first guard shoved his gun in his waistband and drew out a knife. "I've wanted to cut off your head for decades."

Garrett snarled. "I've only lived two decades, asshat. What's your problem?"

The second guard's blade shone bright in the fluorescent lights. "Let's just say the bounty on your head will guarantee we live long and well."

Garrett removed a wicked double-edged knife from his back pocket. "You're not collecting that bounty."

"Drop the knife, or I kill your sister," the prophet said calmly. "Suri will no doubt grant me asylum for killing her, even though I believe he wants to do the deed himself."

"No," Janie whispered. "Keep the knife, G."

Garrett's face hardened. His shoulders went back, and his knife clattered onto the floor.

Terror shrieked through Janie.

Then a voice. "*What's going on?*"

She blinked. A voice in her head. "*Zane?*" she thought back.

"*Yes.*" He sounded out of breath . . . and in pain? "*Where are you?*"

God. It was true. She'd mated, and she could hear his thoughts. So damn quickly. "*Help. We're in the infirmary, and they're trying to kill Garrett.*"

Quiet reigned for the briefest of moments.

Then all hell broke loose.

Zane and Dage dropped into the infirmary, taking in the scene quickly.

Dage went for the two guards, while Zane grabbed Guiles's arm and yanked. Two hard, quick punches to the prophet's face, and he went down.

Zane turned back toward Janie, his face pale, his eyes furious. "Hold still." Reaching out, he grasped the syringe and yanked.

Pain pricked her skin, and she winced, her hand going to the injury. "Holy ow." Then she turned to help her uncle, but Dage already had one guard on the ground, while Garrett repeatedly punched the other in the face.

Zane crossed muscled arms. "I thought we agreed you'd go underground while I took out Suri."

"You ordered and I didn't follow," Janie snapped. Enough was enough. She had a job to do, and her mate would damn well figure that out. Putting her hands on her hips, she took a deep breath.

Guiles jumped up from the floor and grabbed her from behind. Pivoting, she elbowed him in the gut. He doubled over and yanked a knife from his boot.

Silver flashed.

Zane pummeled Guiles to the floor and plunged a blade into his neck. Cartilage crunched. Blood sprayed. The atmosphere morphed.

"Zane—" Janie cried out.

He was beyond listening. Zane straddled the prophet, dug in, and twisted both ways. Guiles's head rolled away from his body.

"Oh, shit." Garrett leaped off the downed guard, blood covering his chest and hands.

Janie backed away from the dead man, gazing wildly around.

A blue light lifted from the prophet, sliding around almost gracefully. Dage ducked as it wove around him.

Garrett backed toward the door. The light slid through the air toward him. "No," he whispered.

The light zagged to the left and then right, finally circling around on itself and wisping out.

Janie let out a sigh of relief. Thank God.

Electricity cracked. She cried out, ducking as sparks flew. The light returned, swelling to such a true blue it hurt to see. She covered her eyes with her forearms.

Heat seared into her.

Then a cooling balm. She slowly opened her eyes and straightened. "What happened?"

Zane glanced at her and leaned forward to tug her shirt away from her neck. He was pale and sweating, probably from the numerous jumps. "No prophesy marking." He turned toward the group. "Anybody?"

A quick chorus of "no" echoed as the collected group double-checked their necks for the mark.

Janie reached out with shaking hands to view Zane's neck. Nothing. She bit her lip. "Who was marked?"

Zane shook his head. "No clue."

Dage wiped his blade clean on his cargo pants. "Fascinating. Well, I imagine we'll hear soon enough."

Janie clenched her hands together. "When a prophet is killed, I thought somebody in the immediate vicinity gets marked?"

"Not always." Dage kicked one of the downed guards, who didn't move. "Sometimes it's just a person close to the prophet. We'll find our third prophet soon enough."

Janie tried to mellow her racing heart by concentrating on Zane. Her eyes swelled. He was alive. But dark circles marred his gorgeous eyes, and fatigue cut into the sides of his mouth. Pain curled his lip.

"Are you all right?" she asked.

Dage eyed Zane. "You've transported too many times this last week. It's a miracle your insides haven't exploded."

Zane nodded. "Yeah. I'm done for a while." His eyebrows drew down in the middle, and his lips tightened. "Although I'm strong enough to have a little talk with my mate."

Janie stilled. Oh no, he had not used that big bad bossy vampire voice with her. "We can talk later."

"Now." Zane took her arm and helped her over the unconscious guards.

Garrett moved to intercept them, but Dage stopped him with one broad hand.

Zane nodded to Dage, some manly look passing between them.

Now her uncle was on her shit list, too. Janie went along with Zane, biting her tongue, more than willing to give him hell in private.

The entire Realm didn't need to hear their dispute.

Chapter 20

They walked in silence through the quiet subdivision, reaching Janie's home much too quickly.

Zane held the door open for her, and she swept inside, head held high. They truly needed to set some ground rules, although her mind was still spinning from Guiles's death. The death of a prophet. The fact that the prophesy marking hadn't branded her neck shocked her.

Deep down, she'd always assumed she'd be a prophet. Especially after the visions Guiles had had last year of her wearing such a marking.

Zane closed the door quietly. Too quietly.

Janie whirled. "I take it you're mad about something."

He lifted one eyebrow. "Try a different approach."

She tapped her foot, trying to dispel her nervousness. "Get over it."

"Bad try." He leaned back against the door, clearly blocking her exit. "You're still human and won't have immortal chromosomal pairs for weeks. Thus you can die. I told you to go underground because I thought something might happen while I was away. I was right."

Yeah, he'd been right. "I can handle myself, Zane."

He glowered. "You lied to me."

"No I didn't." She eyed the distance to the bedroom door, which had a lock. "I didn't promise to go underground, and you know it."

Arrogance marked his every move. "No, but I trusted you'd obey me in a time of war—at least until you're not so vulnerable."

Damn but the *o word* just pissed her off. "I'm glad we got this situation out of the way, because I don't just obey. Period."

A dimple winked in his left cheek. "Oh, you'll learn."

She stiffened. Who the hell did he think he was? Yet finally, he was talking about a future. What had happened with Suri? "Get over yourself."

He cleared his throat, obviously choosing his words carefully. "We mated, and that means something to me."

"Me too." She frowned.

He overwhelmed the small entryway. "You're my responsibility now. Hell. I think you've always been mine."

Vampires. They thought they could control the world. "You're mine, too," Janie said softly.

Zane nodded. "Maybe. But for now, you're human, which means you could die. I'm a soldier, I'm a fighter, and I give orders so people *don't* die. It's all I know, and it's all I can control during this damn war. So for now, you follow orders."

The poor guy had been raised in different militaries since day one, and he'd kept his brothers safe by giving orders. He probably didn't understand another way. Janie shook her head. "No."

That quickly, his expression moved from earnest to soldier hard. "You have everyone fooled, don't you, baby?" he drawled.

She shook her head and backed up. Her every nerve shot into overdrive, making her achingly aware of her body. Of the need suddenly coursing through her. Why did she react like this to him and to that tone of voice? "I don't know what you're talking about."

"Yes, you do." He pushed off from the door and headed toward her. "You're the sweet Janie Kayrs, the fragile human everybody protects and love. The woman who nearly gets killed and yet doesn't express fear. Nobody has ever drawn lines for you, have they?"

She caught her breath and fought the urge to flee. "I'm not some scared, spoiled kid, Zane."

His eyes darkened. "No, you're an interesting mix of competent doctor, loving family member, and reckless brat. While the first two characteristics intrigue me, the final one will get you killed, and it's time that ended. Charm and sweetness have gotten you out of any amount of trouble around here, thus putting you in danger."

Irritation blew up into anger as she backed into the living room. "You're an arrogant idiot."

He shook his head, continuing his advance. "Only brats call names."

"Oh yeah? The doctor in me thinks you're a complete dumbass." She held up a hand to ward him off. "Stop there."

"No." Amusement glittered along with a dark determination in his emerald eyes. "Unlike your relatives, I don't find your defiance cute. Not for one second will I allow the brattiness to continue—especially since it nearly got you pumped full of cyanide earlier."

Allow? Did he say allow? The last thing she needed to think about was the poison that had almost killed her. So much heat roared through Janie, she feared she'd detonate right then and there in a riotous flame of female outrage. "Who the hell do you think you are?" She jumped as her rear pressed against the cool window.

One of his dark eyebrows lifted. "Don't ask stupid questions, Belle. You know exactly who I am."

But did she? The force cornering her in her own living room held far more power and male determination than she'd ever encountered. And she'd mated him! The man was correct. Charm would not get her out of this one, and her own body was betraying her. Her nipples couldn't possibly get any harder than they were right now.

She dropped into a fighting stance.

Two hands slipped under her armpits and yanked her upright. Zane leaned in close, his eyes sparking. "Don't you ever try to fight me."

"Why? Afraid you'll lose?" She turned to aim a good kick to make her point. For years she'd trained, and she could defend herself.

He propelled her forward, plastering her against the glass. "Last chance, Janie. Lose the brat or you'll regret it."

How dare he. She struggled against him, her fury increasing at her failure to get free. "Fuck you, asshole."

Then things happened too quickly to follow. Wind rustled, he lifted her through the air, and oxygen whooshed from her lungs as her chest met his thighs.

She had one second to figure out he'd sat and thrown her over his lap before the first slap hit.

Hard.

Pain ricocheted through her ass, and she gasped. She bucked and struggled, but he held her easily in place, one hand flattened across her upper back, while the other one smacked her butt. *Smack. Smack. Smack.*

He didn't go easy on her, and he sure as hell didn't hold anything back. Her thin yoga pants weren't any match for his hard hand.

A dangerous warmth spread through her extremities. She fought against him as long as she could, finally going limp. Then, and only then, did he cease.

She remained in place, panting, tears filling her eyes.

He caressed one hand over her rear, spreading a warmth that made her moan. Then he lifted her up onto his lap and rubbed his nose over hers. A tear slid down her face, and she batted it back.

"No." He pulled her close and tucked her head under his chin, his broad hand sweeping down her back. "Let the tears out, Belle."

At the soft command, her body ignored every blazing warning from her brain and started to cry. Hard. Sobs racked her, so out of proportion to the silly spanking he'd given her.

Through the storm, Zane held her, rubbing her back.

She wound down with a small hiccup, exhausted and maybe a little embarrassed.

"Were you scared by the cyanide or when Garrett got shot?" Zane's warm breath brushed her hair.

She snuggled closer into his rock-hard chest. Over-the-top vulnerability swamped her, and she needed to draw some protection around her. "Yes."

"Hmmm. If I hadn't been here, what would you have done after the attack?"

Janie wiped her eyes. "I don't know what you mean. I guess I would've gone back to work."

"So you would've hidden your fear from everybody?" Zane's voice remained low and soothing as he caressed her back.

She shrugged. Why talk about all of this?

"Janie?"

She sighed. "I guess."

He leaned back and tried to lift her face. She struggled against him, burrowing deeper. Strong fingers tangled in her hair and tugged, pulling her head back.

God, he was stubborn. Janie knew full well she wasn't a pretty crier, and she really didn't want him to see her blotchy, swollen face. She blinked against his tender green gaze. "What?" she asked.

He frowned. "Why do you hide your emotions? You're completely justified to be terrified of cyanide."

She didn't have time for fear. Thinking about it, she sniffled. "We've been at war for so long, and everyone has too much to worry about. I don't need to be coddled like some . . ."

"Human girl?" Zane finished for her.

"I guess." The vampires had moved heaven and earth to keep her safe, and the least she could do was not burden them with a bunch of emotion.

"When was the last time you cried?" he asked, brushing a soft kiss across her forehead.

She thought about it. "I have no idea." There just wasn't time for crying.

"We're mated, and we're going to give this a shot, Belle." While the tone remained gentle, an underlying thread of steel wound through his low voice.

Her breath caught, and her abdomen tingled. "What about Suri?"

"I'll kill him, but maybe there's a way to end him without getting myself killed. I'm working on it." Zane's fingers unfurled to rub her scalp. "No more hiding your feelings. They're mine, as are your fears."

She shook her head, suddenly feeling fragile.

His slight smile failed to mask the intent in his dark eyes. "You might want to just learn to share without having to be spanked first, but I'm fine with the alternative."

She scowled. "I thought vampires were bossy. Demon vampires are far worse."

"You'd do well to remember that." He brushed hair off her face. "So how are you feeling right now?"

She breathed out. "Well, my ass hurts, my head hurts from crying, and I'd like to punch you in the face."

"What else?" he murmured.

She sighed and her body relaxed as she gave in to him. "Calm and at peace. I'd forgotten how a good cry can help."

"See?" He kissed her nose. "I wonder if I can take your pain away yet." Reaching out, he brushed two knuckles across her forehead.

Her skin tingled, and the pain melted away. Her eyes widened. "You did it."

He closed his eyes and then reopened them. A full smile curved his lips. "Excellent."

She played with the top of his T-shirt. "How about you take away the pain along my butt?" She'd love for him to take that pain into his own body for just a moment, even if he could dispel it.

He grinned. "I think I'll let you live with that one. Keep it in mind next time you put yourself in danger or try to smother your feelings." He stood, keeping her cradled in his arms. "For now, how about we head to the bedroom and I show you what I'm feeling?"

Janie softened in Zane's arms as he strode toward the bedroom. How could he be such a hardass one minute and a sweetheart the next? Her new mate had layers of complexity she'd never imagined. Bringing him into the real world, into her world, would take time and patience.

And a big baseball bat if he ever tried to spank her again.

Although—and she'd deny it to her grave—she did feel much better after letting it all out. Her fear, her fury, her fate . . . she'd forgotten how cathartic a good cry could be.

He entered the bedroom and kicked the door shut behind them.

She'd seen that move in a movie once, and it had given her tingles. Having Zane do it so casually as an afterthought while he carried her to bed? Full-on wings flapping through her abdomen. She reached up to tangle her fingers in his hair as the dark waves curled over his nape. "I like your hair this length."

He set her down as if she was made of breakable china. "Then I'll leave it this length."

She smiled. "Now you're being agreeable?"

Strong hands tugged his shirt over his head. "I'm always agreeable."

She gasped at the pulsing black bruise covering his abdomen. "What in the world?"

He glanced down and winced. "My fault. I teleported too many times, and my internal organs decided to bake themselves."

"Does it hurt?" She leaned closer to determine the bruise was more deep purple than black.

"Hurts like hell." He took advantage of her movements to remove her shirt. "In fact, I can't teleport now." His brow creased.

She shook her head. "Why aren't you in the infirmary?" Scooting toward him, she tried to stand.

He grasped her waistband and tossed her back, easily removing her pants. Pure sin lifted his grin. "I'll heal."

"No." The man was crazy. "If you've damaged your internal organs, you need rest. Not lifting me, not fighting, and certainly not sex."

He kicked out of his cargo pants. "Sex heals. Didn't you know?"

She snorted and scrambled away from him. "That is a dangerous bruise."

"So be gentle with me." He came over her, a massive, muscled soldier, and flattened her on the bed.

Her eyes wanted to roll back in her head, and her legs really wanted to part. But he was her mate, and she needed to take care of him, too. "Zane, we can't do this."

He brushed her lips with his. "I need you, Belle. Make me forget the pain."

The drugging kiss and whispered plea softened her very bones. Lightly, she skimmed her fingers over his upper chest, marveling at his strength. Heat fluttered through her along with a surge of emotion that swept more tears to her eyes. One escaped to roll down her cheek. "You're sure I won't hurt you?"

Zane caught the moisture with one finger. "I promise, baby."

Biting her tongue, she tried to stop crying. "I'm sorry." She shifted beneath him, groaning when her nipples scraped across his chest.

"No apologies and no hiding emotions," he said, pressing at her entrance. "You're wet."

"Maybe a little." She opened wider to take him.

Amusement creased his cheek. "You've been wet since I spanked you." He shoved in a couple more inches.

She rolled her eyes, her heart thrumming. "Not even."

"Nothin' wrong with a little kink, darlin'." He held himself off her with iron-hard arms that clenched as he took it slow.

She dug her nails into his chest, and fireworks detonated inside her. "That wasn't kink."

He nipped her nose. "No, it wasn't. That was my making a point." As if to make another one, he shoved all the way home.

Janie gasped, her body rioting. Slowly, she forced herself to relax and adjust to his girth. "Your point?" she breathed.

He studied her. "You need to stay safe. This is home. Finally."

The words wound right around her heart and dug deep. Another tear rolled down her cheek.

He kissed this one away. "I love you, Janet Isabella Kayrs. Always have and always will."

She gasped, so full of him she couldn't breathe. "Why?"

He grinned. "You're stubborn, sexy, brilliant, beautiful, kind, determined . . . and mine."

She returned the smile as her body accepted his. "That's a large list."

"You have a big presence in a tiny body." He kissed her, taking his time, making her head spin. "Your sense of duty and loyalty intrigue me as well."

She ran her hands down his flanks. "You're just as loyal as I am, but you don't like to admit it."

He frowned. "I'd do anything for my family."

"What about your people?" She saw beneath his anger and hurt, and it was time he did as well. "You care about them and want the war to end."

"Of course, but I'm not a demon."

She lifted her head and kissed him again. "Then what are you?"

He frowned. "Yours." His shaft pulsed inside her, a constant reminder of his strength and masculinity.

She inhaled through her nose, trying to concentrate. "You're also theirs, and if Suri is as crazy as he seems, the demon people need you. There's nobody else."

"Don't talk to me about fate, baby," he whispered, sliding out and then back in.

Her eyes wanted to roll back in her head from the devastating friction, so she blinked to concentrate. In about two seconds, she was going to beg him to move. For now, she needed to get her point across. "Screw fate." She gasped as he slid out and then back in. "I'm talking about loyalty to people and duty. That you have to choose."

He leaned down and nipped her lips with his. "The demons aren't my people."

"You're part demon, like it or not. And who else do they have?" She leaned up and kissed him hard.

"Enough talking." He started to move. Slowly at first, with long desperate drags. Then faster.

Flash fire uncoiled inside her, and she tried to climb the cliff just to fall over. Definitely enough talking. He either understood her or he didn't. For now, her body completely took over. "Harder," she moaned.

He reached under her to clasp her chest against his and started thrusting deep. Hard and deep.

She shut her eyes, lost in the incredible sensations.

A tiny explosion rocked inside her, and then the world blew up. She arched into him, crying out his name, pleasure capturing her and throwing her back into Zane's body. He growled her name, grinding against her as he came. Finally, the pummeling waves lulled, and she flopped back onto the bed, her body satiated.

Her hands shaking, she pushed his hair away from his damp face. The guy was a throwback who needed to learn how strong she was, who had to learn to trust her to take care of herself. She could teach him. For now, all she could do was feel and have faith. "I love you, Zane Kyllwood."

Chapter 21

Zane paced the large conference room, an itch of warning tingling down his back. Sam sat at the conference table with Dage, Talen, Moira and Simone, who represented the witch nation. Nick Veis leaned against the wall by the door, staring at Simone, who pointedly ignored him.

The damn place was overrun with witches and vampires.

Moira Dunne Kayrs sneezed. The witch was pale compared to her cousin.

Zane wondered again if witches sneezed when irritated. Shrugging off the question, his gaze focused on the map projected across the entire wall. Several demon landholdings and outposts were marked . . . but even more were absent. "What do you want, King?" he asked.

Talen answered for his brother. "We want it all. Finish the map for us."

Zane's mind whirled. While Suri was an asshole who deserved to die, the demons were still his people. His shoulders straightened and he stood taller as the mantle of responsibility nearly knocked him on his ass. "No."

His brother lifted his head in a subtle acknowledgment of support. Sam always supported him.

Nick Veis smiled wide, lacking anything subtle. "Good to hear."

Dage rested his elbows on the table. "I thought we decided to be allies."

"We did." Zane kept an eye on the witches in case one of them started throwing plasma balls. He'd been burned once, years ago, and he still had the scar.

Talen leaned back in his chair. "So give us the Intel, and we'll take them out. That's what allies do."

Zane shook his head, and destiny filled him. His mate had been correct, and it was time he followed her lead and stepped up. Duty and loyalty mattered. "You became allies with the demon *nation*. Not just with me."

"Hell no," Talen said. "Suri has too many supporters, and we need to take them out now. We finally can get the Intel to take him down."

Zane nodded, fully understanding Talen's anger toward the demon nation. "You have to remember that *Suri* kidnapped your brother, and *Suri* tortured him. The majority of the demon nation still doesn't even think it happened."

"Oh, it happened," Talen growled.

It'd be a miracle if Zane survived the day without Janie's dad punching him again. "The majority of demons are good people and shouldn't be attacked by you—or betrayed by me."

Dage studied him, silver eyes thoughtful. "You're stepping up to rule?"

"I am." God, he didn't want to. Not in the slightest. But Suri had to be stopped, and to prevent further bloodshed for both of his species, Zane would do what had to be done. Janie had shown him that.

Talen pushed away from the table. "The only way you step up is if you kill Suri."

"I know," Zane said.

"That will leave my daughter as good as a widow." Talen stood tall and formidable across the table.

Zane exhaled slowly. "So you know how much power Suri will release upon death?"

"I'm the fucking strategic leader for the fucking Realm." Talen nearly vibrated with irritation. "The second you talked about Suri's power, I began researching everything I could find. Of course I understand the power."

But he didn't, not really. Zane could barely comprehend the power, and he lived with his own. "For years, Suri hasn't been able to pierce my mind. I've practiced and I've trained mentally. If anybody can contain him upon death, it's me." Yeah, it was a damn long shot, but it was all Zane had. "Janie understands." But did she? Really?

Simone smoothed back dark hair. "This is the closest I've sat to three demons in over a century, and I'm not even twitchy. While Nick has had eons to perfect his ability to refrain from harming the brains around him, you and Sam aren't even a century old. Do you not have the power?"

"We have the power," Zane answered. "I think our vampire lineage gives us more ability to control our impact on others."

Simone leaned forward. "I do not think you have the power. Prove it."

"*Zaychik moy*," Nick muttered, shoving off from the wall. "He'll hurt you."

"Little Bunny?" Zane lifted an eyebrow at his friend. The dangerous, rather bitchy witch was nowhere near a bunny.

"Shut up, Zane," Nick said.

Simone's black eyes flashed. "I doubt the fledgling demon can harm me. Let's see what you've got, boy."

Zane couldn't help smiling. The woman might be over a century old, but she appeared twenty-five, and he looked every single one of his thirty-one years. And he felt ancient sometimes. "I won't hurt your lady, Nick."

"I'm not his," Simone hissed.

The lady definitely protested too much. Zane smirked. "Of course you're not." Taking a deep breath, he centered himself and allowed an energy to flow from him toward Simone. Contained and nearly gentle, he probed into her brain and gave her a slight electrical shock.

She jumped.

Nick growled.

Besides the physical pain, demons could conjure nightmarish scenes to plague their prey. Zane eschewed images of death and destruction to create a very sexy make-believe scenario of Nick kissing the hell out of Simone. Then he put Simone in a bunny outfit and Nick nude as could be.

Her mouth dropped open. "That's enough," she said, her voice going hoarse.

"Of course." Zane calmly closed his mind and shut off his power. Nick focused on the witch. "Are you all right, Simone?"

"Fine," she said, not looking at him.

Nick turned his rigid attention on Zane, who nodded and winked. He'd never hurt his buddy's woman. Any woman, really. Nick gave him a look that clearly said he'd be expecting an explanation later.

Moira stood, her gaze on the table. "Um, we could practice shielding by twisting quantum physics. Kane and I have been working on something similar in the lab for years, and perhaps our research could help Zane when the moment comes." She sneezed. Her eyes widened, and she swayed. All color slid from her face, and even her lips lost their pretty pink. Her eyelids fluttered shut.

Talen reached her just as she started to go down. "What the hell?" he asked, lifting her high.

Dage jumped to his feet, quickly reaching the door to swing it wide open. "Somebody call Conn and tell him to meet us at the infirmary."

Zane stepped out of the way and turned toward Nick. "Do witches just faint?"

"No." Nick watched the vampires disappear with their sister-in-law. "Witches rarely become ill, as far as I know. This can't be good."

Zane shared a look with Sam. He might not understand what was going on, but every battle instinct he owned all but screamed to get ready for hell to descend.

It always did.

Janie finished examining the little girl's ears and handed her a lollipop. "Your ear infection is all gone, Sasha," she said, winking at the girl's mother. "But no swimming for another week."

Sad brown eyes twinkled up from a pretty heart-shaped face. "A whole week?" Sasha asked, her bottom lip pouting.

Janie pretended to consider the question. Feline shifters sure knew how to pout, now didn't they? "Well, how about two days?"

"Yay!" Sasha jumped up and hugged Janie. "You're the best." She turned and ran from the room, her pink tennis shoes squeaking.

Her mother sighed and pushed away unruly blond hair from her face. "That girl." She hugged Janie as well. "Thanks for taking such good care of her. She'll only come and see you, and she usually listens to you. Bye." Moments later, she'd hurried after her daughter.

Janie smiled. "I love that kid," she said to her aunt across the empty examination tables in the lab.

Emma kept her eyes nearly attached to a microscope at the far end. "Uh huh."

Janie tossed the rags in the garbage and inhaled the scent of lemon bleach. "And, as I was saying, there's a new vampire law being discussed that will prohibit the queen of the Realm from working in a lab coat."

"Definitely," Emma said, leaning over to scribble on a note chart.

"But your mate, the king extraordinaire, has decreed that the queen can work nude. You like being naked, right?" Janie turned and leaned back against the counter, arms crossed.

"Sure." Emma jotted something else down and then stiffened, standing to turn. "What?"

Janie chuckled. "Nothing. Just making sure you were paying attention."

Emma rolled deep blue eyes. "Very funny." She glanced around as if surprised to find the lab empty. "I've been meaning to talk to you."

Janie had wondered how long it would take the woman who'd known her since birth to make sure all was well. "I figured."

Emma nodded. "How are you doing with finally having met and mated Zane?"

Talk about a loaded question. Janie shrugged, more than willing to share with her aunt. "I'm overwhelmed and happy and kind of worried."

Emma smiled. "Sounds like you just mated a vampire."

"A demon vampire blend, actually." Janie studied her aunt with new eyes. The adults in her life had always seemed so sure of themselves and so happy, but now that she was an adult, she wondered. "I bet mating Uncle Dage wasn't exactly a walk in the park."

"More like a stroll through a hurricane." Emma rolled her neck. "Vampires are overbearing, overprotective, and waaaay over possessive, and it takes a while to mellow them out."

Janie snorted. "You're saying you've mellowed Uncle Dage?"

Emma coughed. "Not exactly, but once he figured out I can take care of myself, he backed off a little." She rubbed her eye. "Is Zane giving you the caveman act?"

"Oh yeah." But the sex was a nice side effect of his intensity, now wasn't it?

Emma nodded. "He'll come around. Do you love him? It's so much easier if you love the dimwits."

Janie swallowed. "Yes. I've loved him for so long, but the reality is more intense, you know?"

"I do know, and if you ever need to talk, I'm still your favorite aunt." Emma sighed and rubbed her shoulder, glancing back at her notes.

"Always," Janie said softly. "How often do you call the king a dimwit?"

Emma chuckled. "He needs to be kept humble, you know. So every time I want to get tossed into the pool, I make sure to call him a name. My favorites are dimwit, dipshit, and asshat."

Janie laughed. Her aunt was a brave woman, to be sure. She nodded to the papers. "What are you so preoccupied with?"

"I was just examining your latest blood tests and can't believe how quickly your chromosomal pairs are multiplying. This speed is unheard of."

"So I'm immortal?" Pleasure caught on Janie's breath.

"Not yet, but soon." Emma blinked and wiped off her forehead. "I have had the worst headache all day."

Janie peered closer. "Your brow is damp." Her aunt never perspired, and the lab was kept cool. She hustled across the room to feel Emma's forehead. "You're all clammy."

Emma blinked. "Now that's odd."

Immortals so rarely became ill that Janie felt for her aunt's pulse. "Your heartbeat is sluggish. What is going on?"

Heavy footsteps echoed outside the doorway, and Janie's dad rushed inside with Moira in his arms. "She passed out," Talen said, laying her down on an examination table.

Moira? Janie ran toward the table. Moira was one of the most powerful people Janie had ever met. She didn't just pass out. "Was there any warning?" Janie asked, feeling for a pulse.

"No," Talen said.

The door banged open again and Conn Kayrs ran inside, his gaze immediately landing on his mate. "What the hell happened?" His green eyes flashed a deadly threat, but when he reached out to hold Moira's hand, his movements remained gentle.

Janie frowned at the slow pulse. "How long has she been out?"

"Not even a minute," Talen said, staying close to the table.

"Excuse me?" said a quiet voice from the doorway.

Janie turned to see her aunt, Amber Kayrs, leaning heavily against the door frame. "Amber?" she asked, just as the woman started falling.

Talen pivoted and caught her before she could hit the floor. "What in holy hell?" he muttered, turning and carefully placing her on another examination table. "Somebody call Kane."

Janie nodded. Kane was not only Amber's mate but the smartest vampire on the planet. If something was going on, they needed him in the lab. Now. "Emma is near the phone." Janie turned and gasped.

Emma sagged against the counter as if the granite could hold her up. All color had deserted her face, leaving even her lips nearly white. Her eyes fluttered closed.

"Emma!" Janie cried out, just as her aunt pitched forward.

Chapter 22

Janie retrieved data spit out by the nearest printer, her heart aching. Nearly her entire family had converged in the lab, heating the oxygen, but at least now everyone had regained consciousness.

Emma pushed off from a table, and Dage slipped an arm under her shoulder to half-carry her toward Kane. "What do you see?" Emma asked.

Kane turned around, his violet eyes nearly as dark as the natural cotton shirt he wore. It looked like silk, but with a vegan as a mate, he'd quickly discarded all silk in favor of plant-based materials. "You all are infected with a mutated Virus-27."

The room roared into silence. Deadly, stunned silence.

"How?" Talen growled.

Cara hustled inside the room. "What's going on? I'm getting reports from all over the world about an illness. Witches, mates, and even a few shifters who haven't been inoculated."

"Oh God." Janie sagged back against the counter. "The virus has gone airborne. It's the only explanation."

Emma finally reached the row of microscopes. "How did we get infected? We triple-check all food brought in, and the air vents prohibit any addition of contaminants."

Janie's mind ran through the last week, and she gasped. "The peace talks." Janie rubbed absently at her aching temple as she flashed back to her last interaction with Kalin. He'd pretty much admitted the truth without giving her any details. "We warded against chemical and physical weapons. It would've been easy for Kalin to bring in a biological sample and infect Moira and Vivienne. The rest dominoed from there." So that's what Kalin had been talking about in the dream world. Bastard.

"Coward," Talen hissed. "Going after mates and witches. Have the balls to come after us."

But Kalin had struck and well. Vampires loved completely, and killing their mates would destroy them. Their extra chromosomal pairs protected the vampires, so they'd have to live on alone. The witch species as a whole might be wiped out.

Zane loped inside the room. "I'm getting calls from vampire allies around the world that their mates are dropping like flies from Virus-27. As are demon mates who'd once been a different species. What's going on?" He directed the question toward Dage but kept his focus on Janie.

Dage stilled. "You have vampire allies."

"Of course. Not everyone is aligned with you, King," Zane said.

Dage scrubbed both hands down his face. "Purebred demon females are safe, but mates must not be. We need the data on how many chromosomal pairs a demon mate who was formerly human now has."

"Same as a vampire mate," Zane said slowly. "Twenty-seven pairs." Then he frowned. "Belle? You look pale."

Cara gasped and rushed for her daughter. "You're a mate now. You're susceptible."

Oh God. Janie swayed. "I hadn't thought of it." She automatically held out her arm for Kane to quickly take blood. "I do have a headache."

Zane paled and crossed the room. "You're fine. We've only been mated a short time, and there hasn't been enough time to contract the virus. You're fine." Desperation lifted his eyebrows. He slipped an arm around her shoulder and pulled her into heat and safety.

Kane used a dropper to place her blood on a slide to slip under the specially modified machinery before turning around, his gaze sober. "You have the virus."

Cara gasped, her face paling as she stared at her daughter. "Oh." Then she took several deep breaths. "Okay. This is going to be okay. I've had the virus for decades, and I'm still standing. The first year sucks, and you'll feel horrible, but it gets better after that. And the attack on the chromosomes slows down. We have time to fix this."

Emma and Kane exchanged a look.

"What?" Cara asked, clasping her hands together.

"The mutation," Emma said, brushing a limp piece of hair from her forehead. "The virus attacks much more quickly now. It might unravel chromosomes at a faster rate. We need to do testing." She hummed and then coughed. "We haven't even found where the damn thing gets in. If only vampires had studied genetics instead of weaponry the last few centuries." She shot a hard glare at Kane.

He shrugged. "Why? We're immortal. Until this virus, we didn't give a hoot about chromosomes."

"I know," Emma nearly spat. She frowned and focused on Janie. "Did you know that before your mother and I started working on this virus issue that the vampires didn't even map their chromosomes? They thought they had either an XV or a ZV setup. Morons."

Janie bit her lip. "You're kidding me."

Kane shuffled his feet. "Like I said, we didn't really care. Nothing hurts us but beheading, so we concentrated on protecting our damn necks." He shook his head. "Now, thanks to your cranky aunt, we know that vampires have a combination of a V and a Y chromosome. Period."

"So no girls. Ever." Emma nodded. Janie stayed within the circle of Zane's strong arms, her mind spinning. "Maybe now the virus has been weakened by the mutation. Maybe we can finally cure it."

Kane nodded. "Here's the plan. I need a full workup from every mate as well as every vampire. We'll compare to old samples." He nodded at Dage. "Get on the horn and have studies conducted all around the world with our associated medical facilities. Tell them to concentrate on the differences between the old version of the virus and the new . . . and not to waste a bunch of time tracking back the infection. At this point, we don't care about carriers. Everyone susceptible to infection will get it."

Dage nodded, his gaze concerned on his mate. "Love? Why don't you come with me?"

Emma smiled, her lips trembling. "I need to work in the lab, sweetheart. I promise I'll rest."

The king brushed her lips with his. "I'll be back." Turning, he strode out of the room, the weight of rule darkening his features.

Kane immediately set everybody present to the task of collecting, analyzing, or retrieving samples. The group worked tirelessly and silently, each caught in their own thoughts.

Hours upon hours later, Janie, Kane, and Emma sat on examination tables, tense and tired.

Everyone else had been dispatched to other areas of the compound on jobs.

"I'm exhausted," Emma said, stretching her arms. "This virus sucks."

"I'm tired without the virus," Kane said, tapping his foot on the tile floor even while sitting.

Janie swung her legs, nowhere near reaching the floor. "It was a productive day." Though a pretty shitty one. "The virus is speeding up, is easier to contract, and so far doesn't respond to any medication in the petri dishes. Even my mom is infected with the new version of the damn thing." Her shoulders slumped. "We need a cure."

Kane nodded and slid from the table. "I'll go and update Dage. You two, ah, have a nice talk." He patted Janie's shoulder as he walked by, grooves cutting into the sides of his mouth.

Janie stilled and frowned. "What was that about? Am I different because Zane is a demon?" God, was she going to unravel into a vegetative state overnight? Panic roared the blood through her head, echoing in her ears. "Emma—"

"No. You're not different—at least not yet." Emma cleared her throat, having the same expression on her face as when she'd told Janie her pet turtle had died twenty years ago. "Kane left because he thought you and I should talk alone. I mean, it's girl talk, and I'm your aunt and have been in your life forever. I love you."

Emma was babbling. Janie stiffened. "What is going on?"

Emma swallowed. "We did a full blood makeup on everybody."

"I know." Janie leaned forward. "Did you find something odd in mine?"

"Not odd." Emma exhaled slowly. "You're pregnant, Janie."

* * *

Zane stopped himself from knocking on Janie's front door and instead smoothly slid the heavy oak open. She'd said to make himself at home, and now they'd mated.

He had a mate.

Truth be told, any time in his life he'd ever considered a mate, he'd always seen Janie's face, but he'd never really believed he'd live long enough to mark her. Suri had been threatening to kill him for so long, he'd figured his fate had been set.

For the first time in so long, he wanted to kick the ass out of fate. The only way to do so was to take out Suri. But surviving his uncle's death would definitely be a long shot.

Zane stepped inside and closed the door, immediately scenting a delicious aroma. Long strides ate up the distance to the kitchen, where he stopped short.

Janie stirred something in a Crock-Pot, her butt wiggling as she danced to some tune she hummed.

His lips twitched as he recognized the song as "Baby Got Back."

She stiffened as if sensing him and slowly turned. Still pale, her skin nearly glowed, while those blue eyes that had haunted his dreams for decades shimmered with wisdom. "Hi."

"Hi." A quick glance at the table revealed she'd set places for two. He removed the gun at his waistband. Where should he put it? With a shrug, he placed the weapon on top of the fridge. The gun in his boot and the blades hidden along his body would remain in place. "Smells delicious." He had to stop talking in incomplete sentences, but he wasn't sure what to say. They'd only been mated a short time and were still actually getting to know each other.

"Thanks." She smoothed her hands down worn jeans that hugged her delicious hips. "Um, have a seat." Turning, she dished out two large bowls of what looked like stew.

"Let me help." He grabbed a platter of biscuits from the counter as well as a bowl of rice. The woman didn't need to serve him. "It was nice of you to make dinner." Could he sound any more damn polite?

She grinned and led the way to the table near a wide expanse of windows. "This is awkward."

Relief brushed through him. "I know. We've been friends for years, and I've never had trouble talking to you." He thought she muttered "just wait" under her breath, but when she sat down, her face remained calm.

She'd placed a beer at his place. "It's Guinness, but I have other kinds."

"This is great." He'd rather have a Scotch, but it was nice of her to get him a drink. "Aren't you having any?" He nodded at her water glass.

"Ah, no." She took a bite of stew. "I'm fine with water."

"Okay." He took a bite of the stew and nearly moaned out loud. The flavors exploded on his tongue. He was starving. Several moments later, he smiled. "You are an amazing cook."

A smile lit her pretty face. "It's just stew, but thanks." Her fingers drummed on the table. "So, I figured we should talk."

He nodded. "How are you feeling, anyway?"

Her shoulders slumped. "Tired and kind of achy. Virus-27 is like the flu but tunnels deeper."

His chest tightened. "I've had all medical facilities I know of report to Kane and Emma."

"Even the demon facilities?" Janie asked, her eyebrows rising.

"No. Suri won't allow that." Zane rubbed the rigid muscles at the base of his neck. "But I still have some allies in vampire and shifter nations that aren't aligned with the Realm. Maybe through this, they will."

Janie's smile wavered. "Is there any way to reach peace with Suri? Now that we've mated, and your family is safe, maybe Suri will move on."

Zane rolled his shoulders. "That's a nice thought, but Suri's not a man who'd take my betrayal well."

"But couldn't you try?" Janie grasped his hand on the table. "Since the virus has gone airborne, even demon mates are susceptible. The Kurjan-Demon alliance is dead in the water because you and I mated. At least give peace a chance with Suri."

Zane studied her. Intelligent and hopeful was a sexy combination. More than that, he wanted to see that smile on her face again. "I can try," he said slowly.

The smile bloomed. "Excellent. Peace is not only the right solution, it's the smart one. We all need to work together to cure this virus."

He finished his stew and leaned back to study his stunning mate. She'd pulled her sable hair up into a messy bun, and no makeup covered her pretty face. She didn't need makeup. "Dinner was wonderful, and I appreciate your feeding me. Now would you like to tell me what's on your mind?"

She blinked and set down her water glass. "How did you know?"

He smiled. The woman should never play poker. "You have several tells." He flipped his hand over hers, trying to warm her chilly skin. "You can tell me anything. No matter what, I'm on your side, Belle. I promise." Whatever was bothering her would be a pleasure to fix, even if it meant reaching out to his damn uncle. "What's going on?"

She took a deep breath. "We ran a full blood panel on me today in the lab."

"Of course." He frowned and leaned closer. "Did the results concern you?"

She barked out a quiet laugh. "Concern? No, but they surprised me."

"How so?" He rubbed his thumb across her knuckles, trying to offer comfort.

"I'm pregnant."

Adrenaline roared through his blood, while his entire body froze in place. He jerked his head. Had he heard her right? "You're *what*?"

Janie stiffened and then let out a rolling laugh. Her face scrunched up, and her eyes watered as mirth overtook her. Deep, belly-rumbling laughs rolled from her. She tried to cover her mouth with her free hand, but she kept laughing. "Pre-pregnant," she gasped out.

Zane remained in place, his mind spinning. Was she getting hysterical? As she wound down, he tried to keep his voice calm. "How in the hell did this happen?"

Her eyes widened, and then she let loose another round of laughter. "I can get you a book on how babies are made," she finally coughed.

He frowned and tried to make sense of the situation. First, he had to calm Janie down. "Are you all right?" he asked.

She yanked her hand free and leaped to her feet. "All right? Am

I all right?" Her eyes widened, and her arms swept out, all humor gone. "No. No, I am not all right."

Ah. Okay. "Janie, let's—"

"I've been mated for all of a second, and I've only had sex twice. In addition, I'm now being attacked by a virus that wants to turn me into turd slime, and I'm pregnant. Pregnant with a demon, vampire, shifter, human baby who probably doesn't want to catch the damn virus." She took a shaky breath, her chest hitching. "And I don't even know you."

Faced with her crisis, he calmed. "Okay." He slid back his chair and stood, quickly reaching to lift her into his arms. She gave a half-hearted struggle, and he tucked her closer, striding into the living room to drop onto the sofa. Pregnant? She was pregnant? God. He was going to be a father. His heart swelled while his fears exploded. "Let's take a deep breath and tackle each issue at a time." He forced a reasonable tone into his voice before he started yelling, too.

She tucked her head into his neck, igniting every protective instinct he had. "I'm sorry to freak out."

"You're entitled." He ran a soothing hand down her back, marveling at the fragile bones. Concern softened his touch. Was she strong enough to birth a vampire-demon son? "First of all, are you sure you're pregnant?"

"Yes." She splayed her hand across his chest and above his heart. "Our medical procedures are eons ahead of humans, and Kane performed the test three times. Plus, I guess once he knew, he could actually scent the baby."

Zane closed his eyes and opened his senses. Fresh rain and honey dew. He cleared his throat. "I can smell the baby, too."

Janie sighed. "I know it's rare for a mate to become pregnant so quickly."

Rare? "It's unheard of," Zane said. Vampires and demons took centuries to procreate.

"Except for my parents. Mom became pregnant with Garrett right away," Janie said. "So maybe it runs in the family."

"Maybe." Zane tried to keep his head from blowing off. "What will the virus do to him?"

Janie snuggled closer. "I don't know, but my mom contracted the virus when pregnant with Garrett, and he's okay. Besides, what makes you think it's a boy?"

"Vampires only have boys."

"You're part-demon."

"Doesn't matter." Zane kissed the top of her head. "Through all history, vampire males, regardless of cross-species, have boys. We don't shoot X chromosomes." The raw need to make the world safe for his family heated his breath and weakened his knees. Drawing on strength, and drawing deep, he slowly fortified his thoughts. "Everything is going to be okay, Belle. You have my word."

She kissed his neck, sending emotion through his veins. "That's good. Because we need to tell my dad now."

Chapter 23

Janie drew a deep breath in as Zane knocked on the door to a suite in the main lodge. Would Zane's mom hate her? Their people were technically still enemies.

"Come in," came a throaty female voice followed by a series of loud thunks.

"What in the world?" Zane pushed through first, keeping Janie behind him. "Oh." His shoulders straightened as he pulled Janie to stand next to him. "Janet Isabella Kayrs, please meet my mother, Felicity Kyllwood."

Janie forced a smile. Zane's mom stood an inch or two above five feet tall, dressed in workout gear, her chest damp and her white-blond hair pulled back from her face. Black eyes sparkled in a finely boned face. The woman was beyond beautiful to truly stunning. Two wooden sticks rested easily in her hands, while her bare feet slowed to a dance on workout mats spread across an empty living room. A quick look confirmed all the furniture had been shoved into the kitchen.

Felicity smiled. "Nice to meet you, Janie. You've met Logan, right?"

Logan lay on his side, two sticks by his feet, a low groan erupting from his chest. He pushed to his feet. "Hi."

Zane snorted. "Mom being too rough on you, kid?"

Logan shoved his brother. "No. We were just training."

Felicity dropped the sticks and grabbed a towel to wipe her hands. "I'm sorry for the lack of sitting area. Can I get either of you anything?" She peered at a sofa end sticking out from the kitchen. "Logan can probably make it to the fridge."

"No, that's fine. Thank you," Janie said, her knees weakening. A flush heated down her back, and she swayed. Even so, she wanted to stay strong in front of the purebred demonness. A real demonness. They were so rare they were almost just legend.

"Whoa." Zane clasped Janie's elbow and helped her to the mat before feeling her head. "You're feverish."

She nodded. "It's all part of the initial stages of the virus. I'm fine."

Felicity bustled forward. "You poor woman. I heard all about the new form of the virus, and it's such a disaster. Logan, go get her some water." As a full demon, Felicity wasn't subject to contamination by the virus.

Janie shook her head. "I'm okay. Sorry to be a pain."

Felicity slid down to sit on the mat in a move beyond graceful. Her symmetrical nostrils flared. Then she lifted her chin, her gaze narrowing on Janie. "Oh my. Um, well—"

"We know she's pregnant," Zane cut in.

A stunning smile lit up Felicity's face, and she grabbed both of Janie's hands. "Pregnant? That's so wonderful. Congratulations."

Janie finally relaxed and returned the smile, even though she still wanted to throw up. "Thank you."

"Oh, I can't wait to meet my grandson." Felicity threw back her head and laughed. "Although, you might be feeling ill from the pregnancy as well as the virus. I was sicker than three dogs on meth while pregnant with Zane."

Janie chuckled. "Why doesn't that surprise me?"

Zane's phone buzzed, and he glanced at the face. "The king is summoning me to Conference Room A."

Janie frowned. "That's the strategic room. What's going on?"

Zane shrugged. "No clue." He looked toward his mom.

Felicity nodded. "Go ahead. Janie and I will stay here and get acquainted, and Logan will fetch us refreshments." She turned toward her youngest son. "Think of it as an obstacle course toward the fridge."

Janie faltered and then nodded. "Let me know what's going on, please."

"I promise." Zane ducked and kissed the top of her head. "You just relax, and maybe my mom will give you some tips on being pregnant with a demon-vampire son."

Felicity smiled. "Boy, do I have some tips."

Janie nodded, a ball of concern unfurling in her stomach. Conference Room A meant something was either happening right now or the vampires were planning a raid. Either way . . . danger.

Zane found Sam and Nick lounging against the entrance to Conference Room A. Sam looked pissed, and Nick looked bored. Which meant Nick was pissed, too. "What's up?" Zane asked.

"Damn vampires won't let us in," Sam said.

Oh, hell no. "Where I go, you go." Zane shoved open the door, the demons on his heels.

Dage, Talen, Kane, and Garrett Kayrs sat around the table.

Dage frowned. "I asked you to appear, Zane. Just you."

"Too bad." Zane had about had it with the Kayrs family as a whole. They needed him more than he needed them at the moment, and he'd include his men.

Garrett snarled. "Need an entourage, do you?"

"I am a rock star," Zane returned amenably. Apparently the young vampire had found out about Janie's pregnancy. "You have something else you want to say?"

Garrett began to stand, and his father placed a restraining hand on his arm. The kid settled back down.

Zane focused on the king. "What's going on?"

"Suri has requested to speak with you." Dage jerked his head toward a massive screen on the wall.

Zane exhaled a heated breath. "Sam, take the right, and Nick the left." At his quiet order, his men fanned out to form a triangle around the table. "Can anybody here shield from a demon mind attack?"

Kane Kayrs nodded. "I mated a woman who can shield, and I've acquired the ability. Somewhat."

Dage lifted an eyebrow. "I can shield as well. Do you think Suri is strong enough to attack via a teleconference?"

"Yes." Zane shook his head. "You still don't understand the extent of his power, do you?"

Talen shrugged. "His power ends when we cut off his head."

"Actually, his power will be released at that point." Nick shook his head, his gaze on Zane.

Zane nodded. The vampires truly couldn't comprehend the issue. "Let's see what Suri wants." Zane widened his stance and tried to center his thoughts just in case he needed to shield. Though he'd never admit it, his full mental strength hadn't returned after his multiple jumps the previous day. Still, between Sam, Nick, and him, they should be able to protect the vampires.

Dage pressed a button, and Suri took shape on screen. He'd dressed for battle, medals decorating his chest. "Traitor," he said without much heat.

"Asshole," Zane returned evenly.

Suri's black eyes glittered. "That's the thanks I get for raising you?"

Zane forced a smile. "You didn't raise me. The woman who did raise me is currently training to find you and kick your ass to hell."

Suri growled. "I'd like to see my sister try."

"Oh, you will." Zane kept his face expressionless. No way was his mother going anywhere near the psycho, regardless of the demonness's strength. "Why are you reaching out to me?"

"Well, it's apparent you've turned your back on the demon nation," Suri said.

"No." Zane stepped closer to the table. "I've turned my back on you, only. The demon nation is mine."

Dage's eyes sparked at the proclamation, but otherwise, he didn't move.

Suri flashed sharp canines. "Are you challenging me?"

Lava flowed through Zane's blood, while a rock the size of Texas landed in his gut. His uncle was crazy and needed to be stopped. "I am."

Satisfaction lifted Suri's lip. "I always knew you'd try to take me out."

"I didn't," Zane said honestly. "In fact, if you weren't such a sociopathic bastard, I'd be fine leaving you in place. But we both know you have to be stopped."

"I look forward to the day you try." Suri glanced around the Kayrs conference room, and the air wavered. Little mental sparks popped throughout. "You'll need your vampire allies, now won't you?"

Zane kept his stance tall and nodded to his men to shield against Suri's mild mind attack. The ruling demon seemed to be just playing. "No. It's between you and me. Always has been."

"Very well. For now, how about you take care of a mutual problem?" Suri withdrew his mental attack.

Zane relaxed. "The Kurjans aren't happy with you?"

Suri sneered. "When you mated that human, you set into motion events that will destroy everyone you care about. Now Kalin has a price on my head."

"How much?" Zane asked, flashing his own fangs. "My bank account could use some storing up."

"Funny. Kalin and his troops are stationed thirty miles outside of San Francisco, preparing to descend upon Kayrs headquarters. I've emailed you the location. Do the job I trained you for and take him out."

"And then?" Zane asked.

Suri sent out a shock wave of pain. "Then you and I will finish our business. Oh, and feel free to decapitate any demon traitors still with Kalin." The screen went black.

Dage Kayrs grabbed his head, swore, and jumped to his feet. "What the hell just happened?"

Zane sighed. "Welcome to a true demon mind-fuck, King. That was Suri just playing around."

Dage nodded to Talen, who was digging a pinkie into his ear. Probably checking for blood. "Get troops ready to go. It's time we took out Kalin."

Zane lifted an eyebrow. "This might be a trap."

Dage sighed. "Trap or not, the risk is worth it if we capture Kalin. We need more information about the new version of Virus-27, and it's time to take that bastard into custody."

Zane shook his head. "You believe Suri's Intel?"

"In connection with the Intel I received a half an hour ago from our shifter allies in northern California, yes." Dage began striding toward the door.

Zane grabbed his arm. "We're going with you."

"Hell, no," Talen muttered, striding toward his brother.

"Hell, yes," Zane countered, standing toe-to-toe with the equivalent of a father-in-law in his world. "If demons have aligned themselves with Kalin, you'll need shields. We're the best there is."

Talen glanced at Dage, his eyes flashing when Dage gave a short nod. "Fine, demon. But you'd better be as well trained as you think you are." Shoving past them, Talen disappeared through the exit.

Dage clapped Zane on the back. "In Talen speak, that meant *welcome to the family.*"

The helicopters stayed low and under the radar, even with a blustering wind whipping around as dusk fell. Rain slashed down into the forest as the helicopters hovered above a small clearing, and a small contingent of soldiers dropped from air to land in a graceful dance. Zane leaped down to the muddy ground next to Talen, pain ricocheting up his legs from the impact. The chilly wind bit into his face. "The humans will notice if we cause too much damage," Zane said.

"Got it covered." Talen ducked low and headed into a dense thicket of dripping trees.

Zane followed, keeping Sam and Nick in his peripheral vision. He'd make sure they returned home. The mantle of responsibility always choking him tightened its hold, more oppressive since declaring his intention of taking over the demon nation. In addition, Zane wouldn't let Janie's father die on his watch.

Talen turned. "Stay on my six. I can't let you die."

"Back at you." Zane leaned against the trunk of a cedar tree while the scents of rain, mud, and wet pine filled his nostrils. "How is this *covered?*"

"Allies in the USA military." Talen signaled a group of soldiers to the west.

Zane glanced back toward the meadow where the helicopters continued to hover full of soldiers. "Why aren't they dropping?"

Talen kept his gaze forward. "They will. For now, keep your head in the game, and get ready to go in."

Zane cocked his gun, his gaze on a temporary camp of rough

cabins and tents littering the forest. "Why didn't we take them during daylight while they're trapped inside?" It was time to use the Kurjans' aversion to sun as a tactical advantage.

Talen shook his head. "Kalin always has an underground escape route, and the cabins are usually booby trapped. Better to draw them out and kick their asses." He shot Zane a hard look. "As much as I hate it, we take Kalin alive if possible. We need to know more about the new version of Virus-27."

"Understood." Zane nodded at his brother to stay close, and then closed his eyes to take stock of mental vibrations. "If there are demons present, they're shielding well."

"Is that possible?" Talen asked.

Zane opened his eyes. "Yes, but I should be able to sense something. Maybe once we go in, I'll be able to tell you how many demons, if any, are here."

Talen hand-signaled to nearby soldiers. A soldier fired a missile into the middle of the camp.

Without warning, the entire forest detonated all around them, land mines and explosives igniting. Trees all around them burst into flame, and fire roared.

"Get down!" Zane yelled, tackling Talen to the ground. Damn Suri had invited him to his own death. Lying piece of demon dung. "It's a trap," he muttered.

"No shit." Talen rolled them over and shoved them both up on their feet. "Run and follow my pattern so you keep your legs." He turned and began to run through the forest toward two just landed copters. Land mines exploded all around them.

Zane ran, his back warmed by fire, his temper heated by rage. What in the hell? How did Talen know where to run? *Wait a goddamn minute.*

As they jumped inside the transport, the helicopter quickly rose into the air. Zane took a moment to make sure Nick and Sam had made it safely to the other helicopter before rounding on Talen. "You fucking ass-wad son-of-a-bastard fucking bitch." Zane's right-cross knocked Talen's head against the metal side with a satisfying thunk.

Green sizzled through Talen's golden eyes, and he slowly wiped blood off his chin. "That was a freebie, demon."

"Fuck." Zane shoved his bulk onto a seat and ran a rough hand through his hair. "You knew it was a trap."

The king turned around from the front seat. "Of course it was a trap. Suri wants you and me dead a lot more than he needs Kalin gone. Think about it."

Zane's hands shook with the need to hit Talen again. "You set this up to *test me*? The full contingent of soldiers, all of the helicopters?"

Talen lifted a massive shoulder. "We had to know we could trust you."

Oh, Zane just might throw the asshole out of the helicopter. The bastard would probably bounce on the ground and then laugh. "So I passed?"

"Well, you didn't fail." Talen crossed his arms.

Asshole. "How did you know the placements of the land mines?" Zane asked.

"Infrared and some damn good satellite technology." Dage turned back toward the billowing storm outside the window.

Zane shook his head. "Still. Suiting up so many soldiers for one test is crazy."

Talen's grin flashed hard and dangerous. "Who said we suited up for just a test? Now, we fight."

Chapter 24

The cliffs of Baffin Island rose from the depths of a cold and merciless sea as the sky began to lighten outside. The Kurjan headquarters for so many years. Zane had spent the journey to Canada deciding to refrain from killing Talen and Dage for the dangerous test in California. Trust had to be earned, and he couldn't blame them too much. Plus, if he killed Janie's family, she'd be seriously pissed.

So the vampires lived for now.

He glanced down. "Our only chance is a full out assault."

"Then get ready for full out," Talen said. "I'm done playing with the Kurjans, and it's time we took Kalin."

Dage nodded and tapped an ear communicator. "Orders remain at level ten. Kill on sight any Kurjan except for Kalin, who's to be taken alive. His second in command, his cousin Dayne, is also to be taken if possible. Leave Kurjan mates alone unless you need to defend yourselves. Even then, kill as a last resort."

"What's the Intel on personnel here?" Zane asked, sliding open the door. Wind rushed him, and he steadied his legs.

"Armed and protected, but Kurjan soldiers are spread around the world fighting right now, just like us," Talen said, strapping another knife to his hip. He tapped his ear. "Fire."

Two helicopters shot missiles into the cliffs, and rocks exploded out in a glorious display of flames and shooting stones.

"Now," Talen ordered.

Zane jumped from the helicopter and hit hard rock. Heat blasted into him from the fires. All feeling, all sensation, he shoved into nowhere to deal with later. Now was for war. He pointed to an opening blown into the rock. "We go there."

Talen nodded and signaled for troops. "The soldiers dropped into the sea should be at destination." He paused and put a hand on Zane's shoulder as soldiers dropped to the ground all around them. "You've been in combat before?"

Humor tickled Zane's lips, but he remained stoic. "For a decade."

"A whole decade?" Talen asked, sarcasm evident in the low tone.

"Not all of us are ancient," Zane returned, adrenaline flooding his veins. His body hadn't recuperated fully, but his mind was ready to go. "I can fight. Don't worry."

Talen cocked his weapon. "Just don't die." He whistled and gave an attack signal before turning to run full bore for the opening.

"Don't plan on it," Zane said, ducking low to follow. Before they reached the opening, Kurjan soldiers poured out, already firing. Zane dropped and rolled, returning fire and nailing one soldier in the neck. He jumped up and ran forward, tackling a soldier off Talen. The soldier punched Zane in the face, and he hit back, reaching for his knife.

The Kurjan shoved up with a blade, neatly slicing Zane's vest.

Zane plunged his weapon down, severing the Kurjan's carotid artery before decapitating the soldier. A Degoller Star whizzed by his head and stuck into Talen's back.

With a roar, Zane lunged up and threw his knife end-over-end into the eye of the Kurjan who'd thrown the star. Fucking Degoller Stars. Zane rushed toward Talen to reach gingerly for the razor-sharp weapon. "So much for the treaty banning these." Zane withdrew the deadly star, which made a squishing noise as Talen's flesh released it.

Talen tapped his ear as hell reigned around them. "Watch your necks. Degoller Stars being deployed."

A series of muttered curses emerged through the ear devices.

Talen rolled his shoulders.

"Your vest protected you mainly." Zane tucked the star into his back pocket. "Although there's blood on it."

"It cut my shoulder blade, not bad enough to worry about." Talen lifted his chin. "Let's go in."

All around them, vampires and Kurjans fought hand to hand with an occasional shot fired. The sky opened up to rain down on the smoky, fiery landscape, making visibility difficult. Zane caught Nick and Sam fighting over on the perimeter. Good. They'd cover each other. He nodded at Talen. "Let's go."

Together, they fought their way to the entrance into the rocks, protecting each other's backs like they'd fought together for centuries. Zane took a Kurjan down to the ground, and another white-faced monster jumped through the smoke to stab Zane in the leg. Talen had the soldier face down in the mud and headless within seconds.

Zane finished off his opponent.

Talen reached down and yanked out the knife from Zane's thigh. "That might hurt."

Agony rippled through Zane's leg, and he shoved to his feet. "Didn't feel a thing."

Talen nodded and turned again for the entrance, pausing at the top step. "Watch your head."

"I know." Zane held a gun in one hand and a blade in the other. Truth be told, he preferred the blade for fighting. "I've got your back. Go."

Talen immediately jogged down the stairs toward blackness darker than any night. Silver flashed, and Zane rushed him, knocking him into concrete blocks that made up the walls. The Degoller Star ripped into the concrete wall. They crashed to the rough stone steps. A slicing pain ripped through Zane's neck from a spinning Degoller Star, and he kept hold of Talen's shoulders while they plunged end over end down the hard stone. Zane grunted with each abusing impact.

Finally, they reached the bottom, and Talen swept a flashlight wide. Nothing. "Thanks," he muttered, grabbing Zane's arms to drag him up.

"No problem." Zane cleared his throat.

Talen stiffened. "I smell blood." He focused the light on Zane. "Shit."

Zane reached up to cover his neck. "The wound isn't deep." Well, except his head felt like it might fall off his body, and his vision wavered.

The light disappeared, and the sound of tearing fabric filled the small cavern. Talen wrapped the sleeve of his T-shirt around Zane's neck and pulled tight. Zane fought not to wince.

"Go above and get medical help," Talen ordered.

"No. This ends now." Zane pushed the vampire aside and ducked low, heading into smoke. A strong hand grabbed the back of his vest, and he was yanked behind Talen.

"Stay behind me, jugular injury," Talen muttered just as three Kurjans poured out of a far doorway. "Fight back-to-back."

Zane gripped his blade and jumped into the fray.

More vampire soldiers filled the steps behind them. Shouts of pain echoed in the distance, and an explosion rocked through the underground labyrinth. The soldiers from the ocean must've breached the cliffs.

Zane fought hard, keeping his head low and watching for any spinning silver discs. He and Talen slowly made their way through the Kurjan headquarters, finally reaching an elaborate hallway lined with priceless oil paintings and burnished antiques.

"Go left," Talen ordered, turning to the right. "If you sight Kalin, detail his location."

Zane nodded and forged down the plush red carpet, sweeping his gun wide, the hair rising down his neck along with fresh blood. The first doorway, of heavy metal, all but vibrated with the energy flowing through it. Kalin. Drawing in a deep breath of smoke and blood-scented air, Zane gathered his strength and kicked open the door.

He immediately dropped, rolled, and came up firing.

A hard body tackled him, and they crashed into a desk, sending splinters of wood flying. Zane's gun spun out of his hands. He punched out, hitting flesh, and back-flipped to his feet.

Kalin slowly stood, blood dripping down his white chin. "I've been waiting for you."

"Here I am." Zane circled around the richly appointed office. One entire wall looked into the dark and fathomless ocean, and he fleetingly wondered how far down they were. All pain, all concern, dissipated. "I'm surprised you didn't meet the fight up above."

Kalin hissed, his eyes churning greenish purple. "I figured the fight would come to me."

"You figured right." The fight raged closer outside, and a battle shriek echoed through the walls.

Kalin nodded toward Zane's makeshift bandage. "Looks like you weren't quick enough to duck."

"Fucking coward, using stars." Zane crouched and attacked, drawing his knife from his boot and slashing across Kalin's neck. Blood arced gracefully through the air, burning Zane's chin.

A double-edged pain slashed into his abdomen, just under his vest.

He gasped and punched Kalin's forearm, which pulled the knife out of Zane's gut. He growled and sent healing cells to the area. The Kurjan had height and reach on Zane, but Zane had speed and muscle. Time to use his demon side, which he'd never thought he'd do. But to protect his woman, he'd do anything. Zane focused a mental attack at his enemy while drawing out his other knife. Silver flashed in both his hands.

Kalin's head jerked back, and he growled.

Then heavy shields shoved back against Zane's brain. "Not bad," he said.

"I've been practicing." Kalin yanked a gun from the back of his waistband.

Zane ducked low and moved in, hitting the Kurjan at his center and driving him across the room to smash into the wall. A painting of Degas nudes crashed to the ground. He increased his mental attack. Though the Kurjan could counter, he wasn't a match for a demon.

Kalin slammed both hands into Zane's ears.

Excruciating pain hacked through Zane's head, and his ear communicator dropped to the floor. His neck still bled, the wound to his gut remained open, and now his brain began to swell. Dots danced across his eyes.

He turned toward the window as the faintest sunlight tried to pierce the deep.

It was past time to teleport the bastard away from safety. Digging deeper than Zane had believed possible, he manacled Kalin in a bear hug, turned, and sucked the universe up through his feet.

Nothing.

They didn't move.

Damn it.

Kalin bellowed and hit him in the gut. Pain exploded inside

Zane's stomach. Zane held on with everything he had. He couldn't transport. He shook his head and drew on every ounce of strength he had left. Turning them, he powered into the heavy window.

Kalin bellowed and shoved against him, his head impacting the window first. Glass shattered, crashing in, and freezing water poured into the room. Zane kept his hold and forced his enemy through the opening, fighting both the Kurjan and the rushing water.

The chill stole his breath but cleared his mind.

He kicked hard, shooting them up to the churning surface. As they broke free, Kalin let out an ear-piercing shriek when the sun hit him. The weak rays poked through thick clouds, yet Kalin's skin sizzled across his face.

Zane coughed out sea water and waved toward a hovering helicopter. Then he grabbed Kalin's vest and punched the Kurjan in the jaw. Twice. Kalin slumped unconscious.

A head popped up next to Zane, and Talen spit out bloody water while reaching for the unmoving Kurjan. "You still bleeding?"

"Yes." Zane helped Talen to support Kalin as the helicopter dropped ropes down. They quickly tied knots around Kalin, and soldiers above lifted the leader into the copter. Minutes later, Talen and Zane climbed up.

Wind battered the vehicle, shoving Zane into his seat.

The pilot flew over a battlefield littered with bodies, their blood seeping into the rocks. He landed quickly, and Dage Kayrs leaped inside, his silver gaze taking in the Kurjan trussed up on the floor.

"Sam and Nick?" Zane asked.

"Injured but healing and en route home," Dage returned. "Everyone has lifted off except one helicopter. We've taken care of the Kurjans and didn't run into any mates. Dayne and his mate aren't here, so we'll have to deal with him another day." Dage tapped his ear communicator. "Salt the earth and burn it down. Then return home."

The helicopter swung toward the south.

Zane closed his eyes, concentrating on healing his wounds.

"You can fight," Talen said.

Zane let his head drop forward to release the tension in his neck.

His new father-in-law sounded somewhat impressed, but only a bone-tiredness swamped Zane. "Yeah. I can fight," he said wearily.

Talen sighed and clapped him on the back in a fatherly gesture. "I know, kid. Believe me, I know."

"My dad was a good guy. You would've liked him," Zane said. Now where in the hell had that come from?

Talen exhaled, the sound somehow reassuring. "I've researched the vampire side of your family ever since you and Janie started meeting in dream worlds. Your father was a great man, a phenomenal soldier, and I think we would've been friends had we met," he said, his hand still on Zane's shoulder.

"Yes." In that moment, in a helicopter racing through the sky to transport the biggest threat known to Zane's mate, to the only woman he'd ever love, he felt the weight on his shoulders spread to those around him.

He didn't have to do this alone.

Chapter 25

Janie pushed her front door open with a sore hip and slid inside to stop short. The scent of male permeated her senses, and a slow flush shivered across her skin. "What's wrong with your neck?"

Zane sprawled in a chair near the fireplace, a bag of ice held to his jugular. "Just a paper cut." Wet hair curled over his collar, while fresh bruises marred his face. Despite his relaxed pose, he still appeared as if he might decide to lunge at any second. After his shower, he'd dressed in worn jeans and a T-shirt depicting a cat falling off a roof.

"Nice shirt." Janie shut the door and toed off her tennis shoes, keeping her face bland. How in the world did the sight of him send her entire body into overdrive so easily? Several deep breaths calmed her.

Zane glanced down. "Logan gave it to me for my last birthday. Said I was being a pussy about taking out Suri."

Men. They never made any damn sense. "So? How was the raid?" She'd already gotten reports about Zane taking Kalin alive, and she'd seen several battered vampires head into the infirmary as she'd trained outside, but she wanted to hear Zane's take.

He flexed his hand, working bruised knuckles. "We took out the Kurjan headquarters and captured their leader. Damn good raid." His eyes darkened, and his gaze swept her training outfit. "Been out hitting things?"

"Vampires, mainly." And a couple of shifters. "Hand-to-hand and some blade training." She rolled aching shoulders and finally padded across the room to drop onto the sofa. He drew her and always had.

"How are you feeling?" he asked, the question and tone loaded with intimacy.

When would she get used to seeing him in person and not in dreams? He was just so much *more* than she'd expected. More intense, more handsome, more dangerous. "I've felt better." She ran a hand down her still flat stomach. "I think the nausea is more from Virus-27 than being pregnant. All mates are sick, but witches seem to be bouncing back already."

Zane sat up, his focus narrowing on her. "Is that significant?"

"Yes." Janie pushed a strand of hair out of her eyes. "Anything that gives us a clue about the virus is important. We don't know what it means, but we can work with the knowledge." She cleared her throat, her mind humming. "How did you feel working with vampires?" Her breath felt tight in her chest.

"They can fight."

Janie bit back a grin. The three tiny words meant much more than most people would suspect. Zane and her family had reached an understanding. Her shoulders relaxed. "How are you feeling?" She returned his question.

His dark eyebrows rose. "I'm healing."

"You know what I mean."

He removed the ice pack to reveal a long scratch along his neck. "Yeah, I know what you mean." His gaze raked her and warmed. "Come here."

Two simple words, said in a low tone that trapped her breath in her chest. Tingles flared alive in her abdomen. "I think we should talk."

"Me too. Come over here and talk." A dimple flashed in his right cheek, below his scar.

"Are you flirting with me?" Her lips tingled with the need to smile.

"Maybe." He tossed the icepack on the table. "Now get over here and do your duty."

She stood and paused. "My duty?"

"Yes. I'm wounded. Kiss it and make it better." His smile could only be described as sinful.

She coughed out a laugh and reached his side, only to be tugged down onto his hard lap. "You poor baby," she murmured, running her fingers through his hair and leaning close to kiss his neck. "Better?" Her voice came out throaty, and her cheeks warmed. Oh, she'd flirted before, but those guys seemed like harmless boys compared to Zane.

"Much better." He shifted her in his arms, settling her closer. "What are we talking about?" He played with her hair.

She spread her palm over his heart, marveling at the hard muscles. "I heard you shoved Kalin into the ocean. That showdown has been a long time coming."

Zane kissed the top of her head. "I know, and I do feel unsettled. We finally have him, and we're going to have to torture him to get information on Virus-27." Zane ran a hand down her arm, and she winced. "What?"

"Nothing. Just a bruise." Janie stretched her arm out.

Zane slid his palm up and over her bicep. "Here?"

"Yes." She'd ducked when she should've dodged a punch. "I'll be fine."

Heat prickled her skin and dug deep, spreading warmth. Zane rubbed the area with circular motions. All pain dissipated. "There you go, Belle," he rumbled.

She shook her arm. "Hey. You took away the bruise." Sliding her hand along his arm, she pushed on his bicep. "Is it here now?"

"No. I took the injury in, held it, and healed the bruise already." He grinned. "See how handy I am as a mate?"

"I did choose well," she said solemnly, trying not to smile.

"We both did." He flattened his hand over her abdomen. "Can you sense him yet?"

She shook her head, placing her hand over Zane's. "No. You?"

Zane stilled and took a deep breath, exhaling slowly. "Yes. He's strong already. Definitely your kid." Concern flickered in Zane's eyes.

"We'll be all right," Janie whispered, and leaned in to kiss the now faded scratch on his neck. "We'll get the information on Virus-27 from Kalin, and we'll find a cure."

"I don't want you going near Kalin." Zane sighed.

Janie lifted her head and leaned back. "But?"

Zane's eyes darkened. "What do you think we should do?"

"I think I should talk to him. Alone." Janie exhaled slowly. "He's contained, and if he'll talk to anybody, it's me."

Zane closed his eyes and exhaled, his entire chest moving. "I agree."

Janie blinked. "That's surprising." She'd figured she'd have to fight Zane and the entire Kayrs family to get to Kalin.

"I know." Zane opened his eyes. "The thought of you and our child so close to the Kurjan Butcher makes me want to kill. But that virus inside you is as dangerous as Kalin is, and you're the only person who has a chance at getting information. Torture probably won't work with him."

"So you trust me to handle Kalin?" Her chest swelled. Zane saw her as a woman and not some prophesied fragile human who needed to be hidden away.

"You're smart and you're trained. Of course I trust you." Zane sighed.

She leaned over and feathered her lips over his. "So you've seen the error of your ways."

He tangled his hand in her hair and tugged until her head lifted and her gaze met his. "What error?"

"The whole *do as I say or you get spanked* error."

He grinned. "No. You're going to talk to Kalin because it's a plan we're mutually agreeing on, and I'm going to keep you as safe as possible. It's our only chance with him. But if I give an order in the future regarding your safety, you damn well better obey it." Even through the smile, possessive determination glowed.

She rolled her eyes. "You're impossible."

"So long as you heed my warning, call me anything you want." His hold tightened just enough to show his intent. "For now, we need to figure out a safe way to gain Intel from Kalin without me standing in front of you, which is what I'd much rather do."

Holy crap. She was actually going to face Kalin. Dots danced across her vision. With a grimace, she pushed to stand. "I'd rather do this now than later. Let's go talk strategy with my dad. Maybe I'll take a nice picnic lunch down to Kalin in his cell."

Zane stood and wove his fingers through hers. "I'm sure the king and your father will love that idea as much as I do."

Janie waited while the guards finished sweeping the Realm's secured cells in the mountain. Her family had been surprisingly accepting of her idea to speak with Kalin. In fact, when she and Zane had arrived at the conference room, they'd already started making a plan. Their trust in her abilities warmed her.

She couldn't let them down.

Now she stood deep in the mountainous headquarters. She loved being inside the earth and let the sense of surrounding rock center her. Peace filtered through the earth that held them all so tight. Unfortunately, the peace failed to diminish the headache pounding at the base of her skull. She'd barely kept the agony at bay since contracting the virus, and the pain was becoming more insistent.

Zane, Talen, and Dage manned control panels in the adjacent room, recording everything.

The guards exited, and Chalton gave her a terse nod. Dage had decided to send in guards Kalin didn't know and not family—not anybody Kalin knew. "We'll be right outside," Chalton said.

Sweat slicked her palms. She nodded and tugged down her bullet-proof vest before striding inside and shutting the door.

Lighter brown rock made up the walls of a square room bisected in the middle by pure iron bars. A cot and toilet made up the cell. Kalin stood, dressed in a plain black jumpsuit, and drew near the bars. "Janet." Satisfaction rolled his consonants.

"Kalin." Her heart beat hard enough to rattle her ribs. She chose one of the two chairs on her side of the bars and sat, taking a moment to study him. "Please, sit." Damn, he was tall. Almost seven feet. His black hair had grown out longer than the last time she'd seen him, the red tips seeming brighter. Green and purple commingled in his eyes. Gone was the boy who'd visited her dreams.

He sat gracefully at the end of the cot, his burned skin already healing. "Might you bring your chair closer?"

"No, I might not." She had strict orders to keep out of arm's length, and she was smart enough to heed them. Uncle Conn was the ultimate soldier, and he knew what he was doing.

Kalin laughed and glanced at her combat outfit. "Are you expecting to be shot?"

"No."

"How many knives do you have hidden?" Curiosity darkened the purple in his eyes.

"Five."

He nodded. "Good number."

"Thanks." Her hands trembled, so she rested them lightly on her legs as she waited. Some of her training had included interrogation and interviewing techniques, and every instinct she had told her to let Kalin lead the discussion.

Kalin lifted his patrician nose and sniffed. "Ah. Peaches and . . ." He launched himself at the bars, wrapping long fingers around them. "You've contracted the virus."

She barely kept herself from shoving back in her chair. "Yes." Showing trust, she leaned toward him. "I'm hoping you can save me."

He glanced up at one of several security cameras. "Let me out of here, and I promise I will."

"No. Save me anyway."

"Have your *mate* save you," Kalin spat, fangs slashing low. He swallowed and drew them up, visibly inhaling. "I apologize for my outburst, but you shouldn't have mated Kyllwood. A *demon*, for God's sake."

Finally, Janie's body calmed. Her mind took over. "He can't save me. You can. So do it." But could Kalin help? "You altered the virus enough to make it go airborne, and in doing so, you had to be smart enough to create a cure."

Kalin's blood-red lips curled. "Oh, I know the cure. But for now, I like you unraveling and getting rid of that nasty demon-vampire marking." He released the bars. "The mark is fading, is it not?"

Yes, the mark seemed lighter by the hour. "No. Sorry."

"You're a terrible liar." Kalin tsked his tongue. "We'll have to work on that when we're finally together."

"So you really think we're going to be together?" she asked softly, tilting her head.

His smile warmed. "I'm immortal, Janet. We're not confined to a little lifetime, and I have no doubt we'll end up as one. The sooner the better, of course." He stilled and blinked. Then he took a deep breath, his eyes widening and his gaze dropping to her stomach. "Baby powder and fresh rain." His fangs dropped again, glinting in the fluorescent light.

Janie swallowed as her pulse picked up again. Her chin rose. "Yes."

Kalin staggered back and dropped to sit. His eyes narrowed, clearly calculating. "You can't be pregnant this quickly."

"Yet I am." She covered her stomach protectively.

He shook his head, dark hair flying. For several long, tension-filled moments, he just studied her. Then he swallowed. "This new version of the virus will destroy a baby. You won't make it nine months—not even close." His voice roughened.

Was that panic? Janie stood and stepped closer to the bars. "Then help me. For our friendship as kids, if for nothing else."

"I can't," he whispered. His shoulders slumped. "The mutation of the virus happened quickly and infected several Kurjan mates."

Janie's knees wobbled, but she stayed upright. "What happened to them?"

"They died. Within a week to a month of contracting the stronger virus. All of them." Kalin stood and stepped up to the bars again, sorrow lining his face. "Our scientists are working around the clock, but as of right now, there's no cure. I've lied and tried to cover that fact, thinking we'd eventually find a cure, but . . ."

Fury soared through her and she grabbed the bars. "Then why the hell did you set the virus free? Why infect the witches during the peace talks?"

"We're at war, and the peace talks represented the only opportunity to infect witches, and thus vampire mates." He wiped his smooth chin. "We had no choice."

"Oh, you had a choice." Raw anger lowered her voice. "We could've found peace."

He snorted. "Peace after war? Never. War is meant to be won."

"Or lost," Janie hissed.

Kalin moved quicker than possible and wrapped his hands over hers, holding tight. "We'll just see who loses."

The door banged open, and Zane entered, firing three shots into Kalin's shoulder. The Kurjan fell back on the cot.

Zane grabbed Janie's arm and shoved her behind him, the gun still pointed at the Kurjan.

Kalin grabbed his bleeding shoulder and chuckled. "You may have knocked her up, but you're going to lose her. Soon."

"Bullshit." Zane aimed and shot Kalin in the knee.

The Kurjan hissed in pain. "No cure, demon." Even with the fresh wound, he stood, looking down. "All of your power, all of your strength, and you can't save one little human mate. If you were a true ruler, you could save your woman. How helpless you must feel, Kyllwood."

Zane's body tensed, and Janie set her hand against his waist. Zane settled, his shoulders going back. "We'll see about that, Kurjan. Have fun bleeding." He turned and hustled Janie from the room, slamming the door behind them.

Chapter 26

Zane tipped back his head and swallowed the entire tumbler of Scotch.

"That's fifty years old," Talen grumbled, refilling Zane's glass. "Slow down or start drinking the cheap stuff."

Zane would bet his left shoe the vampires didn't have cheap stuff.

"It's over by Garrett and Logan," Talen said, jerking his head toward the kids playing pool. Then he turned and strode across the room where his pale mate sat on a sofa, talking to Zane's mother.

Zane straightened and leaned back against the bar, his drink in hand. When he'd been summoned to a strategic meeting, he sure as hell hadn't expected alcohol, pinball tables, and a comfortable fireplace fronted by heavy furniture. When Suri planned, the demon kept to conference rooms—and no women. Nobody playing pool or arguing good-naturedly about the football playoffs.

The Kayrs family ruled as a family, now didn't they? Oh, there was no doubt the king was in charge, but he relied heavily on his brothers as well as their mates.

Zane glanced at Sam, over playing darts with Jase Kayrs. Maybe Zane should include his brothers more and stop trying to shield them. They were fine men and even better warriors.

Janie slid onto a bar stool, her shoulder nudging his arm. "My dad is sharing his good Scotch?" She wiggled her eyebrows. "You must've made quite an impression in battle."

Zane took another sip. It was good.

"Check out the sunset," Janie said softly.

Floor to ceiling windows showcased the rather calm Pacific Ocean and a spectacular pink and orange sunset. "Beautiful," he said. Then he brushed a hand over her silky hair, allowing himself to touch freely. To reassure himself that for now, she was all right. "I thought you were very brave facing Kalin alone earlier."

She sighed and leaned into him. "I thought he'd want to help me. Foolish, I know."

Zane slipped an arm around her shoulders. So fragile and yet so strong. "I thought he'd help you, too."

"Do you believe him? That there's no cure?" Janie asked.

"I'm not sure." Zane caressed her neck. For so long, Janie had been his only lifeline. It felt damn right to hold her close. "We've been poring over the recordings, and if there's a clue in what he said, we can't find it." Frustration heated up Zane's throat, and he tried to mellow it out. Kalin had been correct that Zane was helpless to cure Janie, and that truth spiked through him like a hot poker.

Janie's chin dropped to her chest. "That feels good. Constant headache."

Zane frowned and rubbed harder, yanking her pain into his neck. Agony flared along his vertebrae and down his spine. He coughed. "God." Sucking in air, he forced healing cells around the pain and shoved it into nothingness. "That was more than a headache."

She lifted her head, her eyes clearing. "I know. Everyone keeps getting them from the virus. Earlier I wanted to rip my own head off."

Yet instead, she'd calmly entered the cell of a killer. Zane shook his head, his chest puffing out. Yeah. His mate was awesome, brave, and so damn smart. He'd underestimated her before, mistaking a fragile body for a delicate spirit. His woman was a warrior. "You're perfect, Belle."

She snorted. "How much have you had to drink?"

"Not enough." He glanced down at her cup. "What's that?"

"Green tea." She sighed and eyed his tumbler. "I already miss red wine."

He faltered. "Ah, maybe I should give up alcohol, too. Just to be fair."

She turned her head and a saucy smile lifted her pink lips. "Drink all you want. You can make it up to me later."

He smiled through the worry. "Now that's a deal." God, he had to save her. The idea of Janie being taken from him poked the beast inside him to action. To fight any danger.

The king stood near the fireplace and cleared his throat. "Let's have a quick meeting. Does anybody think the Kurjans have a cure for the virus?"

"No," Janie said softly. "I think Kalin was telling the truth." She frowned. "At least some of the truth. He seemed cagey."

Dage nodded. "Agreed. I don't think he has the actual cure, but I believe he knows something. Perhaps his scientists are on the right path." The king turned toward his mate. "What's the status in our labs?"

The queen pushed black hair from her pale face with trembling hands. "The virus is definitely attacking faster, but the witches are holding their own. Unlike mates. We don't know why yet, but I think it might be the key to curing the bastard." She sighed and stood, looking thinner suddenly. "The virus comes with a blinding headache, and my vision has come and gone several times all day. The thing spread unbelievably quickly. At least fifty percent of mates are infected across the globe, and we believe about seventy-five percent of witches are as well."

"Any difference between male and female witches?" Zane asked.

"No. Males are infected at the same rate as females, and so far, they appear to get a bad cold and then recuperate somewhat," Emma answered.

Janie nodded. "But even so, they're still infected?"

"Yes, and the virus keeps unraveling their chromosomes, so although they feel better, they're still under attack," Emma said, swaying. Dage grasped her arm and settled her back on the couch with a worried growl.

Zane clawed a hand through his thick hair. Frustration welled up inside him, and he tried to calm himself. Kalin's words kept rolling around in his head, taunting him with the raw truth. "Any news on Suri?"

"He seems to be consolidating power in Idaho," Dage said slowly. "Our first focus here is the virus, and then we need to discuss Suri and a possible attack."

Zane shook his head. "No vampire attack on demons. This is between Suri and me. That outcome will determine the future relationship between our peoples." He kept Dage's gaze until the king nodded.

"Your choice. We'll back you," Dage said.

Zane didn't smile, but relief filled him.

Janie pushed off the stool, her gaze on her mother. "Mom? You don't look so good." She moved to cross the room and stopped in the middle. "Oh." She wavered and put a hand to her head. "Zane?"

Shit. Her vision. Zane reached her in one stride and slid an arm around her. "It's okay, Belle."

Janie shook her head, a sob rising from her throat. Her knees buckled.

Zane swore and caught her, so much fury bombarding through him, his ears rang. *If you were a true ruler, you could save your woman.* Kalin's taunt ripped through Zane's head. "Enough of this shit." Losing her was not a fucking option. He laid her down and pressed both hands to her chest. Drawing on the universe, drawing on every ounce of stubborn strength he owned, he pulled on the pain inside her. On the fucking parasite trying to hurt her.

Nothing would hurt her. Ever.

His stomach lurched, and his liver pulsed. His spleen might have exploded. Yet he pulled harder, his eyes closing so he could concentrate. Something gave inside her.

His eyes flipped open. Pressing against her chest, his fingers went rigid. He could do this. Picturing her strands of DNA, of her very essence, he searched for what didn't belong.

Finding the anomaly, he wrapped himself mentally around the intruder. His fangs dropped low and nicked his lip. The muscles in his arms and chest undulated, tensing with strain as if he tried to pull a truck by himself. An oily sense of wrongness fought him. With a hoarse shout, he tore the intruder from her body and into his own. The effort threw him onto his back, and his head smashed into the floor.

His breath panted out, and his vision went gray.

Sam reached him first. "Zane?"

Zane shook his head and slowly sat up with his brother's help.

Janie sat up, wiping her eyes. Her very clear eyes. "It's gone," she whispered.

The entire room went still. Nobody even breathed.

Zane shut his eyes and wrapped healing cells around the virus before shoving it away. He coughed and opened his eyes. "I got the bastard."

The queen gasped. "Oh my God. The mutated virus is faster but weaker. Mates can pull it free, unlike the earlier version. We didn't even think to try."

Every vampire in the room focused on his mate.

The queen held up both hands. "Whoa. We need to study—ack." Her voice cut off as Dage all but tackled her into the couch. "No, Dage, wait—" Thunder rolled outside as the king concentrated solely on curing his mate.

Zane allowed Sam to help him up before reaching to assist Janie.

Sam glanced around at the odd motions of vampires yanking the evil from their mates. "This is just weird," he muttered.

Zane nodded.

Janie turned and burrowed into his arms, tears in her eyes. "You did it. My God, you figured out how to save us all."

Janie sang softly as she made the bed, her mind finally clear. No virus. Zane had taken the little bugger right out of her body. Emma had confirmed her blood results hours ago. All the mates were clear, and the news had gone out to the world.

By morning, the virus would be banished from all mates.

Mated witches would also be cured, and soon a cure for all witches would be found. For the first time in years, Janie could take a deep breath. Watching her mother suffer for so long had taken a toll on her. Now Cara could heal.

Zane paced into the bedroom, and Janie's breath caught. "I didn't hear you return," she said, holding a pillow to her chest.

He glanced at the bed and then up at her. "The queen finished taking my blood. Damn, that woman likes needles."

Janie chuckled and tucked the pillow into place. "Emma is dedicated. What did she find?"

"No virus in anybody's blood, although the main test takes another ten hours to develop fully." Zane nudged the door shut. "I thought we should celebrate." His voice roughened.

Amusement and desire bubbled up. "Dinner and a movie?"

He blinked. "After."

Her grip tightened on the pillow. "You've never taken me on a real date."

"Yet here you are, locked in a bedroom, totally at my mercy."

She lifted the pillow again, laughter filling her. "I'm not helpless."

"No." He angled toward her. "You're damn strong. Impressive, really."

She lifted a mocking eyebrow, while pleasure burst inside her. "Not weak. So, do you have any weaknesses, Zane Kyllwood?"

"Only you." He stepped closer, his gaze thoughtful. Even flirting, an intensity danced on his skin.

"I make you weak." She slid one foot back an inch.

"You knock my feet out from under me."

Now that was the sweetest compliment she'd ever received. Her heart thumped, full of him. "Let's see about that." Throwing the pillow at his head, she rolled across the bed to land on the other side.

He beat her there and tossed her back on the bed, sprawling over her.

She laughed and pushed at his chest. "Get off."

"Plan to." He went limp, crushing her into the bed. "See. Swept off my feet."

She gasped for breath, chuckling with each pant and trying to shove at his chest. It was like being pinned down by a car. He'd immobilized her entire body. "You weigh a ton."

He lifted himself up onto his elbows, pressing his groin more firmly against hers. "You calling me fat?"

"Hmmm." She pursed her lips, pinched his flank. Or tried to. Nothing but smooth muscle over pure hard steel. "I have a couple of exercise tapes you could borrow."

He grinned. "Have any leg warmers I could wear?" The tension riding his shoulders lessened.

She skimmed up his back to play with his thick hair. "I see you in pink."

He chuckled, and his mental guard relaxed.

Images slammed into Janie's brain. Strategy and danger. She stilled.

His smile faded. "We shouldn't be able to read each other's minds so quickly."

Yet they could. She shook her head against the pillow. "We're finally in a good spot. You have to find peace."

Granite hard muscle pressed against her chest as he took a deep breath and exhaled slowly. "There's no peace if Suri lives."

Fiery heat ignited her nerves. "Then send an army and let's finish this." Her voice rose, and her mind reeled with the need to find a solution without so much danger to him. They'd just found each other, and they finally had a chance to live. To be together. "Please."

"An army of vampires taking on an army of demons? That's not peace." Zane spoke softly, but the firmness of his jaw left no room for negotiation. For reason. "The only way to find peace is to take Suri down and agree to a treaty as the new leader. Otherwise, we'll always be at war. The two sides of me, the vampire and the demon, will be fighting each other. I have family on both sides."

The truth made sense but there had to be another way. A way that wouldn't get him killed. She coughed out frustration. "Even if you beat Suri one-on-one, his death will send out shock waves, right?"

"Definitely." An apology shone in Zane's emerald eyes.

"Can you survive it?" Janie whispered, her gaze dropping to his full lips.

They formed the words she really didn't want to see. "I don't know," he said. "I have a better chance than anyone else, though."

That wasn't exactly reassuring. She sighed, curiosity battling with fear. "What about you? There's power in you, too. If you, ah, died, would you send out shock waves?"

He shrugged. "Not at this point. You need to be at least five hundred years old to accumulate that much mental power, and frankly, after the last two wars, not many demons have lived that long. Suri and Nick are among the few."

So Suri had nothing to fear if Zane died. Janie swallowed. "You're still regaining your strength from battle and from teleporting so many times. Surely you're going to give yourself time to heal before taking on Suri."

Zane lowered his head until his nose nearly touched hers. "I leave tomorrow, Belle."

Her body flared into motion, struggling against him, trying to fight. "No," she breathed.

He held her in place, not moving, letting her work it out of her system. Against him.

But every move, every touch, every strike of her body against his blasted desire into her nerves. Into her very being. By the time she wound down, she panted with more than exertion.

Need filled her, desperate and hungry. Finally, she stilled. "Why can't we just relax and have a soft time? There's always so much fire." Vulnerability and fear made her feel small. Helpless.

His gaze melted. "You want gentle?" Soft as a whisper, his lips wandered against hers. "I can give you gentle." His groin settled more comfortably against hers, hard and ready. Tempting.

Warm and strong, his palm cupped her jaw, his thumb caressing her cheek. "Let me show you, Belle," he rumbled. His mouth covered hers, kissing slow and deep. Tears pricked the back of her eyes, and she let him take her languidly where he wanted to go. His senses opened, letting her inside his head. Inside his heart.

His fears as a child, his hope as a teenager, his determination as a man, all filled her mind. Memories of his thinking about her, of his wanting her, filled her heart.

He gave her everything, holding nothing back.

She accepted him, opening herself. Sharing every secret fear and hope. Somehow Zane smoothly removed their clothing with minimal effort, his hands caressing her breasts, his knees nudging hers farther apart.

He pushed inside her carefully, his mouth constantly working hers, his power keeping her with him. The sensations bombarded her—*his* sensations. What he felt, he shared with her.

The second he'd embedded himself completely inside her, and her internal walls gripped him, a devastating sense of peace and rightness centered him. She rode the feeling, both humbled and amazed. They shared far more than most couples, even immortals. She felt everything he was and everything he hoped to be. At the center of him . . . was her.

She lived in the heart of Zane.

The thought threw her body into a hunger that quickly gripped him, too. He thrust harder, faster, both of them beyond the moment. He drove inside her, one hand tethering her hair, the other clamping her hip. He half-lifted her, increasing his pace.

Flames scorched through her, forcing her higher, searing her nerves. A small explosion detonated, then another, and then her body ignited into an orgasm so strong her skin burned. She cried out and dug her nails into his skin, her body arching into his. Energy uncoiled from her core to singe outward and consume her entire body.

She shut her eyes and held on tight, trusting Zane to keep her safe. To keep her tethered to the world.

The surge took everything she was, finally releasing her to drop onto the bed, panting. Shaking. Eternally fulfilled.

Zane dropped his head into her neck, still pounding, and then groaned her name as he came.

The sound of their ragged breathing filled the room. Zane lifted his damp head and kissed her, slowly and thoroughly. "It'll all be okay, Belle. I promise," he gasped.

She nodded and kissed him back. Prophesied for centuries, she had power of her own. Now it was time to figure out how to save her mate.

Chapter 27

Zane cracked his neck, trying once again go get rid of the dull ache spreading from his shoulders to his temples. His bulletproof vest was cinched too tight, and his feet felt as if he'd donned the wrong boots. He kept his gaze on the dark screen spanning an entire wall.

All of the Kayrs men stood around the conference table, nobody bothering to sit. Sam and Nick kept to the wall behind Zane, as if already covering his back.

The king punched in a couple of numbers on a keyboard, and slowly, a Kurjan took shape.

"Kayrs," the current Kurjan leader said. His hair was a blood red with black woven throughout, and his eyes darkened to a pure purple. A pregnant woman handed the white-faced soldier a drink and then quickly disappeared from sight.

"Dayne," Dage replied. "Congratulations on your child."

Dayne smiled with sharp canines. "Thank you. We do want our race to continue."

"We all do." The king gave a regal nod. "Right now, we have your ruler in a cage. Want him back?"

Zane bit away a smile. Dage sure knew how to get to the point.

"No," Dayne said.

Dage's dark eyebrow rose. "Excuse me?"

"The Kurjan Butcher can stay in your cage. Keep him. I've found I like ruling." With his own regal nod, Dayne cut the connection.

Dage blew out air and turned to the group. "Can't say I'm horribly surprised." Turning back to the keyboard, he punched in several more numbers. "All right. For the next part of our meeting, let's talk about Zane's crazy idea to go after Suri."

Zane lost his smile. The room seemed to waver. What was wrong with him? It had to be all the teleporting he'd done lately. Hopefully there wouldn't be permanent damage, because he'd hate to lose the ability. Shaking his head, he forced himself to concentrate as the king mapped out Suri's current location on a huge wall screen.

Talen growled. "You need to take me with you."

"No." Zane tried nonchalantly to wipe sweat from his brow. "The presence of any vampire in the vicinity of Suri's death will be taken as an attack on the entire demon nation."

"You're assuming Suri will be the dead one," Conn said evenly.

Zane lifted an eyebrow. "Assuming any other outcome will get me killed."

"Good point." Talen's hard features flushed. "Somebody turn down the damn heat in here."

Zane nodded. God, it was hot. Maybe the furnace was on the blink. He eyed the terrain around the Idaho compound, where they believed Suri was still located. "I can't kill him there."

"No." The king tapped the tablet in his hand, enlarging the screen to show Idaho, Colorado, Montana, and Utah. "If Suri sends out the power surge you believe, you have to get him to a more secure location."

Kane Kayrs pointed a laser at the map. "A dormant super volcano lies just beneath Yellowstone National Park, and if it blows, it'll take out a good part of the Pacific Northwest before the ash is spread to the east. It'd be a disaster and would kill many."

Zane nodded and peered closer as his vision wavered. Just how stressed was he, anyway? "The shock waves sent out by Suri might wake up that volcano." He blinked several times to focus. "Looking at fault lines, that area is subject to a pretty bad earthquake."

Dage tapped his tablet again. "The Borah Peak earthquake moved the mountain sixteen vertical feet, and we think the fault line connects to the San Andreas."

So many fragile humans to protect. "So we're talking about millions of deaths. Many cities destroyed. California might even drop into the ocean," Zane said. He shook his head. "There's also a nuclear facility in Washington State, right?"

"Hanford," Kane said.

"I understand," Zane said. "It's almost as if that bastard chose his location carefully, now isn't it?" Leave it to Suri to cover all contingencies. If things went bad, millions would die.

Sam came to his side. "I'm not part of the Realm, so I'm going with you."

Zane turned and put his trembling hand on Sam's shoulder. "You're a good brother, but I need you to take the reins if I don't make it back." Frankly, he wasn't completely sure he could transport Suri out, but it appeared he didn't have a choice.

"This is a bad idea," Talen growled, grabbing the back of a chair and leaning heavily on it. "I said to turn the damn heat down."

"It's off," Dage muttered, rubbing the back of his neck. "I think it's chilly anyway."

Talen shook his head, and his shoulders rolled back. "Zane, if you do manage to get to Suri—and don't think we don't know you're having trouble teleporting—where do you plan to take him to fight?"

"Alaska wilderness, somewhere away from the Denali fault line." Zane's hands began to tremble. A rush of energy rolled up from his feet, swirled around, and landed hard in his gut. Bile burned his throat.

What the hell was going on?

The king pulled out a chair and fell into the seat, his breath hitching. His skin lost all color.

Talen frowned. "What's wrong with you?"

"Dunno," Dage whispered, his eyes flashing a sizzling blue through the silver. A shudder racked his massive shoulders.

Talen turned to Conn, who was leaning over, sucking in air. "Get Dage out of here." The chair back beneath Talen's hands crumbled in his grip, and he swayed. His golden eyes rolled back. Then the biggest badass Zane had ever met dropped to the floor.

Zane moved to help him when the world tilted. Blackness assaulted his vision, and gravity took over. His last thought as his head impacted the stone floor was to look for the attack.

* * *

Janie ran into the first room in the infirmary, her heart thundering. She nearly skidded into Garrett, who turned to grab her arms. His eyes glowed a primal aqua.

"What's going on?" she gasped, leaning to see her father and Dage both on examination tables while Emma and Cara bustled around. "I don't understand."

Garrett shook his head, worry lining his face. "We don't know yet."

"Where's Zane?" she asked, frantically trying to look into the adjacent room.

"He's in room B with Conn," Garrett said soberly. "Kane, Jase, and Max are in C."

Her ears rang. "They're all afflicted?"

"Yes." Garrett released her to turn back toward his father. "We've been attacked."

Janie rubbed her chin. "Only mated vampires?"

"Yes." Garrett rushed forward as Talen stirred.

"Dad?" Janie followed, grabbing her father's hand.

His golden eyes flipped open, he stilled, and then leaped from the bed. A quick glance around had him shoving both Garrett and Janie toward Dage and behind him before he settled his stance and faced the door.

Garrett angled to the side and reached for his father's arm "There's no immediate threat, Dad."

Talen turned, confusion wrinkling his brow. He swayed.

"Whoa." Garrett helped him back to the table just as Dage slowly sat up.

"What the hell?" Dage asked, focusing on Emma as she peered into a microscope.

"Just a second," Emma said, her voice high and tight.

Janie gave her brother a look. "I need to check on Zane. I'll be back." God. If every mate had been affected, there was really only one possible reason. She bustled into room B, where Zane already sat on a table flanked by Sam.

Conn perched on an adjacent table with Moira all but sitting in his lap.

"Any news?" Moira asked, green fire dancing on her skin.

"Not yet," Janie croaked out, reaching Zane in quick strides. "I heard you passed out."

"We all did," Zane said. "I have Logan and Nick locked down with my mom until we figure out what's happening."

"It's obvious what's happening." Janie slid her hand into his, needing to touch him. For once, his palm was cold and clammy. "When you took the virus from me, you didn't destroy it."

"Impossible," Conn muttered. "Vampires don't become ill."

Emma strode into the examination room, her tennis shoes squeaking on the bleached tiles. "Janie's right. Virus-27 is thriving in all of your bodies, slowly attacking your chromosomal pairs."

"Oh God." Janie swayed, and Zane drew her between his legs. "Vampires don't get sick. The only way a virus could infect you would be if you *purposefully* drew the illness into your own body."

"We can get rid of pain and illness," Zane said, running a hand down her back as if trying to comfort her.

Janie turned to face him, still bracketed by his long legs. "So maybe you just need to try harder. Can you sense the virus inside you?"

He closed his eyes. "Yes."

She put her hands on his chest, trying to get inside his body. "Now try to trap the virus and send it away like you did my headache." Closing her eyes, she tried to send every ounce of strength she possessed into him.

His chest lifted beneath her palms, and he breathed out evenly. "I've got him."

Thank God. "Now wrap him up and away from your chromosomal pairs."

Zane shuddered.

Janie kept her eyes closed, but she could sense Sam drawing near, giving his brother support.

"You've got this," Sam murmured.

Janie nodded. "You're stronger than this bug, Zane. Kick it the hell out of your body."

He coughed and pitched back suddenly.

Sam caught him before he could drop to the floor and quickly shoved him around. Janie jumped back and out of the way of Zane's legs before grabbing them and lifting.

Zane lay on his back, convulsing, his eyes rolling back.

"Zane!" Sam pushed down on Zane's shoulders, holding him against the table, his eyes wide and his jaw determined. "Hold on."

Janie ran to the counter and clutched a tongue depressor, hurrying to slip the small disk into Zane's mouth so he wouldn't bite off his tongue.

Emma ran toward them. "Keep him settled so he doesn't fall." She felt for the pulse in his wrist and counted silently. Her concerned gaze fastened on Janie. "Make him stop. Tell him to relax for a moment."

Janie's breath caught, and she squared her shoulders. "Zane?" She caressed his whiskered chin. "Please let the virus alone for a minute. Just let go and come back to me."

His body went rigid as if fighting invisible ropes. The seizure kept him shaking, his head thumping the table even with Sam restraining him.

Janie leaned closer, tears falling from her eyes to his chest. "Please, Zane. Let go for me."

He slowed, the convulsions lessened. Then he flopped back on the bed.

"Zane?" Sam slowly relaxed his hands.

Zane didn't move.

Janie removed the depressor and kissed him softly. "Please wake up."

His eyes slowly opened—all black. No green showed.

Janie swallowed. "You in there?"

He nodded and stretched his neck. "What happened?" he croaked.

"Do you still feel the virus?" Emma asked, her fingers remaining on the vein in his wrist.

He blinked several times as if trying to get his bearings. "Yes. The bastard is still there."

The earth rumbled in displeasure all around, and small shards of rock dropped from the ceiling in the underground headquarters. Janie sandwiched herself between Dage and Zane, not sure she could stop either one of them if they went down. "I think I should speak to Kalin alone." Her voice bounced back from the smooth metal door secured in the stone. "He won't talk to either of you."

Dage straightened his shoulders much too slowly. "If he knows anything, he'll want to gloat to me, and he's pissed at Zane for mating you, so we can use Kalin's anger to glean information."

"If we don't pass out again," Zane muttered.

"Yeah. That." Dage nodded toward a camera set in the far corner. "Let's get this over with."

Janie said a quick and silent prayer for the men to remain standing. The door silently clicked open, and she led the way inside.

Kalin sat cross-legged on the floor, his back to them, his chin down. Several deep breaths later, he lifted his head and stood, turning around as if completely serene.

The door shut, and both Zane and Dage made a move to put Janie behind them.

She halted their progress, staying in the middle but a foot back. "I hadn't realized you meditated, Kalin," she said.

He bowed his head, his angled features almost seeming at peace. "We haven't truly had time to get to know each other yet, Janet." His smile revealed sharp fangs.

She cleared her throat, nerves dancing through her stomach. "We have a question or two for you."

Kalin frowned and glanced at Dage and then Zane, both sweating and pale. Suddenly, his eyes sparked. His red lips curved. Both hands swept out, he threw back his head, and a huge bellow of laughter rolled up from his chest. Deep and hard, he laughed until he was gasping for breath.

Dage sighed. "I take it you're not surprised?"

Kalin wiped his eyes and stepped closer to the bars. "You foolish, sentimental, dumbass son-of-a-bitch. I can't believe it worked."

Zane growled low. "Explain."

Kalin shook his long, dark hair. "You fucking vampires are so led around by your dicks." Fire lit his greenish-purple eyes, and he reached for the bars. "King Kayrs, twenty years ago, did you really think we created an entire virus, a biological weapon, so we could steal your fucking *mates*? Really?"

Janie's knees trembled. "Then why?" she whispered.

Kalin kept his gaze on Dage. "To take out the Kayrs family. You're fools for your mates. The only way to infect you was for *you* to make it happen."

Janie stepped up between Dage and Zane, their protection warming her. "You infected mates just to hurt the Kayrs family?"

Kalin lifted a powerful shoulder. "As well as the majority of vampires. It took years to make the virus both airborne and *weak* enough to be drawn out by a mate." He sighed dramatically. "Just years." He snarled. "Yet here we are, finally."

Unbelievable. Janie shook her head. Kalin had played her when they'd talked, warning her that the virus would kill her baby. In fact, he'd pretty much taunted Zane to save her. Damn liar. "We'll find a cure," she said, lifting her chin.

Kalin's smile was almost gentle. "No, you won't. I promise."

She edged in front of the men she loved. "Why not?"

"Virus-27 is a simple little creature like the common cold in humans." Triumph lifted Kalin's chin, even while he kept her gaze. "The natural antibodies exist on the X chromosome of any species. For you female mates, the illness would've lasted about a hundred years, which for immortals, is like a couple of weeks for humans. Simple. Common. Cold." He brushed invisible lint off his black jumpsuit. "And just as incurable."

So they had just needed to wait out the illness. Fury rushed through Janie, and she moved toward the bars.

Zane stopped her with a hand on her arm. "Stay back," he said.

Janie trembled she was so angry. "We'll find a cure."

"No." Kalin stepped away from the bars. "Witches will eventually be fine because even male witches have one X chromosome. You know who doesn't?"

"Vampires," Janie whispered.

Kalin jerked his head in a short nod. "Yes."

She frowned. "Wait a minute. Neither do Kurjans."

Kalin smiled. "True. But Kurjans aren't stupid enough to force the virus into our own bodies. Well, except for the few we experimented on before turning the virus loose."

"Let's go," Dage growled, turning for the door.

Janie followed with Zane on her heels. At the door, she turned for one last chance. "You can stop this, Kalin. Please."

He studied her, his features set in serious lines. "Even if I wanted to, Janet, nobody can stop this. Say your good-byes now."

Chapter 28

Month 1: Jase

Janie finished cataloging the most recent slides in the empty lab and stood to stretch her back. Morning sickness had set in with a vengeance, and she moved carefully. A rustle echoed by the door, and she turned as her uncle strode in.

Jase Kayrs moved with the grace of a cougar, although more slowly than usual. His copper eyes had clouded, and his skin paled so the ever present scar lining the side of his face appeared deeper. Darker. His short hair was finally growing out, making him look every bit as dangerous as she knew him to be. "You fix this virus yet?" he asked.

"I'm working on it." She leaned back against the counter and forced a smile. "How are you feeling?"

"That's my line." He crossed broad arms. "Do I need to kill the demon?"

Janie brushed her hands down her jeans. "Stop calling him a demon."

"So . . . no?" Jase gave her the look he'd used in her childhood when she'd borrowed his favorite socks.

"No beating the tar out of Zane. You like him, right?" Her lungs trapped her breath.

Jase scratched his whiskered chin. "He's a good fighter."

Janie put both hands on her hips.

Jase sighed. "Fine. Yes, I like him. He reminds me of a cross between Dage and Talen, especially since he has to step up and rule the damn demons and doesn't want to." Jase absently rubbed the scar along his ear. "Although I think the mating happened way too quickly. You should've been given time to think the whole matter through."

Her lips instantly tipped into a smile. "Like most vampire matings."

Jase chuckled. "I know. Good point. So far we've talked him into waiting to take on Suri until after he's cured of the virus, but at some point, Zane will have to go."

"I know," Janie whispered. "But he needs to be at full strength to even think about fighting Suri."

"You love him."

"Yes." Her chin lifted, and her heart thumped hard. In fact, she'd really like to get married when things slowed down. Just like those human girls in the romcoms she watched.

Jase nodded, his gaze mellowing. "So, no regrets?"

"No regrets." Well, except for not uncovering Kalin's master plan to take down the Kayrs family. Janie peered closer at her youngest uncle. "What about you? I mean, you and Brenna mated quickly and now everything is going wrong."

"I need Bren more than I need a certain number of chromosomal pairs," Jase said. "In fact, screw the virus. You're brilliant, Emma is fastidious, and Kane is obsessed. Talk about a trifecta for curing the damn thing."

Hope was all they had at the moment, and it was nice hearing Jase express it after knowing so much pain in his life. Janie tilted her head toward the other lab. "Speaking of Emma . . . she's waiting for you."

"Great. More needles." Jase pushed off the counter and began rolling up his sleeve. "I did want to let you know how much you mean to me, Janet Isabella Kayrs."

All the oxygen left the room. "We are not saying good-bye." Panic heated Janie's throat. Jase couldn't give up.

"We'll never give up. But while I can, I just wanted to say that the best thing that ever happened to our family was when Talen brought you home." Jase leaned in for a one-armed hug. "Don't ever forget that."

Tears pricked Janie's eyes. "I love you, too."

Jase nodded and turned away. "If you change your mind and want me to beat the crap out of Kyllwood, just let me know." He sauntered toward the other lab, his gait hitching slightly.

"If this morning sickness gets any worse, I may take you up on that offer," she called after him.

"What offer?" Zane stood in the doorway, his eyes nearly glowing in his pale face.

"To beat you up." Janie drank him in, flutters cascading along her skin.

Zane slowly lifted one dark eyebrow. "What did I do?"

Janie moved toward him as if drawn, needing to touch. Needing reassurance that her uncle hadn't just said good-bye to her. She slid her hands up Zane's chest. "Nothing . . . yet. Let's go see what we can do about that."

He grinned and ducked a shoulder to lift her against his chest. "Now that's a plan."

Month 2: Kane

Janie retrieved the samples from the humming medical device to place them back in the small fridge. The AC clicked on in the large lab located in the main lodge, and she shivered.

Kane dropped a sweatshirt around her shoulders. "Sorry it's so cold." His fingers brushed her neck, several degrees more chilled than the air.

She turned to study the dark circles under Kane's magnificent violet eyes. "When was the last time you slept?"

He reached for a stack of papers being spit out by the nearest printer. "There's no time for sleep. According to this, we've all lost an entire chromosomal pair already. At this rate, we'll be human or even dead by the time your baby arrives."

How odd that everyone had begun measuring time in terms of the baby's arrival. "Then we need to get you healthy so my son can learn science from his uncle Kane," Janie said slowly. "If you don't get some rest, the virus is going to win. You know that."

"The virus is winning anyway." Even ill, Kane Kayrs moved with the grace of a panther, crossing the room to reach for more samples. He'd unbuttoned the top of his dress shirt, and muscles shifted beneath the natural material. Muscles noticeably smaller than they'd been the previous month.

"Find a cure yet?" said a chipper voice from the doorway.

Janie turned to see Amber Kayrs glide inside the room, reaching her mate in several long steps.

Amber leaned up and kissed Kane's smoothly shaven chin. "You need rest."

"That's what I was just saying," Janie said.

Kane tucked Amber into his side, his darkness a fascinating contrast to her reddish hair and tawny eyes. "My resting doesn't solve anything, and you two know it." He looked down at Amber, love in his eyes. "Nor does my preoccupation with this virus mean I don't follow the trouble my mate creates."

Amber blanched and tried unsuccessfully to step out from under Kane's arm. "Trouble? What trouble?"

Janie settled in for the show.

Kane tugged on one of Amber's curls. "Apparently an Internet campaign was just launched against a leather factory last night, bombarding personal emails, business accounts, and even some governmental sites with images and names of executives."

Amber blinked. "Wow. No kidding."

Kane focused on Janie, who shook her head. "Don't look at me. I know nothing about this one," Janie said.

Amber hip-checked Kane. "All right. Garrett and I may have created a teeny campaign a while ago, before everyone became ill, and the Internet launch date was last night. Don't blame Janie."

Kane pressed a hard kiss to the top of Amber's head. "I know exactly who to blame, don't worry. And I will deal with you accordingly when I get home tonight."

Amber finally extricated herself from Kane's hold and flounced toward the doorway. "Promises, promises." She turned and blew Kane a kiss before winking at Janie. "Later, Jane." She disappeared.

Janie smiled. "Amber is trying too hard."

"I know." Kane sighed and grabbed another stack of papers. "She's scared to death and wants to put on such a brave face. I'll have to ease her mind somehow tonight."

Janie swallowed as nausea rose from her belly. "I'm scared, too."

Kane, the smartest man on the planet, turned toward her, a stack of useless papers in his hand. "You're strong and brilliant. No matter what happens, you and little Kyllwood in there will survive. I have faith in you."

A rush of energy rippled through Janie. "You need to survive, too."

Kane nodded. "I'll do my best. You make me proud, little niece. You always have." He turned back toward the printer.

Emotion welled and fuzzed Janie's vision. Why did that sound like another good-bye?

Month 3: Conn

"Harder," Conn muttered, stepping back and twirling the wooden pole. "Hit harder, Jane."

Janie's feet danced on the mat, and she tightened the hold on her own pole. "I'm trying."

Conn slid to the side and clapped her thigh with the pole. His normal scent of gunpowder and sage filled the room. "No, you're not."

She stepped back and huffed out a breath, dropping the pole to the mat. "Listen, buddy. You're pale as hell, shaking, and slow. I'm pregnant, nauseous, and getting mad. Drop your pole."

His eyes flashed an amused green, and he threw the pole across the room. "Want to grapple?"

"Not unless you want barf all over you." At the moment, she'd like nothing better than to throw up on her pushy uncle. "What has gotten into you?"

"Meaning?" Conn reached down for a towel to wipe his forehead.

Janie kept her expression bland. They hadn't worked out hard enough to even remotely break a sweat, and Conn appeared as if he'd just run eighty miles. Backward. "Why the new training schedule?" The schedule had appeared the previous day for pretty much all Kayrs mates and Janie.

Conn shrugged. "We've gotten complacent. The demons are consolidating their forces under Suri, and the Kurjans just won a big battle in Iceland and should be wanting another good fight soon. We all need to train."

"That's not all," Janie said softly.

"No."

She stared at her uncle, trying not to wince at the deep lines of fatigue and pain cut into his chiseled face. Conn was the strongest soldier ever born, and now loose skin sagged on what used to be steel-tough muscles. Gray sprinkled liberally through his brown hair. "What else?" she asked.

He dropped into a fighting stance. "If we don't cure the virus, you all need to know how to fight. Even better than you do now."

She shook her head. No way was Conn saying good-bye to her. Losing the Kayrs men as well as the myriad of vampires across the world who'd taken the virus into their bodies to save their mates would be a huge blow to the Realm. Personally, Janie couldn't even consider the cost. "We will find a cure."

"I know."

Running footsteps echoed down the hallway, and they both turned as Moira Kayrs, Conn's mate, ran inside. Moira's wild red hair cascaded around her face, her eyes glowed a brilliant green, and blue flames danced on her bare arms. "Conn?"

Conn rushed toward her. "What, Dailtín? What's wrong?"

Moira swayed and grabbed both his forearms. "You're, ah, not going to believe this. I mean—"

He yanked her into him for a hug and rubbed a huge hand down her back. "Whatever it is, we'll figure it out. What's going on?"

Moira levered back. "I'm pregnant."

Conn stilled. Completely. "Wh-what?"

Moira nodded vigorously. "Emma just confirmed it in the lab. I'm with child."

A brilliant smile split Conn's face, and he bellowed a champion's cry. He swung her up and around before holding her tight.

Janie wiped away tears and discreetly headed for the doorway to give them space.

A baby.

She and Moira would both have little ones. How exciting. And how very terrifying—especially if the virus took their mates and left them all alone.

Straightening her shoulders, she marched through the building to the lab. She was going to kill this little fucker of a virus and now.

Month 4: Max

Janie knocked on the large metal door set into a contemporary oceanfront home and smiled when Max Petrovsky opened it, dressed in worn sweats and nothing else.

Even ill and leaner than ever before, Max's cut figure looked every bit the hunter he was known to be.

"I need your help," Janie said.

Max stepped aside to allow her entry. "Anything."

She moved inside the comfortably furnished home. Thick, cushioned sofas angled toward a rock-wall fireplace with colorful pillows strewn throughout in a welcoming chaos.

Max shut the door and rubbed the back of his neck. "Sarah isn't here."

"I know. She's in school right now." The vampires were trying to keep the routine as normal as possible for everyone, and that included school for the shifter and vampire kids. Sarah was the main teacher for the Realm. Janie sank into the sofa with a sigh of relief.

"How are you feeling?" Max retrieved a shirt from a pile of folded laundry on an ottoman and yanked it over his head. "I thought the second trimester was supposed to be better?"

"I feel better," Janie lied. It was hard to feel anything but nauseated by the obvious decline in the vampire men. "How are you feeling?"

"Fantastic. What can I do to help?" Max asked, his formidable concentration solely on her.

"Zane wants to go fight Suri, and I need you to stop him."

Max lowered heavy brows. "Why me?"

Because the king and her dad agreed with Zane. "You're the voice of reason and always have been. Dage listens to you when things get emotional. This is emotional."

Max had been more than a bodyguard and more than another uncle to Janie through the years. He was good and kind and truly saw the world in straight lines.

"I need you to talk to Dage," she said.

Max shook his head. "Dage isn't the key to this. Zane is."

As if on cue, a heavy knock echoed on the door.

Max gave her a look and opened the door to reveal Zane. "What a surprise," Max muttered, gesturing him inside.

Zane's gaze caught Janie's and held as he stomped inside. "I'd rather have this discussion in private." His voice held a low threat.

Max rolled his eyes. "This is my house. I'm not leaving."

"We are." Zane nodded to Janie. "Let's go, Belle."

Janie stood, her own temper pricking the back of her neck. "Fine."

Max eyed Zane. "How are you feeling?"

"Fine. You?" Zane glowered back.

"Like shit, actually. My head hurts, my heart is beating too slowly, and my fucking knees feel weird." Max leaned back against a jam-packed bookshelf. "Sound familiar?"

Zane's shoulders relaxed. "Very."

Max clapped him on the back. "So teleporting to Suri, teleporting him out, and then fighting him sucks as an idea right now. Right?"

Zane shut his eyes. "Yes."

"It's okay, Zane. We're family, and we'll figure this out," Max said.

Janie clutched the back of the sofa. Max had just called Zane family. She hadn't realized how badly she'd needed Max to acknowledge Zane. "We'll come up with a plan."

Max nodded and reached for a small package next to all the books. "I agree. Now, you two get back to work so I can make a nice dinner for my Sarah." He handed the package to Janie as Zane drew her outside. "This is for you." Without another word, he shut the door.

Janie stood on the porch, her gaze on the package. Slowly, she slid out a picture of her and Max at her fifth birthday party. They both wore party hats, and delight filled her young face while amusement danced on Max's deadly features.

She turned toward Zane. "Why would he give me this now?"

Zane faltered and then kept silent.

Yeah. The shot was a remembrance of better times. "This is not good-bye," Janie yelled.

Month 5: Dage

Janie rubbed her protruding belly in circular motions, humming to her son. She lounged on the sofa in the main gathering room of the lodge, watching the tumultuous ocean outside. The baby kicked

her hand, and despite her sorrow, she smiled. She'd kill to have an
ultrasound of the little guy, but vampire babies created too strong an
amnio sac, and waves couldn't permeate it.

But her psychic abilities granted her some comfort. She could
sense the spirit inside her—strong and good. Probably stubborn as
heck. Just like Zane.

"I'm glad to see you resting." Dage crossed into the room, leaning
heavily on a handmade walking stick.

Seeing the king moving as if decrepit stabbed harsh nails into
Janie's heart. After months of searching, months of trials, they hadn't
found a cure for the virus. The Kayrs men were practically human
by now. "The baby is kicking. Want to feel?"

Delight flickered in Dage's eyes, and he carefully spread a gnarled
hand on Janie's belly.

The liver spots were new.

The baby kicked. Hard.

Dage chuckled and removed his hand. "He's strong. Definitely a
Kayrs."

"Kyllwood," said a low voice from the doorway as Zane hitched
into the room. While he didn't require a cane, he moved like an old
man. "I have Sam and Logan reaching out to any demon allies we
might still have out there."

"Is Sam going to take on Suri?" Dage asked.

"No." Zane sat next to Janie and slipped his thin fingers through
hers. "Talen and I have come up with a plan. We're waiting another
month, tops, and then we're sending in a full assault with healthy
vampires and shifters to Suri's Idaho compound."

"Then what?" the king asked wearily.

"The orders are to take Suri alive, and then, we'll have to figure
it out. Kill him somewhere safe." Zane's hand trembled.

Janie straightened up. "A month?"

Dage and Zane shared a look.

God. "Kane finished mapping the virus's path." Janie slid a comforting hand over her belly, her heart cracking. "Two months is what
you have left."

"Maybe less." The king leaned heavily on his cane; silver had overcome the black in his hair. "We've received the first reports of vampires succumbing to comas this week. We're not far behind."

"No." Janie struggled to her feet. "Let me talk to Kalin again. Please."

Dage sighed. "We've talked to Kalin until we're blue in the face. We've tortured him. We've even tried to bribe him. The bastard is telling the truth. There's no cure."

Janie stood tall, mentally telling fear to fuck off. "Then we contact his people again."

"Already have," Zane said wearily. "Dayne has taken over as leader, and if you ask me, he doesn't want Kalin back. If he wanted to save his cousin, he would've mounted an attack by now."

"So what the hell do we do with Kalin?" Janie asked.

Dage's weathered face tightened. "He dies before we do."

Zane nodded. "I won't leave him here to be a threat to you or my child."

"I'm not giving up," Janie said, her heart thundering. The men in her life couldn't leave her alone—she needed her family. Her son deserved to know these incredible people.

"Neither are we, sweetheart. But we have to be proactive." Dage tugged a folded piece of paper from his back pocket to hand it to Janie. "I had a vision."

Janie slowly unfolded the paper to see a drawing of a handsome, sixteen-year-old male vampire. Make that a vampire-demon. "This is our son?"

"Yes." Dage tapped the kid's chin. "Stubborn chin."

Zane leaned around to see. "He has my good looks."

"Definitely." Janie's lips trembled when she smiled. "So this is the guy inside me?"

"Chances are," Dage said. "He's definitely from the two of you."

"But maybe it's not *this* baby." Janie's teeth clenched as she scrambled to find hope. "This could be our third son. Heck, our eighth son. We're going to cure this virus, and Zane is going to give me a barrel of sons."

Zane lifted an eyebrow. "Eight kids?"

"Yes." She reached up and kissed his chin. "I'm going back to work."

Dage reached for her and enveloped her in a hug. "I'm not saying good-bye. Just that I love you and I'm proud of you." He nodded at Zane. "And I'm so pleased you've found your mate."

Janie swallowed past a huge lump in her throat. "I love you, too." The words were soft, but they really did feel like good-bye.

Month 6: Talen

Janie rubbed her aching belly and knocked on her parents' home, a plate warming her hands. The wind bustled around her, and she shivered.

Her father answered, a smile splitting his face. The sight of his pale skin threw her, as did the lightening of his warm golden eyes. It was as if the gold wasn't strong enough to stay.

She held out the plate. "I made your favorite cookies."

"Chocolate chip?" He drew her inside and led her to the kitchen before accepting the treats.

"Yes." She reached for him, and he enveloped her in a hug of warmth and pine. The feel and smell of safety.

"How are you feeling?" he asked, his voice a deep rumble around her.

She stepped back and forced a smile. "That's my line. Any better?"

"Much." He leaned back against a marble counter, the lie obvious on his blue-tinted lips. "Any interesting theories or results from today's blood draw?"

"No." She'd give anything to find a cure for him. "But we're working around the clock. Don't worry, we'll find a cure." She patted his thin arm. "You're too tough to keep down for long."

His grin flashed a perfect dimple in his right cheek. "I'm too mean, that is."

She nodded, her lips trembling. "Exactly."

"Sweetheart, stop worrying so much. Love is the one thing that makes Kayrs men stronger, so it could never be the thing that takes us down. Trust me." He pushed back to sit on the counter, his feet still touching the floor.

"I do." She stretched her neck and studied the man who'd made the world safe while also giving her a family. "Do you ever wonder what life would've been like if you hadn't rescued Mom and me from the Kurjans?"

Talen lifted one gray eyebrow. "No."

Amusement bubbled up, easing the constant pain of worry for a moment. "No? Not at all?"

"No. Some things are meant to be, and some people are meant to be. You and your mother were meant to be mine."

Janie kept her smile. Her dad was one of a kind and had no intention of ever hiding himself. "I don't think many women in the world would've accepted your, ah, outdated approach."

Talen smiled. "Your mother is one of a kind. Evolved and brilliant."

And happy. Talen had made Cara happy for decades now. Janie cleared her throat. "So, you and Zane have reached peace?"

Talen sighed. "Yes." The strong planes of his face sobered. "It's difficult seeing your daughter grow up. If I could, I'd have you still be five years old, fascinated with ponies and faeries. Not demons."

"I know." She shuffled her feet, her stomach aching. "Does Zane's lineage bother you?"

"No. He's a good man, a good fighter. I couldn't care less about his lineage." Talen pushed away from the counter to stand.

"What about the pregnancy, Grandpa?"

Talen shook his head. "I'm not old enough to be a grandfather."

"You're three and a half centuries old."

"Exactly." Talen nodded, his gaze dropping to her abdomen. "We'll protect and love this little guy with everything we are and everything we have. He'll have a good life."

"I know." Janie moved forward to touch her father's arm. "Thank you. For rescuing me, and for being my dad."

Talen straightened. "I'm not going anywhere, Janie. No goodbyes here."

She nodded. "Some things just need to be said sometimes."

"In that case, thank you for being my daughter. My life meant nothing before you and your mother came home with me."

Like they'd had much of a choice. Janie stepped into her father's arms, the one place she'd always been safe. "We'll fix this, Dad. I promise."

"I know." The doorbell rang, and Talen's head lifted. "You expecting somebody?"

"Yes." She slid her arm through her father's as they made their way to the door. "I asked Zane to pick me up here on the way to the lab. He's due for another round of tests." She opened the door to find her mate looking as pale and elderly as her father, so she forced a smile. "There's my guy."

Zane slipped his hand over hers. "Talen. How you feeling?"

"Great. You?"

"Perfect," Zane said.

Talen pressed a kiss to Janie's forehead. "I'll be along shortly. If your mother's at the lab, please tell her I'll meet her there and then walk her home." With a nod to Zane, he shut the door.

Janie bit her lip to keep from crying.

Zane sighed and tightened his hold on her hand. "Talen will be all right."

"I know." The only way to heal her father would be to find a cure. She held Zane's hand and turned to go down the steps and onto the sidewalk. The wind whistled, and leaves dropped from colorful trees.

Death was all around them.

They walked in silence, both lost in thought. Minutes later they escaped the wind in the massive lodge, and Janie led the way to the main lab. It was empty. "Mom and Emma will probably be back soon." She suddenly felt numb.

"I know. Keep hope, Janie. We'll find a cure." Zane shivered, even in the warm lab.

Desperation tasted like raw acid pouring down her throat. She wanted to fight, and she wanted to hit something. The baby bounced inside her. Could he feel her fear? Her horrible panic?

Zane pulled her into his lean body. So lean—no fat and hardly any muscle. His odd blend of demon and vampire blood had made the virus grow more slowly in him than in the vampires, but it was still taking its toll.

She inhaled his scent, his very essence. Why wasn't she strong enough to save him? There had to be a way. The baby kicked her, bouncing against Zane's flat stomach. He chuckled.

She leaned back, tears blurring his face. "Please don't leave me."

He opened his mouth to answer, and the room rocked.

A series of explosions ripped through the peaceful day in such rapid succession it was impossible to tell where one ended and the next began.

The floor rolled, and they fell.

Zane turned so she landed on him.

A blaring alarm roared through the building.

Zane helped her up, his face pale, rage filling his nearly colorless eyes. "We're under attack. Run."

Chapter 29

Janie scrambled down the hallway, ducking flying glass and slivers of wood. The earth rocked, and she fell. Pain vibrated up her palms to her shoulders. Her knees ached.

Zane grabbed the back of her shirt and hauled her up, pushing her into the janitor's closet. Shoving cleaning supplies and a mop out of the way, he revealed a silver keypad. His fingers flew over the pad, and a secret door snicked open.

"Go, go, go," he said, pushing her inside and yanking the door shut behind them. "Run, Belle."

Her mind swirled, and panic heated her breath. The full out assault would destroy Realm headquarters and alert nearby humans. She shoved open another door and jogged down a long flight of stairs cut into the rock, her hands finding purchase on the smooth stone walls.

Zane labored behind her. "Do you have your phone?"

"No." She'd dropped it when the first bomb had hit. "You?" she gasped, trying to see through the dim lights.

"No. Keep running."

The steps took a sharp turn at the bottom, and she barely made it without smacking into the wall. Her center of gravity was off with the big baby bouncing inside her. Finally, the tunnel widened, and they reached a small alcove and another door with a keypad.

Zane turned. "I don't know this code."

Janie swallowed and typed in the correct code. The heavy metal door unlocked, and she struggled to open it. Zane added his weight, and the door slid open.

They hurried into another hallway, this one leading even farther down into the earth.

Zane paused and looked behind them. "I don't hear anybody. Do you?"

A boulder crashed down, shattering into pieces. One cut into Janie's neck. "No," she said, shoving the door closed. "There are several tunnels into headquarters. Let's go."

Zane grabbed her hand and pushed her behind him. "These are steeper. Stay behind me, so if you trip, you'll hit me and not fall."

She loped into a run behind him, fully trusting he'd catch her if necessary. Even weakened, even dying, Zane Kyllwood wouldn't let anything happen to her or their baby.

The air chilled as they descended.

A wisp echoed around them. "Missiles," Zane muttered.

Relief propelled Janie faster. "That's good. Somebody's in the main control room firing back. That's really good."

An impact rocked the earth, and the lights wavered.

"That's not good." Zane glanced over his shoulder. "You okay?"

"Yes. Two more doors, and we'll be in the inner headquarters. It's safer there." She tried to nod while keeping a hand on the cut in her neck.

His eyes widened. "How bad?"

"Just a scratch. Go."

He turned and continued running, reaching yet another fire door. "Code?"

She punched it in and followed Zane into the eastern part of the underground headquarters. A gun cocked.

They both stilled, and Zane backed her against the stone wall, covering her.

She peered around him at several demon soldiers, all in combat gear. A gaping hole in the wall showed the Pacific lapping peacefully against the rocks.

The soldier in front pointed his gun at Zane's chest and fired three times.

Zane flew back against Janie, and her head knocked on the stone. "No," she cried out, reaching for him.

He slid to the ground, silent.

The demon smiled, flashing sharp fangs. "Suri will be pleased."

Janie tried to bend and administer CPR, but a demon hauled her away from her mate. She fought with everything she had, but the soldier easily pulled her toward the opening.

She frantically glanced around for an escape, just as several more demons jogged up with Kalin between them. They'd bound his hands behind his back, and a myriad of bruises marred his pale face. He'd lost weight during his captivity, but his eyes remained clear and his body ready for battle.

Apparently the Kurjan had put up quite a fight.

He reached them, his gaze dropping to her stomach. Then he focused on the motionless Zane, and the oddest look of regret flashed through his eyes.

Kalin's broad shoulders straightened, and he focused on her. "Stop fighting them. You'll hurt your child."

Tears streamed down her face, and she tried again to free herself from the soldier. He shoved her through the opening, and she stumbled on the rocks, barely keeping on her feet.

She flipped around and shot a hard punch to the demon's trachea before finishing up with a kick to the groin.

He reared back and punched her in the face. Pain exploded along her jawline, sparks flew behind her eyes, and she dropped into blackness.

Janie awoke, her head cushioned somewhat on a hard thigh. She blinked. An ache pounded in her jaw.

Reality slammed home with a rush.

She sat up, her head spinning.

"Take a deep breath," Kalin said.

She blinked and turned. The Kurjan sat on a stone floor, his hands behind his back. Oh. She'd been resting on his leg.

Brushing her hair from her face, she looked around the underground cavern where the peace talks had been held. Without all the occupants, the room seemed hollow and somehow dangerous. Unnatural. Right now, only she and Kalin occupied it.

"How did we get here?" she mumbled, not quite understanding.

"Helicopter and then lift. The demons blew the Realm headquarters to hell," Kalin said without any inflection.

Panic jolted Janie wide awake. "Who survived?"

"I don't know. Depends entirely on how well enforced the underground headquarters were."

Zane. God, Zane. Janie rubbed her eyes. He'd been shot in the chest, and he'd been in a weakened condition. "And Zane?" she asked, her voice wavering.

Kalin swallowed. "I don't know, but he didn't look good. He never moved."

Zane couldn't be dead. He just couldn't. Janie bit back a sob and tried to focus on getting out of there. The walls seemed to waver around them. "What's going on?" she asked.

Kalin sighed. "The quantum physics are failing, and the center fire went out."

They'd all be incinerated. Panic threatened to choke her.

Janie rubbed her belly, which didn't move. Was the baby all right? She tried to focus in on his essence, but fear inhibited her. She slowly stood. Four of the five exits had been barricaded with heavy rocks, and only one remained. Over to the right, the Prophesies of Arias spun eerily, bright flames dancing on the heavy leather cover.

The sheer sight of it sent chills coursing down her back.

"Yes. I suppose that is why we're here," Kalin said, shoving to his feet.

Janie turned and frowned. "I'm probably here for the book. Why are you here?"

Kalin shrugged. "I don't know, unless Suri has a plan."

Janie focused. "What's your plan, Kalin?"

He pursed his lips. "Immediate plan or long term?"

"Both."

"For the moment, I plan to listen to Suri. If he wanted me dead, I'd be dead, so he must have an offer. I'll negotiate, maybe kill him, and then you and I will go to a secondary Kurjan headquarters." He spoke calmly, as if already seeing the future.

Janie swallowed. "That's quite an offer, but I think I'll head home." She turned to study the barricades, seeing rocks all the way back. It appeared as if the demons had filled the entire passageways, except for the one lift. "Looks like there's only one way out."

"Your home was destroyed," Kalin said, wandering over to the now demolished entrance he'd used during the peace talks. "Time to let fate have her way."

Janie shook her head, anger fighting with focus inside her head. "Fate can kiss my ass."

Kalin chuckled, and kicked a smaller boulder out of his way. "That'll be my job."

Janie swallowed and turned to face him. "It's not going to happen."

"Sure it is. From day one, you were meant to be mine." Kalin wedged his hip against a rock and shoved. "I don't suppose you can unbind me?"

Janie glanced at the silver handcuffs. "Not without a key."

"I figured." He grunted and pushed the rock a foot. "After we get out of here, I'm killing my cousin and his pregnant mate, and then you and I will rule the Kurjan nation."

Wow. He was really not listening. "I said no."

"Your wishes are irrelevant."

That was it. "Listen, Kalin. I know we've been in each other's lives for years, but you're a serial killer. You like to kill women."

He shrugged. "The killing isn't important. It's the hunt that matters."

The cold, nearly bored tone of voice sent chills down Janie's back. "So someday you'll hunt me."

He turned, his eyebrow lifting. "Not you. Never you."

"Why not?" She forced a chuckle. "Don't tell me you love me."

"Love?" He rubbed his smooth chin. "Love is an emotion I haven't experienced. But I do like fate, and I like that you're special. I'll keep you safe."

Was he crazy or just lacking in empathy? "You feel nothing?"

He studied her. "I don't really know. It's always been you, Janet."

Janie shook her head. She'd never understand Kalin, but someday, like it or not, he would want to hunt her. He wouldn't be able to stop himself. She had to get back to Zane.

The rocks rattled, and a lift hurtled down. Suri stepped off, tall, powerful, and mean.

"You're finally awake," he said. "Now get the book."

Janie looked from the demon leader to the book and back again. The second she released the book, he'd kill her. "No."

Suri smiled, the sight truly evil. "You'll get that book, or I'll cut that baby out of you. Decide."

Janie convulsed as if she'd been hit. Terror clawed through her.

Kalin growled low and angled himself in front of her. "Why the hell am I here?"

Suri clasped his hands behind his back. "I thought to trade you to your people for a nice sum. But apparently your cousin has taken control and doesn't wish for your return. Pity."

Kalin lifted his regal chin. "So?"

Suri clicked his tongue. "So, I have a plan. Like you, I'm against any uprising or disloyalty to a true leader. Your cousin lacks vision, and you don't."

Kalin stilled. "Meaning?"

Suri shrugged a wide shoulder. "The vampires are done, and the witches and shifters are regrouping. Let's form an alliance, a permanent one, and take out your competition."

Kalin's eyes darkened to a deep purple. "I'm amenable to your plan." He glanced toward Janie. "She comes with me."

"Of course," Suri said.

Lie. Even without superhuman senses, Janie discerned the lie. "You want me dead," she said, facing her opponent and refusing to show fear.

Suri glanced down at her pregnant belly. "I have to admit, I'm rather curious to see Zane's vampire-demon son be raised by Kurjans."

Baloney. Janie angled closer to the lift, fear ringing through her ears.

Belle?

She stopped. *Zane?* So much relief flooded her that her knees wobbled.

Where are you? His voice filtered through her thoughts like the softest of whispers.

Cavern for the peace talks. Despair weighed down her shoulders.

They couldn't possibly get to her in time, even if any of the Realm helicopters had survived the attack. *Is everyone okay?*

Battered and bruised. Headquarters is just a crater. I'm coming to get you.

Tears filled her eyes. *There isn't time. I love you, Zane. Always.*

Suri frowned. "Get the goddamn book, or I'm taking that baby myself."

Janie turned her coldest gaze on him. "You will die, and I'll be there." She turned back to the crazily spinning book. The cavern's protective spells wouldn't remain in place for long.

She stepped toward the book, and the cover opened, its pages fluttering in a nonexistent breeze.

Creepy.

Drawing on strength, trying to remember her lessons with Moira and Brenna, she chanted in a language even she didn't understand.

The book snapped closed.

Rumbles shook the earth, and a schism wound along the floor. Janie shoved herself away from the split, her gaze wildly rushing to the lift.

"Not a chance," Suri said. "The book. Now."

If she gave him the book, he'd leave her underground. Every instinct she had yelled at her to stop him. Maybe with the book?

"You can't read the passages without me," she said slowly.

"I don't need the passages. I just need the book," he returned, his eyes gleaming as his gaze alighted on the now still book. "Get it, or I promise pain you can't even imagine."

Her imagination was excellent. She rubbed her belly and took a step closer to the book. Warmth brushed her face and wandered down her front. A pure warmth.

She couldn't let Suri have the power of the book.

Heat rushed through the cavern, and the earth quaked. Another fissure ripped along the floor. Janie fell down. Kalin jumped to her right.

Agony rippled along her abdomen.

Gasping, she shoved herself to stand. Another pain hit her, and she bit her lip to keep from crying out.

The air shimmered. Oxygen split in two, and Zane Kyllwood

heaved himself through space and time to land hard on the stone floor. He rolled at the last second to avoid the fissure.

Blood coated the earth.

He stood, pale and gasping, raw fury darkening his face across the cavern. "Let her go, Suri."

Suri snarled. "You're supposed to be dead."

"Not even close." Zane rose to his full height, his chin lowering. Red matted his vest. "Stop hiding behind my woman, and let's finish this."

Janie eyed the book. Only pure stubborn will was even keeping Zane upright. She had to do something.

Suri glanced from Zane to Janie. "If she gets me the book, I'll let you both go."

"Bullshit." Zane didn't even look her way. "Stop being a coward."

Suri frowned. "You know, I have a better idea. How about I kill her, and you watch?" Silver flashed, and a Degoller Star filled his palm. He flexed his hand and threw.

"No!" Zane yelled, leaping across the cavern.

Janie cried out and tried to duck, but Suri was too fast.

Kalin growled and jumped in front of her, his hands still bound. The star slashed through his neck, and he fell to the ground.

Janie dropped to her knees, reaching for him.

Shock covered his face. His eyes closed, and his head rolled into the fissure.

Chapter 30

Zane blinked, his gaze focusing on his pregnant mate. She sat on the floor, pale and trembling next to Kalin's headless corpse.

The Kurjan had saved her.

Suri swore, and the world narrowed to the threat he posed.

Zane lunged across the schism and tackled his uncle, throwing them both into a series of boulders. Pain ripped down his spine, and rock splinters stabbed his neck. Blood still poured from his chest wounds, and his knees felt like rubber from transporting one last time.

But if this were his final moment, he'd take Suri with him.

He turned his head to capture Janie's attention and get one more glimpse of the woman who held his soul. "Get to the lift and then run."

Suri grappled him into a headlock, and Zane had to concentrate on living long enough to give Janie a chance at survival. A slim chance, but if anybody could live through this, it'd be Janie Belle Kayrs.

Just the thought of her name awakened something inside him. Deep and strong . . . and beyond his current limitations.

Using Suri's chest as a fulcrum, Zane flipped his feet over them both, landing on his knees above Suri's head and jerking free his neck. He clapped both hands into a solid fist and drove down into Suri's nose.

Blood arced almost in slow motion across the cavern.

Suri punched up. Zane's jaw cracked, and unbelievable pain

threw him back into a solid sheet of rock. His head hit and then his shoulders, the impact ricocheting down his body.

The earth rumbled in absolute fury. The fissure widened, and several smaller branches broke from the main one.

Zane blinked and fought for consciousness. Across the cavern, Janie had risen to her feet, her hands settled protectively across her belly, a look of hard determination blanketing her delicate face. She leaped across the widening gap in the earth and dropped to scrabble through the rocks shifting and falling all around.

"Get out of here," Zane yelled.

Suri turned and stood, his chin down, the promise of death glowing in his black eyes. He stood tall and formidable—an ancient demon with unimaginable power. "I gave you everything."

Zane snarled and spat blood. The monster had beaten him, threatened him, and made most of his childhood hell. Even worse, he'd turned Zane into a killer. "I thank God every day my father had years with me before you stepped in." God only knew what kind of beast Zane would be without his father's guidance and his mother's love. And Janie's. "You're never going to have the chance to harm any of my family."

Suri's fangs shot out. "I should've killed you on day one."

Zane allowed his fangs to descend. "You really should have." Drawing on a strength taught by his father, he crouched and then attacked. Fists flying, knees lifting, elbows swinging, he went at Suri with everything he'd ever had.

Suri countered, crushing Zane's rib with one hard punch.

Zane dropped to one knee.

Suri chuckled and drew a Degoller Star from his back pocket. Silver glinted in the dim light, brighter than possible.

Janie cried out.

The Prophesies of Arias volume flew across the room and smashed into a wall. Pages whipped open. A shriek of unimaginable decibels roared from the pages.

Zane's brain swelled against his skull.

Suri growled at the book and then advanced toward his nephew, lifting the deadly weapon.

"Zane!" Janie threw the other star toward him. Still coated with Kalin's blood, the star spun wickedly through the air, spraying red.

Zane ducked, and the weapon wisped by his ear to embed itself in rock.

Suri laughed and lifted his arm.

Zane shoved pain, fear, and humanity to hell and let the demon inside him trump all else. His eyes stung, no doubt turning all black. He twisted on his one knee, yanked the star from the stone, and drove up just as Suri swung down.

Suri's star sliced across Zane's shoulder.

Zane's aim stayed true, and he sliced the sharp disk into Suri's trachea. The demon leader gasped, his hands grabbing the star. Zane let his momentum propel him into his uncle, and they both crashed to the ground. Another fissure opened up beneath Suri, spreading out from his waist.

Suri bucked, his hands sliding through the blood on the weapon.

Zane straddled him, his vision wavering. He wrapped both hands over Suri's on the star and turned to seek his mate. She stood on the other side of the cavern, pale, visibly trembling. "Get out, Belle. Before he dies, get out."

She looked down at her protruding stomach and nodded.

Zane shut his eyes. He could kill Suri and take the responding explosion into his body. To save Janie and their son. He could do it. Suri's struggles gained force, and Zane's hands lost dexterity.

He leaned up and stared directly into his uncle's black eyes. "For my family." Letting out a warrior's battle cry, he shoved with all his weight. The star cut to the stone—through muscle, tissue, and bone.

Blood gurgled from Suri's mouth, which dropped open in an expression of pure shock.

Zane released the star and grabbed Suri's hair, yanking his head from his body with a sickening wet sound.

For the smallest of moments, death held peace.

Then a wave of deadly power exploded out, throwing Zane into a table. Agony lanced down his back. He dropped to his knees. The air morphed and turned brown, the oxygen flashing with sparks. Wind somehow burst through the cavern with a painful keening.

Blood dripped from Zane's eyes, turning the world red. The earth bucked in displeasure, ripples turning into earthquakes.

God. What had he done?

Pressure built, heavy and devastating. The earth began to fold in on herself, sending out shock waves for miles.

Janie emitted a powerful cry of denial, hopping over fissures to reach him in a low tackle, landing on him. "Hold on." Grabbing him tight, she yanked him out of hell.

Peace and warmth. Zane opened his eyes to the oddest sense of safety. He blinked and sat up on heated sand in their dream world. "Belle?"

She lay next to him and pushed herself up on hands and knees, looking around. "Oh."

Zane glanced down at Suri lying beneath him. "How?"

"I don't know." Janie stood up and brushed sand off her jeans. "But we only have seconds."

Zane stood, battered and bleeding, and kicked his uncle over onto his back. Suri's mouth remained open, his eyes wide in death.

"Ouch." She grabbed her belly and grimaced.

"What?" Panic swelled and choked him.

She shook her head. "Not now. God. We have to get out of here."

Zane tried to force thoughts through his muddled head. How many concussions did he have, anyway? The sky opened up above him, red lightning flashing against black clouds. The entire dream world wobbled.

The air chilled to freezing.

A figure hovered near the tree line. Kalin? Zane shook his head, trying to focus. The Kurjan was almost transparent, and his greenish purple eyes glowed through a rapidly thickening mist.

Janie stilled. "Kalin? Why are you here?"

The Kurjan smiled with blood-red lips. "I'm just passing through." His image faded in and out. "This isn't how I saw destiny."

"Thank you for saving me," Janie said, rubbing her belly. "For saving us."

Zane cleared his throat. "Thank you."

Kalin gave a short bow. "Life. What a surprise. I see the future, and it's a shocker. Thank you both for being the closest to childhood friends I ever had. Live well." He flickered in and out, his gaze dropping to Janie's stomach. "Maybe tell your babe about me, so someone remembers me?" His voice trailed off at the end, and he disappeared.

The ocean began to boil and turn black.

Suri leaped to his feet.

Zane shoved Janie behind him. "But you're dead—"

Suri smiled. "Kind of."

Janie grabbed the back of Zane's demolished vest. "I forced us all in here to keep the world from exploding."

Suri advanced. "In the dream world all rules are gone."

Thunder bellowed into a shriek. Lava bubbled up through the sand, hissing toward the ocean. The environment rose under pressure, pushing in, adding gravity to the very oxygen.

Zane faltered.

Red filled the sky and spiraled down, thundering through the heavy atmosphere. He sensed that the second its energy touched the lava, the dream world would detonate. By taking Suri's power from the real world, Janie had sacrificed their dream world.

Suri snarled, his face contorting.

Zane turned and grabbed Janie close, opening up a space in time and dimensions. One more jump. Just one more to save his mate. The dream world exploded, burning his feet just as they jumped through.

He turned instinctively to land on his back and cushion Janie's fall. The ground rocked beneath him. He opened his eyes, his nose filled with the scents of dirt and death. "We're back in the cavern. Damn it all to hell." Struggling to his feet, he fell. His head dropped to his chest.

Janie struggled to stand and grabbed his arm. "We have to get out of here."

The earth continued to rumble, even with the power surge caused by Suri's death removed. Zane nodded, blood sliding from his ears. "I'm not gonna make it, Belle."

"The hell you're not." She propelled him toward the lift and around the opening schisms in the ground.

He glanced down to see lava and red core. The physics keeping the cavern safe were about to fail, and his woman was fighting to get him to the lift. Taking a deep breath of heat, he forced himself to put one foot in front of the other. Reaching down, he grabbed Suri's head by the hair.

Janie blanched.

"Trust me." He moved like an old man onto the lift and sat.

Janie sat and then stood back up. "I need the book."

He grabbed her arm just as the book spun round and round, finally dropping into the largest schism.

"No," Janie cried, struggling.

"Yes. Let's go, Janie."

She shook her head but tugged the gate closed. "Well, I guess we figured out my big destiny," she groaned, sliding onto the seat next to him.

Zane closed his eyes and surprised himself by grinning. "Saving millions of humans by forcing Suri's power into the dream world is a hell of a destiny." He slipped an arm around his woman. "Although, don't take this wrong, I figure you have more than one destiny."

She paused. "I have more to do?"

"You are the Prophesied One." His chuckle turned into a cough for air. It'd be a miracle if he lived past the day. He leaned down and grabbed a bunch of dirt to rub in his hair. Mixed with the blood, it'd hide the gray.

"What are you doing?" Janie asked.

He finished by patting some dirt onto his face. "Taking years off my life. Push the button, Belle."

She frowned, hit the button, and the lift sprang up through rock. Then she hissed. "I can't believe I lost the book."

"Forget the book." As far as he was concerned, the damn thing was cursed.

Janie peered over the edge but didn't stop the lift.

"Stand behind me when we get to the top." Zane tried to find strength, but only pain filled his mind. This was a long shot, but it was all they had.

The lift reached the top, and he forced himself to stand. Stepping out of it, he counted the number of demon guards flanking the exit. At least twenty. Shit.

He staggered to the opening, very conscious of the woman covering his back. Wind and rain pummeled the area, and trees swayed as if furious. The earth continued to quake. Several helicopters rested at the far tree line; there was no way to get to them without fighting.

One by one, the demon soldiers turned their focus on him. They were the elite of the elite, all wearing flashing medals across their chests. All close followers of Suri.

Zane blinked blood and rain from his eyes and lifted Suri's head high in the air. "Follow me or die."

He sensed a wave of pain behind him. From Janie. "Are you okay?" he muttered.

"Peachy," she said, stepping to his side. "I'll take out the right side of soldiers and you take the left?"

"Funny." He kept his gaze hard as Suri's blood dripped onto the earth. "Decide. Now." The demon in him came out full force in the harsh command.

A couple of the soldiers eyed each other.

Dread dropped into Zane's gut. He could barely stand, much less take them on.

A whir of sound echoed through the sky. He lifted his gaze. One by one, several helicopters dropped Realm soldiers onto the ground. A chopper landed, and the king stepped out, followed by Sam and Logan.

Zane's brothers ran toward him.

The demon soldiers slowly dropped their weapons. "Looks like you're the new leader," a well-decorated soldier said, respect filling his eyes.

Relief buzzed through Zane.

He threw Suri's head back into the earth and grabbed Janie, starting for the nearest transport. "We still need to get out of here."

She cried out and doubled over.

"What?" he asked, holding her upright.

Her eyes widened, pain turning her face pale. "I don't know."

He stilled. The entire world stopped spinning. "How bad is the pain?"

"Shit. Bad. Something's wrong." She bit her lip, tears filling her eyes.

Sam shot him a worried look and slipped an arm under Janie's shoulder. Between the two of them, they got her to the helicopter, where the king quickly put everybody in seats, and Janie sat next to a worried looking Talen.

As if choreographed, the Realm helicopters and the demon helicopters all rose into the air and then split into two different directions. Zane held Janie close, his body bleeding, his heart breaking. It was way too early for the baby, so she must've been injured somehow in the jumps. Pain racked his mate, and he tried to draw it into his body. But between the fight, the virus, and teleporting, he was done.

He'd see Suri soon in death.

Zane looked up to see the king, worn and wan, and so damn ill, staring at him with regret in his silver eyes. "How did you get transport?" Zane coughed.

"Allies. Mainly shifter allies," Dage said. "We'll head to our secondary headquarters for now."

So they all could die. Tears clogged Zane's throat, so he stopped talking.

An explosion echoed like deadly thunder behind them, heaving up red, orange, and yellow smoke. The cavern was toast, although no humans in outlying states would be harmed. Zane comforted himself by brushing his hand through Janie's silky hair. His mate had saved millions.

She doubled over again and gasped. "The baby is coming."

Panic ripped through his chest. "Now? He can't be coming now."

"He is." Janie took several deep breaths, her eyes a wild blue. "I want to get married."

"What?" Zane shook his head. "Now?"

She grabbed his hand, her nails digging in. "Yes. I wanted to before he came, or before I die, but everything has been so crazy. I want to get married. Now!"

Sometimes he forgot her human ways, but he'd move the fucking earth himself if it'd make her happy. "Okay." He looked at the ground below. "We can probably find a preacher on the way."

The king turned around and rolled his faded eyes. "I can marry you."

"You can?" Zane asked.

"Why does everyone forget I'm the fucking king?" Dage asked Talen.

Talen shrugged, looking a thousand years old. "I almost never forget."

Dage growled and placed a hand on Janie's arm. "Do you take—"

"Yes," she gasped, her face pinching in pain.

Dage frowned, concern wrinkling his brow. "Zane Kyllwood, do you take Janet Isabella Kayrs as your wife?"

"Hell, yes." Zane patted her hand, trying to send healing vibes her way, although he lacked the strength.

Dage nodded. "I now pronounce you husband and wife."

Talen leaned over and shook Zane's hand. "Welcome to the family. Again."

Zane nodded and kissed Janie's forehead. "Feel better?"

She smiled. Her eyes widened. Then she doubled over, vibrations of pain shooting away from her shaking body. "The baby is coming. Right now."

Chapter 31

Janie lay back on the makeshift bed, her heart thundering. She eyed the rough stone walls of the Colorado underground facility. After it had been attacked years ago, Dage had quietly rebuilt it as a backup if necessary. "Why are we here? Another hour and we could be at the Realm hospital in Canada."

Cara grimaced. "The demons hit the hospital at the same time as headquarters. There is no hospital."

Cramps gripped Janie's rib cage, and her stomach rolled. "We have to stop this."

Her mother and Emma scrambled around the narrow room for medical supplies.

"We've contacted Doctor Morose," Emma said, reaching for a blood pressure cuff. "He's en route from Maine."

Janie sucked in air and tried to stop the next contraction. The doctor was the best gynecologist in the Realm, having delivered babies for seven centuries. He'd agreed to move to headquarters during her eighth month—in just a few measly weeks.

But headquarters no longer existed, and it looked like she wouldn't be pregnant much longer.

The Colorado facility wasn't functional yet and lacked medical necessities. Her baby could not be born right now. "He's too early. He's way too early," Janie gasped, the pain making her light-headed.

Cara smoothed back her hair. "You're at seven months, sweetheart. The babe is early, but he's strong."

Janie tried to take comfort from her mother's soft words. But had the baby's early exposure to the virus weakened him? Or the falls she'd just taken during the fight? Now she lay in an unfinished facility, half-nude, covered by a sheet, because they didn't even have hospital gowns. "Don't you have anything to stop the contractions?"

"No." Emma felt for Janie's pulse and looked at the ceiling. "You need to take several deep breaths and try to slow your heart rate. It's way too fast." She eyed Cara. "A stethoscope won't work on the baby, and neither would a monitor. If we had one."

Cara nodded and patted Janie's arm. "I know. Vampire babies are too well insulated."

So there was no way to see if he was doing all right. Janie tried to hold still and not move. Maybe if she stopped moving, then the contractions would ebb. "Where's Zane?"

Emma wiped Janie's brow with a wet towel. "He's getting patched up in the next room and will be here soon. We can't have him bleeding all over everything." Her smile trembled on her lips. "Women have been giving birth in fields forever, Janie. This is fine, and your son will be perfectly healthy."

Janie nodded. "If there's a problem? What do we have here?"

"The lab is stocked," Emma said. "We were moving on to the medical facilities next."

So basically . . . no medicine.

Cara leaned in and grasped Janie's hand in hers. "I gave birth to Garrett in an underground jail cell. Remember?"

Janie forced a smile. "That's right. Simone and Moira helped you." Maybe they should get a witch in the room. Although manipulating quantum physics wouldn't help right now. A contraction ripped into her, and she cried out.

Emma cleared her throat and reached for the sheet. "Let me just take a gander, Jane." She looked for a moment and then gently felt Janie. "You're dilated at about a four." Emma stepped back to the narrow counter to wash her hands in the small sink. "This little guy is showing up today."

Zane kept his face stoic and tried to concentrate on a tiny spot on the rock wall. The needle dug in again.

"You doing okay?" Talen Kayrs asked, his thick fingers working the thread through Zane's flesh.

"Yes." Although he might pass out from loss of blood. He sat on an old folding chair in a large, empty cavern in the rock. The emergency headquarters lacked pretty much everything. "Thank you."

Talen chuckled, his gray head bent at the task. He looked like a ninety-year-old human, and he moved as slowly. "Thank you for saving Janie. It's a miracle you were able to teleport."

"Or fate." There was no way Zane had made it on his own, was there?

"Or you." Talen slapped a bandage over Zane's chest wounds. "There's no stronger drive in the universe than the need to keep a mate safe." He stood and straightened his back, the vertebra popping loudly.

Zane nodded, trying once again to force his wounds closed. Nothing happened.

Sam and Logan hastened into the room.

"Mom's secure with a couple of the witches closer to the center of the mountain," Sam reported.

Logan frowned, worry glinting in his eyes. "Are you okay?"

No. In fact, Zane could feel the energy leaving his body. He had to live. Just long enough to see his kid.

Dage strode into the room followed by Conn, Kane, Jase, Max, and Garrett. The king's gnarled hands shook on a stack of papers. "How is Janie?"

"Getting settled," Zane answered. "Emma is coming to get me as soon as they have her in place. The baby is coming today."

Dage smiled cracked teeth, lifting new wrinkles at his eyes. "Good. I'd like to meet your son. Before . . ."

"Before what?" Garrett shoved away from the wall, panic filling his tone.

Talen turned toward his son. "We've had reports of five vampires across the world dying during the last week. Apparently the virus works very quickly once death is close." He turned, and a crack echoed through the room. Shock opened his mouth, and he fell flat on his butt.

Garrett rushed forward. "Dad?"

Talen growled and grabbed his hip. "Broken."

Shit. That easily? Zane wanted to get up and offer his chair, but his legs refused to move. He ran a weak hand through his hair. Strands of gray fell to the floor. "I'm almost dead, and now I'm balding?" He snorted. "Apparently I am a superficial bastard. The hair loss bothers me almost as much as death."

Talen leaned his head against the wall and barked out a laugh. His nearly colorless gaze met Zane's. "Me too. I would've liked to have known you over centuries, Kyllwood, not just a few short months."

Zane nodded. "Ditto."

Garrett growled and shook his head. "We're not giving up. Please don't tell me we're giving up." He looked around wildly at the group.

Conn, Kane, Max, and Jase all leaned heavily against the wall, death dancing on their pale faces. Their eyes had lost all color, and their bodies all strength.

Talen reached out a hand for his son. "I'm sorry, G. I need you to be strong."

Garrett blinked, tears in his metallic-colored eyes. He looked so much bigger and stronger than the indomitable Talen that something in Zane's gut hurt. Bad.

Dage hobbled toward Zane and handed him a stack of papers. "Treaty."

Zane took the pages and a pen. His head hurt, and his vision sucked. "Tell me it's fair."

"It's fair." The king wiped sweat off his sagging chin. "Treaty between the Realm and demon nations, sharing all information, and banding together against any enemies. If the Prophesy of Arias is ever found, we share it." He pointed to a second page. "This page turns over your rule to Sam." The king glanced at his nephew. "I've transferred mine to Garrett. The Realm is yours, kid."

That quickly and in front of Zane's eyes, Garrett Kayrs changed. His head lifted, and his shoulders went back. A wounded desperation filled his gaze, while pure Kayrs power tightened his jaw. "I'll protect the Realm." The pain fled his eyes, leaving a hard determination that made him look centuries older.

Zane nodded at his brother. "Sam?" he gasped.

Sam stepped toward him and dropped to one knee so they could see eye to eye. "Thank you for being my brother."

Tears pricked the back of Zane's eyes. "I couldn't have made it without you and Logan."

Logan knelt by Sam. "You protected me. Thank you."

Zane blinked, not caring that tears slid down his face. "Take care of each other, and protect Mom, Janie, and my son."

Sam held a hand over his heart. "With everything I am."

"Me too," Logan said, choking up.

Zane tried to hold his shoulders up. "My child."

Sam's and Logan's heads snapped up, while Garrett pushed off from the wall. "My life," they said in unison, their deep voices a vow to protect and defend.

Tears clouded Zane's vision. He'd never thought he'd request the oath, but as it was given, something eased inside him. They'd take care of his son.

Jase cleared his throat. "I'm going to spend my last moments with my mate. Somebody text me when the baby is born." He moved toward the doorway and stumbled. Conn reached for him, while Kane and Max assisted each other, and the four inched their way into the hallway.

Fuck the virus. Zane scrubbed his face with both hands. One little bug had taken the toughest predators in the universe and turned them into old men. The Kurjans should all be shot for creating the virus.

The queen hustled into the room, her gaze landing on her mate. "Dage?" she asked, her voice breaking.

"I'm fine, love." The king slowly lifted his hand.

She ran to him, snuggling into his chest. "I'm so sorry."

Dage ran a hand down her dark hair. "You gave me joy for longer than I deserved." He slowly put her away from him. "Janie?"

Emma swallowed and turned toward Zane. "The baby is coming. Now."

Panic and hope flamed through Zane. He struggled to stand.

Emma hurried for him and slipped a shoulder under his arm. "Let me help."

Dage padded across the room and slid down to sit by his brother. Two skinny former warriors during their last moments. "We'll be here. Let us know the good news." He slung an arm around a swaying Talen.

Talen exhaled and leaned his head back on the stone, his eyes closing. "I'm almost a grandpa."

Emma swallowed and turned to stare at her mate. "I'll be back. Please be . . . here."

Dage slowly winked.

The room spun. Zane caught his breath and tried to remain upright.

A scream rent the day. Janie!

Emma tightened her hold. "We need to hurry, Zane."

He stumbled along next to her into the hallway and toward the makeshift medical room. "What's wrong?"

"I don't know. I think maybe the baby is breech." Panic filled Emma's voice.

They reached the room, and Emma helped him into a chair by Janie's head.

Pain filled Janie's face and blood scented the room with sulfur and copper. Her sable hair was plastered against her forehead, and tears streaked down her pale face.

She truly was the most beautiful thing in the world.

Zane clasped her hand in both of his. "Belle?"

She turned toward him and sobbed. Her back arched, going rigid. With a cry, she closed her eyes and seemed to push.

Cara fumbled beneath the sheet, her hair a wild mess, her eyes a panicked blue. "Don't push yet, Janie. I think I can turn him."

Janie groaned and subsided into the bed. "Oh God."

Helplessness coated Zane's throat, and his body trembled. "You're so strong, baby. You always have been and always will be." He leaned his face closer to hers. "Trust me."

Her eyes widened, and then she nodded.

"Okay. Push now, Janie," Cara urged.

Janie drew in a deep breath and bore down. A vein filled with purple in her neck.

Zane whispered soft words without meaning, trying to stay conscious. Just to help Janie through the storm and to see his son. Just once.

Janie flopped back onto the bed, gasping for air.

"Again," Emma said. "Whoa. Tons of black hair on this little guy."

Janie's eyes widened, and she hissed out air before bearing down again. Zane counted seconds to her until she sank onto the barely padded table.

"You're doing so well," he murmured, drawing in her scent. "Think how special he will be. Human, vampire, demon, and several shifter species. Plus, you're enhanced, so you're a cousin to the witches."

Janie gave him a pained smile. "He'll be a man of the world."

From the world and to the world. Zane rubbed his cheek on hers. "I'm proud of you."

"One more time," Cara said, her hands full of a towel.

Janie shook her head. "I can't. No more."

Zane kissed her hand. "One more time. For me. So I can meet him."

Tears spiked into her eyes, changing them to a dark, desperate blue. "Don't leave us."

He closed his eyes against the reassurance she needed. Not once would he lie to her, not even now. "I love you, Janie Belle."

Her mouth opened, the cords in her neck stretching. A contraction gripped her stomach hard enough Zane could see it. Crying out, she sucked in air and bore down. Hard. For what seemed like minutes.

Cara ducked low and reached out.

Janie fell back to the bed, a sigh of relief echoing on her scream.

Cara cooed and wiped off a little bundle.

A gurgling cry came from the towel. Not a scream so much as an interested hello.

Zane chuckled into Janie's neck, tears sliding down his chilled face. He turned his head to see his child.

Cara wiped and wiped. "You have a beautiful . . ." She paused on a gasp of air.

Zane lifted his head. "Cara?"

Her eyes went wide, and she swayed. "Emma?" she asked.

Panic filled Zane.

Janie struggled to sit up. "What is it?" she asked, her voice cracking.

Emma shook her head and frowned, looking closer. "Ah. It's a girl."

Zane coughed. "No. That's impossible."

The baby gave another gurgled sigh.

Emma smiled and rubbed the babe's head, quickly snipping the umbilical cord to place on a tray. "Possible or not, this is a girl." She took the bundle and laid the babe on Janie's chest, covering her with a fresh towel. "Oh my." Emma wiped off the baby's back. "A baby girl prophet. Interesting."

The blue prophesy mark wound over her little neck and down her back. Zane blinked. "That's impossible," he repeated.

Janie's face softened, and she rubbed the baby's back. "We were in the room when the prophet died, and I was pregnant. I guess it makes a sort of sense."

Zane shook his head. "Not the prophesy. She can't be a girl. A vampire girl."

Janie inhaled the baby's scent, smiling. "Well, demons have girls."

"But vampires don't, and as a cross-breed, I'm a DV blend. No X." Zane reached out a trembling hand to touch his . . . daughter. She blinked, black eyes focusing on him. He could've sworn she smiled. "Never."

"When have we ever done things the normal way?" Janie asked softly. "You must somehow have an X chromosome in there. Unless I gave you one of mine. Who knows."

She was so fucking perfect his heart swelled, just for her. He had a daughter. Thank God.

Janie smiled, wonder filling her pretty eyes. "A baby girl. *A girl vampire.*"

Emma gasped, her gaze slashing to Cara. "Vampire. Girl."

Cara dropped the towel still in her hands. "No."

"Yes. Oh God. Do you know what this means?" Emma asked.

Cara clapped a hand over her mouth.

Emma ducked her head. "Push again, Janie. Let's get the afterbirth. Cara, grab the cord."

Janie pushed, her gaze remaining on her baby.

Emma stood. "Oh God, Oh God, Oh God."

Zane tried to focus on her, but his head lolled on his shoulders. "What?"

"An X chromosome. A baby girl vampire with an X chromosome. The cure." Emma turned to grab a syringe, drawing blood from the cord. Her eyes intent, she turned toward Zane. "This may pinch."

He frowned to ask a question, but the world gave out on him before the needle reached his arm.

His head fell forward, touching both Janie and his daughter. A perfect place to die.

Chapter 32

Seven hours. Seven long, impossible, fear-filled hours had passed since Emma had injected Zane with stem cells from the baby's umbilical cord. Janie perched on a folding chair and cradled her baby, watching the man she loved.

Her silent, too still, in-a-coma mate. Zane lay on the one table, his long legs extending over the end. Blood and dirt still matted his hair, but the gray shone through. His chest barely rose with shallow breaths.

Completely out—but not dead. A coma he could awaken from . . . or not.

She patted the sleeping baby's back. "That's your daddy," she whispered to her beautiful daughter, glancing down at the full dark head of hair. Just like Zane's. Janie kissed the soft head. "I think you have my chin, though." How was it possible to feel such contentment and such incredible fear in the same moment?

"Wake up, Zane," she said softly. "Please."

The warrior didn't stir.

The virus had stolen the deep color of his hair, the muscles in his body, the youth of his eternal skin. But even after the virus had weakened him, he'd drawn enough strength to teleport and save her from Suri. With bullet holes spitting blood from his chest. A man who could dig deep enough for such strength deserved to survive.

Emma strode wearily into the room, shoving black hair from her face. "Any change?" she whispered, her gaze on Zane.

"No." Janie shifted her weight on the hard chair.

Emma glanced at her. "We should get you into a bed."

"I'm not leaving him." Janie snuggled her nose into her daughter's soft hair, keeping her gaze on her aunt. "How is everybody else?"

Emma sighed and reached for Zane's wrist. "The same. Dage and Conn are basically in comas. Talen, Jase, and Max are unconscious but breathing better than the other two. The other vampires in the facility are in similar states. We haven't lost anybody." She released Zane's wrist. "Yet."

Janie's stomach swirled, and her entire body ached. "Do you think we have a chance?"

"Yes." Emma smoothed gray hair off Zane's broad forehead. "If the antibodies are associated with the X chromosome, then we just injected a *vampire's* blood, including the X chromosome, into our mates. It has to work."

Janie said a silent prayer for the cure to work. "Where's Dr. Morose?"

"After he declared you and the baby perfectly healthy, I put him to work in the lab synthesizing the cure. The baby's blood is . . . unique." Emma smiled. "Of course, she is the youngest prophet ever claimed."

"She'll be her own person, prophesy or not." Janie tucked the baby closer.

"Totally agree. You choose a name?" Emma asked.

"Not until Zane wakes up. God, I hope he wakes up soon."

Emma's eyes softened. "Me too."

Janie drew in a deep breath. "All right. Most of the vampires here are out cold. How vulnerable are we?" If she had to take up arms to protect her child and Zane until he awoke, she was going to need a painkiller.

"Nobody knows we're here," Emma said. "Even so, the healthy vampires have suited up and are ready to fight. You should see your brother—quite the leader Garrett has turned out to be."

Pride lifted Janie's chest. "I have full faith in Garrett."

"Me too. Sam has made public the treaty signed by Dage and Zane, so for now, the demon nation is holding tight."

"Waiting for Zane to make an appearance," Janie said. If Zane didn't step up soon, would the demons turn on them again? Or could Sam hold the nation together?

"Yes, and Felicity has sent out a video showing support for the treaty and pretty much threatening anybody who rises up against Zane. Then she gave orders for the demon nation to attack the Kurjans at their secondary location. That should buy us more time." Emma smiled. "I like Zane's mother. A lot."

"Me too," Janie agreed. Felicity had instantly sniffled tears at seeing her granddaughter, declaring her to be the most beautiful baby in the world. Felicity had good eyesight, and the street smarts to pitch the demons against the Kurjans while the Realm recuperated.

If it recuperated.

A rustle sounded, and Cara Kayrs moved into the room. "I came to check on my baby." She smiled and brushed a hand through Janie's hair. "And her baby." Delight somewhat lifted the worry from her eyes as she tucked the blanket more securely around her granddaughter. "She is perfect. Just perfect."

"I know," Janie said softly to her mother. "She has your eyebrows."

Cara chuckled. "I think she does."

Emma headed for the doorway. "I'll be back. Just want to check on Dage." She disappeared into the hallway.

Janie blinked. "How's Dad?"

Cara lost her smile. "The same. Garrett is with him now. Talen hasn't awakened." She focused on a too-silent Zane. "How about him?"

"Nothing." Janie's shoulders drew back. "He's still alive, so that has to be good. Right?"

"Right." Cara touched the sleeping baby's cheek and then straightened. "I'll check on the doctors in the lab and then go back to—"

"Mate? When I wake up, I expect you there," said a rough voice.

Janie's head jerked up. Talen stood at the doorway, an arm around his son for support.

Cara gasped and ran for her mate, sliding both arms around his waist. "You're awake."

Talen lifted an eyebrow. "I noticed." His gaze took in the room and landed on Janie. "My granddaughter?"

"Yes," Cara said, easing to his side and helping him forward.

Talen reached the baby, awe filling his eyes. "Look at her," he breathed. "A little Kayrs baby."

"Kyllwood," came a hoarse rasp from the bed.

Janie jumped to her feet. "Zane?"

Zane blinked several times and shoved himself to sit. He groaned. "How am I still breathing?"

"That's a long story." Janie smiled through her tears. "For now, meet your daughter."

His chest rose and he held out his arms. Janie placed the baby in them, a sense of rightness clicking into place. She turned to include her parents, but they'd disappeared with Garrett. No doubt giving her space. "How are you feeling?" she asked.

Zane's gentle smile filled her with hope. "Better. I can feel the healing cells awakening in me again. I'd forgotten the tingle." He rubbed his nose into the baby's hair. "You fulfilled your prophesy by first negating Suri's power and then by having a girl vampire who just may have saved the Realm."

Janie shook her head. "No. The first destiny was mine—the next was hers. She's less than a day old, and she's already fulfilled a fate."

"My girls. Overachievers." Zane sighed and pulled Janie up next to him on the table. "I have no doubt the two of you are just getting started."

Janie smiled through her tears, hope welling in her. God. Had they cured the virus? Could it be possible she could have a life with Zane and her baby?

Emma poked her head in, a huge smile curving her lips. "Just finished taking blood and running analysis. We've got it. The virus is going down." With a happy hop, she disappeared from sight again.

Janie's chin dropped to her chest. Emotion rushed through her so powerfully, she let out one low sob.

Zane held her closer, their baby protected between them. "We're all going to be okay, Belle."

"I know." And she did. For the first time in so long, she believed. "I tried to be strong, but I don't think I could've made it without you."

"You'll never be without me." He turned his head and brushed her cheek with a soft kiss. "I promise."

Janie lifted her chin and met his lips with hers before drawing back. "You can't make that promise."

"Sure I can." Green began to sizzle through his pupils, filling them with color. "I've loved you every second of this life, and if I died, I'd love you every second of the next. That, my beautiful Janie Belle, is something neither fate, destiny, nor stubborn will can change. Ever."

She closed her eyes, love washing through her with a completeness she'd never imagined. Then she opened them, not wanting to miss another moment with her family.

Zane stared at their daughter. "What should we name her?"

There really was only one possibility. Janie smiled. "Hope."

Zane smiled. "Hope Kayrs Kyllwood."

The baby, the future, awoke and looked up with serious, dark eyes full of light—and smiled.

Chapter 33

One year later

Cara Kayrs finished tucking in the African violet in a green pot, humming softly to herself in the small atrium off her kitchen. The lake outside shimmered in late fall weather, boosting her already good mood. She added a little jiggle to her butt.

"Now that's a damn fine sight," Talen said from the doorway.

She yelped and turned around. "Don't startle me like that." Taking off her gloves, she glanced down at her casual skirt and blouse to ensure she hadn't spilled any dirt. "We have a party to attend."

"A quick party. Then back here, and I'd like to see that dance again." His gorgeous golden eyes darkened.

Heat filled her face. On all that was holy. After two decades of marriage, after she had birthed his son, the vampire still had the ability to make her blush. Her empathic abilities allowed her to feel inside his skin, and sometimes his passion burned hot enough to singe them both. "I'm not missing a minute of my granddaughter's first birthday party, Talen. You'll just have to control yourself."

Big mistake. Or rather, a big challenge, which she'd meant wholeheartedly to throw down.

He advanced toward her, all male intent.

She chuckled and looked frantically for an escape. The vampire was between her and the door.

He grinned. "You didn't plan this room well, did you?"

She shook her head and drank him in. Healthy, virile, and strong. The gray hair had fallen out, leaving a world of bald vampires for the briefest of time as the virus cure took effect. Then health had descended upon them, and the color had returned to their eyes and skin just as their hair had begun to grow. Talen's thick brown mass now curled over his collar, although a gray strip remained as if a grim reminder of how close he'd come to dying.

"You know, I kinda liked you bald. You were a Mr. Clean badass," she teased, angling to the side for her one shot at the door.

He lunged and caught her about the waist, swinging her up with one arm. Easily.

The renewed, much darker brand on her hip began to burn. The Kayrs marking in full force after Talen had mated her again. Her golden cuff encircled her wrist again, and she clunked it against his jaw as she wrapped her arms around his neck. He pushed her up against the wall, settling comfortably between her legs. "Why do you always try to run?" he asked.

"So you can catch me."

He pressed a gentle kiss to her lips. "I'll always catch you."

"I know." Happiness burst through her chest. "Thank you for the atrium. I love this room." She wiggled against him, gratified when his eyes flared.

"The structure is sound and will withstand any blast." He smoothed her hair back from her face. "Although maybe we should've included another exit to the tunnels in our aboveground home."

She smiled. "We have six passages from our home alone. That's enough." The vampires had built a subdivision at the northern end of an Idaho lake, burrowing another headquarters underground into the massive mountains. This time they'd included missiles and defenses in the lake itself. "We're safe here."

"Unless there's another full out assault." Talen shook his head. "We had to bribe and threaten too many humans last time to keep our nation secret."

Cara pressed her breasts against his chest to distract him. "Who'll attack us? We're allies with everyone except the Kurjans, and they're so wounded, it'll take centuries to rebuild. Now stop worrying and start making me happy, mate."

One dark eyebrow rose. "Keep talking like that, and we won't make it to Hope's party."

She grinned. "It's our party, too. We started everything—all the matings, all the love. It was us, Talen."

His gaze gentled. "No, mate. It was you. All the love—only you could've created this for the Kayrs family and for me. Always you, Cara."

Well now. That was the sweetest thing ever. She bit her lip. "I think I might be getting baby fever."

"You want another baby?" Talen gripped her butt, opening her to him. "With Garrett and Logan going off to explore the world after Christmas, it's going to be lonely. Maybe it's time to have a few more sons."

Cara fingered his dark hair. "Or daughters."

Talen chuckled. "Vampires only have sons. Although Zane and Janie had a girl, that was a one-shot deal, I'm sure. Because of Zane's lineage."

Cara lifted a shoulder. "Oh, I don't know. You've had a vampiric X chromosome put into your bloodstream that actually changed and healed your pairs; it might be possible for you to have a girl. We won't know until we try."

He blinked. "Another daughter?" Then his smile split his face, and his head lowered toward hers. "Let's give it a shot." Then the sexiest, most dangerous, heavenly vampire leaned in and kissed her until she forgot to breathe.

Finally, he lifted his head. "I promised you forever, mate. Here it is."

Emma Kayrs sat on the settee in their bedroom, reading from a stack of printouts and swinging her leg. "Our scientists haven't found a way to use the virus cure for any human diseases. So far, we've only cured vampires."

Dage nimbly buttoned up a black dress shirt. "I don't see how the cure would apply to any other species."

"It hasn't." She sighed and set the papers on her dresser to study her mate. Very nice muscles filled out his shirt, while he'd tied his black hair at the nape. Even with the sliver of gray remaining mixed among the black, he looked young and virile. She smiled. "Talen is ticked your hair grew out faster than his."

"I know." White teeth flashed in Dage's grin as he fetched a grape energy drink from the dresser and took a big draw. "I texted him earlier and asked if I could borrow a hair band. He told me to bugger off."

Emma snorted. "You were in serious meetings with the witch, shifter, and demon nations earlier, and you took the time to mess with your brother?"

"Of course."

"How did the talks go?" Emma asked.

Dage toed on dress shoes. "They went well—mainly because of Zane. He has the demon nation well under control."

Emma shifted her weight to get more comfortable, glad she'd chosen a light dress for the party. The expertly cut material was sleeveless and showed off her beautiful Kayrs marking on her shoulder blade. "You sound impressed with Zane."

Dage nodded. "I am. Zane's a good leader, even though he doesn't want to rule."

"Maybe that's the key," Emma murmured. "Where did you go after the meetings? I thought you'd be home sooner."

He chuckled. "You're the psychic. You tell me."

She shrugged. "I get visions but never when I want them. My last vision included seeing Garrett and Logan partying next spring break with a bunch of human girls. Believe me, I saw more than I wanted."

"Now that's funny." Dage rubbed his chin. "Earlier, Jase and Conn were training in the southern gym, and I went to watch. They kicked the crap out of each other." Joy filled the king's laugh this time.

Emma shook her head. "It's amazing to see everyone back to normal. Healthy and ready to hit somebody." She gasped. "Oh my gosh. I forgot to tell you the news."

Dage lifted one dark eyebrow. "News?"

"Yes. We managed to synthesize Virus-27. The characteristics of the virus that negate the allergy aspect in mates."

He blinked. "So you can take away the mating aspects in widows and widowers?"

She nodded. "Yes. Well, and conceivably even in mated couples if wanted."

"Immortal divorces. Not sure I like that."

She'd figured he'd be concerned. "Freedom matters, King. You know that."

"I agree." He sighed. "Though you haven't tested the new serum with mated people still alive, now have you?"

She couldn't help but smiling. "No."

Triumph filled his gaze. "So it might not work—I mean, if both parties are still living."

She winked. "Thanks to everyone's hard work, we have so many vampires healthy and living now. Finally some peace."

"It is good to be alive." Dage's graze dropped to her barely swelling tummy. "Speaking of life, how are you feeling?"

"Better." She'd thrown up for the first three months of her pregnancy, leaving Dage worried and as grumpy as a wounded bear. "The moment I hit the second trimester last week, I just felt hungry. No more nausea."

"Thank God." He finished the drink and tossed the empty into an antique trash can.

Emma rubbed her belly, warmth cascading through her. "So long ago, when we were running through that scary forest from the Kurjans, did you think we'd end up like this?"

"Like what?"

She glanced down, her heart expanding. "Happy?"

The king strode toward her and dropped to his knees between hers. One large hand flattened over her abdomen. "Yes."

She looked up into shining silver eyes streaking with blue. The blue was just for her. The most powerful being in the world, possibly ever, knelt in front of her, giving her everything. Giving her him. "I love you," she whispered.

The blue overtook the silver. "I dreamed of you for centuries, and the reality of the true you blows every fantasy I created out of existence. Without you, love, I don't have a life."

The words slid right into her soul. "Dage—"

"With you, I have the universe. Only you, Em. Always."

Sarah Petrovsky straightened up the lesson plans spread across the kitchen table, taking a moment to feel the vibrations from an old stack of geography maps sent by a shifter teacher in Wyoming.

Warmth and happiness cascaded from the paper. Apparently the elderly wolf liked teaching as much as Sarah did.

"Milaya?" Max strode into the room, holding a bouquet of yellow daisies.

Sarah gasped, pleasure sparking through her from the nickname as well as the flowers. "For me?"

"Of course." Max handed them over. "My pretty one."

The name sounded just as lovely in English as Russian. "Thank you." She inhaled the flowers' rich scent and plunked them in a vase on the counter. "I love them."

His massive shoulders relaxed. "Good." He tugged his shirt over his head and turned for the laundry room. "Do I have a dress shirt anywhere?"

"Hanging up and already ironed," she said, her gaze eating him up and landing on the jagged tattoo of a phoenix winding over his right shoulder. Those shoulders, fully healthy now, could probably shield a village.

The scars lining his lower back, raised and white, spoke of his difficult childhood.

He reached in and grabbed a pink shirt, and the smile he flashed spoke of a happy adulthood. With the Kayrs family and with her. "I am not wearing pink."

"Come on. Hope giggles whenever you let your vampire eyes show." While all vampires had a secondary eye color, only Max had pink. A beautiful, stunning, sizzling pink that was only a shade lighter than it had been before the virus had nearly taken him away.

Max scratched his head. "Yeah, she does. Well, okay." He shrugged into the shirt and rapidly buttoned it up.

Sarah grinned. Even in the delicate color, the vampire looked deadly. A strong and rugged face with messy brown hair swept back made him look like he'd never even been sick a day.

He moved toward her, ferocious and wild, completely solid. "Keep the smile. You owe me for each and every dig I take from my family today over the pink shirt."

"Sounds like a plan," she murmured.

He reached her in two strides, both hands grasping her waist and lifting her onto the table. "We trying for a baby again tonight?"

"What? Twice this morning wasn't enough for you?" She pressed her thighs in on his, her hands flattening across his muscled chest.

"No." He tangled a strong hand in her hair. "It would've been three times, but I had to check on Hope."

Sarah nodded. The second the vampires had begun to heal, she'd followed him as Max had shown up outside Janie and Zane's temporary room and declared himself bodyguard to the baby. The demon had taken one look at Max's serious face and had nodded. That Zane was a smart guy. "Little Hope is still smiling the most at you?"

"Of course." Max's chest puffed out, and amusement filled his rapidly pinkening eyes. "Ticks Zane off every time."

"You're terrible." Sarah laughed.

"That's not what you said this morning." Max leaned in and nuzzled her neck, shooting sparks directly south to her sex.

She pushed. "We have to get moving. The party starts in just a few minutes."

"I bet I could change your mind."

"Yes." She levered herself back to cup his whiskered chin. "Always." Then she glanced at the pretty flowers. "Although you don't have to keep bringing me flowers, candy, and presents. I mean, I love it, but you can relax."

He shook his head. "I made you a promise, years ago, that I'd court you."

Love for him welled through her. "We've been mated for decades."

"I know. After I mated you, I promised I'd still court you. Then the virus hit, the war went crazy, and we had to go into survival mode. Things are good now. So, Sarah?"

She smiled, her gaze on her one true love. "Yes?"

"Be prepared to be courted. A lot."

Connlan Kayrs leaned over the crib to tickle his son's belly. Bright green eyes sparkled up from the babe's seven-month-old face, full of fun and a little craziness. Yeah. Definitely Moira's child.

His brother kicked pudgy feet next to him, his gaze more thoughtful and serious. His eyes glowed a burnished silver.

Twins.

Conn winked at the little guys. His wild witch of a mate had given him twin boys. One had already set the nursery on fire. The new nursery in the subdivision was fireproof, as was most of the house.

Moira's boots echoed on the tile outside, her lilac scent preceding her arrival. "You mixed up the food in the refrigerator again."

He grinned and turned. Yeah, he'd placed the limes in the cold-cut drawer just to mess with her. "You really need to let go of the fridge organization problem."

She lifted a creamy shoulder. "Food should be organized. You know that."

Crazy and compulsive. No wonder he loved the petite little witch. Red curls cascaded down her back, showcasing smooth skin. For the party, she'd donned a crimson blouse with black skirt and matching boots. "You look lovely, Dailtín."

She blushed. "I'm the mother of two boys. Perhaps it's time to stop calling me *brat*."

Not when it brought such a glimmer of pleasure to her stunning eyes. "At this point, it's tradition." One he liked and she'd definitely earned.

Moira frowned and strode to touch his still aching jaw. "Who hit you?"

"Jase." Pleased humor tipped his lips. "We trained earlier." Like the old days before they'd all taken ill. "It was great. I threw him across the gym and dented the new wall. Dage was pissed."

Moira smiled and slipped her hands down his chest. "Aye. I do so appreciate your stamina returning."

As did he. With a sigh, he sent healing cells to his chin. "How was your teleconference with the other witch enforcers?"

"Good. Kell is afraid the news about phanakite has gotten out to the Kurjans, but I think he's worrying unnecessarily. Plus, he insists we call it planekite when discussing it, and that's just silly. The mineral has several names." Moira leaned to the side and cooed to her babies. "Oh, so cute. You dressed them in the outfits Brenna bought in Ireland last month."

Conn looked over his shoulder at the matching green and white jumpers. "They'll outgrow them in a month, so I figured they should wear them at least once." He couldn't believe how quickly the little guys had already grown. "Plus, in between throwing punches at my face earlier, Jase hinted it would please Brenna to see the outfits."

Moira grinned. "Aye. Bren has been out of sorts because some loony group in Ireland still wants her to be their leader. A total bunch of nut jobs."

Conn shrugged. "Makes me happy you're a witch enforcer and not on the Council. Probably makes the loony group safer, too."

Moira smoothed down his T-shirt. "I wouldn't say that. Apparently Jase knocked one of the loonies into the Liffey. It's cold this time of year."

Her soft hands on him sent desire straight to his groin. "We have a little time before the party," he said.

Those soft lips curved in sin. "No, we don—"

His mouth took hers, delving deep into warmth and woman. Turning, he sank his fangs into her neck. Honey and spice exploded across his tongue, followed by a punch of real power. She sighed against him, elongating her neck to allow him deeper access. He drank and then licked the wound closed.

Her eyes shone dark and unfocused. "Connlan," she breathed.

"You're the best choice I ever made, Dailtín. I love you."

Tears glimmered in her eyes. A powerful woman sharing her emotions. "I love you."

Conn tucked her close and caught sight of his babies before rubbing his chin on her unruly hair. His chest settled as he kept hold and kept watch over what mattered most in this world or in any other.

Family.

Kane Kayrs was running late. As usual. After taking a fast shower, he hustled through the bedroom into his sprawling closet, a towel wrapped around his waist. "Amber?" he called out.

A rustle echoed, and she skidded around the corner, paint caught in her wild blond hair. The scent of wild heather, just blooming, came with her. "What?"

He grinned and shook out his wet hair. "One of us needs to be conscious of the time. I vote you."

She wiped paint onto her jeans, her freckles standing out on her stunning face. "You're the logical one. Time is logical." She paused. "Right?"

"Some say time is merely a theory."

"Let's go with that." She stepped out of her peasant blouse and kicked her jeans to the side. "You showered without me."

He dropped the towel and reached for his woman. "I erroneously thought you would've already showered." Though why in the world he'd thought she'd be more organized than he was beyond him. "Weren't you supposed to drop by the lab and remind me of the party?"

She pursed her pretty pink lips. "I think you were supposed to pop by the new rec room and get me. We've been painting it all day, and the kids are gonna love it."

"I'm sure, *Beag Gaisscioch.*" His *little warrior.* "Guess what?"

"What?" Her eyes lit with the hope of a good surprise.

He loved her bizarre enjoyment of surprises, considering he couldn't stand behind taken off guard. "We figured out how to negate the mating aspect today."

She clapped her hands together. "My grandma Hilde can get re-mated! Oh my."

The *oh my* was a freakin' understatement. "Yes. God help the male vampires." His wife's grandmother had been mated in her early forties and would no doubt go on the prowl as soon as possible. Although Kane knew a certain badass soldier named Oscar whom he'd bet on. "Let's not tell Hilde today."

Laughter bubbled up from Amber. "That's a deal."

He lifted her and retraced his steps to the stone-wall shower, twisting the knob and setting his mate under the warm stream.

She gasped and shut those stunning dark eyes, emitting a low, sexy moan of pleasure that shot straight to his cock.

What the hell. Kane stepped into her, pressing her against the wall.

Her eyes opened, and pleasure curved her smile. "I thought we didn't have time."

"I thought we agreed time didn't exist." His lips captured hers, and he coaxed her into relaxing. Into submitting. The second she softened, he pressed harder, lost in the whirlwind created by his mate.

His illogical, disorganized, emotional mate who loved so completely. He didn't deserve her, without a doubt. But he was keeping her.

Slowly, he released her lips and drew back to gaze at the woman who'd taught him he had a heart. "I love you."

Her smile rivaled any scientific discovery ever made. "I love you more."

"That's impossible." He reached for cinnamon-scented shampoo to rub through her curls. "I'm a scientist and know quantitative analysis."

She tilted back her head and closed her eyes. "You know it turns me on when you use such big words."

"You turn me on just by breathing." He helped her rinse her hair and then washed her head to toe. By the time he was finished, she was panting and he was in pain. He lifted her, impaling her in one smooth move.

Her eyes widened and she gasped. "Well now. We're going to be late to the party."

He kissed her again, trying to find the right words. When he'd thought the virus was going to make him leave her, he'd been full of more pain than he'd thought imaginable. Now, healed, he wanted to spend each day keeping her safe and loved. She continued to amaze him. "Not once did you give up hope, did you?" he rumbled against her mouth.

"Never." She clasped her ankles at the small of his back, her fingers curling over his shoulders. "There's no way you'd leave me in this life alone."

Such absolute faith both intrigued and humbled him. "You're right. Wherever you are, I will be." He didn't lie or evade, so when he gave the words, they were a vow. "I promise, Amber."

Jase Kayrs stretched his jaw and rolled his dislocated shoulder back into place as he pushed open the front door to his home. Sparring with Conn had been fun. Over the top, joyous, hit after hit fun. Damn, it felt good to be strong again. He'd even commanded the oxygen to rip open and drop water onto Conn's face. His brother was lucky he hadn't created a snowstorm.

Chuckling, Jase shoved inside and shut the door.

His mate sat next to a crackling fireplace, a cup of tea in her hand, her face pale.

"Bren?" he asked, reaching her in long strides, her vanilla scent soothing him. "What's wrong?"

"Nothing." She swallowed and gestured toward the sofa. "Have a seat." Her gray eyes were veiled, and her hand shook as she lifted the cup to her lips.

He faltered and then sat, his knees brushing hers as he faced her. "Whatever it is, I'll fix it."

Her smile lifted his spirits. "That's a sweet thing to say."

"I'm not sweet." Nobody in the world would accuse Jase Kayrs of being nice.

"Sure you are." She reached up with her free hand and ran a finger down the long scar extending from his forehead to his jaw. Her very touch seemed to heal him. Then she sighed and removed her glasses, revealing those pretty gray eyes that held such kindness. "Very sweet."

He took the cup from her and placed it on the table before taking both her hands in his. "What has you worried?" Though he could probably read her mind, that usually ticked her off, so he stayed out. For now.

"Our lives have been a whirlwind."

"Yes." He kept his hold gentle on her fragile hands.

She swallowed. "We mated to save my life, and between the war and the virus going airborne, we really haven't had time to reevaluate."

Panic lifted his chin. "There's no reevaluating. Period." His voice came out a low command, one most people would heed.

Bren merely lifted one dark eyebrow. "While the treaty may have covered all contingencies, we have still made our own way. But we haven't discussed everything."

His shoulders shot back. She'd heard about the trials to reverse the mating bond. "Oh baby, I have no idea where your mind is, but if you even think of negating my mating bond, I'll have you on your knees to discuss it."

Her eyes darkened to the color of storm clouds. "Last time I was on my knees, we decided to mate."

"Exactly." He'd put her there again until she agreed to stop talking about reevaluating anything. "What's going on, Bren? You love me."

"Of course I love you." She pushed a strand of hair out of her eyes. "And I'm keeping your marking."

"I know." Yeah. He sounded arrogant. "Spit it out so we can get to the party."

She tried to remove her hands, and he tightened his hold. She sighed and looked him right in the eyes. "We never discussed this, and we haven't planned. But I'm pregnant."

His mouth dropped open, and he released her hands. "Pregnant?"

"Yes." Her hands fluttered in the air. "It seems like you all healing has somehow brought on a baby boom. I know we haven't discussed children, not really—"

"Pregnant?" Joy caught him around the throat and squeezed. He leaped and picked her up, swinging her around.

She laughed.

He buried his head in her neck. A baby. Bren's baby. For so long, he'd been tortured by demons, and he'd welcomed death. Then he'd been ruled by revenge until he fell for her. Finally, the virus had all but guaranteed his demise. Now he lived.

And he was having a baby.

Elation filled him until his chest hurt. He fell back onto the sofa, cradling everything he loved. "Well, I guess we should discuss this."

Her eyes sparkled as she settled against him. "You're happy."

He shook his head, his lips curving. "There isn't a word for what I am. Nothing comes close to how I feel." He pressed his lips against hers, trying to show her how precious she was to him. "Thank you, Brenna."

She kissed him back, love shining in her eyes when she drew away. "You had a part in this."

"No." He sobered, his gaze remaining on hers. "You saved me, and you gave me this life. Only you, Bren." He didn't know how, but he'd spend the rest of his days showing her what she'd done and how much she meant to him. "You're my light in a very dark world, and you always will be."

Chapter 34

Zane handed his baby girl over to his mother, who sat on the sofa next to Cara. They cooed together, completely charmed by the one-year-old. A pretty white dress decorated with bows made up her outfit, while bright green sandals adorned her tiny feet. Max stood a few feet away, always near, and somehow Zane had not only become accustomed to the big lug's presence, he'd started to take reassurance in the idea.

A huge stack of presents sat next to a stone fireplace that almost served as the focal point in the main rec room in the largest lodge. It was close, but the stunning lake outside the floor-to-ceiling windows took center stage. Balloons danced in the air, and party streamers cascaded from wall to wall.

He leaned against a wall and accepted a beer from his younger brother. "Thanks."

Sam nodded, his gaze encompassing the large gathering. "Shifters, witches, and vampires . . . oh my."

Zane grinned and tilted his head toward a prowling cat and a gorgeous feline shifter. "That's Jordan and Katie Pride, the heads of the lions. They have twin girls around here somewhere."

Sam took a long swig of beer. "I met Jordan earlier on the shooting range. He's a good shot."

"Should be." Zane pointed over at a bunch of wolf shifters. "Terrent and Maggie Vilks, as well as a bunch of their clan. He's one dangerous bastard." Yeah, Zane liked Terrent. A lot.

Sam nodded. "Yet they're all here to celebrate our girl's first birthday. Weird world you've joined."

"We've joined," Zane returned. It hadn't been easy splitting his time between Realm headquarters and the new demon headquarters, but since he'd made sure they were located within a mile of each other, it hadn't been overly difficult, either. "Thanks for having my back, Sam."

"Of course and always." Sam gave a half-nod to a pretty witch flirting with him from across the room. "Now, if you'll excuse me." He grabbed two more bottles from the bar and sauntered through the crowd.

Zane grinned.

"What's so funny?" Janie asked, sidling up to him.

"Sam's about to get shot down by a witch."

Janie pursed her lips, her gaze across the room. "Not from where I'm standing. Sam may get lucky."

Zane turned his focus on Janie's sky blue eyes. "What about me?"

Her smile revealed even white teeth. "Depends if you play your cards right."

"Meaning?" He lowered his voice to a demon growl, knowing full well how it affected her.

A visible shiver wound up her shoulders, and a pretty blush covered her cheeks. "You clean up Hope after she eats cake."

He grimaced. "We're really not going to give her a whole cake, are we?"

"Of course." Delight lifted Janie's lips.

His life had been colorless before Janie had joined it. Like the dream world, he'd just existed without real light. Now light and love surrounded him. "Tomorrow morning our mothers are taking turns watching Hope for a week," he said.

Janie blinked. "Why?"

"We're going on a vacation."

"Really?" She looked around the festivities at family and friends. "Can we just take off like that?"

He slipped an arm over her small shoulders. "We can. It's time we had some fun without war, without ruling, without worry. Just a week."

Her smile warmed his heart. "Where are we going?"

"It's a surprise." A warm, very nice, extremely private villa on an island where clothes weren't necessary. "It'll be our new dream world."

She turned and stretched up on her toes to kiss him. "Sounds lovely."

He kissed her back. "Do you miss the dream world?" Since they'd blown it up, they hadn't been able to re-enter. The place, wherever it had been, no longer existed.

"No." She rubbed his chin. "Real life is so much better now that you're in it."

Her sweetness knocked his knees out from under him each time. Every time. "I love you, Belle."

She sighed and snuggled into him. "I love you."

Yeah. Life was pretty damn perfect.

Janie laughed, her heart full, trying to wipe frosting off her daughter's nose. "Maybe letting her go at the cake was a bad idea."

Zane nodded, grimacing as he removed a frosting-covered sandal. "It was your idea."

Prophet Lily Donovan clapped her hands together. "No, it was wonderful. She enjoyed herself so much, and we took lovely pictures."

Her mate, Caleb, stood well back and away from flying frosting. "You're all crazy."

Hope turned sparkling black eyes toward him and let out a giggle.

Caleb smiled, the harshness of his features disappearing. "The girl has good taste." Then he lowered his chin and gentled his gaze. "Forget that marking on your neck, little one. If you want to be a prophet, great. If not, tell Fate to . . . push off."

"Nicely put," Zane said dryly, shaking the second sandal.

Caleb ducked as frosting flew by his head to stick to the stone mantel. "Let's hit the bar, Lily." Holding out his arm, he waited until his mate slipped hers into place. Then he winked at Hope and headed off.

Talen arrived with more towels. "You made a nice mess, sweet girl," he cooed to Hope.

Hope grinned, showing one new tooth. "Tayen."

Janie stilled, and Zane's head jerked up.

"What did she say?" Zane asked. He leaned toward his daughter. "Hope?"

The girl waved chubby arms. "Tayen."

Janie laughed and turned toward her father. "You taught her to say your name."

Zane shook his head. "Her first word. *Talen.*"

Talen rubbed his whiskered chin. "Well, I . . . don't know. I've been saying 'Realm' and 'vampire' to her. Not my name."

Janie shrugged. "She is smart."

Cara bustled up with a wet washrag and quickly went to work on the girl's hands. "I've been trying to get her to say Grandma."

"Tayen," Hope said, clapping her now clean hands together.

Talen leaned down and kissed the girl's frosting-covered hair. "Just perfect."

Cara threw the rag at him and stood. "You're buying me dinner."

Talen grinned and grabbed her hand. "I happen to know a wonderful buffet—just across the room." Sweeping her up, he barely kept her legs from hitting several people as he hauled her across the room.

Zane shook his head. "Your parents."

"Your in-laws." Janie finished with Hope just as Felicity showed up to take the girl.

"Good timing," Zane said.

Felicity patted Hope's dark hair. "Your mother is no dummy." Then she smiled at Janie. "Take a moment and have some fun. I've got our girl."

Janie grinned and stood. "There's frosting in your hair, Felicity."

Zane's mother laughed as she took her granddaughter toward the buffet.

Janie slipped her hand in Zane's. "We're so fortunate to all be here."

Zane nodded and opened a door to the deck, nudging her outside into peace. With a wisp of sound, he lifted her and maneuvered around deck furniture to drop onto a wide chair facing the sparkling lake. The late afternoon sun glimmered on the soft waves, and a rather warm fall breeze stirred the colorful leaves surrounding them. "Ah. Quiet."

Janie fingered his thick hair, settling in to home. "Remember the first time we met?"

"In a dream world. You were so small and brave." He ran a large-boned hand down her back. "Even then, I knew we'd end up like this."

"Like what?"

"Happy." He turned the most beautiful green eyes toward her. The virus had lightened the inner part of his iris, leaving a darker green ring around it. Very sexy, actually. "You and me."

Janie inhaled his rugged scent. "I always hoped we'd find and keep each other."

"Keep?" He kissed her, pouring so much passion and love into her she forgot where he ended and she began. She could barely breathe when he lifted his head. "We belong with each other. In each and every world. My Janie Belle."

Epilogue

Six years later

Hope Kayrs Kyllwood snapped her fingers and turned the sky a light blue. She wrinkled her nose and then changed the hue to a darker blue that made the yellow sun seem brighter. Yeah. That was better.

A bubbling stream wound next to a grassy bank, so she added a bunch of flat rocks around.

The forest behind her remained green and quiet, so she took a moment to sit on a rock and wait. A few pink birds hopped by her feet, and she waved at them.

The second he entered the forest, she straightened. Her hands smoothed down her new jeans, and she hoped her new sweater fit nice. She'd received both for her birthday the day before. The blue of the sweater matched the prophesy marking on her neck.

When he strode out of the trees, she straightened. Wow. He was a lot taller than she'd expected. Even so, she stood bravely to meet him.

His head swiveled left and right, and he crouched low as if waiting for a strike.

"Um, you're safe here," she called out.

He glanced up at the sun, which shone off his black hair and brought out the many strands of red woven throughout.

"The sun won't burn you." She clasped her hands together, wondering if she should've waited another year before meeting him. But seven was a lucky number, and she'd just turned seven. "I promise."

He frowned and stalked toward her like one of the shifter boys about to pounce on each other. When he reached her, she had to stop herself from stepping back.

"You're super tall," she breathed.

He looked down. "I'm seven."

"Me too."

He shook his head. "You're too small for seven." His voice was nice, and he smelled like the trees. This close, she could see the purple ring surrounding his dark green eyes. Pretty. Very pretty.

"I'm seven," she repeated. Maybe she should stand on one of the rocks.

He glanced at the sun again. "Am I dreaming?"

She sighed. "No. I mean, not really. Well, you're kind of asleep, but not completely." She didn't understand how it worked, but someday she would. When she was older and studied all those big books of Great-Uncle Kane's.

"Okay. Who are you?" the boy asked.

Oh yeah. She held out a hand like her teacher, Sarah, had taught her. "I'm Hope. I'm a vampire."

He blinked. "You're a girl."

"Yes." She smiled. He was quite smart.

He scratched his chin and then shook her hand, keeping his grip super gentle. "I'm Drake, son of Dayne. I'm a Kurjan."

"Oh. I'm daughter of Zane." She hadn't learned that way of saying her name. "Hey. Our daddy's names rhyme."

He smiled and let go of her hand. "Yeah."

What a very nice smile.

He pointed toward a big rock in the center of the stream. "What's that?"

She didn't need to look to see the large green book lying on the rock. "That's my book."

"What's in it?" he asked, squinting to see better.

"Dunno." Someday the book would open for her, but she wasn't ready yet. "Maybe it's our book."

He coughed. "I doubt it. We're enemies."

She shook her head, her hair flying. "Only if we want to be. I don't wanna be." She patted his big arm.

He looked at the book, then at her hand on his arm, and finally at the sun. "Then what are we?"

A bird screeched in the forest, and he jumped, putting himself between the noise and Hope. A waddling cockatoo slid out from behind a tree, and Drake relaxed.

Hope smiled. He had wanted to protect her. That was good. Although she'd protect him, too. She waited until he looked back at her. "Want to walk by the stream and feel the sun?" she asked.

He cleared his throat. "Okay."

They started to walk, and before long, Hope slid her hand into his. "You asked what we are."

He glanced down at their joined hands and then up at the grassy trail in front of them. "Yes."

"How about we be friends?" She held her breath, making sure not to trip on small rocks as they walked.

He was quiet for several steps. Finally, he nodded and tightened his hold on her hand. "Okay. Friends."

The air whooshed out of her lungs. Happiness filled her, and she gave a little hop. "That's good. Okay. Because you and me, Drake?"

"Yeah?"

"We're gonna change the world."

Please read on for a sneak peek at Book 1 in a new related series, the Realm Enforcers, coming next June.

Chapter 1

Kellach Dunne held his fire at bay and turned the corner, keeping his prey in sight. Rain smattered the concrete sidewalk in a weary Seattle fashion, while garish lights from bars and massage parlors marred the comforting darkness of the midnight hour. He stepped over the legs of a bum and ignored the stench of piss, absently wishing for his bed and a good night's sleep.

Instead, he'd left his Harley parked in a side alley to follow the bastard who stalked a woman through the city's underbelly.

The woman scurried ahead, glancing over her shoulder, her instincts obviously kicking in. Her tight neon blue minidress hampered her movements, but he could appreciate the outfit. The kind that curved in just under the ass . . . and the woman had a hell of an ass. Too bad she tottered in her five inch heels—and from what smelled like Fireball.

He opened his senses to the night and the universe, scenting what humans couldn't even imagine. Yep. Fireball and tequila. Dangerous combination. Although a lingering scent, just under the surface, sped up his blood.

Woman. Fresh and clean . . . all woman.

The man ahead of him stank of body odor, cheap cologne, and cigarette smoke. And something else, something that made Kellach's temples pound.

Damn it, hellfire, and motherfucker.

The bastard had taken the drug. The human had somehow ingested the drug right under Kell's nose.

Kell had hung out in the Seattle underground bar for nearly a week, and somehow, the dealer had gotten past him. No wonder the human was hunting the woman. He wouldn't be able to help himself.

She broke into a run.

Surprisingly agile on those heels as she reacted to the imminent danger, she leaped over a mud puddle and turned down a barely lit alley.

Why the fuck did they always run down an alley? Shaking his head, Kellach increased his strides while the human male in front of him did the same. Idiot didn't even know Kellach was tracking him.

The woman ran by two overflowing Dumpsters, a couple of garbage cans, a cardboard box housing a vagrant who smelled like pot, and an odd arrangement of yellow flowerpots perched on the back stoop of a porn shop.

The woman reached the end of the alley, found herself blocked by a brick building, and whirled around.

Gorgeous. The moonlight slanted down through the clouds, highlighting a stunning face. Even with a ridiculous amount of blue eye shadow, pink blush, and bright red lipstick, the woman was a looker. Deep blue eyes, the color of the witching hour, stared out from a fine-boned face.

A woman like that not only didn't belong in a fucking alley . . . she didn't belong in the bar she'd just left.

The human male slowed and let out a low chuckle that sounded slightly manic. He towered over the woman, even in her heels, and before Kell's eyes, his shoulders seem to broaden in his flannel shirt. "Looks like you're at a dead end," the guy said.

The woman sucked in air, her chest moving nicely with the effort. "Wh-what is wrong with your eyes?"

The human shrugged.

Yep. His eyes should be all sorts of fucking crazy at this point. The skin down Kell's arm sprang to life, and the hair rose in warning. The atmosphere changed.

Flames, morphing and an unhealthy dark blue, danced down the human male's right arm. He gasped and shook out his wrist. Then he threw back his head and laughed. "Did you see that?"

The woman gaped and then slowly shook her head. "Did you just set your arm on fire?"

"No. I am fire." He held out his arm again, and flames licked down.

The woman inched to the side of the alley and stumbled over a loose brick. "What drug are you on?" Her focus narrowed to the guy's eyes as she regained her footing.

"Who cares? I'm invincible, and I can create fire." More flames danced. The guy formed a ball in one hand. "Take off the dress, or I'll burn it off."

"That's not going to happen," Kell said, moving to the other side of the woman.

The guy whirled around, fire whipping. "What the hell?"

"Been following you." Kell kept his hands loosely at his sides while fighting back the urge to alter matter with quantum physics and create his own fire. Just being in the same vicinity as another fire starter, one who didn't have a clue what to do, made him itchy. "Get lost, lady. I have business with the gentleman here."

The guy squinted. "You Australian?"

Kell drew himself up. Australian? Fucking moron. "No. Move. Now." He spoke the order for the woman, who'd frozen in place.

The guy shook his head. "If she moves, I'll burn her. Even through the rain, I'm all powerful."

"Wh-what's your business?" asked the woman as she took a tentative step along the building. Water sloshed up her shapely leg, and she had to shove wet hair away from her face.

"Doesn't concern you." Kell angled deeper into the alley so the guy would have to partially turn to keep him in sight, thus giving the woman a chance for freedom. Rain spattered into his eyes. "Just get moving, would you?"

"No." The guy shook out both hands, and fire danced. Blue and yellow stripes cut paths through his brown eyes, and red bloomed in the white parts. "I'll kill you both."

Kellach sighed. "How much of the drug did you take?" If the guy had only taken half a dose, he might live.

"The whole damn thing." The guy spun around, and plasma fire shot into a Dumpster, ripping a hole in the metal. "They'd said I'd be a god. I'm a fucking god."

The woman cringed back against the brick building. "I don't understand. What kind of a weapon throws fire?"

Kell shot forward and slid an arm around the guy's neck, spinning him into a headlock, their backs to the woman. Fire burst along the guy's arms, burning Kell. Pain dug under his skin. With a low growl, Kell allowed his own fire free. Deep and green, it crackled along his body, shielding him from harm. With a puff of smoke, Kell's fire quelled the human's.

The human convulsed. Hard and fast, he shook against Kell, who held him upright. It was too late to help the guy—he had taken too much. Way too much. A wretched scream spilled from the human's throat.

Kell released him and stepped back.

The guy fell to the wet ground, still convulsing. Red poured from his ears, his eyes, and then his nose. He hit hard, shook, and then went still. His eyes retained the bizarre colors as he looked sightlessly up at the cloudy night. The rain mingled with blood across his face.

Kell sighed and pushed wet hair out of his eyes. He needed to get rid of the body and then somehow convince the woman she hadn't just seen what she'd just seen. Plastering on his most charming smile, he turned around and froze.

"Seattle PD. Freeze, asshole," she whispered, her stance set, a Glock 22 in her hands and pointed at his head.

Detective Alexandra Monzelle kept her balance on the ridiculous heels and her gun pointed at the definite threat.

Well over six feet tall, muscled, graceful as hell . . . the guy facing her showed no fear. No emotion, really. Black hair fell to his broad shoulders, the darkness a perfect match for his eyes. Chiseled face, huge-ass hands, and feet big enough to waterski on. Yet he moved with the smoothness of a trained soldier.

He lifted one dark eyebrow. "Seattle Police Department?"

She nodded and tried to keep from shaking from the chill in the air on her bare skin. Way too much bare skin, but she'd been undercover. "Get on your knees."

Intrigue leaped into his glittering eyes. "Not garing ta happen."

Was that a true Irish brogue? It fit him somehow. "I will shoot you."

He shrugged a massive shoulder beneath a leather duster. "'Tis your choice, lass."

Did he just fucking call her *lass* like some lady from a century ago? "Oh no, Irish boy. Get on your knees—now." She put every ounce of command into her voice that she possessed.

"Well, now. At least ya knew I was from Ireland." He glanced down at the dead man and his foot slid forward as if to kick him. Then, apparently changing his mind, he focused on her again and smiled. "As opposed to Australia."

Okay. She really didn't want another body on her hands, but in the dress and heels, she was at a physical disadvantage. The last thing she wanted was to spend all night filling out more paperwork than had already been created. "Down. Now."

He cocked his head to one side. "I can't help but ask where you were keeping your weapon." His gaze, dark and intense, roved over her entire body.

Tingles. Damn weird and very unwelcome tingles cascaded wherever his gaze landed. She might just have to shoot the bastard and fill out the paperwork anyway. "I don't want to shoot you, but I can live with the decision. So get on your knees or say a quick prayer to your Maker."

He glanced over his shoulder. "I don't suppose you have backup coming?"

No. Her backup had followed the dealer. She shook her head to provide warning and lowered her aim to his right leg. "I guess losing one leg won't kill you."

His focus returned to her. "You shoot me, and we're going to have a problem." He spoke slowly and clearly, without a hint of distress.

A chill wandered down her back. The man was damn serious . . . and damn scary. Yet she couldn't let any fear show. So she sighed and tightened her arms to shoot. "If you'd just get on your knees, this night would go so much more smoothly."

"Say *please*."

She blinked. Seriously? Hell, if it got him to cooperate, she'd chirp a Haiku. "Please."

"As you wish." Graceful as any dancer, he dropped to his knees. Water splashed up.

Funny, but the guy didn't seem any less dangerous. She cleared her throat. "Cross your ankles."

He sighed and crossed huge-ass boots. "Why were you trapping this guy?"

Her handcuffs were in her purse in the bar, and she hadn't had a chance to grab it before rushing out so the guy would take the bait. Her gun, on the other hand, had been strapped to her inner thigh. "Clasp your hands together on the back of your head."

He kept her gaze and clasped his hands on that thick black hair. His shirt pulled tight over defined muscles in his chest, and now he seemed more in control of the situation than ever. "You don't have cuffs."

Yep. Might just have to shoot him. "My partner will be here soon." God. She hoped Bernie would be there soon.

"Aye, I'm sure." The man glanced at the body. "Do you know how he died?"

"Overdose." Duh. "What's your name?"

"Kellach." He lifted both eyebrows. "What's yours?"

"Detective Monzelle." Everyone called her Lex. Between waning of the adrenaline rush, the chilly rain, and her aching arms, the gun became heavy. Yet she didn't twitch. "What do you know about the drug?"

"What drug?" The man's eyelids half-closed as if she were boring him to sleep.

Man, she'd like to plug him one in the leg just to get his attention. "You asked about the drug. It's too late to play dumb."

He shrugged.

"Okay, then how about explaining all of that fire. Did you douse yourself with some weird accelerant?" She couldn't quite come up with a reasonable explanation for the strange glow along both his and the corpse's skin, so he'd better damn well explain. "Where's the weapon?"

"No weapon. It's a chemical that looks like fire but obviously isn't."

True—no burn marks marred his skin or the dead guy. So who was

Kellach? Was he a rival dealer or something else? He wore a leather duster, flack boots, and faded jeans. Motorcycle gang member?

His head lifted, and his nostrils flared just like a German shepherd she'd seen scouting for drugs once.

Two long shadows mingled along the alley floor, and two men drew nearer. Deep blue flames morphed along the arm of one of the guys. More of the damn weapons?

"Ballocks," Kellach muttered before launching himself off the asphalt and right at her. He cleared the dead body, wrapped his arms around her, and tackled her to the ground. One hand cushioned her head, while a rock-hard arm banded around her waist and kept her from injuring, well, anything. He rolled, released her, and jumped to his feet in front of her.

The scent of salt, ocean, and pine surrounded her.

No way. No fucking way should he have been able to move so quickly when she'd had him contained on his knees.

She scrambled up and kicked off the heels. Shit. She still held her gun in her hand. Despite being one of Seattle's most dedicated cops, she was acting like a fucking rookie.

"Gentlemen?" Kell asked, his stance casual. "Can I help you?"

The guy with the blue arm glanced down at the corpse and hissed. "We came to help Charlie." His face contorted and turned an ugly red. "You killed him."

"No. The drug he took killed him." Kellach's stance widened. "How much of the drug did you take?"

Lex peered around the solid brick of a man toward the two guys. The light illuminated them from behind, so she couldn't see their eyes. What was Kell seeing?

"Enough to be a god." The first guy lifted his hand and threw what looked like a ball of fire at Kellach.

A massive fireball instantly crackled from Kellach's hand, and he threw it toward the other ball. They smashed into each other with an unholy bellow of steam, fire, and energy. Kellach's ball encircled the other ball and snuffed it out before disappearing.

What the holy fuck? They did have some new weapon that threw fire, and she hadn't had a chance to frisk anybody.

Lex slid to the side to keep all three men in sight while lifting her weapon. "Everyone get down on your knees."

Kellach shook his head. "Not again. Just stay out of the way, darlin'."

Oh. He. Did. Not. She focused the gun on him.

The first guy shot again, and fire slammed her way. She pivoted, turning and catching her foot in a pothole. As she started to go down, another ball flew toward her head.

"Enough." Kellach jumped in front of her, his right shoulder slamming into her cheekbone. Stars exploded behind her eyes, and she hit the ground. He groaned, and the scent of burning flesh filled the rainy evening.

She blinked, her brain fuzzing and her body going numb. He'd saved her. Unconsciousness tried to claim her, but she fought against the darkness with her remaining strength.

Kellach shoved to his feet, his back to her, and balls of what truly looked like green fire shot out from him. The fire hit each of the men dead center. They both flew back about three yards and crashed to the ground.

Lex groaned as rain continued to beat down on her face. She couldn't pass out. If she passed out, she'd be dead. Her hand trembled on the asphalt. Where was her gun?

Kellach turned and started toward her—a massive hunter in a darkened alley.

"No," she whispered just as the darkness won. The last thought she had as she succumbed to oblivion was that she was about to be killed by a predator with the face of a fallen angel.

New York Times and *USA Today* bestselling author REBECCA
ZANETTI has worked as an art curator, Senate aide, lawyer, college
professor, and a hearing examiner—only to culminate it all in
stories about alpha males and the women who claim them. She
writes contemporary romances, dark paranormal romances, and
romantic suspense novels.

Growing up amid the glorious backdrops and winter wonderlands
of the Pacific Northwest has given Rebecca fantastic scenery and
adventures to weave into her stories. She resides in the wild north
with her husband, children, and extended family who inspire her
every day—or at the very least give her plenty of characters to
write about.

Please visit Rebecca at: www.rebeccazanetti.com/
www.facebook.com/RebeccaZanetti.Author.FanPage
twitter.com/RebeccaZanetti

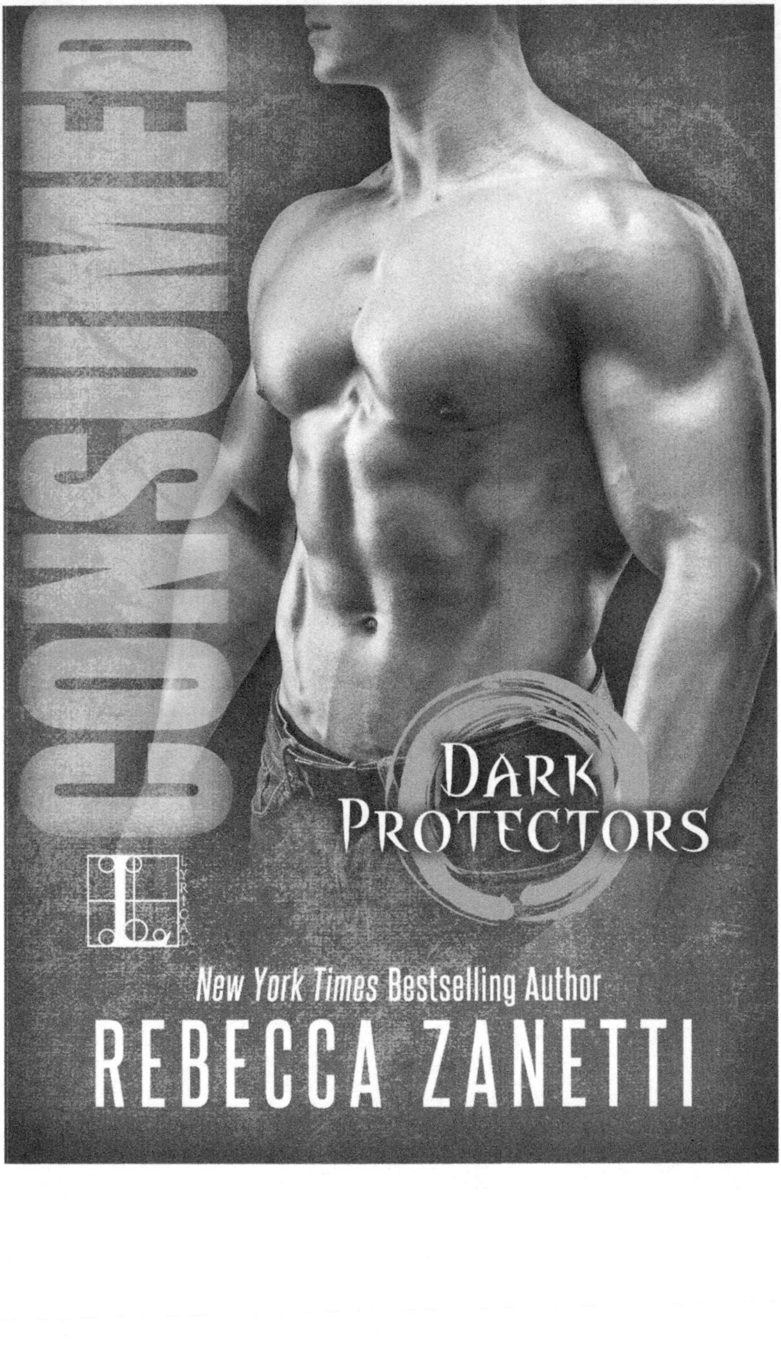
CONSUMED
DARK PROTECTORS
New York Times Bestselling Author
REBECCA ZANETTI

PROVOKED

DARK PROTECTORS

New York Times Bestselling Author

REBECCA ZANETTI

SHADOWED

DARK
PROTECTORS

New York Times Bestselling Author

REBECCA ZANETTI